AT YOUR SERVICE

Sandra Antonelli

At Your Service

For Elle Gardner who understands what it means to Bond.

For Megan Whalen Turner who read and liked this book, and knows its seeds were planted many years ago.

CHAPTER ONE

The text message Major Kitt sent the previous evening had been brief: *Home. Breakfast at 7. Please.*

Fresh food and other supplies in tow, Mae arrived at the rear entrance of her employer's Maresfield Gardens flat at 5:30 and let herself inside. She found his luggage beside the front door, which meant he'd only be home a short time and was likely to depart for another destination quite soon. Or he'd been preoccupied by something soft and perfumed. She tended to the things that indicated the latter, hanging up a woman's satin trench coat left on the floor, tossing out a moist copy of *The Times* that had been used as an umbrella, returning throw pillows to the window seat in the sitting room.

In the butler's pantry adjoining the kitchen, she slipped off a messenger bag holding a thin laptop, an envelope of bank documents, and an iPad. She stored the items in the small cupboard that housed cleaning supplies, aprons, and two extra sets of work clothes. After tying on a fresh apron, she organised the groceries and mixed sweet dough, which she put aside to rise. At the breakfast table near the big bay window in the sitting room, she arranged his vintage gilt-edged blue and white Minton china beside Jersey butter, little crystal pots of strawberry jam, Corsican honey, and her homemade orange and ginger marmalade.

By 6:50 the coffee was ready and the Béarnaise was done. By 6:55 Mae began to scramble his eggs and her employer ambled into the kitchen wearing a dressing gown, in need of feeding, a purplish welt below his damp hairline.

"Good morning, Mae," he said, gravelly voiced.

Mae didn't ask about the livid bump on his head or the red, raw scratches on his neck. A retired army officer, at present the Major was a Risk Assessment Specialist for Regent's Park Consortium, a company dealing in precious metals, chemicals, and fuels. The job sometimes sent him to dangerous parts of the world, places where people tried to kill each other for land, valuable commodities, or different religious beliefs. He met with of all sorts of hospitality in his travels. At times, the hospitality turned hostile, resulted in his harm, and he returned home with a split lip, black eye, and once, a detached retina. There was also the fact the man had two vices: the drink and women.

Rather than misunderstandings with antagonistic tribal landowners, hillbilly moonshiners, or religious zealots hell-bent on world domination, Mae suspected that the majority of his injuries were sustained by overindulgence in spirits and a penchant for married or attached women, which resulted in misunderstandings, brawling—and an occasional unhappy boyfriend or husband with murder on his mind.

"Good morning, sir," she said. "Nice to have you home again."

"Did you miss me, Mae? You must've. You're making scrambled eggs with Béarnaise." He poked a finger into the Béarnaise to have a taste, sucked the sauce from his fingertip, and a low, appreciative sound vibrated in his throat.

"Eggs for two then?"

"For one. Miss Samarakkody's taxi is waiting. She had a coat?"

Mae set the bowl of eggs aside. She wiped her hands on her apron as she went to the foyer to meet the waiting beauty, who was finger-combing lustrous dark hair.

Striking, the young woman was tall, had brown skin and blue eyes. She looked Mae up and down, taking in her preferred uniform, the supportive Doc Marten Mary Janes, unassuming dark blue shirt-dress, apron, reading glasses on chain, the French plait that kept the hair from her face—and dismissed her as any competition or threat. Miss Samarakkody's perfect brows arched expectantly.

Mae retrieved the satin coat, helped the woman into it, and received a slapping faceful of gleaming umber hair as Miss Samarakkody turned about and stretched out her arms to the man she'd spent the night enjoying.

"*Naan poga véndum, anpe,*" Miss Samarakkody said, embracing him. "*Ellām naṉṟi.*"

He kissed her cheek.

Quietly, Mae left the lovers to their farewell and returned to the kitchen to continue cooking. He would not be long. He was never long with goodbyes.

Abhorring tea, the Major made espresso when he was alone, but when she cooked for him Mae made the dark roast brewed coffee that she preferred to drink. She filled her cup and took an empty one out for him. Then she placed a pan on the gas cooktop, spooned in a knob of butter and whisked the eggs, pouring them into the pan once the butter had melted.

The chair at the small table in front of the bay window squeaked softly as he sat. She served him wholewheat toast, the scrambled eggs topped with Béarnaise, and set his coffee beside his blue plate. He smelled clean, of orange, bergamot, and a whisper of spicy nutmeg that blended with the aroma of coffee. The scent suited him.

"Will you join me for a cup?" he asked.

"Yes, of course." Mae pulled out the chair opposite his, sat with him, and sipped her mug of black Sumatran-Latin American blend, while he ate his breakfast with gusto.

"Why are you so good to me, Mae?" he said, savouring the simple plate of food as if he'd never eaten anything more heavenly.

"Because you pay me."

"I pay, you care, just like a patient who visits a psychologist."

"Yes. Except you don't tell me any dark secrets about yourself."

"No, you figure those out all on your own."

"Miss Samarakkody," she said. "Indian, or perhaps Sri Lankan?"

"Sri Lankan."

"Single?"

"Would you approve if she was single?"

"It's not my place to approve, sir. You pay me, remember? I care for your clothing, scrub your toilet, and cook your breakfast."

"Would you approve if I paid you more?"

"Are you offering me a pay rise?"

He chuckled and found untold delight in another mouthful of scrambled egg. "How long have you been with me now, Mae?"

"It's been three years since your previous man left your employ and retired, so three years as your butler, sir."

"It seems much longer."

"Like eternity in hell."

The Major laughed again. "I'll be home in Hades for the next six weeks. It'll be a month and a half of compiling reports for head office, paperwork, and such other hellishly mind-numbing bits of boring, so I'll be needing you here to keep me fortified."

"I'll make certain you're appropriately well-fed to deal with the dullness, sir."

"See that you do." He gulped a mouthful of coffee then returned the cup to the table and lifted his fork. "What did you get up to while I was away this time?"

"I finally finished painting the downstairs flat, and discovered Caspar left an indecently large sum of money in a trust."

"Define indecently large."

Mae told him the figure.

A forkful of egg paused at his lips, his brow quirked and he gave a little nod. "I'd say that's decidedly indecent."

"I ought to get the financial documents and show you. It's taken some time to absorb the size of the sum. I've a mind to give the money away."

"I had no idea being a Master Gardener could be so lucrative. Clearly, I've chosen the wrong career. Well, with that amount you're set for life."

"I'd be set for life if Caspar were still with me—and if property maintenance on old buildings didn't involve plumbing. Two weeks ago, there was a leak in your bathroom that warranted repair. I had to replace your toilet and retile the floor around it. It was better that you weren't here. Quite messy. Would you have any idea how the toilet cracked, sir?"

Neatly, with a cloth napkin, he blotted Béarnaise from his lips. "You are rather deadly with a toilet brush, perhaps you scrubbed it too hard."

"I hadn't thought of that, sir."

He sighed, and returned his napkin to his lap, a shrewd little smile on his lips. She knew it amused him that she was both his butler and landlady who lived in the converted period house next door. "Mrs Valentine," he said, "will you be increasing my rent to cover the cost incurred in this minor renovation to the lavatory?"

It amused her that he addressed her formally when their roles shifted from employer and employee to lodger and property-owner. "I hadn't considered that either, sir."

He spread her homemade marmalade on his toast. "Sir," he sniffed. "My previous man scorned the idea of calling me *sir,* and yet you call me nothing else, despite our arrangement."

"I know nothing of your previous man's education. However, I trained in buttling and house management. Any other form of address would be inappropriate, sir, unless you would prefer I always call you *Major.*"

"Only if you salute," he said with a grimace, and then his mouth was full of toast and the grimace had turned to a grin.

"You look tired, sir. Perhaps you might be ready for a holiday."

"You're so eager to be rid of me already you suggest a holiday. Is that your way of sugar-coating that I'm beginning to look old?"

"If that were the case I would have said you look *distinguished.*"

"Where would you send me on a holiday, a spa, or a detox health spa such as Champneys at Tring or Henlow?"

"As if I would ever deny you a Kentucky Straight Bourbon. No, no. I'd send you to Castello di San Marco in Sicily, near the Ionian Sea, or Ojo Caliente in the high desert of New Mexico, where distinguished gentlemen go to be pampered."

"Is that where you would go?" he said as he watched her sip her coffee.

"I'm not a distinguished gentleman."

He chuckled and the timer she'd set in the kitchen peeped.

"Have to knead the Chelsea buns, sir," she said as she rose, mug in hand.

"Chelsea buns? Oh, you do spoil me so, Mae. You are an Irish pot of gold. Is there more coffee, Mrs Pot O'Gold?"

"I'll brew more. It will be ready before you finish that cup." She turned towards the kitchen, smoothing her apron over her hips.

"Mae?"

"Sir?" She faced him.

"What do you think of me?"

"What do I think of you?" Mae felt her brow arch.

"Yes. And be honest. Don't tell me that I don't pay you to give me your opinion."

Mae considered his request for a moment. He was attractive—in an ugly-handsome sort of way. His body was well toned, with defined muscle and a rather remarkable arse, but his face...his face was somewhat cruel with blue-grey eyes that were stony, and a mouth that was perpetually stern until he smiled, which wasn't often. Somewhere between ginger and dark blond, depending on the amount of time he spent in the sun, his short hair emphasised his pitiless features. As for his disposition, he was immensely trust-worthy, possessed a cracking sense of humour, but... She tipped her head. "You're very like Mr Rochester, sir."

"Mr Rochester?"

"From *Jane Eyre*."

His head tilted, mirroring hers. "You consider me moody and brooding?"

"At times."

"That's a fair observation, although I can assure you I don't keep a madwoman hidden away in the attic."

"It's been a while since I've been up to the attic, but we all have secrets, sir."

"Ah, back to secrets again. I suppose you keep secrets too, Mae?"

"All women do."

He nodded, his hard mouth suddenly pursing. "Are you in love with me, Mae?"

That was not a question she'd expected, but she kept a straight face. "No, sir."

He pretended to look wounded. "Not even a little?"

"Not even a smidgen."

His expression turned quizzical. "But if I'm Rochester, wouldn't that make you Jane Eyre?"

"No, sir. It makes me Mrs Fairfax, the housekeeper." She turned again toward the kitchen, but paused, looking over her shoulder. "Although, if truth be told, I am rather fond of you, sir."

The coffee cup at his lips did little to hide his little smirk. "Thank you. Your fondness has restored my crushed ego."

ETIQUETTE DEEMED twenty minutes to accommodate a person's late arrival, but to hell with protocol. She'd been more than polite. After waiting three-quarters of an hour with no call or message, Mae signalled the waiter and ordered a salad of arugula with pear, walnuts, and Parmesan. She expected better service in an upmarket South Kensington establishment, expected the staff would have received proper training, yet the waiter left the place setting across from her—even after she told him she would be dining alone. The presence of the extra stemware and bread plate irritated her far more than the absence of Daniel Pierce.

She'd met Daniel at the bank. He'd assisted her with the trust fund Caspar had set up sometime before his death. She had had no clue such a trust had existed until she'd received a letter from Zurich-based Suisse Global Bank. At first, she thought it was a hoax, one of those Nigerian Prince scams that tried to bamboozle money from gullible widows. Then another letter arrived—a registered letter—from Suisse Global Asset Manager Mr Pierce, who directed her to his office at the local Suisse Global branch on Cabot Square. Mr Pierce had been patient, attentive, and flirty. By the end of their meeting Mr Pierce had become Daniel, and Daniel had asked her out. Deceived by his charm, well-cut suit, and pretty brown eyes, she'd accepted.

It turned out the money had been real and the date had been a hoax. She'd rung Daniel, left a message on his voicemail, sent him a text as well, but both had been ignored. He had seemed so eager to get to know her, genuinely interested, but she now believed that Daniel was married, or engaged, or had a girlfriend. Or he'd simply changed his mind about being interested. Whatever the case, Monday's afternoon meeting to finish the last details for the transfer of the trust's funds would be... succinct.

Instead of dwelling on the fact Daniel was an ill-mannered, insincere prat, she took a book from her handbag and cracked open the worn spine of a Charlotte Brontë classic. She ate and read. When the waiter came to clear away her dishes she ordered dessert and black coffee, and asked that he bring them at the same time. As he hurried off, leaving the soiled dinner plates on the table, she caught a glimpse of a familiar figure walking to the bar across the room.

If ever a man suited a dinner jacket it was her employer, and he looked decidedly more handsome than ugly-handsome at the moment. His companion, a redhead, wore a low-cut, open-back gown that matched the shade of her hair. While the restaurant was posh, it wasn't dinner suit posh and, for a moment, Mae wondered where they'd come from or where they would be going so formally dressed.

Although she looked after his household accounts, she did not keep her employer's social schedule, as others in service often did. She saw him in formal attire now and again, but it was a rare occasion to catch a glimpse of his evening companion fully dressed the night before. Mornings after, with the woman sans make-up, clothes rumpled, hair tousled were more typical.

She watched them have a seat and then resumed reading until the waiter returned with her dessert, but no coffee. Politely, she pointed out his mistake. With a huff, he flounced off like a drama

SANDRA ANTONELLI

queen, leaving the dirtied dishes behind once again. Mae found her place on the page and continued to read until a shadow appeared at the table's edge. She glanced up, expecting the waiter with a cheese platter and martini she hadn't ordered.

"Good evening, Mae."

"Good evening, sir."

The Major's eyes moved from the untouched place setting, the balsamic-stained plate to her left, and the dark, sweet-filled dessert glass to her right. "You've been stood up," he said.

"Yes. I suppose he changed his mind and decided I was too old, too short, too blonde, too smart or something, but if you think I'm going to sit here and cry into my chocolate mousse over bad manners and being stood up, then you know nothing about women and chocolate, sir."

"I know a little about women and chocolate, and that dark Belgian mousse looks as decadent as you in that little black dress."

She held his very direct gaze. "Thank you, sir. Would you like a taste?"

His mouth twitched. Once. "I'm afraid that might spoil my dessert, Mae."

"Good evening, sir."

"Good evening," he said, half turning. "And the man's a fool. You look lovely, Mae."

Mae would have watched him cross the dining room to his date, because he moved so well, with such confidence, but the waiter arrived with a café latte.

She sent it back immediately.

Three chapters and two proper black coffees later, she asked for the bill. "It's been taken care of," the waiter scowled, "and the gentleman did *not* leave a gratuity."

"That is a shame," she said.

Outraged, the waiter scuttled off, muttering something about *stupid cows* under his breath. Mae set down her book and looked to the bar on the other side of the room. She scanned the crowd for her employer, to thank him for his thoughtful gesture, but did not see him or the flame-haired beauty. Resigned, she collected her wrap and handbag and exited the restaurant into the reception hall of the Baldessare Hotel. She was in the foyer when she remembered the much-prized Brontë. She turned back to retrieve it, although the change in direction hadn't been necessary.

"You've left your book behind," he said. His thumb tapped against the small, hardbound volume pressed to his chest.

"You've left your date behind."

"My date has left me behind. She's finished with me."

"So we're both sorry losers at love tonight."

He shook his head. "I didn't say anything about losing."

"Apologies, sir. *I'm* the sorry loser at love tonight. You're the gentleman whose date has *finished* with him."

"Feeling sorry for yourself, Mae?"

"Didn't we already have this discussion?"

"Some things bear revisiting."

"Well, I've had enough chocolate for the night, but if you need some to bolster your flagging ego I would recommend the dessert I had, and a good book."

"Ah, my cue." He extended the small hardback. "Really, Mae, *Jane Eyre*?"

Mae took the book and tucked in into her boxy little handbag. "I'm trying to make headway into understanding men who possess a black, black soul, like your own, sir."

"Yes, I suspect mine may be a very deep, dark hole."

"I haven't decided if yours is a bottomless pit as Caspar's and my brother Sean's, but I suspect it's close."

He reached for the pink silk wrap looped through the crook of her elbow and stepped behind her to settle it upon her shoulders. "May I give you a lift home, dear Widow Valentine?"

"Not that I wouldn't appreciate a ride in your girly sports car, but I was going to have a little walk and get a taxi."

The shawl halted a few centimetres above her shoulders. "My girly sports car?"

"Sir," she gave him a pitying look. "A Bentley GT is too pretty for a man to drive."

"Too pretty? What should I be driving?"

"Something Italian, like a Maserati." Mae reached for the edges of her wrap and jerked it from his fingers to pull it around her cool skin.

"A Maserati. Yes. A *Maserati*." He shook his head, his expression suggesting she understood nothing about men and their automobiles. "Come on. We'll have a walk and then I'll take you home. My girly sports car is parked in Kensington Palace Gardens, near the Embassy of Nepal."

They exited the hotel and walked along Kensington Road, crossing near the Albert Memorial. They strolled into the park, the summer evening pleasant. Locals, tourists, and couples were out enjoying the mild night and they filled the footpath that skirted the park. Everything smelled fresh and green and it reminded Mae of when she'd been fresh and green—and newly married. She wasn't nostalgic for the handful of months she'd had with Caspar, but the bright, clean scent of summer emphasised that the sixteen years since his death had passed in what felt like ten minutes. One day he'd been there, his beard tickling her nose, the next he was gone. Mae sighed at the expedience of time.

"Thinking about the black souls of men again, or the," he sniffed, "manliness of a Maserati?"

"Have I insulted you, sir?"

"No, you've perplexed me."

Mae looked up at him as they walked. "Then let me explain. There are two sorts of cars men should never drive. Anything made by Bentley or Rolls Royce, and anything referred to as a 'hot hatch'. A hatchback, no matter who makes it, is not sexy or manly."

He laughed. "What about a Mini or a Fiat 500 like yours?" he said, taking her elbow to steer her out of the way of oncoming pedestrians.

"Do you ever see men driving Minis and Fiat 500s? No. You don't. Because they're girls' cars."

"That's rather sexist, but I see you feel quite strongly about this, don't you? You're gesturing like an Italian mama scolding her son."

"Forgive my flailing about, sir. It's very bad manners."

"Your manners are always impeccable, Mae."

Abruptly, Mae stopped walking. He was incorrect. "I haven't thanked you, sir."

"Thanked me for what?"

"My dinner. You were very kind to pay for it. I appreciate the gesture."

He released her elbow. "As much as I'd like to take credit, I didn't pay for your dinner."

Now Mae was perplexed. "You didn't?"

"No. But I should have."

Mae began to laugh.

"What's so funny?"

"My waiter was miserable. He never got my order right. I'm certain he confused me with another woman in a black dress at different table when he said a gentleman had paid my bill. It would serve that little weasel right if the restaurant took the cost of my dinner out of his wages."

He crossed his arms and looked smug. "Who's the black-hearted one now?"

Mae lifted her right foot and rotated her ankle. "I call it natural justice for poor service. There is no excuse for poor service." With a grimace, she shifted her footing and repeated the ankle rotation. "So much for a nice walk. It's probably best we head home. These pretty shoes are killing me."

Amused, he put his hands in his pockets. "Wait here. I'll get the girly sports car and pick you up."

"No, no. I'll come with you. It's only a little way to the embassy."

Hands still in his pockets, he offered his arm and, as unorthodox as it was considering he was her employer, she took it.

They let a family of noisy tourists pass where the Flower Walk met the Board Walk near the mouth of the Palace Gate, and made their way towards the residences and embassies of Kensington Palace Gardens. They passed through the police checkpoints and went along the quiet, dimly lit avenue. Fine gravel crunched beneath their feet as they ambled by Kensington Palace and the embassies of Israel and Romania.

Another couple walked ahead of them, going the same direction toward the Notting Hill Gate. The woman had a head of blonde, Shirley Temple ringlets. Her purple, knee-length A-line dress had a square neckline. It was a lovely, sixties-inspired garment and she had the body to wear it. She'd paired the dress with opaque white tights and hideous, five-inch bug green patent leather platform shoes with a spill of tiny plastic tropical fruits at the toes. Her dark-haired, moustachioed companion was more classically dressed. His suit was navy or charcoal and fit him well. They walked and canoodled, weaving slightly, leaning on one another as they laughed, the man's hand on the woman's arse. The smell of whiskey trailed behind them.

Mae said quietly, "I wonder which one of them is going to fall over first."

"He will."

"But he has better shoes."

"Don't underestimate those things she's wearing," he said, his voice low. "They'll maintain her balance better than his slippery leather-soled shoes."

"You can see his shoes have leather soles in this light?"

"I have the same shoe. They're Ferragamos. They have a leather sole. By the way, Mae, you'll have to drive. I'll be quite over the limit."

"It was your plan all along to have me drive, wasn't it, sir?"

He chuckled.

They neared the house of the Finnish ambassador. Several countries maintained missions on this small, tree-lined avenue, one of the most expensive and exclusive areas in London. A little further along were the embassy of Nepal and Russian Consulate. Mae said, "I had a friend who worked in the Dutch embassy. I believe that's around here somewhere, isn't it?"

"The Dutch embassy is back that way, closer to the hotel, to the left and down. It's the other side of the Hyde Park Gate." He glanced in the direction they'd just come. "It pays to have friends in high places. Knowing embassy staff means parking in the city is never an issue."

"Is that what you've done? You've parked at the Nepali embassy."

"More like across the driveway." He stopped. They were right in front of his Bentley.

Mae withdrew her arm from his. "The key, sir?"

"The key is inside the embassy, should the car have needed to be moved. I'll just be a moment." He stepped to a gate set into a white wall and pushed the button on the intercom. He gave her a nod as he was buzzed inside. Mae stood beside his Bentley and let her eyes travel over its sleek lines. Graceful, lean, it was a feminine-looking thing and no one would ever convince her otherwise.

There was movement near the Bentley's boot. The drunken

couple they'd walked behind had backtracked. The pair swayed closer on unsteady feet, although the woman had removed her ugly shoes. She wore them on her hands like bulky green gloves. As they drew near, the man asked, "Excuse me, is the Dutch embassy around here?"

"No, it's back the other way, the way you came, down Kensington Gore, towards that Italian Hotel. It's the other side of Hyde Park Gate."

"The other side of what gate?" The man shuffled closer, stumbling a little, his hand slapping the Bentley as he regained his footing.

Mae repeated what she'd said.

"*Grazie.*" The woman nodded politely. Her head tilted, her teeth very white as she smiled and leaned in close, saying, "Thank you so much. You are very helpful. Easy. *Cosi facile.*" Her hideous shoes clattered to the footpath. Mae half bent to pick them up and her handbag was torn from her fingers. The bag's clasp parted, mobile and tube of lipstick tumbling out to the gravel, and the woman bolted towards Bayswater Road, the square bag under her arm.

The man mumbled a curse in Italian, Mae took a single step, and a backhanded wallop pitched her sideways. She banged into the side mirror of the Bentley. The silky wrap she'd had about her shoulders slithered to the ground beside the blood that slopped from her mouth. She staggered to right herself, to run away, to get away, but the heel of her shoe broke. She lurched against the car, banging her forehead, and the fist meant to smash into her eye hit the Bentley's side pillar instead.

The man swore and swung at her again. The blow went too wide as Mae moved toward him, surprising him, doing the opposite of what he'd expected, clawing at his face, grabbing for an ear to tear off because her brother had taught her to never back away, to never be cornered. Sean had told her, *always move forward*, and when the man seized a handful of her lacy neckline and dragged her toward his body, she shoved forward, using his momentum to overbalance him, hoping his leather soles were slippery. He stumbled backwards, the lace tore, and he was gone. His body slammed onto the Bentley's bonnet.

And her employer began to beat the living hell out of him.

CHAPTER TWO

M ae watched one man thrash another and enjoyed the brutality. The sound of fist splitting skin and the man's nose cracking made her smile. She knew she'd smiled because the action had stretched her ragged, bleeding lips across her teeth and pain set in, triggering the realisation of her delight.

Bemused by her glee, she fingered the tattered neckline of her dress and caught her breath as she tried to reconcile with her absent morality.

Suddenly it was over. Floodlights illuminated the street. Diplomatic Protection Officers and embassy staff rushed outside. Her employer had swooped down like the avenging hand of God and now the DP officers held her assailant. Eye swelling, nose broken and bloodied, he smiled the whole time they handcuffed him.

The Major's expression, on the other hand, remained unaffected. From the first blow to the last, his face had been fixed, ruthless, his mouth flat. The ugly-handsome cruelty of his features did not alter until he came to her, and then only imperceptibly. The blue-grey eyes that were typically cold held a faint flicker of warmth. He looked down at her, at the blood she felt on her chin and throat, and swore.

"As bad as that bad, is it?" she asked.

"You've spoilt your little black dress."

"And ruined my pretty shoes as well," she fumbled with remnants of black lace to try to cover her half-exposed breasts, "but at least I have all my teeth."

"Are you hurt anywhere else?"

"No, are you? You've blood all over your hands."

"His, not mine." He crouched, retrieved her wrap. Darker, wet splotches stained the pink silk he held in his fingers. "And now yours as well."

Mae watched him rise. He wasn't even winded. He looked neat, bow tie still perfectly tied, jacket uncreased, Marcella shirt pristine except for at the double cuff. There was a smear of crimson on his right cuff. She flinched as he draped the pink wrap around her, covering her gaping neckline. A muscle along his jaw pulsed. Another pulse touched his brow. He swore again. "Did I frighten you?" he said.

"Please pardon me," Mae said. She turned away and spat out blood. Immediately, a metallic taste flowed back over her tongue again and she swallowed the hot, iron taste. "Did you frighten me? No, the man who tried to smash in my face frightened me. You, for want of a better word, amazed me."

He withdrew a plain white handkerchief from a pocket and slipped it into her hand. "And you astonished me. Mae, you give a mugger your money, your wallet, your watch, whatever he wants. You don't fight him. The police will tell you the same thing when they arrive."

Mae wiped away spittle. Blood surged over her teeth and

tongue. "Please, don't lecture me, sir. My brother Sean taught me that a girl—no matter how old—needs to know how to protect herself from the big bad wolf, and this wolf hit me first. So I hit him back. But thank you for coming out to tan his hide and save mine. I always knew you were a bit of a brawler, sir. Something I suspect you learned in your misbegotten youth."

"My misbegotten youth. You have no idea."

"I think I have now."

He opened the Bentley's passenger door. Mae flinched again as he laid a warm hand on her shoulder. His eyes narrowed and he observed her for a moment, cautious, concerned, but his hand did not move. He led her to sit inside the car. "Let me have a look," he said and bent forward to lift her chin, his fingers soft on her tender skin. He took the handkerchief from her hand. Surprisingly gentle, he prodded then dabbed the white cloth at her bloody lips. Despite his gentleness she winced, her eyes began to water and his jaw compressed, rippling as it had before. He said, "Your tooth has punctured the left corner of your bottom lip. You're going to need a few stitches."

"They'll be my first."

"You've never had stitches before?"

"Until now, the injuries in my life have all been internal, you know, the sort you don't see, the sort time is supposed to heal, but never does. In your vast experience with," she glanced at the bruise on his forehead, the one that sat just below a scar hidden by his hairline, "physical harm, are stitches painful, sir?"

His little laugh was a puff of air. "Not as much or for as long as the other sort of wounds. Try not to swallow so much blood. It can make you sick. Spit as much as you can." He stopped dabbing and nodded as she turned away. "There's a girl. Does it hurt very much?"

Wetness trickled from her burning eyes. "Yes, it bloody well does now."

"We have no need to wait for the police, the embassy staff can give them the details," he said as he took her hand and placed the handkerchief in it. "Press it to your mouth. Apply as much pressure as you can stand. I'll have one of the officers take us to St Mary's."

Mae held the cloth to her bottom lip.

"That's a good little girl."

Mae bristled, sniffling. "I'm *not* a little girl."

"No. You most certainly are not."

"Well, you needn't rub it in." She leaned aside, spat again, and wiped her running nose on the vermillion-tainted square of cotton.

"Excuse me, I didn't mean to suggest anyth—"

Exhaling, she held up a hand. "No. Excuse *me*, sir. Clearly, I'm a little out of sorts. I was stood up and then mugged. I've ruined my dress and it was vintage. I've broken my shoe, lost my wallet, my keys, my mobile, and my book. Damn it, I've lost my book, but I apologise for being rude to you, sir."

It was evident he tried not to grin. "Which one finally tipped you into feeling sorry for yourself?"

"I don't feel sorry for myself. I'm angry. The *Jane Eyre* was an early edition that Caspar gave me, and it's probably in a rubbish bin with my bag somewhere by now."

"Mae?"

"Sir?"

"You still have all your teeth."

Mae laughed, her mouth a little too wide. It made her stinging eyes water even more.

"On second thought," he said, "We should walk to St Mary's."

"Walk?"

"It may help diffuse all the adrenaline left in your system." He removed her shoe and paused for a moment to reach under the car. "This is yours, isn't it?" he said, lifting up a mobile phone with a cracked screen.

She looked at the mobile in his grip, at her naked toes, at her discarded broken shoe, at the droplets of blood on the ground, then back to the drying scarlet that stained his hands, and finally to his intense gaze. There was little difference to what she'd witnessed and viewing a boxing match with mismatched opponents, yet his bare-knuckle bout encompassed something foreign, something bizarre. Despite her pain, she felt another coil of incomprehensible, misplaced pleasure. It made her shiver.

He rose and the flicker of warmth that had seeped into his cold eyes glowed brighter. He took off his perfectly uncreased jacket, and slipped it over her shoulders.

THE NEXT FEW minutes passed rather quickly. He changed his mind about walking and herded her into an embassy car, instructing the driver to head to Accident and Emergency at St Mary's in Paddington. Once they'd reached their destination, her employer cast a single glance at the throng in the hospital waiting area. "No, this won't do," he said, clasped her hand and turned about, taking her back outside, before she could protest. He hurried her along the side of the hospital to the ambulance bays, where he paused for a moment to look around at ambulance technicians, EMTs, and hospital staff. His eyes settled on a portly, ginger-haired, middle-aged man who'd just leaned against the brick wall away from the entrance.

The man closed his eyes. The ID around his neck swung on its lanyard as he lifted an unlit cigarette to his mouth.

Mae was pulled along a few steps.

"Doctor..." her employer peered at the plastic ID badge, "... Grove. We'll be needing your assistance."

Grove's eyes flicked open. He looked at Mae and then her

companion "The A&E entrance is around the corner," he said, cigarette bouncing on his lips. He took a lighter from a pocket.

"I see you pay little attention to the warnings and believe smoking may not be hazardous to your health, but I can assure you if you light that cigarette, it will be."

Mae didn't think she'd heard that quite right. "Sir?" she said, not certain if she cared about understanding as much as she did the searing pain in her swollen mouth.

Grove seemed to be very interested in the meaning. The flame that had sprung to life below his nose halted a millimetre from the tip of the tobacco and then winked out. He blinked, his confused brown eyes darting from blood-caked hands, to Mae's face, to a cold stare. "Are you...threatening me?"

"Yes."

"Oh, sir, really..." Mae said, rather feebly.

Grove glanced at her again, as if for confirmation this was really happening, and she rolled her eyes and nodded. Grove stammered, "Wh-what...what is it you want?"

"The lady's bleeding and in pain."

"Yes?" Grove said.

"Help her."

"Of course, of course," Grove's cigarette fell to the ground and he gestured to sliding doors outside the ambulance entrance. "Just this way. Just this way."

Once they were tucked away inside in a little cubicle full of medical things, Grove quickly cleansed her wound. While the doctor busied himself preparing sutures, Mae looked at her employer. He'd perched on a swivelling stool, a vigilant bird of prey. "You're a bully," she said.

"I was hoping you'd see me as heroic."

"Heroic. Which means you expect me to leap up and cover you with kisses to thank you profusely?"

"I think I've enough of your blood on me already."

"Heroic. Maybe you're a little of that, but mostly, you're a bully."

"I can live with that," he said and cast an eye at the needle Grove held ready in his right hand. "Would you like to hold this bully's hand while the nice doctor gives you an injection?"

"I thought you said stitches wouldn't hurt very much."

"The stitches don't. The needle with the lovely lidocaine, well, Mae...it's a needle. Are you as fond of needles as you are fond of me?"

She glanced at Grove, who had relaxed. A little. Mae didn't like the look of the sweat on his upper lip. "Give me your damn hand, sir."

IT WAS after midnight when they got a cab from St Mary's back to the Bentley. The lean embassy guard who handed over the car key fob leaned in close to the Major and murmured something. Her employer's head snapped up as he swore. "How the hell did that happen?"

The guard shrugged, muttering an apology.

His mobile came out of his pocket. It had buzzed frequently while they'd been at St Mary's and he'd ignored it. The Major spoke into the device. "I'm not in the mood. Give me the abbreviated version, Lazenby," he said, and walked a few paces, his back to her. "It's not my cock-up... I'm sure he is... Yes, I can hear him... Monday. I'll be there Monday... No...I said, *no*... It's called doing the right thing." Turning, jaw set, the Major's eyes settled on her. Mae watched him reel in his anger. Tucking his mobile away, he moved toward her. "Somehow, Mae, as we were on our way to St Mary's, the man who attacked you got away from police guards in Accident and Emergency."

"You're joking."

"No, I'm not."

"Well, aren't the police about as much use as a back pocket on a shirt," she said.

Jaw tight, the Major held the key fob in his outstretched hand. "You'll have to take us home, as I'll still be over the limit."

Mae drove the big V8 back to Maresfield Gardens. She pulled to the kerb near the front wall and dragged the stained silk wrap from about her neck. The local anaesthetic Groves had administered before he'd proceeded with giving her three tiny stitches continued to deaden any discomfort. She was weary, but when she opened the door to climb out of the Bentley and looked towards the front of her house, Mae didn't know how she felt.

But flabbergasted was a good start.

The exterior door was wide open, the lights in the entryway blazed. Fixed in her seat, Mae stared for a moment. Her employer made an impatient sound. She heard him rummage in the glovebox and then exit the car. When the passenger door shut, Mae finally got out of the Bentley and he stood beside her, a hand in his pocket. He fixed a stern gaze upon her. "Is Stephens home?" he said.

"No. Mr Stephens is in Santa Fe making another movie."

"Then wait here."

Ignoring his domineering tone, her bare feet slapping on the footpath along the white fence, Mae pushed through a little black gate and headed for the front door. He was a half-step behind, she heard him on his phone ringing the police.

She went inside, past Mr Stephens' undisturbed flat. All appeared to be fine in the foyer. Mae knew the story upstairs would be different. She hurried towards the staircase that led to her apartment. Hard fingers gripping her elbow brought her to an abrupt halt.

SANDRA ANTONELLI

"Wait here," he said again, harshly. He released her and started up the steps.

Mae waited. For three seconds. Then she went upstairs, tiptoeing on the treads. Streetlights shining through the window above the stairs cast a dim spotlight on her front door, which gaped open. She saw the Major go in into her dark apartment. Mae reached in through the doorway and switched on the lights.

He spun around. "I told you to wait."

"Yes, you did," she said, staring at the little black gun in his right hand. "Where did you get that?" she asked and heard something about "risk assessment and military reserve," but she'd already forgotten about the Glock or whatever the hell it was in his grip because she'd taken in the scene behind him. She swore like an Irish dockworker, which seemed to amuse him. He tucked his weapon into the waistband of his trousers, and she considered what a descriptive word *ransacked* was.

The contents of her home lay strewn about. The sofa on its back; the cushions divested of their insides. Tables and chairs upended, pictures were knocked over or ripped from the wall. Books had been swept off shelves and the desk and flung higgledy-piggledy. The entire contents of the antique filing drawers had been tossed about, insurance and financial records, Caspar's death certificate scattered atop or beneath the furnishings. Cupboards and drawers hung open in every room. Sheets and towels from the linen press had been shaken out and dumped in a pile. The contents of the medicine chest had been strewn about the bathroom tiles. In the kitchen, drawers had been emptied and cooking utensils littered the floor, worktop, and table.

As they moved from room to room, cautiously, and she surveyed the damage, she realised little was actually missing. If she'd left her laptop and iPad here instead of in her employer's pantry, those would have been taken, yet beyond a few pounds and change she kept in a biscuit jar, and three pieces of inexpensive jewellery, nothing of real value was missing.

She crossed from the kitchen into the sitting room. With a huff, she righted a side table and picked up a silver-framed photo of Caspar. The glass was cracked; spindly lines disfigured her late husband's face. She touched the image, running a finger over the brown eyes that smiled back, and set the picture back on the table, carefully.

"You should leave things as they are, Mae," the Major said, from the kitchen doorway, mobile phone in hand, tapping on the little screen.

"I can't leave Caspar on the floor."

"I understand, but the police prefer that you don't disturb the scene of a crime." He pocketed the mobile.

"Are the police going to clean up or make more of a mess?"

"Make more of a mess."

"Then what's the harm?"

With a shrug, he bent to pick up a few books and began to stack them near the bookcase.

The police came.

There wasn't much they could do, beside leave dark grey finger-printing dust in various places, and suggest she cancel her credit cards and change her locks. There were no fingerprints, no jimmied windows or locks. There'd been no need. The key that had been in her handbag gave entry to the burglars. The constables said thieves were probably looking for ready cash rather than items to pawn or sell. It was a crime of opportunity brought on by her earlier mugging.

The police went.

It was nearly two when Mae found herself sitting on a sofa in her employer's flat. He stood across from her, a crystal tumbler of amber liquid in his hand. "Don't argue with me, Mae. You see the logic. You know I'm right."

The scotch liqueur he insisted she drink was infused with tangerine and cinnamon sweetened by honey. Yes, he'd been right about the Glayva. It hadn't set aflame the stitches she'd received. Each sip had been pleasant, warming, and did not make her choke or sputter as she usually did when swallowing spirits. He was also right about seeing logic. She saw it and was going to argue with him anyway.

Head shaking, she placed her empty glass on the Empire side table and rose from the comfortable Chesterfield in his sitting room. "All right. I won't stay in my house. I'll ring the locksmith and *then* go to a hotel."

He downed what remained of his Glayva and set the tumbler beside hers. "A locksmith at two o'clock on a Sunday morning will cost a fortune."

"I think I can afford a locksmith, what with the fact I'll soon be coming into Caspar's indecently large trust, sir."

"How will you get to the hotel? You're certainly not walking. I can't drive you. I've been drinking. And so have you. You've had two of those."

Mae followed his line of sight to the crystal on the side table. "You're devious. You're not drunk. You haven't been drunk this whole night. Steady on your feet, steady with your hands, steady with your words."

"You'd be surprised just how drunk I was and how drunk I still am, but it would be careless of me to let you walk, drive your little Fiat or my girly sports car now."

She took the key fob to his Bentley from the inside pocket of his jacket, which she still wore, and lay it beside the empty tumblers. "I'll take a taxi. After I ring the locksmith. Mr Stephens may not be home, but I have a responsibility to tenants who don't have the fancy internal electric keypad lock and monitored security system you do. You are a few flights of stairs and a garden away, and it's only my door and the outside front door. I'll have the locksmith come back later to replace the locks for Mr Stephen's flat."

"Mae." His gaze was cold, hard, adamant, but she was too worn out for it to have any effect and too tired to go on arguing.

She moved into the foyer. He was a step behind. When she reached the door and pulled it open, he pushed it shut with a flattened palm. Beyond his knuckles being somewhat pink, he'd washed his hands clean of any evidence of the fight—except the smear of blood on the cuff of his dress shirt, which was still there. It had turned brown. Mae stared at the dulled colour and heard fist strike flesh, the crack of a nose breaking...

Hours ago. That had been hours ago. Now her employer's hand was plastered on the heavy oak, just above her head. She was in his flat. He'd boxed her in at the door and stood close. The heat of his body warmed her back. His scent, that slight hint of orange, bergamot, and a whisper of spicy nutmeg blended with the honeyed sweetness of Glayva in his breath, warm on her neck.

Sensations were juxtaposed. Man, bully, hero... Mae trembled in a ridiculous but natural way she understood—and in an utterly alien way she did not.

She turned to face him. Strands of her hair, which she'd worn in loose curls for her date, stuck to the stiff stitches where her tooth had gone through her bottom lip. She was certain she'd wind up with a scar there. Before she tugged at the errant locks, he lifted the hair away. The tips of his fingers brushed her cheek.

"Mae," he said again. The smooth tone of his voice made it rather plain he thought her trembling meant she was still feeling the effect of the night's events. His words indicated the same. "You've had a fright. You were hurt. Your home was invaded, your

29

privacy invaded. You're worried about feeling secure, and this is the safest option for you."

"I had a fright? I'm worried about feeling secure? Don't he-man me and tell me how I feel. Please." Fight or flight, her central nervous system had been overstimulated, and now she was tired, so very tired. Being unaccustomed to more than a little alcohol, she was probably a wee bit tipsy as well. Fatigued and slightly drunk was enough reason for the inappropriate ideas she had and the bizarre way she felt. Fight or flight, she was too weary for either. Instead, she was honest. She took a deep, measured breath. "I would be uncomfortable staying here, sir."

"Ah. There it is. Can we set aside the fact that our arrangement, our...relationship is based on service, salary, and rent, and simply be friends? Can't we be friends tonight, Mae? Although I have secured the exterior doors to your place for the night, I would be uncomfortable if you didn't stay here. You visiting a hotel, even the luxury one a half block from here, would emasculate me."

"Emasculate you? I don't think there's any danger of that happening. I've seen you brawl. I've seen you bully. I've seen your gun. Yet...there is the matter of your Bentley."

His laugh was tired, but genuine. "Friends it is then?"

"Yes, friends. You're very kind to give up your bed to a friend."

"What makes you think I'm giving up my bed?" He frowned.

She pursed her mouth.

"Right. I see. I'm giving up my bed." Finally, his hand came away from the door and he scratched his neck. He'd undone his bow tie hours ago. Twin black tails sat against the crisp white of his open collar. "Don't look so smug," he said as he stepped aside.

"I'm not smug, I'm exhausted." She took off his jacket, which had smelled wonderful and had been a lovely consolation to a dreadful night. She'd worn it long enough now. She held it out to him. "Thank you, sir."

He crossed his arms. "I never knew you were so damned contrary, Mae."

"A line has to be drawn somewhere, sir."

His eyes travelled from her bare feet and paused at her breasts before continuing to her aching face. "Yes, I see. Put the jacket back on, Mae. You may think the Bentley equivalent to being gelded, but I haven't been completely unmanned yet."

CHAPTER THREE

Mae reached for Caspar. Then, as every morning for the last sixteen years, the disorientation passed. Slowly. Caspar was dead. She was alone, and there remained a new sort of pain. Her head pounded, her mouth throbbed without mercy, the space she found herself in was endless, and she was drifting, caught in a net of cool Egyptian cotton, lost in a vast sea of blankets and pillows, drowning in a bed far too large for one small woman.

With a gasp, she opened her eyes.

The Major stood at the foot of the enormous king bed, his left side lit by light spilling in from the hallway. As was his routine when he was home, he was dressed and ready for a run. "Wake-up call," he said, "as you insisted last night. Now, tell me. Do you feel like joining me for a run, as you also insisted last night?"

When he was home, she sometimes accompanied him for three miles of the ten-mile route he took, but not this morning. This morning, all she wanted to do was lie still, in the dark. She made a sound somewhere between a moan and a sigh.

"The locksmith will be here at seven." His voice held the same smug tone it had less than three hours ago. He laid a thick dressing gown near her feet, gave a nod, and left the room.

Mae wanted to shut her eyes to the summer morning sunlight that peeped through the slats of the blinds. In a little less than an hour, he'd return and after a shower and shave the man would be ravenous. She sat up and scooted to the distant edge of the mattress —or tried to. The shirt he'd given her to sleep in was bunched up and twisted with the bedclothes. She kicked at them to free her legs. A moment later, swamped by his dressing gown, she entered the en suite. On a little chair beside the deep claw-foot bathtub were the shoes and change of clothes she stored in the butler's pantry. The garments sat folded neatly alongside a new toothbrush, towels, and a crystal jar of Epsom salt. On top of the glass urn was a note that said: *Add bath salts. Soak 20 minutes.* Steam rose from the hot water that filled the tub.

Her employer had run her a bath.

She gazed at the bathwater, lured by the hypnotic suggestion of a long soak. She threw in a handful of grey-tinged salt, drew the shirt over her head, and winced as she wiggled out of her knickers. Mae stepped into the bath, her aching body met the soothing warmth, and she groaned, not with pain or pleasure, but with the realisation there was no time for a leisurely bath. Before the lock-smith arrived, she had eggs to poach, Hollandaise to prepare, and coffee to brew. There was also the matter of lifting the bloodstains from her employer's Marcella shirt and changing his bed linen.

She allowed herself ten minutes of luxury, then dressed and stripped the bed, her body stiff and screaming for her to stop. Her movements slow, she gathered dirty garments, the sheets, his shirt and dinner suit to ferry them into the butler's pantry and into the machine for washing. Arms loaded, she entered the kitchen and stopped dead in her tracks, laundry plans instantly waylaid. On the bench beside the coffee maker was one of the Chelsea buns leftover from yesterday, a glass of orange juice, and another note written in large, block letters: *EAT*.

Her mouth throbbed, her muscles ached, and her skin prickled with annoyance. She glanced around and found he'd washed the crystal tumblers they'd used last night. He'd brought up the newspaper too, and it lay front page up, the juice on top of the lead story. Mae stared at the headline upside down, pursed her lips, and found that doing so hurt. She exhaled with a huff.

This would not do.

Yes, she'd had a fright. Yes, she'd been knocked around. Yes, the gesture was intended to be kind, as kind as his bullying the doctor had been, as kind as the offer of his bed had been, as kind as the bath had been, but this was too much. This would not do.

He was well aware she had survived far worse, albeit less physical injury than this; she was no feeble, little, contrary widow and he was *not* doing her job. She worked for him. Not the other way around.

This would not do *at all*.

Irritated, she went into the little butler's pantry and shoved the bed linens into the washing machine. The fitted sheet was three-quarters inside the drum when she froze, breath caught in her chest. A moment later the soles of her shoes squeaked on the pantry tiles as she hurried back to the kitchen. She snatched the juice off the newspaper. A wave of orange liquid spilled over the edge of the glass. Droplets marred the photo of the man who'd stood her up last night, but not the headline *Investment Banker Found Dead in Hyde Park*.

HIS BUTLER SLEPT in a single bed.

As Kitt ran, his mind had wandered to the odd fact he'd discovered last night. The seven-mile route he usually followed went along the outer perimeter of Hampstead Heath, but this morning, as he contemplated the tiny mattress most adults shunned, he compressed his course and opted for a shorter four-mile run, wondering how the hell Mae got a night's rest on a bed so small.

It was strange that he judged her choice of mattress. He could sleep soundly standing up, in a cramped, jostling armoured vehicle, swinging in a shipboard hammock, on a filthy or hard dirt floor, covered in mud while mosquitoes and other insects stung him, but, as he realised last night, not at home on a quilted leather sofa with a deep buttoned back. Kitt knew his pitiful night's rest had little to do with where he'd slept. Rather than the size of a bed, or uncomfortable sitting room furniture, what perturbed him was the matter of his butler.

After twenty-five years in service as a butler and household manager for three different families, Mae had retired. But when he'd returned from a near-disastrous trip to Rome that left him with a detached retina, his new landlady brought him some excellent homemade Chelsea buns, suggested that he needed help with day-to-day tasks as he recovered, and left with a job previously filled by a surly Scotsman.

Her two and a half decades as a butler had set her up for a comfortable life. She had invested her income shrewdly. She owned property in Italy and several sought-after areas of London, and managed the residences herself. She'd retired from service a wealthy woman, and it had been a surprise to find, after being in her home for the first time last night, that despite her wealth, Mae lived simply. A dead man, a man she still loved, had given her the things she valued most.

Butler, housekeeper, chef, household manager, occasional chauffeur, Mae was fiercely loyal to him and to her deceased husband, a fact Kitt respected, appreciated, and had no desire to alter. Regardless of her insisting the contrary, he had frightened her last night, more than the mugger who'd split her mouth open. And that had surprised him too. She'd done quite a good job of hiding her fear, of denying her revulsion, tossing out her little quips, but she'd quaked when he'd touched her, her hands shook, her hazel eyes widened, and the pulse at her throat jumped. The matter of his butler was...inconvenient.

In his line of work intimidation was a valuable tool, but terrifying his prized pot of Irish butler gold did not sit well on his conscience. Her fright spun the direction of the moral compass he'd forgotten he'd ever had and pointed to not wanting to blemish her faithfulness, the one thing in his life that existed without any sort of artifice. With Mae, there was nothing he sought to gain, no deal he had to make, no compromise to agree to, no arrangement to be met. And there was no one else whose scrambled eggs were such tiny bites of absolute joy.

He laughed at himself as he approached the front of his flat. It was ridiculous, waxing lyrical over eggs. For the next five or six weeks, he'd enjoy tiny bites of joy and the company of Mae reminding him he still had a conscience.

He keyed in his front door security code, entered the foyer and began to climb the stairs to his flat, expecting the tantalising scent of breakfast and coffee, yet the air was perfumed by nothing more than a hint of the wood polish on the balustrade. The lack of aroma concerned him for a moment. He paused on the steps.

Perhaps Mae had fallen asleep in the bath and forgotten his breakfast. Christ, he hoped not. He was famished.

He continued up the steps and considered the least embarrassing ways he might wake her from a therapeutic soak and nap in his tub—had that indeed happened. He could call out to her, rap on the frosted glass en suite door, or ring the apartment buzzer, which would undoubtedly pull her from the bath. He liked that idea. She'd open the door, pink-faced, groggy, her hair wrapped in a towel. He'd say he'd forgotten his front door code, and she'd give him that look, the one that said he was 'full of shite,' then she'd step aside, and hurry into the kitchen to tend to his breakfast while he showered.

When he reached the landing, he considered the inappropriate ideas. The first challenged her suggestion that his choice of automobile classified him as foppish. The other played on the fact he'd never seen her with her hair down before last night. Her hair had been soft and loose and it seemed so old-fashioned, such a Victorian thing to fix upon, but he thought about her hair anyway before conceding that inappropriate notions would see him out of having her homemade marmalade, her Chelsea buns, or her eggs ever again.

Hunger, it seemed, was his true moral compass—the moral compass that apparently only operated when it came to his butler —and the damned thing quelled his indecorous considerations.

Amused with himself, with how simple his ruin could be, he entered his flat to find her dressed and sitting at the dining table. An expression of worry furrowed her brow, crow's feet crinkled beside her pretty hazel eyes. Absently, her thumb rubbed across the stitches in her lip. She stared out the window beside the table instead of at the newspaper spread open before her.

She never ironed the newspaper the way other butlers and housekeepers often did to keep the ink from smearing. He thought the ironing was silly; after all, it was only ink and it washed off. She'd put a smudge of ink on her chin. He watched her preoccupation for a moment and took in the greyish mark on her chin and the bruising on her jaw. He had missed the discolouration when he'd woken her at dawn. In the bright morning light, the mottled bloom on her skin was ugly, the stitches worse. He had moved too slowly last night and now she wore that tardiness on her face. Anger filled his empty stomach. He said softly, "I wasn't certain if you'd be up."

With a start, she turned. "I beg your pardon. I didn't hear you come in, sir."

"I'll be sure to make more noise next time I return early. Is the coffee ready, Mae?"

"Coffee? Yes. Coffee... Oh... I haven't..." she glanced down at the paper and back up at him as she rose. "I apologise. I haven't put on the coffee or your breakfast. I thought you'd be a while still and..." She pressed her lips together in a flat line, found that painful, and grimaced the way he did whenever he drank wine, which always left him with a cracking headache.

He studied her again. Meticulous, authoritarian, she was an independent woman of strong character, and lived life on her own terms, but plainly she wasn't her usual self. Did he need to cancel meeting Bryce and take Mae for a CT scan to check for concussion? He hadn't thought she needed a scan last night and didn't really believe she needed one now. She wasn't so much flustered or startled as she was irritated, as if she'd been trying to work out some kind of mathematical theorem and was just on the verge of understanding when he'd interrupted. "Are you all right, Mae?"

Nodding, she took a breath, ready to speak, but paused, frowning before trying again, only to look back down at the newspaper.

He found her perturbation amusing and concerning, and his laugh was slight. "Perhaps I should put on the coffee and...get my own breakfast."

That suggestion shifted her chaotic deliberations. Her head snapped up. She rose, broadsheet crinkling beneath her hand. "I am not in your employ to look after myself."

"You know, I have some tablets that will help take the edge off the pain and grouch."

She looked at him, her expression oscillating through a range of eyebrow arrangements, rapid blinks, and a small cough. "Please pardon my foul mood, sir," she said, and her butler-trained veneer of calm returned. "The story on the front page is rather...distressing."

"Has a member of the royal family died or have there been social media-organised riots in London again?" He moved to the table to cast an eye over *The Times*.

"Neither, but, as you can see, there is a rather good reason for why my date stood me up last night."

Kitt lifted the paper and scanned it. "Mm, he was a banker felled by a heart attack."

"Yes, sir."

"A banker is commendable choice for an evening companion."

"You approve of my dead date?"

"Do you need me to approve, Mae?"

"I only wish not to embarrass you, sir."

He chuckled. "I think you deserve a man of distinction."

"Caspar was a man of distinction," she said and made a soft, sniffling noise that drew his attention back to her crinkling brow.

Damn, he thought, and his own brow furrowed. "Have I spoken out of turn? I only meant you deserve a man of the highest calibre rather than an insensitive idiot or a lout who would stand you up." Kitt waited for that little smile of hers to appear, for her to make a quip about his manners, but the groove between her brows simply deepened. She untied the strings of her white apron. Rather than a full cook's apron, she favoured short, half-waist chef's aprons, and she smoothed the sides of the one she wore over her hips after she retied the garment. It was a simple action, one he always enjoyed watching, but this time the act held a note of frustration. He set the paper back on the table. "Mae?"

Mae exhaled. Hands clasped behind her back, she looked at the Major, sheepishly. "It may be abundantly obvious, sir, that I am, shall we say, a little twitchy and out of sorts this morning."

That odd flicker of warmth, the flicker she saw last night was back in his eyes. "That's completely understandable. Take the day off, Mae," he said.

"And what would you eat if I did that, sir?"

"I'd...make do."

"With a stale Chelsea bun? Yes, of course you would." She left him chuckling beside the dining table, and went to make his eggs.

A little later he went to watch a match at Wimbledon and she spent the rest of Sunday afternoon cleaning up the mess at her place, shifting the mattress back onto the bed, restoring the upended couch to its rightful place, reorganising her desk and kitchen. By the time she'd finished, the Major had returned from the tennis. For his dinner, she made him lamb cutlets with buttered peas and new potatoes, which he ate with great relish.

After she did the dishes, she went outside with a small pair of secateurs to tend to the roses beside the staircase. She cut back spent blooms and gathered a few fresh blossoms for inside, then moved on to the lilacs at the gate.

She glanced up from her gardening as the Major came down the steps. Dressed casually in jeans, a lightweight jacket over his arm, he moved along the footpath and paused. "Oh, Mae, I'd like something from Barrett's for lunch tomorrow."

"Of course, sir."

"And breakfast at half-seven. Miss Astor will be joining me and..." He looked over her shoulder and she turned to follow his gaze. Two police constables walked along the footpath at the front of her place. The Major tilted his head and continued. "If Barrett's has them, I'd like those apple and boar sausages again."

"As you wish, sir. Have a pleasant evening, with Miss Astor." He headed up the street. A few seconds passed before Mae realised she'd been watching the movement of his arse, and squeezing spring-handled secateurs in one hand.

CHAPTER FOUR

F ive o'clock Monday morning, Mae entered the butler's pantry adjoining the kitchen and slipped off her messenger bag. In the small cupboard that housed brooms and the Hoover, she put a fresh set of work clothes on the shelf beside the laptop and envelope she'd left there previously. After tying on a fresh apron, she mixed sweet dough for Chelsea buns and set it aside to rise. She cleaned up remains of an intimate party her employer had the night before, picking up empty bourbon and wine bottles, and a trail of carelessly discarded women's clothing, placing the underthings and a thin dress into a cotton garment bag that she hung off a rack in the pantry. The empty bottles she took down the back staircase and outside to recycle. She retrieved the newspaper and brought it upstairs. Then she arranged two places of blue and white Minton china at the breakfast table near the big bay window in the sitting room. She laid the newspaper on the table and set out the Jersey butter, the little crystal pots of strawberry jam, Corsican honey, and her homemade orange and ginger marmalade.

By 6:50 the coffee was ready and the Chelsea buns were done. By 6:57 Mae was ready to scramble her employer's eggs, and he ambled into the kitchen in his dressing gown, in need of feeding, hair damp, a small, purplish love bite below his left ear.

"Good morning, Mae," he said, gravelly voiced.

"Good morning, sir." Mae set aside the coffee she'd been drinking and handed him a bottle of cold water, anticipating his need. The speed at which he guzzled the liquid was a plain indication that he was hungover. It was also the only sign that he'd drunk too much he ever displayed. She gave him another bottle and he downed it with the same haste.

He said, "How are you feeling this morning?"

"A wee bit sore, but fine."

"Do I smell Chelsea buns?"

"Yes, you pay, I bake," She passed him a steaming cup of black coffee and took the empty bottle from him.

"Ah, we've returned to standard operations this morning."

"Yes."

"Oh, goody. I missed my eggs yesterday." He perched himself on the tall stool at the end of the kitchen worktop and drank deeply from his cup. "Will you join me for coffee, Mae?"

"Of course. I know how you hate to drink alone." Mae retrieved her cup and finished what was left inside.

"Miss Astor may have left some things in the sitting room."

"I have them in the pantry, sir. Would she like her clothes laundered?"

"I think she'd prefer to wear them now. She doesn't like my dressing gown." He frowned. "Worse, she loves wine, drinks tea, and hates coffee. Have we any tea, Mae?"

Mae set her cup on the workbench, drew a wooden tea box from the cupboard beside the dishwasher, and pulled out a lone, ancient

Darjeeling tea bag. She filled the kettle with water and switched it on to boil. "Were you aware of Miss Astor's partiality for wine and tea before now, sir?"

"I was more aware of her partiality for me."

"Might I make a suggestion, sir?"

"Find a woman closer to my own age?"

Mae lifted the Chemex carafe of coffee and poured more into her cup. She turned to him and topped up his mug as well. "While you are skilled in many things, sir, you have yet to master mindreading."

His mouth pressed into a smirk that put the tiniest dimple in his left cheek. "You were saying?"

"Perhaps having a ladies' dressing gown on hand as a permanent fixture would be in order."

"The only permanent fixture I want on hand is your scrambled eggs. Can you believe Miss Astor doesn't know how to scramble an egg, Mae? One imagines that's why her husband is so unhappy with her."

"Yes, an inability to scramble eggs is a sure sign of marital strife," Mae said over the rim of her cup. "Is that why you are unhappy with Miss Astor, her lack of egg-scrambling aptitude?"

Her employer gave an impatient sigh. "I had enjoyed her company until the moment she divulged she despised coffee." He rose from the stool. "Forget the tea. I'm famished, and she's leaving. Her things?" When Mae didn't move, he looked at her, mirroring the way she'd tipped her head, brows lifted. "Yes, I see." he said. "You think I'm a sexist cad."

Mae took the empty mug from his hand. "Your mindreading ability has failed to develop in the last few minutes."

"Then what? What is it you think? Out with it, and don't pull your punch. My brother never has, so why should you?"

"You have a brother?" This was what he did, fed her tiny morsels about himself at the oddest times. She knew so little about his childhood and family, but it wasn't her place to make further enquires when he guarded his privacy in such a way. She refilled his coffee.

He took the cup. "Yes. A half-brother. He's older, your age in fact. Never pulled his punch because I was younger. Don't pull yours."

Mae removed the kettle from the burner. "It is my observation that wine gives you a very sore head and you truly hate sharing your breakfast."

Three minutes later, the Major bid his female companion a fond, hurried farewell, savoured every bite of his scrambled eggs, and ate two Chelsea buns, alone.

THE LITTLE BELL above the door rang as Mae exited Barrett's butcher shop in Belsize Park and tucked boar and apple sausages into a canvas shopping bag. Her mobile rang. She took it from the pocket of her dress and looked at the cracked, but readable screen. The name above the display read *Daniel Pierce – Suisse Global Bank.*

She'd forgotten she'd put his number into her contact list, their final appointment scheduled for this afternoon. She raised the mobile to her ear. "Hello?"

"Mrs Valentine?"

"Yes."

"Mrs Valentine, this is Ernst Largo with Suisse Global Bank at Cabot Square," he said, with an Austrian German accent. His manner was cordial and formal. Mae pictured him as a bald man with a pencil moustache and bow tie.

"Yes, Mr Largo?" she said.

"Mrs Valentine, I understand you had an appointment this afternoon with Mr Pierce."

"I did, Mr Largo."

"I am afraid I have some rather unhappy news to convey."

The stitches in her lip rubbed against the phone as she said, "Yes. I understand. I saw the report in *The Times*. It's very sad."

"Thank you, we are all distressed at his passing. *Ach, ja*, it came as such a shock. He was such a young, healthy man and...well, I am sure you can imagine we at the branch are distraught."

"He was an asset to your bank. Forgive me, that wasn't meant to be a joke. Mr Pierce was very helpful, a nice man and I li—" Mae decided that there was no need to mention that Daniel had been on his way to meet her the night he'd died. A dead man whose life had just been splashed across the newspapers deserved to have some privacy. She said, "Thank you for ringing to let me know. My condolences to you and to his family." She halted at the corner and waited for a car to pass before she crossing the street.

Mr Largo said, "You are very kind. Contacting you is a courtesy on our end, albeit an unhappy one, but as they say, life goes on, especially in the world of finance. I also ring with regard to your appointment today. Oddly enough, Mr Pierce had taken responsibility for some of my accounts while I recuperated in hospital after an unfortunate dining experience. Had I not fallen ill I would have handled your account from the start, and here it is in my hands now and...it seems quite unreal, so unreal and..." His voice had begun to crack. "I beg your pardon. Mrs Valentine..."

Mae adjusted the canvas shopping bag on her shoulder and winced when it dug into her sore muscles. She hadn't expected to still be sore two days after being assaulted, yet she ached all over. "Not a worry, Mr Largo," she said.

Largo exhaled unhappily and began again. "As I was saying, your account was one that Mr Pierce had undertaken to manage for me. I understand that he had been discussing the details of a trust with you. Is that correct?"

"Yes, that's correct." Mae said, heading along Englands Lane.

Mr Largo coughed and made a weedy, asthmatic sound. "I am afraid there are some documents Mr Pierce neglected to have you sign, which indicates to me that he may have failed to explain the conditions of the deposit's execution. It is embarrassing that such a thing happened here at Suisse Global. Perhaps he had Fridayitis."

She said, "Yes, perhaps it was Fridayitis."

"It is also conceivable he was not feeling well then. I cannot say, but I apologise for the oversight, and I am terribly sorry to ask if you might drop by Cabot Square today before noon, to sign, rather than at two o'clock as you had arranged with Mr Pierce? This way I can properly process the transfer for you by close of business today. If that is troublesome, I could pop 'round to your place and we can take care of it later this morning. I have your address here. I am visiting another client who lives not far from you, in Regent's Park, and it would be no effort to visit you as well. Would eleven suit you?"

Mae glanced at her watch. It was a little past nine. The Major liked to have lunch at one o'clock. She pulled a shopping list from her pocket and scanned it. Dry-cleaner, butcher, baker, off-licence, Sainsbury's—she'd done the first two. There was still the fresh bread, Gordon's gin, Basil Hayden's bourbon, the expensive French aperitif her employer liked, and a new toilet brush to replace one that had seen better days. Yes, she had plenty of time, but tending to Caspar's trust earlier meant that, instead of taking a cab to Cabot Square after lunch, she could spend the afternoon reorganising the spirits in the sideboard and washing blood from the Major's Bentley. She should have washed the Bentley yesterday. "Yes, eleven would suit me nicely. I appreciate you making the trip, Mr Largo."

"Wonderful. I will see you then," Largo said. "Ah, Mrs Valentine, one more thing. It would be a great help if I could look over any documents that Mr Pierce left with you, to ensure that nothing else was neglected."

"Of course, Mr Largo."

It was close to eleven when Mae parked her little Fiat in front of the Major's place and went around to take the shopping from the car's boot. A black Mercedes halted at the kerb on the other side of the road. A thin, tall man climbed out of the passenger side, a black, zippered compendium in one hand. The stocky, dark-haired driver exited the sedan and said something to the thin man, who replied with a nod. The driver leaned against the car, lighting a cigarette. The flame from his lighter reflected in his mirrored sunglasses.

The thin man crossed the street. Mae watched him head for the little gate at the front of her house. Three-piece conservative suit, shiny black shoes, club tie; he dressed like an old-fashioned banker. "Excuse me," she said. "Might you be you Mr Largo?"

He turned. "*Ach, ja.* I am. Mrs Valentine?" He smiled. Largo had a full head of light brown hair, and no moustache or bow tie. "Please," he said walking toward her, "let help you with those things."

"Don't trouble yourself. I need to take them to my employer's flat next door, upstairs. I won't be long."

"It is no trouble, I assure you. I am happy to help. If you could you please take this?"

She took his compendium and he took the box with the gin, bourbon, and Lillet, leaving her the sausages and toilet brush. Typically, she went around to the back of the building and used the rear stairs to her employer's flat, but Mr Largo was doing her a favour and the front steps were quicker. He followed her up the brick path and stairs, through the security door and the internal staircase to the Major's flat. She keyed in her code, opened the heavy door, and ushered Mr Largo inside to the kitchen.

The man was out of breath, puffing from the exertion of climbing the steps with an armload of heavy bottles.

She switched on the lights. "Just there is fine," she said, and he slid the box onto the worktop. Mae placed the compendium, new toilet brush, bread, and meat on the butcher-block surface. "Excuse me for a moment." She took the dry-cleaned dinner suit into the butler's pantry and hung it on a hook on the outside of the cupboard with the Hoover. After tying on an apron, she headed back to the kitchen, but turned about, and returned to the cupboard. Inside, on the shelf beside her laptop, was the envelope she'd left there several days ago. She returned to Mr Largo.

Moisture gleamed on Mr Largo's forehead, trickling around his brown eyes. He wiped both with a folded handkerchief, slid on a pair of reading glasses, and turned for his compendium.

"There's no reason for us to go anywhere else," Mae said. "Everything Mr Pierce gave me is right here." She pulled documents from the envelope. Daniel had given her the papers the morning of the day he'd died. "My home was burgled the other night. Quite a mess was left behind. Everything was so jumbled up I'd forgotten I'd left these papers here."

Largo swallowed, touched a hand to his throat, turned his head and coughed when she handed him the documents. "*Ach, ja,* so much has been jumbled and fumbled and..." He made a little humming noise as he leafed through the pages. With a satisfied nod he put aside her documents, mopped his brow again, and lifted the compendium embossed with *SGB*. "This is convenient and welcome. I'm a little winded and was not looking forward to climbing more stairs." With a cough, he unzipped the leather folder, flipped it open, revealing a thin pile of papers held together with a tiny fold-back clip.

Stuck on the top left corner of the first page was a yellow sticky note listing a neat, hand-printed column of names Mae read upside down. *Mr Bianco, Man, Torrisi, Russo, Valentine. Torrisi* was a brand of Italian coffee, *Russo* was a very common Sicilian name, and *Valentine* was the name she shared with Caspar.

Largo began coughing more. "May I trouble you for a little water?"

"Are you feeling all right?"

"To be honest, I am slightly light-headed. I am still recovering from a terrible bout of salmonella. It appears I am not quite as robust as I had hoped. I may have returned to work a little prematurely, but it was necessary, considering the circumstances."

She gave him a glass of water. He sipped it carefully. "Thank you," he said. "What is it you do, Mrs Valentine?" He drank more as he waited for her response.

"I'm a butler. Butler, housekeeper, chef, and," she smiled, "occasional chauffeur."

"A woman butler, how unusual and enchanting." With a tired smile, he drained the glass, set it on the worktop and lifted the sheaf of papers in the compendium. He undid the clip, removed the yellow note, and set a single page in front of her. He took a small pen from inside his jacket, removed the cap and held the black Montblanc out to her. "Please sign at the bottom, where you see your name printed. I shall then sign the document myself."

Politely, Mae took the ridiculously expensive gold-tipped fountain pen and scanned the paper. "I beg your pardon, Mr Largo, I don't quite understand. This is a revocation of lasting power of attorney."

"Yes, it is."

"Why would I sign a revocation?" Mae set down the pen. "Mr Pierce never mentioned anything like this.

"Ah, you see, the bank, acting on behalf of your husband, is granted lasting power of attorney over your husband's trust until the date he set forth came to pass. As the bank's representative, Mr

Pierce, or in this case, I, act on your husband's behalf, as arranged when he had opened the account, to ensure that his instructions are executed. We must both sign the bank revocation."

"You met with my husband?"

Largo dabbed his brow once more. "I'm afraid not. I am merely entrusted with carrying out his wishes, or rather the bank is. I act at the behest of the bank. As per your husband's wishes, Mr Pierce was in the process of transferring the lasting power of attorney to you, yet he failed to revoke *his* lasting power of attorney, meaning he failed to release the bank from acting on your husband's, or in this case, your behalf. I did not see the revocation in the papers you have here. I suspect that is why you had a meeting scheduled with Mr Pierce today. He did explain we had a difficult time finding you, did he not? Your husband's old addresses were listed."

"Yes, Mr Pierce mentioned that. I had no idea of such an account. I have to assume my husband set it up shortly before his death. We weren't married very long and there was nothing in the financial records he left behind indicating he'd left me anything more than what was in our joint account." Mae looked down at the page, reading through the paragraphs again.

"I understand if you would be more comfortable with carrying out this matter at the bank. This is not something to take lightly. Since this is such an unusual circumstance, perhaps it's best that the Branch Relations Manager, Ms O'Toole, explain this to you. I can have my driver take us both to Cabot Square and we can complete the task there at the branch. Sal will then return you here."

"That won't be necessary." Mae understood what she'd read and his clarification of lasting power of attorney. She signed the paper and extended the Montblanc to Largo.

He looked decidedly off colour as he signed his name on the line beside hers. He replaced the Montblanc's cap and his hands shook. He laid the pen on the worktop and licked his bottom lip, wheezing.

"Would you like another glass of water, Mr Largo?"

"Oh, please, yes, Mrs Valentine." Largo groped for the empty water glass, but pushed it farther away. He tried once more and knocked the glass against the bread and the plastic bag holding the toilet brush. The fountain pen and brush rolled off the worktop, the bag drifted off and the scrubber fell to the floor, bouncing into the dishwasher as Largo gave a little moan. "Mrs Valentine...oh, Mrs Valentine..."

Mae moved to his side. "Mr Largo, you're not well. *Sie sind nicht gesund.*"

"I am not. The world is going around and around. And you speak German. How nice. I must sit. I must sit and ring for my driver's assistance."

"Perhaps I should ring an ambulance?"

"No, no, I am just light-headed. The doctor said this might happen. My driver will look after me. I am afraid we must conclude this business at another time."

"Of course." She helped the wheezing, shaking man to the foyer and eased him into the chair where the Major sometimes left a sports bag. Mr Largo took out his mobile. His hand shook as he dialled his driver. Mae went to fetch the man another drink of water, returning with the glass as the downstairs door buzzer rang. She pressed the button to release the security lock and opened the upstairs door as soon as the driver knocked.

The stocky man reeked of cigarettes. "Largo?" the driver asked.

"I am here, Sal." Mr Largo placed the glass beneath his chair.

Head cocked, the driver said, "Okay?"

When Mr Largo nodded, the driver turned around. Sal looked at Mae, rubbed his nose, and shrugged. She saw his hand flash, light exploded and everything fizzled to black.

Ears ringing, Mae tasted blood. She heard, Largo, very faintly, "*Gott im Himmel*, Sal, put that bottle down and look at the mess you made. And did you have to be so rough with her? Wake her. Delicately, Sal, do it delicately. Oh, and while you are here go to the Revolution Exhibit at the Victoria and Albert Museum. Enjoy your holiday. Everyone should see London. Tell me about your trip next week."

Groggy, nauseous, Mae opened her eyes and found the kitchen tiles cold against her smarting jaw. The toilet brush and shiny black shoes were close to her nose. Her hazy gaze shifted from gleaming leather to the well-dressed man towering above.

The progression of time turned to individual photographs in three-second bites. In one picture Largo straightened all the papers. In the next, he zipped up the compendium. One more photo and he crouched down to her. In the short film clip she watched, he helped her sit up, propping her against the dishwasher, putting the toilet brush on the worktop above her head.

Largo said, "I promise you. He will be gentle. It will not hurt. Sal will not hit you again. It will not hurt. *Es wird wie Einschlafen sein.*"

"I don't want to go to sleep," Mae said, and something cold and wet splashed her face, stinging her eyes, her vision as foggy as her brain. In strobe-light images she saw Mr Largo leave the kitchen. Sal, his driver, screwed the top back onto the bottle he'd been drinking, and put it on the worktop beside the box with the bourbon and Gordon's gin. Then Sal knelt beside her and she heard the door to the flat close. He slipped his arm through hers and lifted her upright, as though she weighed nothing. He smelled of bourbon. Or maybe she did.

"*Allora,*" he said, turning her gently, slipping her into his embrace and then into the crook of his elbow. "Shhh, *tesora mia, vai a dormire.*"

Go to sleep, my treasure? His Italian snapped reality into sharp focus and Mae understood his intention. In a rush, before the man began to constrict the flow of blood to her brain and the breath from her body with a chokehold, she sagged dead weight, Sal adjusted his hold, and she bit him, flesh and blood filling her mouth.

"*Puttana!*" he yelled, shoving her hard. She crashed sideways into the edge of the worktop between the sink and the dishwasher and he pulled something from his pocket, flicking it one way and then the other. His knife glinted in the overhead lights. "*Delicatmente? O cazzo delicamente!*"

Forward, she had to move forward, to advance not retreat. She needed to advance with force and a target, to protect herself, to get away. The box with the bottles of gin and bourbon sat on the opposite worktop, right in front of the frying pans that hung on the wall, all out of reach. Mae did the best she could, grabbing whatever there was on the worktop behind her, and Sal stabbed the loaf of sourdough bread instead of her throat. She tried to dart to the right, to jerk open a drawer full of cooking utensils, but Sal slashed out, slicing her forearm. He slashed again, cut into her arm once more as she twisted to the left. She threw the packet of sausages into his face, but the meat hit him and tiles with a soft *plut*.

Advance, force, target, run. She dipped, snatched up the toilet brush, tightly gripping the staff of the white, bulbous, nylon-bristled mace.

Sal took one look at her began to laugh. He spread his arms out wide. "*Si. Sono un gabinetto sporco, lava mi*! Hai ham a dir-ty toilet, scrup me!"

Force and target, Mae pivoted and jabbed down, driving the toilet brush into his balls, putting all her weight behind one single step forward as she shouted, "*Vaffanculo!*"

Mouth open, Sal staggered, stepping on the soft packet of boar and apple sausages. The paper wrapping split, the plastic bag inside ripped apart, wild pig meat smeared across the tiles, and he slipped on sausage, crashing into her, falling forward, pushing her against the worktop, his dead weight dragging her down to the floor. He landed on her hard, the brush in her hand snapping.

With a twist, she scrabbled from beneath him, scuttling backwards, grabbing the handle on the oven door and everything slowed as she hauled herself to her feet. Ghost-like, Sal's breath rasped and rattled as he rolled onto his side, holding his testicles. Then he pawed at himself, his face contorted, his dark eyes feral. His feet kicked in a childish, stamping tantrum run at half-speed. Sal finally screamed, the noise long, and distorted as the spiked head of the toilet brush rolled a lazy path across the floor to become an island surrounded by gleaming scarlet surging along the tiles.

Mae watched the ruby red rivulets meander and stain the grouting. A rushing ocean, a howling wind, a roaring freight train combined to fill her ears and drown out Sal's high-pitched half-speed warble as the man tried to get to his knees. She back-pedalled out of the kitchen in slow motion, sluggishly untying and wrapping her apron around her bleeding arm. Near the door, she pounded the square red button at the base of the home security pad. When she made out the weak buzz of a voice she said, "There's been an incident in my employer's flat. There were two men. I may have killed a man."

A faint murmured reply came from the little speaker beneath the other end as droplets of crimson hit the polished oak floor.

"I can't hear you. I can't hear you." Starburst patterns exploded on the gleaming blonde wood of the foyer. Those marks on the wood would come up easily, but the blots she'd trailed across the sitting room, she'd have to tend to soon with dishwashing soap and water—or ammonia and water if it dried. Her heart thudded in her chest, in her mouth, in her arms, in her head as she reached for the front doorknob. Her hand slick with blood, the knob refused to turn, then it yielded all at once and the door opened.

The Major stood on the other side of the threshold. Immediately, his smart little grin flattened, his eyes hard and cold. He said something. His lips moved, but she couldn't hear him above the deafening clamour in her head.

CHAPTER FIVE

S wearing, Kitt lifted Mae's bloody chin. He drew her to the chair near the door, the place he usually dumped his sports bag, and sat her down. Blood smeared her chin, but the stitches she received in her lower lip the other night were unbroken. The blood darkening the front of her navy-blue dress, neck, and forehead had originated from her arm, which she'd bound with one of her aprons. He took her left hand and unwrapped the scarlet-mottled white cloth spooled around her forearm. The cuts were deep and not the usual sort that occurred in a kitchen accident. They might need stitching, but they were not life threatening. The fact she was speechless, dazed, suggested she'd cut herself, fallen, and hit her head. A possible concussion concerned him more than her bleeding arm.

"What happened, Mae?" He re-tied the apron around her wound, her expression as blank as it had been when he'd opened the door. He shook her shoulder. "Mae!"

Blinking, she looked beyond him, over his shoulder with an abrupt, reedy laugh. "There's a man. He stepped on your sausages and I killed him."

"Did you ring the police?"

"Sorry?" She rubbed her ears and looked up at him.

"Did you ring the police or use the security alarm?"

"In the kitchen," she said, and pressed shaking hands to her ears.

He yanked a brass-tipped walking stick from the antique umbrella stand near the chair and headed to the kitchen. He stopped in the doorway, realising there was no need for the stick. "Right," he said, and estimated there were about seven centimetres of clean tile between the entrance to the kitchen and the slick of bright red that began where a dark-haired man lay slumped against the dishwasher. A white bristled object lay in the bloody pool beside the man, the plastic handle in two pieces. "Well, I did I say you were deadly with a toilet brush," he muttered.

He went back to Mae, returning the cane to the umbrella stand. The dazed look had vanished, but her breathing was shallow and rapid. "Your lunch is ruined," she said.

"Yes, I saw that." Gently, he pushed her knees apart and shoved her head down between them.

"I'm not going to faint," she grumbled. Loudly.

Kitt crouched beside her. "You will if you keep breathing like that. Slow down, inhale, and count to five before you release the breath. Good. Yes. Like that." The perfume that rose from her neck was good Kentucky bourbon. He knew then how this was going to unfold. He muttered a vulgar word under his breath.

"Is he dead?" she said.

"I'd say so."

Mae looked at the Major's shoes. His toes were terribly scuffed. Muffled ringing penetrated the thrum in her ears. Then the Major spoke into his mobile as he rose. Mae thought he sounded as if he were underwater, in the bedroom, with his head stuffed in the wardrobe, but he was right beside her. In between her deep breaths and fluctuating levels of clarity, she heard him saying, "Yes...entire... One...female... Five minutes..."

Hunched over as she was, she watched his feet move across the carpet where she'd dripped blood. A moment later, he opened his front door and left it that way.

Mae righted herself, and immediately wished she hadn't. The muffled thickness in her ears vanished, but her face was on fire and she was going to be sick, which meant there'd be more than blood to clean from the wool and Persian carpets. She stood, legs as unsteady as runny egg yolks, and hurriedly wobbled her way toward the kitchen before the Major corralled her, turned her for his bedroom and escorted her to the ensuite.

It was bad enough she'd slept in her employer's bed, soaked in his bath, and killed a man in his kitchen, but now she was about to be ill in his pristine lavatory—in front of him.

It was not professional.

It was not appropriate.

It was happening anyway.

She was on her knees in front of the toilet, heaving, emptying her spleen, liver, kidneys, lungs, and whatever else was contained inside her body until she was as limp as overcooked pasta. All that time he was there, setting a cool, damp flannel on the back of her neck.

When she was through, he washed his hands, sat on the edge of the bath, and waited.

Mae leaned against the tiled wall and wiped her eyes with the flannel from her neck. "There were two of them," she said. "The first one said he was with Suisse Global Bank. He rang me earlier this morning, saying there was a matter with Caspar's trust that Daniel Pierce had failed to implement. We'd arranged to meet at my house, but this man was early. He was there when I got back from my errands for you. He helped me bring things upstairs. We discussed bank matters. I signed documents with his fountain pen. Then he pretended to be ill and asked for his driver. The second man, the one in the kitchen, was his driver. The first man left. The second man was Italian and he...stayed. He stayed to...put me to sleep, to kill me gently, *delicatamente*. I bit him."

"You did more than bite him."

"He tasted like an ashtray."

"Was that the reason for the toilet brush?"

"I snatched what was at hand. It was new, it was there, I grabbed it and belted him in the yockers. Now I'll have to buy another brush." She looked at drying smears of blood on her legs and rusty-looking sunbursts across the top of her feet. She'd lost a shoe and had no recollection of that happening. "Did you ring the police?" she said.

"I didn't need to. You pressed the security alarm."

"Did I?"

"Yes. An investigation team is on the way. It's automatic. That's what happens when you use the security system. Once it's activated they ring back to check with me."

"I didn't touch anything. I left everything as it was, not like with Caspar's photo the other night." Mae placed her hands on the toilet and hoisted herself up to stand, leaving bloody smears on the white porcelain—more to clean. She moved to the sink and rinsed her mouth, grimacing, dabbing a trickle of pink-tinged water with the damp cloth. "The first man was Austrian or Bavarian German, and he knew things. He knew things and he seemed credible. He said he was replacing Mr Pierce, the investment banker who stood me up. He had documents. Bank documents. Like the ones I'd left in your pantry." She looked at her employer's hard face reflected in the mirror above the sink.

He looked back at her with cold eyes that held a furious glint and yet he said nothing.

"I'm a fool," she said. "I let them in, sir. I let them in to *your* home. It was a stupid thing to do. Very stupid. I'm so sorry, sir. I understand if you'll want to let me go."

"Let you go?"

"Yes, sir. I killed a man in your home, in your kitchen. Of course you'll let me go."

"The others who employed you, Mae, the media mogul, the Danish royal family, and the head of the Gelsomino Pasta Company, is that what they would have done in a circumstance such as this, let you go?"

"Yes."

"Is that what you would do, let you go?"

"I would."

He crossed his arms. "Let you go? I worried that your hearing loss was a result of a head injury, yet it was only temporary, and understandable given the circumstances, but perhaps you are concussed. Does your heard hurt, Mae? Did you at any time black out?"

"Only when the Italian struck me, and only for a moment or two." She turned back to the basin, ran cold water over the cloth, wringing it out before laying it against her swelling face.

"He hit you in the jaw. Rather well." He rose and came to stand beside her at the sink, very gently taking the cloth from her hand. "We should clean those cuts on your arm properly, and you need ice."

"The ice is in the kitchen. I don't want to go into the kitchen."

As he had the night before last, he turned slightly and his chest pressed into her back. He reached over her head and opened the medicine chest hidden behind the mirror, taking out a flat, white and green packet. He squeezed the Insta-chill pack with one hand, shook it, and laid it against her jaw. "Let you go," he said, meeting her eyes in the mirror.

Mae returned his unwavering gaze; pain, fear, and lingering nausea were replaced by sensations and thoughts even more bizarre than the things that had caused the pain, fear, and lingering nausea. She forgot herself, mumbling, *"Are you feckin' jokin'?"* but the words were masked by a man calling out, "Major Kitt!"

The Major put the cold pack in her hand and hurried out of the bathroom. He returned several minutes later, his jaw tight with fury. There were two men with him. One was tall, had a cleft chin, and brown hair he wore with an old-fashioned side part kept in tidy place with hair product. He had a medical kit in one giant hand. The other man was tall as well and built like a soccer player. He too had a cleft chin, but his black hair was slightly curly, and he had the greenest eyes Mae had ever seen. Dark brows rose above those incredibly green eyes as he said, "This is Mrs Valentine?"

Kitt ignored Bryce's tone of incredulity and jerked his chin at Hindmarsh. "Mrs Valentine, this is George Hindmarsh. He's Australian, but don't let that put you off. He'll have a look at you and take a few photos for his report. I'll be with Bryce and the rest of the investigation team, in the kitchen."

Bryce gave Hindmarsh a nod and looked Mae up and down for a second time. "I've been told you'll need to join us there when you're done, Mrs Valentine."

Kitt exhaled harshly, watching Hindmarsh pull bandages and a hypodermic from a medical chest. "Is all this really necessary, Bryce?"

"You know it is," Bryce said. "Without exception."

As Hindmarsh fished out a small glass phial, Kitt took a step toward Bryce, saying "Not this time."

"Without exception." Bryce shook his head slightly. "Without exception, Major Kitt. Would you like Hindmarsh to explain the procedure?"

Kitt's hands were tied and he knew it. He'd complicated the

matter with his butler by not acting with restraint, by not following protocol, and Bryce addressing him as *Major* was a friendly reminder to rein in his temper and ego the way he should have Saturday evening. Glaring, Kitt said, "Sod it," and looked back at Mae.

Her attention was on the green-eyed Welshman rather than the hypodermic that Hindmarsh was filling. She said, "I'm glad to finally put a face to a voice on the phone, Sergeant Bryce."

Bryce turned to her, nodding. "You too, and it's Timothy."

Mae gave the man a weak half-smile. "If I may, Sergeant, please ask your people to try not to track blood all over Major Kitt's carpet."

"Come sit here, love," Hindmarsh said, patting the little stool, "and let me have a squizz at ya." He held an antiseptic swab in one hand and a syringe in the other. "I'm going to take a little blood sample, so we can differentiate your type from the man in the kitchen, but first, can you tell me the last time you had a tetanus shot?"

"A tetanus shot? Saturday."

Kitt loosened his jaw. He watched Mae regard the damned needle, her eyes cut to his before she scrunched up her face and accepted her fate. "I'm sorry," he said. He wanted to take her hand, to offer her something to grip while she cursed under her breath, as she had with the needle the other evening. Instead, he conceded to her destiny, left Hindmarsh to tend to her, and gave Bryce a push out the door.

They had got as far as the bedroom doorway when Bryce said, "What was that about?"

"She's been through enough already."

"And you wanted to make it worse?" Bryce shook his head. "What's going on here? You told me your housekeeper was an older woman."

"Butler. She's my butler, and she's older than me." Kitt moved through the door, into the short hallway, and headed for the kitchen.

Bryce followed. "By what, a few hours?"

"A few years."

"Let's go back to what happened Saturday."

"She was mugged, in Kensington Palace Gardens, her keys were stolen, and later her house was robbed."

"After which you rang in Saturday night, irritated the Station Duty Officer and stepped on some toes. Have you ever considered you might be past your use-by date, Kitty?"

"You'd be close on my heels."

"I am well aware I am your senior and junior, Major."

"And when will you retire, Sergeant Bryce?"

Bryce evaded the question with a statement. "I heard Casino was very unhappy."

"Your friend Casino can go to hell."

"Well, you did step on his toes."

"I stepped on his toes?"

"Llewelyn said it escalated. I figured toes or fingers were involved. And this break-in, this—"

"This, from what she just told me, is follow-on assault."

Bryce rubbed his chin. "You know, I'm wondering how she was mugged in Kensington Palace Gardens with all that Diplomatic Protection Group security around."

"You tell me."

"What a cock-up."

The pair moved past two police constables and a detective waiting at the breakfast table in the sitting room. "Gentlemen," Kitt gave the men a glance.

"Morning, sir," the detective said.

"There's one more thing." Bryce fell into step alongside. "Why does it sound like you think you're responsible for her mugging?"

"I was with her. And I left her for a moment. That moment was enough for her to be attacked. Why are you here, Bryce?"

"You hit your panic button. Office was notified. Hindmarsh and I were notified."

"Llewelyn cares. How nice."

"Your housekeeper, Kitty." Bryce cleared his throat. "Have you enjoyed her company in other ways as well?"

"Butler." Kitt paused, turning to Bryce. "No, Bryce. I was out with Ursula Green and I ran into Mrs Valentine at the same restaurant."

"Redheaded Ursula from Henderson's section?"

"Yes."

"How'd that go?"

"Her boyfriend asked her to marry him. She cried all over me about it."

Bryce chuckled. "She cried because she was disappointed he asked her to marry him and you didn't?"

Casting a sidelong glance, Kitt walked on. "We never discussed marriage."

"Well, why would you need to when you've got your housekeep —butler to keep you warm and...holy hell that's a lot of blood." Bryce gaped at the kitchen entrance.

Two team members in pale blue coveralls, facemasks, and safety glasses were processing the scene. Crouched in front of the dead man was Soames, black liner tipping up at the corner of her brown eyes. She said, "Ah, Major Kitt. This is your place. No wonder Llewelyn told Special Branch to get a team over here so quickly."

Kitt shrugged. "It's never what you know, Soames..."

"But who you know. I'm glad to see you well. So who is this man? His femoral artery was severed."

Bryce pointed to the broken toilet brush that Moore, another Investigative Service team member, placed inside a plastic bag. "With that?"

"Possibly."

Kitt said, "Mrs Valentine told me she 'belted him in the yockers'. She has deep cuts on her arm. Mr Hindmarsh is processing her."

"Mm-hm, defensive wounds. The blood pattern and pooling here indicate he was down low when the perforation occurred. My guess is she incapacitated him with the brush and killed him with this." Soames held up a flick knife. "I'm going to assume this is what caused the cuts on her arm, but I can't be certain until I look at them myself. Who is he?"

Kitt shrugged. "I didn't enter the kitchen and go through his pockets to find out. I didn't touch him. It's a crime scene. I know how these things work and that's why you're here."

"Is this your pen?" she said.

Kitt looked at the Montblanc. It was a beautiful, very expensive writing instrument he'd never waste money buying. He exhaled and put out his hand. Soames passed the pen over to him and he tucked it into his pocket.

With a snort, Moore's eyes turned squinty. "If you didn't touch him, how could you be sure he was dead?"

Kitt smiled. "Experience."

"Define your *experience*." Moore sniffed his disgust.

"Afghanistan, Kuwait, Bosnia, Rwanda, Iraq, Colombia. Take your pick."

Moore threw up his hands. "What in hell does that mean? This man might have been alive when you found him!"

"Yes, he might have been."

Despite the mask and safety goggles, Moore was bug-eyed apoplectic. "Y-y-you admit that and yet you did nothing to see if he was? What sort of man are you?"

Amused, Bryce muttered, "Yes, Kitty, what sort of man are you?"

"Mr Moore," Kitt said, ignoring Bryce. "Look at the blood on the floor. The average human body carries about five and half litres of blood. Think about how you buy your milk and pour that milk all over the floor tiles. Now look at the blood again and add that amount of blood loss to a drop in blood pressure. Even if the man had been alive, there was nothing I could do, no assistance I could have offered. My concern was my butler, not the dead man, which he already was, even if his heart was still beating."

All the air went out of Moore's bluster. "I see."

"Good."

Soames held up a hand. "The operator said your housekeeper mentioned two men."

"There *were* two men," Mae said from outside the kitchen doorway. "That man is Italian. His name is Sal."

Kitt turned and wondered how long she'd been there, and what she'd heard. Barefoot, her face washed of blood, clumps of hair were damp and loose about her battered face. She stood back from the kitchen, straightening things on the bookcase. Hindmarsh had given her an injection, seen to her injuries, collected samples, taken the photographs he needed, and then sent her out to the kitchen. Her shoes, blood-soaked dress, and apron had been gathered as evidence. Mae wore blue coveralls similar to the kind that kept Soames and Moore clean, only she'd turned up the sleeves. The wounds on her forearm closed by butterfly plasters, she held the cold pack on her swollen jaw, the fresh bruising on its way to indigo. If the man in the kitchen hadn't already been dead, Kitt would have, regardless of the presence of the police and investigative service, finished the job. With a well-placed foot on the larynx.

Mae's glassy eyes strayed to the activity in the kitchen and darted back to fix on his. Her decompensation was happening quickly. She licked her bottom lip repeatedly. Then she focused, adjusted her mindset to who she was and the position she held. She said, her voice sharp, "Sir, Inspector Sender would like me to accompany him to the station. There may be a delay in my return. I can arrange for a company to clean this mess and have a service send in a temporary housekeeper during my absence, if that is something you would find suitable."

"I would not." Kitt bit his molars together and glared at Bryce.

SHE'D READ about the after-effects of surviving a life or death situation. Or the Major told her about the after-effects of surviving trauma. Mae really couldn't recall which it was, but surreal and frenetic was an accurate description. Since she'd been shown to this room, her mind was abuzz, questions swarmed, and expanded, and took on an energy of their own. She preferred the constant barrage of queries to the horrid disjointed images she had of Sal's blood-soaked hands or his warbling slow scream for help. She had so many questions, but she wasn't the one asking them now, and her mouth was cotton dry. Detective Inspector Sender, a short, middle-aged man, set another cup of water in front of her. She drank the water just as quickly as she had the last two.

Sender removed his jacket before he eased back in his chair. His arms bulged the sleeves of his shirt, the fit of the blue fabric tight across his muscled chest. He was soft-spoken, his voice deep and soothing, a little like Mr Stephens, the handsome actor who lived in the flat below hers. "Now, Mrs Valentine." Sender set a pen on the desk. "This man Ernst Largo told you he was with Suisse Global Bank. He rang you this morning, saying there was a matter with a trust that your husband had set up. You had dealt with another gentleman at the SGB, but he died of a heart attack at the weekend. This morning, you arranged to meet Largo at your house, he arrived early, and assisted you in bringing a box of heavy things upstairs—that would be the box of plonk that was in the kitchen."

"Plonk?" Mae pinched the bridge of her nose and glanced around the grey room with the grey ceiling, grey table, grey floor, grey chairs, and blue-white overhead lighting. Sender refilled her cup and Detective Sergeant Mathis leaned against the grey-tiled wall, picking his cuticles, flicking tiny bits of dead skin to the grey floor. His grey pants and paler grey shirt matched the interview room's decor. She stared at his trousers until they faded into the drab colour of everything around her. Had she been set-up? Maybe there was an irate husband somewhere bent on getting even with the Major and she got in the way? Or was this a crime of opportunity built upon...Daniel Pierce? And *why*? Why her?

"Did this..." Sender shuffled his notes, "...Largo have any bank credentials?"

Credentials. Had she ever asked to see any bank credentials? Had she always been so gullible and stupid and careless an—

"Mrs Valentine!"

"Yes. I'm sorry. Where were we?"

"Let's go back to the plonk in the kitchen. Do you drink alcohol regularly, Mrs Valentine?"

"Erm, I wouldn't call Basil Hayden's plonk, but no," she reached for the water and sipped, "I do not drink regularly. In fact, I seldom drink at all."

"I see," Sender said. "When was the last time you had an alcoholic drink?"

"Saturday evening. Well, technically, it was Sunday morning, after I discovered my home had been ransacked. My employer gave me a glass of Glayva."

"Are you certain that you didn't have that drink this morning, perhaps?"

"I did not," Mae huffed, shifting in her seat.

"You said you discussed bank matters with this man before he pretended to be ill and asked for his driver, the man who died on the kitchen floor. You said Largo was Austrian and the dead man..." Sender looked down at his notes, "...Sal, you say he was Italian. How do you know these men were Austrian and Italian?"

She sipped a little more water, letting it spread across the arid thing that was her tongue. "My husband was Italian. I schpeak —*speak* German and Italian. The Aush—*Austrian* German accent is distinctive. The woman the other night, the one who stole my bag when I was attacked, she was Italian as well. Do you think that's a coincidence or do you think she and Sal, and perhaps even Largo, may have been working together?"

Mathis took a pair of nail clippers from his pocket as he came away from his spot against the wall and moved to stand near the door behind Mae. The clippers *snip-snipping* as he gave a little cough.

Sender glanced over her head and then returned to his notes. "Where's your husband now, Mrs Valentine?"

"He died in a car accident sixteen years ago."

"Yes," Sender nodded at the papers he read. "That accident involved three-hundred cars in heavy fog outside Padua. We checked."

"If you knew, then why did you ask?"

Sender kept his head down. "Let's go back to the other night, when you said you were attacked. Where was that again?"

"In front of the Nepali embassy, in Kensington Palace Gardens."

Mathis exhaled, as if he were the one who'd been assaulted, killed a man, ruined his employer's Persian carpet, and was now subjected to police questioning. "I've had enough of this, haven't you?" he said.

Mae turned in her seat and glared. "Is there something bothering you, Detective Sergeant Mathis?"

Inspector Sender let out a soft little chuckle "Detective Sergeant Mathis is trying to convey, rather impolitely, Mrs Valentine, that there are a few holes in what you've told us."

She faced the Inspector. "I've had a horrible experience, and I'm trying to comprehend it. It seems reasonable if I'm a little... muddled, don't you think?"

"We don't doubt that today's been trying."

"I've told you everything, three times." Or was it four? Mae rubbed her eyes, finding it difficult to concentrate. There were moments of clarity and moments where simple things made no sense, moments where everything drifted, and moments that leapt from one thought to another, and her mouth was dry, so damned dry. Her dehydrated tongue formed words, "If you need me to tell you everything again...what are you looking for to fill these holes you mention? What do you think I'm leaving out?"

Mathis moved to the table and parked his arse on the edge beside her, shoving the clippers into his pocket. "Well, for starters, a record of this...assault and robbery you say happened in front of the embassy, that would be nice to have."

Mae blinked. "What do you mean there's no embassy record of the assault or robbery? Two constables came to my home that night, when my house had been looted. Surely there's a police report."

Sender shook his head. "There was no break-in reported in your neighbourhood."

"Well, of course there wasn't a break-in reported. Whoever took my bag had my keys and let themselves in!" She downed what was left of her water and banged the empty cup on the tabletop.

"And then there's the fact your blood alcohol level is point oh-nine. You like Basil Hayden's bourbon, Mrs Valentine?" Sender shrugged. "Personally, I prefer Jim Beam Black."

"Point oh-nine?" Mae shook her aching head, her heart skittering in her chest. "That's impossible. I...I haven't had...there's been a mistake...a mix-up of some—"

"Right. You don't drink." Mathis smirked. "Your slurred speech, the near empty bottle of bourbon we found in your employer's kitchen, and the blood taken by the paramedic tells us you had a tipple or ten. We checked a few other things too. The Diplomatic Protection Group logged no disturbance at the Nepali embassy last weekend, but Notting Hill Police Station recorded your assault—on Bayswater Road. Suisse Global Bank has no record of an employee named Ernst Largo working at any Branch of Suisse Global Bank, on any continent." Mathis hunched toward her. "So, enough of the porkie pies. Your husband was Italian. You said the man who assaulted you Saturday night was Italian. The man you killed this morning, you said he was Italian too. You like Italian men, don't you, Mrs Valentine?"

The colour of the room shifted from dull grey to blue-white, and Mae squinted against the sudden brilliance as she squinted at the two policemen. "What are you saying? Exactly *what* are you saying?"

"I'm saying you and your Italian boyfriend had a lover's tiff last Saturday, after he stood you up at the Baldessare Hotel. We spoke to several employees at the Baldessare. We know you were there, alone. We know your employer was there as well. How nice of you to use your employer, a decorated military officer, to keep your boyfriend from knocking out your teeth a little later. Your assault at the weekend was a convenient way to explain your actions from this morning, but there weren't two men at your employer's flat, there was only one. The Italian man you killed, he was a bit of company you picked up this morning because you like Italian men. They remind you of the husband you lost. You brought this Italian man back to your employer's flat, had a few...things got a little friendly... maybe a little too friendly for your liking, and it all went balls-up.

You protested, he hit you, and you killed him with the knife he cut you with. Now that's a murder charge, although a judge or the defence will probably introduce the claim as manslaughter, but of course your injuries suggest you used reasonable force to protect yourself, which could mean you make a claim self-defence. That sound about right to you, Inspector?"

Mae thought her mouth had been dry before, but now her teeth stuck to her lips when she said, "No." The light too bright, her heart pounding, she stared at the Detective Sergeant as he sat back and crossed his arms, gloating. And suddenly she was furious. "No, that's not right!" She shot to her feet, hands on her hips, indignation forcing her tongue to unstick from the back of her throat. "Ya insulting, bloody peelers talkin' shite. That is *entirely* incorrect!"

There was a sharp knock and the door opened. A silver-haired woman poked her head into the room. Sender and Mathis exchanged bemused looks. "We're not done yet, Detective Superintendent," Sender said.

"Yes. You're done," She poked a thumb over her shoulder. "She's out."

CHAPTER SIX

Mae yanked on the change of clothes her employer had brought for her and walked out of the Rosslyn Hill Metropolitan Police Station. The Major waited, sitting with an arm draped casually over the back of a bench outside the front of the red-brick building. He rose when he saw her, finished the conversation he was having on his mobile, and shoved the phone into a jacket pocket. She was too frenzied, too pasty-mouthed to decipher if his lack of expression meant he was angry or if his blankness meant anything at all.

The Major said nothing, simply glanced over at his Bentley parked near the pay and display ticket-vending machine. She followed him to his car and climbed in when he opened the passenger door. For a moment, he stood beside the open door, so still, palms on the roof, gazing across the top of the luxury vehicle.

She said, "Have you acted as surety for bail?"

His hands moved. "You've been released without charge for now, into my care, but you'll have to return here on the first."

"Thank you. I'll repay y—"

"I don't need gratitude." He shoved a fist into a pocket. "This will not happen again, Mae."

"No, sir. I'll refrain from making a habit of inviting men into your home and killing them in your kitchen."

His laugh was dry.

Mae stared at a button on his shirt, just above where his navel would be, and remembered Sal's distorted squeal and the fountain of blood bubbling up in his lap. "That was not something I hallucinated. While they said I lied about everything else, the police said I killed that man. On that we agreed. I saw his blood spill out all over the floor. He tried to kill me and I killed him. Do you think it's unusual to feel nothing after killing someone?" She lifted her eyes to find him looking down at her, and then she knew, without a doubt, that he was angry.

The Major swallowed. His jaw moved forward, baring his bottom teeth as he exhaled. "I should let you go. I should spare myself the trouble and let you go, and watch you walk away."

She nodded and her head began to throb. "Yes. You should. If you were smart you'd let me go right now. You'd leave me here to find my own way home and you'd let me go."

"If I were smart I probably would." His anger shifted, his eyes narrowing and then softening. "I'll take you home."

"It might be a better idea to take me to a doctor, sir. Perhaps I did hit my head after all. You asked me if I had blacked out and maybe I did, for longer than I thought. I have a headache that comes and goes, and the police said some things, things that make no sense. They said I was drunk, they said I drank bourbon."

"You don't like bourbon, Mae." He shut the door.

Mae stared out the window as he drove. Too many questions overcrowded her mind for her to settle on just one to ask him.

After a silent ten minutes, he found a space in the car park of the Royal Free Hospital in Hampstead. "I hate hospitals." He shut off the engine.

Mae released her seat belt. "Does that mean you're going to find me a doctor like you did before?"

He glanced at her, left side of his mouth quirking. "Would you like me to?"

"I don't know."

"You would, wouldn't you?"

"Yes... No. This is all wrong."

"Because I'm a bully?" He tapped the wheel with one finger.

"Because you are my employer, because...you are my friend, and because nothing makes any sense."

"Being attacked never makes sense."

"I meant what the police said." Mae touched her tender face. "How can there not be a record of my assault in front of the Nepali embassy? Wouldn't the embassy and the Diplomatic Protection Group have CCTV footage? Why would the report be at the Notting Hill station? You were there. You know it happened, and you know where it happened. How can I have a blood alcohol reading of point-oh-nine when I had nothing to drink? Have I mentioned the police insisted I was a drunkard with a taste for abusive Italian men?"

He shook his head. "We both know you like brooding men with black souls."

Hyped up, bewildered, raw and battered, Mae's laugh possessed a sharp, frenetic edge.

"You're having a very bad week," he said.

"And it's only Monday."

Finger drumming on the steering wheel again, he said, "I think you may have been forced to drink the bourbon, Mae. You reeked of it when I found you."

"Being forced to drink bourbon is something out of an old Cary Grant movie. I'd remember that happening."

"Like you remember hitting the home security alarm? I know you don't recollect doing so, and yet that's exactly what you did. I asked you if you had blacked out. First you said no, and then a few minutes ago you suggested I bring you to a doctor because you decided you might have blacked out. Hindmarsh didn't believe you were concussed. And I don't think you are either." He turned in his seat, leaving one hand on the wheel. "Listen to me. In situations where your life is at risk, time often speeds up or slows down. Your focus can shrink to pinpoint on nothing but your own survival, so that everything else is shut out. Because of that, it's not uncommon to have some kind of short-term memory loss associated with traumatic events. And you've had two in a very short time frame. A similar thing can happen after a spike in adrenaline. The hyperarousal of your nervous system may make you feel more emotional, fatigued once those stress hormones drop off, and your sens—"

"My mind won't stop racing. Does that make it seem I'm more emotional?"

The left corner of his mouth pulsed again. "Mae, you're positively wrecked."

"Don't sugar-coat it, sir."

"I wouldn't know how to sugar-coat this, except perhaps to say that, despite the wispy bits so pretty about your bashed-up face, your hair is perfect."

Mae laughed and felt her eyes burn, but tears did not eventuate. The lack of tears served to further baffle her, added to her anger and numb sense of disbelief that she had killed another human being. She pushed a few strands of hair behind her ears. What she wanted more than anything was an explanation for the things she *knew* had happened, despite the police being otherwise convinced. She wanted answers to the avalanche of questions that slipped and rolled through her mind. Yes, she'd been knocked about, nearly killed, and, as a result, had acted in a way so as to cause a man's death, but she *knew* what had happened several nights ago, and she *knew* what had transpired before Sal had given her a blow to the jaw.

She wanted to know why. She wanted to know how she was put into a position that had driven her to kill another human being. What the Major said about time slowing down and contracting into a sort of tunnel vision was somehow accurate as well, except there were all sort of tunnels to go down, and there didn't appear to be light at the end of any of them.

She prodded at the stitches in her lip. "Why do you think the Nepali embassy and the Diplomatic Protection Group have no record of my assault? That did happen, didn't it? You were there. I watched you break that man's nose...and I liked seeing you do it. I enjoyed the sound it made. It was...satisfying. Why is that?"

"Mae," he said so carefully, confidently, matter-of-factly. "Embassies and consulates prefer to have incidents like car accidents and your attack handled by the local police. It's a form of cooperation, to avoid embarrassment, or unwanted attention because what government wants to be seen sleeping on the job in another country? The embassy is embarrassed that they dropped the ball with the man whose nose you saw me break. The Nepali government wants to save face and the police will shoulder the blame for the mishap. Had you been more severely injured or killed...that would have been different. Trust me on this."

She regarded him for a long moment. "I have no reason to not trust you, but I find myself wondering what it was you did in the army, sir."

"Basic diplomacy."

"You mean you were a government attaché?"

"Everyone in the military is an envoy for Her Majesty."

"I suppose they are." She did not press him further, knowing he did not like to talk about his military career, what he'd witnessed, or how he'd participated in the horrors of war. Sean was the same. What her brother had faced as a chaplain with UN forces in Bosnia was not something he ever wanted to revisit or discuss. Gingerly, she touched her swollen jaw, the stitches in her lip, and shifted her attention to a hedge outside. "Do you think I was set up?"

It was a sparklingly blue, warm summer day and ice ebbed into Kitt's veins as his gaze absorbed her injuries. They were a reminder of how he'd made an error in judgement and complicated this matter with his butler. She was in this position because he'd overreacted when the situation had called for measured restraint. He had bodged this, handled it so poorly. Immediately after the mugging he should have insisted she take a holiday instead of a single day, rather than thinking of himself and his stomach. "What do you mean set up?" he said. "Explain that."

"Targeted, singled out. Or was what happened simply a crime of opportunity, where my being in the wrong place at the wrong time opened the proverbial door and things snowballed into whatever *this* is."

"Is that what you think?" Kitt sat back and a rapid exploratory monologue spilled out of her.

She said, "I don't know what I think, except that I can't stop thinking. I'm, as you said, wrecked, and I can't stop bloody thinking about why and how, and what I did or didn't do, especially since it now involves you. How and where did it begin? It seems so well thought out, so *organised*, there has to be some kind of ring at work here, don't you think? There has to be someone who watches and waits for an opportunity to present itself, like those people who sit and listen to the police radio, or the kind who troll social media sites to see who was stupid enough to put 'we're on holiday' as a status. Did someone notice I was alone at dinner in the Baldessare, and they thought I looked an easy target? Did you think I looked easy?"

"Nothing about you is easy, Mae."

"Yes, I could have been set up." She nodded. "They saw me alone, paid for my dinner and followed me—followed us. They saw a moment and took it. Identity theft. Isn't this what happens with identity theft, someone looks at a driving licence, at credit card statements, financial records, personal details? Someone went through my things, through my personal papers. Identity theft explains how Largo knew about Caspar's trust when he wasn't a Suisse Global Bank employee. Something was taken from my house; something I haven't noticed was missing. And you, you were simply at the wrong place with the wrong person. At this rate, it's conceivable that we could get back to your flat and find that it has been emptied by someone else and the mess I made..." She frowned and drew in a sharp breath. "Oh," she said. "Oh. Your kitchen."

"I've seen to the kitchen, Mae."

"Oh, no. No." She pressed the heels of her hands against her head. "It is not your job or anyone else's to see to my work. It is not your job. I work for you. I am the professional. You pay me."

"Yes, I pay and you care." Kitt opened his door. "I'll find you a doctor."

She laid a hand on his arm. "No, sir. I don't need you to bully a doctor. I need you to take me to the Suisse Global Bank at Cabot Square."

TIFFANY O'TOOLE TAPPED the screen and looked over the top of her purple-framed glasses. "Yes," she said. "My associates confirm you were here speaking with Mr Pierce last week, but as I said, I am unable to find an account in your name. There is no correspondence with you in Mr Pierce's files, no hard paper or electronic documentation or confirmation of any correspondence with you. There is a desk calendar entry for Saturday, the day he passed on. It simply says *Dinner, Mae Valentine, Baldessare, 20:30.*"

Ms O'Toole removed her spectacles. Thin, with high cheekbones, she had dark circles under her eyes and a wan look that came from lack of sleep. "You say there was an account, a trust that named you as beneficiary awaiting transfer, and Mr Pierce was assisting you with that transfer, yet I find no evidence of one."

"And the man, Largo, you have no evidence of him either?" Mae said.

On her desk was a photograph of a toddler dressed as a lion. O'Toole focused on the picture for a moment before she pressed her lips together and slipped her glasses back into place. "None. I told the police the same thing I am telling you, again. There is no employee with Suisse Global, at any branch *worldwide*, named Largo. It's not a mystery why he'd know my name. I am listed as a Relationship Manager on the Suisse Global website, as are several others at this branch. I have nothing, Mrs Valentine. Unless you are able to show otherwise, I cannot help you."

"Show otherwise?" Mae gave a high-pitched snort.

"Show otherwise how?" Major Kitt sat in the leather armchair beside Mae's. He replied to the message he'd received, looked up from his mobile, and waited for O'Toole to respond.

The banker's eyes flicked to the clock on the wall behind him.

"This bank closes at 7:00, Ms O'Toole. It is 6:32," he said, tucking his mobile into his jacket pocket.

The too-thin brunette put a palm to her mouth, tears springing to her eyes as she shook her head. She dropped her hand. "Oh, I apologise for my rudeness, Mrs Valentine. I'm getting back on my feet after a time in hospital. It's been a little stressful for us here today, with Mr Pierce passing on. He was a charming, lovely man, as you might know, seeing as you were...dating. We adored him, but that is no excuse. I can see that this is frustrating for you. And it is for me as well. I am truly sorry. I have no explanation for what you've told me. I have nothing to confirm any sort of dealing that Mr Pierce or Suisse Global Bank may have had with you."

Kitt pocketed his mobile. "You've been ill, Ms O'Toole?"

"Yes. Food poisoning. Quite severe. I only returned to work today. I'm beginning to think I've been premature in doing so."

"Ha!" Mae's laugh was short and, sharp. She looked at Kitt and shook her head. "Largo said he had food poisoning."

O'Toole blinked. "If you...if you could give me something to look over, Ms Valentine, copies of documents you have, the letters you say Mr Pierce wrote to you, the financial information—"

Mae tittered. The woman made an absurd request for an absurd incident that Mae thought left her in precisely the same financial state she'd been before anyone from Suisse Global Bank had contacted her. She'd thought Caspar's 'trust' was a scam. She'd thought Daniel Pierce was a scam, but he turned out to be genuine. The money—the bloody money—had always been the scam. "I have no copies." She tittered again. "What I had was stolen by a man who claimed he worked for this bank. He said he'd had salmonella, said he'd been in hospital like you, and he had Suisse Global papers."

Cackling, Mae looked at Ms O'Toole and the jaunty little scarf she had tied around her neck, the peach fabric knotted in such a way it gave the appearance that Ms O'Toole had a penis sitting beneath her chin, which only served to make Mae laugh harder and louder. Thunderous whoops of gasping laughter rolled from her. The door of O'Toole's office was shut, but bank patrons took notice of the noise, peering through the slats of the plantation-shutters as they stood in line for a bank teller, leaning around privacy screens as they filled out deposit or withdrawal slips, and she kept on laughing. Tears streamed from her eyes, her sides began to ache more than her bloated, battered face, more than her head.

"Mrs Valentine, please!" Ms O'Toole said, fingering her scarf.

Mae stopped laughing and began to rock in her seat because what the hell else could she do?

"What's wrong with her?" O'Toole said, palms cupping her cheeks.

Mae shot Kitt a helpless glance. He knew she was about to hit the wall. He rose and pulled her to her feet. "She's been assaulted, swindled, and robbed, Ms O'Toole, and it appears Suisse Global Bank may have been as well. Perhaps you should notify your head office to look into this. I'd suggest you do it sooner than later." Hand on her elbow, he led Mae out of O'Toole's office, into the bank, the foyer, and outside where he paused to look at the shops and cafés about Canary Wharf.

"Well, now what?" she said, massaging her scalp vigorously.

He took her arm and tucked it into the crook of his. "Let's take a little walk." He began to move her through Columbus Courtyard at an easy speed. Instead of returning to where the Bentley was parked in Cabot Place, Kitt escorted her toward the Thames, leading her along Westferry Circus to Riverside North, and into the Four Seasons Hotel.

"Sir?" She hesitated in the foyer.

"You need a quiet space for a little while," he said. "If I took you home you would go straight back to work. You would rattle about in the kitchen and prepare my dinner. You would inspect the floors for blood. You would look for any bit of labour to keep yourself occupied, instead of resting. You need to rest. And I'd like a drink."

She gave him no argument. "Of course." She pulled her arm from his and headed for the Quadrato Bar and Lounge off the lobby.

Kitt caught her wrist. "I said you needed a quiet space, and that," he tipped his head in the direction of the busy lounge, "is not a quiet space." He turned her around and steered her to the front desk. "Good evening."

"Good evening, sir. Welcome to the Four Seasons. My name is Devon." The desk clerk smiled. Then he noticed Mae.

In the last ten minutes she had somehow...disintegrated. Her French braid had unwound, the front of her dress rumpled, unbuttoned, and a generous amount of her thigh showed. There was scabbing around the stitches of her cracked lips, the bandages on her arms were slightly soiled, and she had what looked like a love bite on her neck. Bruises were livid on her calves, her face blotchy with blue, purple, red and the dark circles under her eyes.

Stiffening, eyes shifting to Kitt and back to her, the clerk frowned. "Are you in need of assistance, madam?"

"I don't *rattle about*," Mae grumbled.

"Madam needs a rest," Kitt handed over a black credit card.

"Madam needs a bath." The clerk stood watching them both, credit card in his hand. "And perhaps a different hotel."

Kitt smiled broadly.

"Uh-oh," Mae said.

"Shall I swipe the card for you?" Kitt placed a hand flat upon on the high desktop. "Or would you like to insult the lady again?"

The desk clerk crossed his arms and glowered.

"And we're back to bully," Mae leaned forward. "Please swipe the card."

With an irritated sniff, the clerk passed the credit card though a reader. As he perused the information that appeared on his computer screen, his disposition shifted from churlish to obsequious. "Major Kitt, it's a pleasure to have you and madam here at the Four Seasons. I have you on level eight in a riverfront suite, as per your standing request. I'll send up a chilled bottle of Bollinger, fresh strawberries, and something soothing from the spa for madam." He handed over Kitt's card and an electronic passkey. "The lifts are to your left. Please have a pleasant evening and do not hesitate to ring me if there is anything I can do to make your stay at the Four Seasons more enjoyable."

"Thank you." Kitt took the cards and moved off in the direction of the lifts. He stopped dead and turned about, going back to fetch Mae where she'd remained at the desk. "What are you doing?"

"I've asked Devon to fetch me a cab."

He pulled her along to the lift and poked the call button. "You do get obstreperous when you're tired, don't you?"

"I don't know what I am right now, but haven't you done enough?"

"Haven't I done enough?" Kitt exhaled harshly, perhaps a little too harshly. Mae took a step back. "I should have killed that man at the embassy, rather than break his nose," he said. "Killing him would have been enough."

Mae swallowed and licked her dry lips. "I liked watching you break his nose and I wanted you to kill him. What does that say about me?"

The lift doors opened behind her. Kitt said nothing as he hooked an arm about her waist and walked her backwards into the waiting car. He left his hand where it was, splayed between her hip and ribs. He thumbed the lighted number 8 and waited for Mae to burst into tears. Tears didn't happen, but she laid her hand over the top of his, and Kitt felt the needle of his moral compass begin to spin. It was still spinning when she came out of the bath twenty minutes later, wearing a dressing gown that would have been too large on him.

Compass needle whirling, he sent the rather lengthy text he'd composed to Bryce and set the mobile aside.

She fumbled with folding up the too-long sleeves.

"Come here and let me help you with that," he said.

"I've got it."

"Yes, it certainly looks that way." He rose from the chair at the desk and went to her.

She huffed and held out her arms.

Mindful of the bandages on her forearm, Kitt began to roll up the sleeves that hung down to the top of her knees. Her face was shiny with the arnica gel the desk clerk had sent up to soothe her bruising. She'd shampooed her hair, combed it back, and used a soap that mixed well with her body chemistry. Kitt breathed in clover, camomile, essence of Valentine, and thought about scrambled eggs, the curve of Mae's neck, her blood on his hands, and murder. "The other side now," he said, once he'd folded the waffle-weave cloth to her elbow.

With another huff, she flopped out her arm.

"You loathe anyone helping you, don't you?"

"I wouldn't be very good at my job if I needed help."

"Ah, we're going to have this conversation again."

"What conversation?"

"The one about our being friends. We've been friends all weekend. Have you forgotten already?"

"No." She watched his hands turn up the large sleeve of the dressing gown, and then cast her eyes over the soft beige linen and fuchsia orchids atop the plush pillows of a king-sized bed to his left, and back to him. "It's kind of you to give up your bed for me. Again. There is only one bed, isn't there?"

The left corner of his mouth curved upwards. "Yes." He glanced toward the mushroom-toned couch near the window. "Go to bed."

"It's still light outside."

Contrary Mrs Valentine was back. Kitt turned her about to face the bed. "Get some rest."

She didn't move; she simply stared at the all the pillows and orchids.

"What are you afraid of, Mae? Do I frighten you?"

She gave him a sidelong glance. "No more than I frighten myself."

"What is it then?"

"The bed's too damned big. I'm lost in a bed so huge, it makes me feel as if I'm drowning."

Kitt left her where she was and moved to turn down the bedclothes. He laid all the pillows in a vertical line, dividing the bed into two sections. "There. It's smaller. Now stop fannying about and get in," he said.

"I never fanny about," she said, curling up on the mattress and tucking her hands beneath a pillow as he drew the soft linens up over her.

His phone buzzed on the desk. He went to check the message, frowned at the screen, and replied to Bryce immediately. Then he switched off the mobile. When he looked over his shoulder, she was already asleep. He turned the mobile like a deck of unopened cards in his hand and watched her sleep. "Damn," he muttered.

Kitt liked women and enjoyed their company. Yet sometimes, as now with Mae, he found women to be a nuisance. In a small way that made him something of a misogynist, only not quite because he didn't see women as less intellectual, less capable, less valuable. If anything, he valued and respected women more than men. Women carried a greater burden in life, across all cultures, and had so much less to show for their strength and perseverance. The fact was he was selfish and had to be. Self-interest tended to be an important factor in his work and was why he preferred the casual, mutually satisfying liaison that never advanced beyond a shallow friendship and lots of sex. He disliked entanglements that were murky with emotion and expectation, where feelings were hurt and bitter tears shed. He was cavalier when it served a purpose, but Kitt wasn't foolish enough to believe that he didn't feel affection or a connection to a few women he'd known. He'd loved a woman once, when he was very young, and bore a scar of that love when she'd literally plunged a knife into his back. He was not unaware of the affection, of the connection he felt for Mae, but egocentricity was fundamental to his way of life. As complicated as he'd made things, as much trouble as she had suddenly become, he was no longer able to ignore what he always had, and it had little to do with her scrambled eggs.

THE EMPTY BOTTLE of Bollinger sat upended in a bucket full of water. Strawberry stems formed a dark mountain in a bowl on the low table in front of the sofa. Light from the partially closed drapes painted a thick bar across her employer's throat. Mae was accustomed to seeing her employer with a black eye or scratch marks like the ones that had almost faded on his neck. Occasionally, she'd been his Florence Nightingale crossed with Jeeves the butler. In a bizarre turn of events she was battered and bruised and her employer had become man, bully, hero...and personal saviour. For a moment she observed how sleep softened the stern face of a man who was anything but Christ-like.

Major Kitt's lashes were long, longer than hers, longer than Caspar's had been. Funny how those lashes gentled and blurred the cruelty of his features, made him.... It was an odd thing, to be aware of him as a man. The violence of seeing him thrash the mugger in front of the embassy activated something primal within her, had reminded her she'd been aware of him in some peripheral way, but is that how it had been with Caspar? Had she relished her employer's alpha-male display because it was an elemental thing, as earthy as Caspar getting sun-browned and dirty, working with his hands as he shaped the land, bent it to his will?

Bending someone or something to your will, that's what fighting was, what violence was, what nature was. Nature was manipulative, designing women to notice men and men to notice women, in the oddest of ways, at the strangest of times, twisting diamond-hard wills to find beauty or comfort or charm in something vicious. Major Kitt's softened face, the fact she found him more attractive than she had before, was nothing but a manipulation of nature. Yet what got her to this hotel room, what caused her to watch her employer sleep and contemplate his appeal, was the result of the manipulation of con men.

"Did you have a nightmare?" Her employer opened his eyes, alert immediately, as if he'd just stretched out on the sofa, and perhaps he had. His voice lacked any trace of gravelly sleepiness. He didn't yawn or sniffle, or rub his face as he sat up, swung his legs over the side, and rose from the couch. "Nightmares are common with trauma."

"I dreamt about papers—filing papers, shuffling papers, stacking papers, signing papers, picking up papers from the floor." She inhaled and let out a long sigh. It was curious that she'd become cognisant of her employer on a new and different plane. What was even more curious was that the last few days had obliterated her sense of decorum and self-consciousness. Bearing novelty and curiosity in mind, she sank onto the pillow where his head had rested. It was still warm. She was surprised how much she needed, how much she wanted that warmth from him. "I woke up because all that paperwork made me think of something else," she said.

He crossed to the minibar, switched on a tiny light, and opened a bottle of water that had been sitting on a tray. "The man you killed?"

"No. Leather compendiums. When I met Daniel Pierce at Cabot

Square, he had a leather compendium on his desk; it had gold embossing on the front. The same sort of leather compendium, with the same sort of gold embossing was on Ms O'Toole's desk, to the left of a picture of her child. The man who called himself Largo had an identical compendium." She began to rub her face and wished she hadn't. Nettles of pain stung through her jaw. She quit rubbing her face. "I don't believe Daniel died of a heart attack like the story in the newspaper said."

The water bottle paused at his lips. "Are you saying you think Pierce was murdered for his compendium, Mae? Is that what you're suggesting?"

"It's the only thing that makes sense to me. Do you find it ridiculous?"

"Ridiculous, no, but not probable either." Kitt came back to the sofa, shoved aside the champagne bucket and strawberry stems, and sat on the table, facing her. In the dim light, the marks on her face stood out like soot, the stitches in her lip black as coal. He refrained from reaching out to touch her, from giving her hand a reassuring squeeze. "As you said, what happened to you was a crime of opportunity. Yesterday, you wondered if you might've been targeted, hacked, set up for identity theft. Any one of those is more likely, more plausible than Pierce being murdered for his compendium." He leaned forward, elbows on his knees. "There are criminals that work in separating people from their money. They move swiftly once they have a foot in the door, and they had both feet in your front door. They found something in your home that they used, information that was easy to copy with a simple snapshot on a mobile. Every detail of your life taken and yet left behind."

She shifted her position, slipping down to lie on her side, pulling the pillow from under her bum and clutching it to her chest. "And what they left behind means I may be charged with manslaughter."

"I can promise you that will not happen."

She put her forearm across her eyes. "Your ability to predict the future is on par with your ability to read minds."

"Here's what I can predict. You are going to have a holiday."

"I don't want a holiday."

"I misspoke. I meant you *will* go on holiday."

She sighed. "Yes, as you wish, sir, I will take a day."

Kitt shook his head. "No. I'll not make that mistake again. You will take a month. Three weeks at the very least. And before you rise up with mulish outrage and protest, or ask how I'll manage without you, this is not negotiable. You will have a holiday or I will take you to the spa at Champneys Forest Mere myself."

"So now you bully me. I've wondered what that would feel like."

"Don't push me, Mae."

His contrary Irish butler withdrew her arm from her eyes and glowered at him for a long moment, mulling over his words or gauging the strength of his resolve, thinking, thinking, and he wondered what she was thinking—or planning—he was certain she was doing a little of both. There was a glint of defiance in her squint, as though she was about to test him, but then she hugged the pillow to herself and exhaled. "Very well," she said. "I will take an unpaid leave of absence."

"Yes. Of course you will." Kitt laughed. "And where will you go to rest?"

She continued to glare. "To hell, I suspect."

"Do you truly dislike relaxing that much?"

"I like it as much as you like being home with paperwork for six weeks."

"Point taken." He gave a slight nod.

"I dislike not being...productive."

He sat up. "A holiday isn't supposed to be productive. It's supposed to be restorative. Where will you go?"

"I haven't decided what I'll do yet, or where I'll go, but I'll let you know when I do."

"Let me know at breakfast or I'll choose for you."

"I beg your pardon. I'll choose for myself. While there is something appealing about a spa, you are not, as of this moment, my employer. Whether I go to a Champneys spa, one on the Ionian Sea, or stay home to manage this affair is my business, not yours, but I am grateful for your concern, sir."

Kitt swiped a hand over his mouth to hide his amusement. "No, you're not, you'd prefer I didn't fuss, but my apologies anyway because you are correct. Despite my...concern, it is none of my business where you choose to spend your free time. Now," he said, "are you going to continue scowling at me, or will you move so I may go back to sleep?"

She gave him a cold, hard look, rolled over, and faced the sofa's backrest.

Kitt left Mae to play the petulant martyr and climbed into the bed that was big enough for them both. He shoved aside the line of cushions he'd laid out to make the space smaller for her and bunched up the pillow she'd used under his cheek. The pillow smelled of Mae, of her hair and neck. It took a moment for him to realise he'd buried his nose in the cotton and down and inhaled that fragrance, real or imagined, more than twice. He chastised himself for being a quixotic dolt.

When a knock at the door woke him four hours later, she was gone, but she had ordered him breakfast. He understood her intention had been to look after herself, but that only came after she'd looked after him. Room service wheeled in beautifully presented shirred eggs, toast soldiers with a rich Danish butter, and strong black coffee. The croissants were a baking marvel and the exquisite damson jam served on the side came from a small farm outside Oxford. While delicious, the meal lacked that essential thing to make it perfect. He contemplated the prospect of Mae denying him a month's worth of perfect breakfasts and chastised himself for being a selfish, quixotic dolt.

He left the hotel and drove to his office in Central London to tend to the paperwork he'd outright ignored yesterday. Before he commenced anything, he was yanked into a blunt discussion with the manager from the Security Section and got chewed out over the importance of going through proper channels. Then came the cool, frank reprimand from Llewelyn for being a bloody-minded Good Samaritan. It wasn't the first time he'd been castigated by a senior-ranking officer, nor was it the first time Llewelyn had threatened to dress him down or move him elsewhere if he did not toe the line. Despite his charitable defensive actions, he was told in no uncertain terms *how things were*. The exchange turned Kitt as surly as a caged animal.

Regardless of his *duly noted* protest, he stalked back to his office —or cell, as he viewed it at present—and slammed the door. The damnable matter was twisted and his hands were tied. Seething, he poured a glass of water from the jug Bryce always put on the desk, drank it, and smashed the tumbler against the wall. That action tempered a portion of his hostility.

The box Bryce had left on the low bookcase beside the coatrack mitigated the belligerence a little more. Kitt left the parcel where it was and had a seat at his desk. His computer powered up, he keyed in his password, and began typing the chronicle of recent events, including the ninety minutes he'd spent in Eritrea and his Istanbul posting.

Tedium set in quickly. Out of the field, behind a desk, chained to paperwork, equalled a soft life. Kitt began to feel doughy in both mind and body. After two hours he wanted to gouge out his own eyes, after three hours he pondered Seppuku, the Japanese ritual suicide. Death was preferable to paperwork. The mundane activity turned his brain to pasty gruel. The only remedy to mind-numbing, doughy boredom was action, physical action. He needed a ten-mile run and a good meal. Paperwork could wait for tomorrow.

With a huff of frustration, he gathered a handful of slim books, stuffed them into a leather satchel, and turned for the box Bryce had placed on the bookcase. Kitt opened it, unwrapped the tissue, and looked at what the Sergeant had restored. Despite a musty smell and grey markings, the item was in one piece. Bryce had done well, very well, and Kitt grinned.

He left his office with the satchel and box tucked under his arm and drove home, climbed the steps to his flat, and put the little box on the chair beside the door. A slight aroma of roasted meat hung in the air. Unable to leave things be and start her holiday properly, Mae had chosen to be *productive* in his absence. A cleaning crew had removed the evidence of what transpired yesterday, but she'd gone about her business, organised spirits in the bottle cabinet, and cooked something for his lunch. Fresh laundry filled his wardrobe; his dinner jacket and Marcella shirt back in place beside his other suits. She had stocked his refrigerator with a variety of cheeses, a fine quiche Lorraine, and beef tenderloin with horseradish-dill sauce. The order in his home was very much typical of her workday. While he was reluctant to admit it, he was pleased she had tended to his things before she had tended to herself.

When he found Mae's note stuck to the bottle of Elijah Craig 23 Single Barrel bourbon, his sense of selfishness vanished, his moral compass began to spin. Kitt knew that, like his butler, he was going on a summer holiday.

CHAPTER SEVEN

The espresso the barista made was too bitter, yet so was coming to this place. Unlike the coffee, the bitterness of this place could never be sweetened or watered down. She glanced at the newspaper and chose to give herself a day to rest and a day to find the resolve to undertake the activities she usually left until September. Mae scanned the headlines of the *Gazzetta del Sud*, the stories all unpleasant. *Anti-migrant Protesters March in Messina. Painstaking Bid to Identify Shipwrecked Migrants. Anti-Mafia Police Begin Investigating Doping Scheme.* Disgusted, she slid the newspaper beside her mobile and touched her throbbing jaw.

A soak in a lavender salt bath had loosened her tight muscles and the massage worked out the remaining kinks. Too bad neither spa treatment had any effect on bruising. Shades of purple, green, yellow, and brown spread a sloppy rainbow along the left side of her face because both men who had belted her had been right-handed. The arnica gel from the Four Seasons soothed her skin, but she wasn't skilled enough in the use of make-up to conceal what brutal hands had consigned. Covering up marks would have prevented staring and the pitying looks the desk clerk had given her upon checking into the spa.

While she preferred to think of visiting here as a series of activities, one activity was akin to getting into a scalding bath or swallowing corrosive drain cleaner. As far as restorative went, day one of her holiday simply exacerbated her sense of restlessness, as she'd suspected it would. Last night, she'd dreamt of papers again. She'd slept fitfully in an oversized bed and searched for Caspar when she woke.

She wasn't certain if the dreams, Caspar, restlessness, or the morning's call from Suisse Global Bank's Tiffany O'Toole, was why she'd felt an impulse to leave—despite acting on impulse to come here in the first place. She hadn't given much thought to coming here at all and mulled over what she wanted to do now that she was. She could check the rental properties like she did every year, see her old friend, Fiorella, and have lunch, but fortifying herself with bitter coffee, in order to confront a bitter reality that burnt and blistered as horrifically today as it had sixteen years ago, seemed like the most logical step. Mae signalled the waiter and ordered a cappuccino and croissant. Espresso alone wasn't enough fortification.

It wasn't quite holiday high season and the café wasn't very busy. She looked about the small outdoor dining area, at the patrons sitting beneath umbrellas that shaded them from the brilliant morning sun. A flaxen-haired man wearing a white tee, drawstring trousers, and sandals sat sketching. His blonde girlfriend had a sunburnt nose and chewed her breakfast with her mouth open. Sunlight glinted off his dark lenses and caught Mae, blinding her for a moment. When the blue-white starbursts faded, Mae shook out her napkin, placing it in her lap.

The fair-haired couple rose and Mae stared beyond them, out over the sparkling water. It was cooler than usual for this time of year, more like May than July, but the sun was still strong and painted the sea a remarkable blue. The waiter arrived with her cappuccino and croissant and placed them beside her. Eyes on the sea, she began to rip apart the pastry.

"You're rather vicious with your breakfast, aren't you?"

She stopped tearing apart the bread and wiped her fingers on her napkin. "Good morning, sir."

"Good morning, Mae."

She looked up at her employer. He wore loose trousers similar to the sandy-haired man's. He also wore a slight smile and a pair of aviator-style sunglasses with lenses so dark she could not see his eyes at all. She would have preferred to see his eyes.

The Major pulled out the chair across from Mae, angled it so that he'd have a view of the Ionian Sea and had a seat. He looked out over the water and waited.

Mae knew what he was waiting for, so she said it. "What are you doing here?"

"You said something last week about my having a holiday, and I thought you might be right. I could not bear another day behind a damned desk, and the timing seemed right, with you away. I remembered your suggestions. I said Champneys, and you said I should try a desert retreat in New Mexico or spend time by the seaside in Sicily. I didn't fancy the idea of a detox or lengthy air travel, so I chose the Castello di San Marco. As did you."

"Quite the coincidence." She adjusted the napkin in her lap.

"Yes. And I'm delighted. I much prefer this to any Champneys spa. Obviously, you do as well. I quite understand why you come here every year. The views are incredible, whichever direction you look, from Mount Etna to the sea. Is that what made you change your mind about going to Champneys, the volcano and Ionian Sea?"

"I never mentioned where I was going." She lifted her cappuccino to her mouth and sipped.

"No. You didn't. Your note said you were going to a spa."

"And Champneys is where you thought I'd choose to go?"

Kitt knew he'd had no cause to ever chastise himself for his lack of mind-reading skill, because Mae had telegraphed her holiday plans the night they'd spent at the Four Seasons, yet he'd missed it. He'd been unmindful of her intentions until he'd read the note stuck to the bourbon. It had become a habit to overlook what had been right in front of him. It was second nature for him to outright ignore what had been right in front of him because of his bloody moral compass. Kitt had been behaving as he was, had shifted the focus of his position, his rank, his work, because of his bloody moral compass, the matter of his butler, and his own self-interest. It was this, of course, that made him a quixotic dolt. He said, "I supposed I did."

"You asked me to let you know when I had something in mind. I considered staying home, but I felt compelled to come here rather than go to a place like Champneys."

"As did I."

"Another coincidence." She brushed crumbs from the front of her pink cotton dress.

"Yes. Coincidence aside, I did believe you'd go to Champneys because of the sticky little fact that you were released without charge under the condition that you remain in my trust. Your leave of absence was well within the conditions set while the police carry out their investigation, yet you did not remain, as was also part of the condition, *in* England. I supposed I should have made that clear, in case the police did not, or if by chance you...forgot what the police told you." He removed his sunglasses and fixed his eyes upon her.

Mae had busied herself spreading cherry conserve on her croissant. She stopped. "I don't recall a conversation stipulating the conditions of bail, either with you or with the police. There was never, to my recollection, any mention of surrendering my passport. But I admit I was muddled at the time. Did we have such a discussion, sir?" She set the jam-coated knife on her plate and licked dark red stickiness from a fingertip.

His flat expression did not alter.

She looked away to the water and exhaled. "I have put you in an awkward position," she said. "I didn't think this through. I didn't think at all. I simply came here to tend to some business. I apologise."

He placed his sunglasses on the table, signalled a waiter, and waited for her clever comments, for her smart-arsed remarks, for the usual amusing tête-à-tête to start, but she said nothing. She gazed out at the Ionian Sea, her colourful face blank. He wouldn't say she was emotionally fragile or depressed, but she was plainly not herself. "Mae," he said. "You have put me in a potentially awkward position. And no one can blame you for not thinking, not after what happened."

With an exhaled half-laugh, she turned her attention to him. "You are ridiculously understanding about this, sir. If it suits you, I'll go home after I tend to what I came here to do. I only need a day or two."

"*Signore*?" the waiter asked, tipping his balding head.

Kitt ordered *caffé Americano* and continued when the man went away. He said, "A day or two. You didn't come here to simply relax and take in the views then?"

She eyed him with a small sidelong squint. "Is that why you are here?"

"Of course. I am here to have a relaxing holiday."

"I can recommend the lavender and salt bath and massage I had

this morning. Perhaps you'd find the therapeutic waters relaxing."
She popped a bite of croissant into her mouth.

"I'll keep the massage in mind for later. What would you recommend to a tourist in the area?"

"Tourist? I can't quite picture you as a tourist."

"Why is that?"

"I have the impression you've already been everywhere and seen everything."

"Do I seem that jaded to you?"

She spread jam on her croissant. "Is there any place you haven't been?"

"Sicily."

"What is it you'd like to do?"

"Be a tourist. See amazing sites, have amazing experiences, eat amazing foods, and meet amazing women."

Mae set the jam spoon on a plate. "I'd recommend Taormina because Taormina is considered the Sicilian Riviera and you have Riviera tastes."

"Do I?"

She arched a brow and dabbed her mouth with a napkin. "Taormina is beautiful if you want something historic like the Teatro Greco, a well-preserved Greek theatre. The views of Mount Etna from there are even more spectacular than from here. If you're feeling literary, D.H. Lawrence and Truman Capote both stayed in the Villa Fontana Vecchia in Taormina. You could visit the Villa. However, just up the road from here is the beach at Giardini-Naxsos, if you'd like to lounge, sunbake, meet sunburnt, bikini-clad women, and have cocktails. But if you'd prefer a more adventurous holiday, there's always trekking Mount Etna. Most of those trips leave from Linguaglossa, the little town where I'm going later this morning."

Kitt shook out the napkin beside his place setting. "When you worked for the Gelsomino family, was their home in this region?"

"They have a villa a little bit south of here, in a tiny place called Macchia, another in Taormina. They also have a beach house near Agrigento and a place in Lugarno. You might like Agrigento. The Greek temples there are in far better condition than the sites in Athens."

"I quite like the more adventurous idea of a volcano trek—despite my Riviera taste," he said, laying the napkin across his lap.

The waiter set a *caffè Americano* on the table.

"*Grazie,*" Kitt said and had a mouthful of volcanically hot black coffee. He drew in a cooling breath to ease the heat. "Perhaps before you leave," he said, "you could show me some of these places."

Mae's cup paused at her lips. "You'd like me to be your tour guide?"

Tongue slightly scalded, he sat back and regarded her for a moment. Then he gave a shrug. "You have local knowledge. I like local knowledge."

"How deep is your local interest? I'm not so sure you'd enjoy meeting my old friend in Linguaglossa, but I could take you there and set you up on an Etna trek. I can even arrange your accommodation. As for being a tour guide... I have a little business to take care of inspecting properties I own here, and I wouldn't want to subject you to anything work related or disagreeable on your holiday." She had a long drink from her cappuccino. It left a little patch of foam in the corner of her mouth, just next to the stitches in her lip.

Kitt refrained from reaching out to wipe the foam away. He licked at the corner of his own mouth. "I should have known this is a working holiday for you. You did say you needed to be...what was the word you used?"

"Productive," she said, pushing her croissant and coffee aside, running her tongue over her stitches. "While I don't believe Linguaglossa would be your idea of amazing, you are welcome to tag along and have a walk about town before we arrange a trip to the volcano for you."

He made an offhand gesture. "I would find that interesting. Old towns are fascinating places. The history, the architecture, the churches tell you a lot about local custom."

"I never knew you were interested in anthropology, sir."

"Anthropological study comprises a great deal of my work, Mrs Valentine."

Her tongue poked over her stitches again, and she said, "Before I do anything, I have to hire transportation."

"I have transportation."

She put an elbow on the table, set her chin into the heel of her hand, arched an eyebrow, and gazed up at him. "Isn't your girly sports car difficult to navigate through tiny villages with narrow cobblestone streets?"

Kitt was pleased her sense of humour was still intact. "What time would you like to leave?" He said and rose, laying his napkin on the table. "Shall we meet at the front desk in an hour?"

Mae watched him walk away. She could not deny that he was concerned for her wellbeing, but she doubted he'd chosen to travel here on holiday because she'd visited every September or had mentioned it was a lovely place. He'd followed her here because she'd been so thoughtless and had, as the Americans said, skipped bail, bail he had financed. Rather than demand she return to England, or escort her back, he was indulging her. He understood that, bail jumping aside, she'd go home when she was ready to. She would not be intimidated and he was not one to be fooled. Major Kitt would accompany her wherever she went, stay close or just a few steps behind. Mae found it oddly...touching. She kept her eyes on him until he disappeared inside, and she finished off her croissant and coffee.

Fifty minutes later she stood at reception. The motherly woman behind the desk spoke English with the slightest trace of an Italian accent. "Our summer has been more mild than usual this year, but I hope your stay with us is pleasant." Then desk clerk cut her eyes to a spot behind Mae. "Signorina." she said, handing the tri-folded schedule to Mae. "A man is looking at you. *Iddu beddu*—he is very attractive, but I am not sure I like the way he looks. Is he the man who hit you?"

"No. I was robbed by a stranger, *un scanusciutu*." Mae glanced over her shoulder, beyond the couple who been at the table near hers outside, to where her employer stood near the carved stone pillar. He gave her a nod and headed toward the desk.

"Is he your *Spielzeug*?" The clerk held up a hand and shook her head. "No, no, that is German word. *Giacattulu...come si dice,* what is the English word?"

Mae chuckled. "Plaything."

"Yes, yes," the clerk whispered. "Like Madonna."

Mae turned to the Major." Have you already checked out, Mr Spielzeug?

"Mr Spielzeug?" Kitt said.

The clerk looked him up and down and grinned as he reached for Mae's travel case. As Kitt turned, the woman leaned over the desk, had a good look at his arse, and made a gesture of approval.

Still chuckling, Mae followed the Major outside to his car. Instead of finding the curved, feminine lines of his Bentley, she found herself looking at the bubbly arches of a convertible Volkswagen Beetle.

The Major tipped his head toward the vehicle. "*Das Auto*," he said.

"Your German," she said with a wry grin, "is flawless."

"I try. How many languages do you speak, Mae?" He placed her small bag in the back seat along with his own larger one.

"German, Italian, Spanish, some Danish, and passable Russian."

"No French?"

"Only enough to get by as a tourist. You?"

"Traveller's French, traveller's Spanish, traveller's Italian, a wee bit of Arabic, and as you noted, fluent German."

"Naturally you'd excel with Romance languages." Chuckling, she opened the driver's side door and slid into the seat.

Head cocked, he frowned. "What do you think you're doing?"

"Sparing you from being emasculated, sir." Mae adjusted the rear-view mirror. "The key please."

"*Mr Spielzeug,*" he grumbled, shaking his head as he handed over the key and climbed into the passenger seat. "You'd better know the way."

Mae did know the way. They were on the *autostrada* less than five minutes before she made a turn and followed a twisting road that climbed in elevation and took them closer to the foothills of Mount Etna. Billowing blue-grey clouds loomed to the north, the low rumble of thunder barely audible. The Beetle's top was down, the distant rain no threat to where they were heading. Their conversation was uncharacteristically innocuous. She gave a running commentary as any tour guide might. She said Etna was the tallest active volcano on the European continent and that the Forges of the God Hephaestus lay beneath the mountain that smoked in the distance. She told the Major bits of information regarding the history of Sicily, how the island had been invaded by the Phoenicians, Greeks, Vandals, Ostrogoths, Arabs, Normans, Spanish, and Germans, and he listened with interest, either feigned or genuine. She was driving and couldn't look at him to gauge his expression. When she hazarded a glance at him, wisps of hair blew into her mouth. She thought she heard him laugh as she dragged strands clear and shoved them behind the ears of her sunglasses.

"Thank you," he said, "for leaving me so well stocked before you departed."

"Did you enjoy the quiche?"

"I did, but what I liked most was how you left your note where you knew I'd find it."

"Pasting it to your bathroom mirror seemed too..."

"Obvious?"

"Boring. I know how you dislike being bored, and you did ask for fortification since you were going to spend a few weeks in the mind-numbing boredom of Hades. But I do confess that it was also a case of my being selfish."

"Selfish?" Kitt looked up from the map in his hand.

"Selfish and helpless." She turned and held his gaze. "I felt helpless after what happened. I dislike feeling helpless. I dislike being in a position that makes no sense, where I have no control. Being active, cleaning, cooking, lets me think, gives me focus."

"I understand," he said and pointed to the windscreen. "But I would very much like your focus now to be on the upcoming sharp bend in the road."

After a few kilometres of winding, the road straightened, and their conversation dwindled. Kitt watched the landscape change and followed along on the map he had. The view shifted from the Ionia Sea to Mount Etna puffing out smoke. Etna was not his first volcano. He'd seen Kilauea, although Hawaii was a geological infant compared to the old man the island of Sicily was. Hawaii was new, whereas the Sicilian countryside had been touched by antiquity, frozen in time by ruins, cobblestones, lava flows, pasture land, oak and chestnut trees. They came to a small town called Piedimonte Etneo, the blue Ionian Sea behind them, timeworn but lively Etna looming ahead, exhaling a steady plume of smoke.

As she drove through the village and progressed closer to Linguaglossa, Mae began to fidget. She shifted her seat. Her pulse kicked up a notch, her palms began to sweat, her mouth started to go dry. Her choice to drive had been deliberate. Rather than ruminate, she preferred to stare down an unpleasant experience when it stood before her. Driving gave her something to occupy her mind, as had her insipid chatter about Sicily's history and landscape. Anyone could have found the same information in a guidebook, on the Internet, or from any tourist information centre. She prattled on about local wineries, told him that granita, the semi-frozen icy dessert, was eaten in a brioche and had originated in Sicily, as did the cultivation of artichokes. He'd said he'd never been to Sicily before so she prattled and her employer listened politely—or pretended to listen politely. He wasn't an idiot; he knew her well enough to ascertain something wasn't quite right with her. Yet he said nothing and she continued to chatter. Then she mentioned the weather. "It's cooler than usual for this time of year in Sicily."

"Yes. It was warmer in London."

"It looks though we may get some rain." She looked to the east and the grey-blue clouds for a moment before fumbling for conversation less mundane and stilted. "You packed light for this trip, sir."

"I did. As did you."

"I'm staying at the spa. I'll take a bus back this evening. Do you plan to be in Sicily long?"

Kitt shrugged. "It depends on how exciting I find it. I suspect driving here would be fun. Much more fun than being a passenger."

"You dislike being a passenger?"

"I dislike being a passenger slightly less than I dislike sitting behind a desk doing paperwork. I'd rather eat glass than do paperwork. Death is preferable to paperwork."

Mae's short laugh softened the line of her mouth, which Kitt noticed had been tight since they'd passed through the little village a few kilometres back. He'd noticed something else as well. Her loose pink dress was bunched up on her thighs, higher on one side than the other. A constellation of brown freckles dotted the inside of her left thigh and formed a sort of Southern Cross on her skin. Before his mind began to entertain ideas, he shifted his gaze back to the road ahead. "I think you and I both like to have a certain level of activity and control in our lives, Mae."

"Then I should tell you about my plans for the day," she said. "I'll make a stop before we come to town. I'll be a few minutes, then we'll continue to Linguaglossa, go to the *Pro Loco* for information, and book you an Etna trek. I'll take you to comfortable accommodation, a studio apartment I own, see that you're stocked with food and whatever sundries you'll need for trekking, and then I will leave you and see to my business—unless you care to visit my friend Fiorella with me. She looks after my property and has lived in the town since she was a little girl. She does love to chat, and she'd *love* you. She'd pinch your cheeks, shove food in front of you, and fuss over you like an old-fashioned Italian *nonna*."

"You're the only one I like fussing over me, Mae."

"I don't fuss over you."

"Exactly."

Kitt watched Mae rub one hand and then the other down her hips. The action was similar to the habit of how she smoothed her apron. She said, "Then I won't take you with me to Fiorella, although she does live next door to the accommodation I have. There's no escape in meeting her."

"Good thing my Italian is so poor."

"But her English is not. She learned from American soldiers during the war, likes saying 'Buddy' and 'kiss my ass' a lot. I can sort out someplace else for you to stay. And perhaps I should since the apartment is rather spartan. The Villa Neri may suit your Riviera taste."

"I'm fine with spartan. How did you come to own a place in this village, Mae?"

She worried her stitches with her tongue again. "Linguaglossa is where Caspar was born." Mae indicated and turned right, taking the VW into an empty gravel lot rimmed by high stone walls. "And it's where he's buried."

A grove of fruit trees grew to the left, framing the smoking Etna. To Kitt's right was a small chapel, and slightly beyond was a tall, wrought-iron gate, a carved stone entrance, and rooflines of marble mausoleums. A noticeboard beside the gate had death announcements of local residents pasted to it. The departed stared out from black and white photos as he stared back.

He heard Mae open the door and climb out.

"Feel free to have a wander and play anthropologist. I don't think I'll be long, but if I am there's a gardening shop across the road, just back a little bit. There's a café inside, or used to be, if you'd rather wait there." Her tone was light but her colour high. The shade matched the pink of her dress. Her hand shook as she handed him the car key.

He watched her head toward the ornate stone entrance and pass inside as another car pulled into the lot. Gravel crunched beneath the tyres. A woman got out of the blue Fiat Panda, a wide-brimmed straw hat in hand, large sunglasses covering half her face. She waited for the man driving to adjust his baseball cap and exit the car. Then the couple entered the cemetery together. Kitt thought they looked like American tourists.

For a moment or two, he sat and sent a response to Bryce's text message. *Done. Need 48-72 hours. Don't give a toss about toes.*

He folded up his small map of the area and stuffed it into the back pocket of his jeans. Then he reached across and inserted the key in the ignition, switching on power, depressing the button to raise the Beetle's roof. After it clicked into place, he locked the car and went into the cemetery to wander, as Mae had suggested. He spotted her and kept his distance, giving the space her body language said she needed. She stood near a pine tree, and he read inscriptions on old grave markers, going between rows of tombs to walk the perimeter of the old municipal cemetery, roaming by high, ornate mausoleums, crypts, and the ossuary. He glanced up now and again. The couple that had entered before he had gone inside a crypt. Thunder rumbled, the sound rolling in softly. Kitt looked at the sky and the bulging grey-blue clouds off to the northeast. He cast his eyes back to Mae. Her shoulders shook as she cried.

What would it take? As far as he could tell, he was finished, but was she? Would she ever be? Perhaps a gesture, a word, a statement of fact, a confession would make all the difference. A confession. A confession reflected poorly on his soul. A confession suggested he had a soul. A confession meant he had something to lose, but how could he have anything to lose if he had no soul, or if his soul was, as they both knew, a bottomless mineshaft of blackened nothing. It was curious to ponder his own worth, to toy with the idea that he had something of value, beyond his loyalty and duty to Queen and country, when he knew he had no soul.

Having no soul, however, did not mean that he had no heart. Despite doing his best to turn the damned thing into a stone, which was essential in his line of work, his heart was there, and it was the core of every irritation he'd ever had in his life. Jesus Christ, self-awareness was a double-edged sword.

Clouds moving overhead filtered the sunlight. His teeth on edge, he watched Mae cry and crossed through rows of graves, passing crosses, statues of Jesus, saints, and the Virgin Mary. He glanced through the doors of a mausoleum with a domed gold roof, and moved closer to Mae, maintaining a degree of distance until he reached a stone angel three graves from where she stood weeping. He leaned against the monument and waited, hoping she might find some sort of peace.

Mae heard thunder again as she gazed down at the long slab of her husband's grave; the low rumble was similar to the sound in her throat. Once. She had been here once and it was still the same. It had been sixteen years since she'd seen Caspar interred, sixteen years since she'd stood at his grave. He rested near the end of the row, between a grey-speckled headstone and a black marble one with a glassed-in statue of The Blessed Virgin. Mae kicked aside pinecones, pine needles and leaves that had collected on top of his tomb. She looked at the small, oval portrait inlayed on the gravesite because that was how generations of Sicilian graves were marked. She stared at the familiar snapshot and sobbed.

There was no point to a funeral, no purpose to burial rituals that she could see. Ceremony, interring a body, paying respects, a bid to say farewell or find closure, they were all things lost on her. Caspar had died, and all those funereal things had no impact on that fact. Living simply reminded her of Caspar. Time moved on, time expanded far beyond the few months she'd spent with him. Everything had moved on, but she hadn't. Although she'd tried to move on, to do new and different things, to meet other men, she remained haunted by Caspar. She'd imagined him beside her and the conversations they would have. She thought of him before she fell asleep and when she awoke. She thought of Caspar every day, every hour, and missed him desperately, vehemently, every damned day. Caspar was both very much alive and very much dead. His grave was supposed to be the final reminder that he was gone, but it only served as a reminder of the life she lived without him. Life without Caspar lacked a real purpose and held very little joy or satisfaction. Except...that *very little* gave the suggestion that there was something, however infinitesimal: her work, her employer, her friend. *Except*...except Major Kitt paid her a salary, had outlaid a substantial sum of money to have her bailed, and wanted to safeguard his expenditure and lifestyle. The perceived infinitesimal something was nothing after all.

"Why am I here?" she muttered, wiping her nose with her arm. "What's the point? There is no closure. No goodbye, no end, no explanation, no clarity, no nothing without you." Raking fingers through her hair, Mae wept and sank to her knees as a roll of thunder masked her choking sobs.

It was ridiculous. She'd come to Sicily two months earlier than usual because she'd believed on a subconscious level that seeing Caspar's grave again would settle her, or somehow answer all the questions about his trust. Naturally there were no answers and being here only served to fill her mind with reminders of Caspar. She'd had a stupid compulsion to travel here, been single-minded in her quest, forgetting she'd been accused of a crime, forgetting she'd killed a man, forgetting her employer had taken on a sizeable financial responsibility for her. She'd been stupid, bloody-minded, and fixated because of a subconscious notion that Freud, Jung, and a whole score of psychiatrists, psychologists and psychotherapists would find laughable. Heart aching, tears hot and bursting with self-loathing, she gaped at Caspar's grave and the graves on either side of his. She stared, snot-nosed, at names that had been carved in headstones, left, right, and centre. *Biagio Torrisi, Stefano Russo, Caspar Valentine.*

Abruptly, Mae stopped crying. *Torrisi* was a brand of coffee. *Russo* was a very common Sicilian name. *Valentine* was the name she shared with Caspar. "Oh, for feck's sake!" she said over a cracking boom of thunder.

Just like in films it began to rain, but the rain was black and not at all wet. Mae rose as dark sand and tiny stones pelted down. She turned, stumbling a few steps over pinecones toward the nearest cover she saw. Like-minded, her employer darted out from where he'd been waiting, grabbed her hand, and hurried her to shelter beneath the arched doorway of the gold-domed mausoleum as Mount Etna erupted.

CHAPTER EIGHT

Kitt pushed her against door, shielding her from the downpour of sandy black pebbles slapping into his back. He looked down at her as she sniffled and met his gaze. With a swallow and a funny frown, she pressed her hands to his chest, sliding her palms up to his shoulders, moving closer, bumping into him before she shoved him sideways to stand beside her against the door. "Don't be such a hero," she said above the noisy torrent. "There's enough room for us both."

Turning, he pulled a handkerchief from his pocket and gave it to her. "Should we be worried about this?"

Head shaking, she blew her nose. "I don't know. I don't know what it means, but it means something."

"Such as?"

Mae rubbed her face. "Something...it's something," she said over the din, looking up at the sky and the ballooning, dark cloud from Mount Etna. "It's ash, but you never know. We may be here for a while, or we may be here for a few minutes. It depends on the wind. For now it's only this ash. If you smell sulphur, then be worried."

Kitt had a look at the sky as well. He pulled the map from his back pocket. Then he shifted right, across the door of the mausoleum. Unfolding the map a bit, he held it against the pane of glass in the door and rammed his elbow into it, breaking the pane. Careful of the jagged edges, he reached through the breach, opened the door from the other side, and tugged Mae into the crypt. It felt cool and smelled slightly musty. He returned the map to his pocket. There was a dusty, pale blue runner beneath a pitted brass cross on a stone shelf above the crypt on the right. Kitt moved the statue, snatched up the cloth, and stuffed it into the hole he'd made in the window.

She said, "This ash is like a black hailstorm."

He looked out through the unbroken part of the glass pane. She was right; it was like hail. Black bits of lava pelted the terracotta roof tiles; dark hailstones hit the ground bouncing, shredding flowers left in urns, strafing the trees and gravestones. "I'm glad I had the foresight to put up the Beetle's roof. Do you want to make a run for the car?" he said.

"Let's give it another few minutes and then we'll see. This sort of ash isn't the worst. The foggy, pulverised stuff is more hazardous."

He fixed his attention on her. Her hair was loose, a little wind-blown, and soft looking. She kept slipping shorter strands behind her ears. As far as expressions went, hers was a mixture of sadness, annoyance, and determination. He thought about placing a hand on her shoulder, the way her brother might, despite how very un-brotherly a few of his other dark and wretched thoughts were. Instead, he stood very still and settled his mind as the black ash settled outside. "Did you experience many eruptions when you lived here?"

"Small ones, but Caspar grew up with them. I remember him

telling me there are usually warning signs for more dangerous eruptions, like large tremors, big clouds of ash, and more explosions." Then she was crying again, her face contorted. She turned away, struggling to regain control. The hair she'd tucked behind her ears fell forward. "Oh, Jaysus," she murmured.

Kitt leaned against the edge of the crypt that held Isabella Patane, who had died in 1901. He watched Mae. "You loved him very much."

"I still love him," she choked.

"I know."

She shoved at her hair and blew her nose again. "Apparently my still loving him the way I do is called *complicated grief*." Her mouth twisted. "I think that's so stupid. I loved Caspar, he died, and I still love him. What's complicated about that?"

"It seems straightforward when you put it that way."

"Have you ever loved anyone, sir?" She faced him, her eyes wet, imploring, which made them appear more green than hazel, even in the dim light. "Have you ever, with any of the women you... Have you ever loved someone?"

"Of course, but..." he slanted his head.

"But what?" She shuddered and sniffled and swallowed.

"I can't say she loved me."

Her laugh was short, sharp. "Was she married?" she said, and then her palms covered her eyes. "I'm sorry. That was...that was unconscionable. That was cruel." She dropped her hands. "You deserve better. I have no excuse. I'm so sorry."

Kitt's smile was dry. "I don't object to your laughing at my misfortune. This last week has been bizarre and you are dealing with it the best you can."

"Yes, that's true, but it is only becoming more bizarre. Do you know why I decided to come here?"

"You prefer the spa at Castello di San Marco."

She waved a hand, the hanky in it a little flag of surrender. "No, I don't mean to Sicily. You know I come to Sicily every year to check on my properties, but I never come here. This is only the second time I've been to this cemetery. I came here because..." She laughed and tears spilled out again, but these tears were ones of frustration, not pain. As she continued speaking, her accent loosened from cultivated English to angry Irish. "I came here because when we were at the Four Seasons I told ya I dreamed about papers, and I haven't stopped dreaming about papers since then. I've been stackin' paper, foldin' paper, filin' paper, takin' paper from a drawer and puttin' it in another drawer full of paper. I didn't know why I thought I had to come here to see Caspar now, as soon as I could. Maybe I thought I'd stand before his grave and ask him why the feck he never told me about his damned trust, and I'd get some kind of ghostly response. Or that just being near him would be comforting, or some gammy shite idea like that. I don't know. I only know I couldn't wait until September. I *had* to come here. I had to. And now I know why. Paper." She pointed, stabbing a finger in the direction of where her husband had lain for sixteen years. "Out there, those names, the dead on either side of Caspar, they were names that bloody Austrian man had in your kitchen. Valentine, Torrisi and Russo, they are all names I saw on a sticky note attached to a sheet of paper that man shoved into a leather compendium, a fecking leather compendium like the skinny bank lady O'Toole and Dennis Pierce had."

"Daniel Pierce," Kitt said, taking his hands from his pockets, crossing his arms.

"Yes. Daniel. The compendium Daniel had." Mae stopped pointing and wiped her face with the hankie. Somewhat out of breath, she looked at Kitt and held out the damp, snotty cloth to him. "Your elbow's bleeding, and the black hail's stopped."

Kitt didn't move.

"Don't you get it, sir?" she said. "Don't you see?"

"I don't see anything." He wiped blood from his elbow with the bottom of his shirt tail and tucked it back into his jeans. He said, "What is it you want me to see, Mae?"

"Torrisi is a coffee and Russo is a common Sicilian name. Torrisi died two years after Caspar, Russo two years before. There were other names on the note, Mr Bianco and Man, but I didn't look to see if either name is anywhere near Caspar. Bianco could be anyone, and Man could simply be *man*." She folded up the hankie and slipped it inside her bra. "It's dodgy. It's dodgy and has to mean something."

"Such as?"

"I don't know, but I'm going to find out."

"Maybe it is dodgy, and maybe it's a coincidence."

"I'd go to the police and tell them what happened to me, but," she gestured like an Italian, using both hands, thumbs to finger-tips, mouth pulled down, shoulders up, "why would the police here care that I was mugged and duped by criminals in the UK? I have no proof of anything, except the names, and they mean nothing."

"Then let me take you home."

Mae crossed her arms. "That's why you came to Sicily, isn't it, to take me home because I was released into your custody?"

"I told you why I am here."

"Yes, to escape the horrors of paperwork." She nodded, her smile artificially wide. "There's something you're not telling me. I am certain of it."

"You're not quite yourself, Mae."

"No. I'm not. After what's happened I'm not sure I know how to be myself."

Kitt moved away from the crypt to push the door open. He expected the air to be rank, as rank as his non-existent soul. Dark sand and tiny stones looked like black snow, and like snow it gave the impression of tidiness.

"Would you help me, sir?" she said softly. "I'll pay you."

He glanced at her over his shoulder and chuckled. "You want to hire me?"

"Yes."

"You can't afford this."

Eyes narrowed, she said, "I am not some widow who's been swindled out of her fortune. I have money. I have accounts that have not been touched. This is not about finding money. It's about finding out what, why, and how this has to do with me."

Kitt grimaced. "That's wasn't quite how I meant it."

"How did you mean it then? What is it I can't afford? What are you sugg—"

"Yes. I'll help you," he said more sharply than he'd intended.

She was quiet for a moment. "Where do we start?"

He faced her. "You haven't a plan?"

Mae shook her head. "Other than finding out more information about Torrisi and Russo, beyond when they were born and died, no. I understand your military career and current occupation have seen you deal with local customs, local officials, with people of all sorts. If this were about how to get bloodstains out of wool or how to make scrambled eggs, then I wouldn't need your help, but this is Italy. Italy can be quite officious. The bureaucracy can be like a maze, even for the simplest thing. Worse, this is Sicily. It still has a certain reputation for corruption and I am assuming you know how to...do certain things."

Kitt said nothing.

"Am I wrong?"

Kitt said nothing.

"Look," she said, "It's common knowledge that the Mafia, that organised crime still operates in Sicily. There's a certain level of tacit extortion that functions. You give the kid on the corner ten Euro to look after your car when you park it on the street and no one smashes the window to steal the Ray Ban sunglasses you left on the seat. You bargain a ransom price with the guy who stole your motorcycle so you get it back in one piece. It's a protection racket, but people around here don't like when you ask questions, and when you're an outsider asking questions they get a little testy. I know how things work here and I know how to get around them."

"If you know all this, why do you need me?"

"Because you possess a certain..." she exhaled and rolled her eyes, "...because you're a man, and this is Sicily."

"Where chauvinism and misogyny are alive and well."

"Exactly."

He wore a tiny grin. "You hate admitting that, don't you? You hate asking anyone for help, but you hate asking me for help even more."

"Yes."

"Why?"

Mae looked at him and swallowed. "I don't like how I feel when you help me."

"You help me."

"I work for you."

"Not at the moment. At the moment, you and I are both on holiday."

She gave a sceptical sounding *tsk*. "I hate to spoil your 'holiday fun,' but there won't be any Etna treks leaving in the next day or two, not while the volcano is erupting and there's an ash cloud. And you can be sure air travel will be disrupted too. So what else had you planned to do?"

"I was going to lounge on the beach."

"You are such a bad liar."

"I'm a very good liar, Mae."

Mae inhaled. "Please," she said. "Please. I think I can guarantee what I'm asking you to do won't put you behind a desk, and there won't be any paperwork."

Kitt exhaled. "There will be paperwork. There's always paperwork."

"So name your price."

"Five pounds."

"Don't be absurd."

"You'd rather I be mercenary?"

She flicked hair from her face. "This is your holiday. You deserve to be compensated for my taking advantage of your free time."

"My free time." He gazed back through the open door to the black snowfall that had subsided. Kitt decided that, like any form of snow, this would soon turn sludgy. Hell, this snow had begun melting the evening Mae was mugged in front of the Nepali embassy.

He took her arm, headed for the Volkswagen, and cleared the precipitation of new earth from the windscreen.

Another short flurry of black sleet accompanied them on the drive into Linguaglossa. The pavement changed and the VW droned over narrow street cobblestones, crushing the lava gravel to powder under the tyres. Dark grit *tippty-tapped* against the windows then ceased abruptly. Like rain, the sandy lava had fallen more heavily in some places than others. The town centre had a mere dusting. A few residents swept the dark grime from the front of homes and businesses. Others left the dirt where it was. Mae wound the way though narrow streets, passing slim houses with window boxes full of geraniums, abandoned structures, several churches, and small piazzas.

She turned the corner and halted near a monument to the war dead. Across from the monument, stood the *municipio*, the town hall. Carved into the neoclassical Greco-Roman pediment, was

Linguagrossa, the Sicilian form of Linguaglossa. Italian and European Union flags waved from the balcony of the stone building. Mae took a page from the locals and parked the VW halfway on the street and halfway on the *Piazza Municipio*, just at the front of the old building.

She made a face, glanced at her watch, and got out of the car. "We have about forty-five minutes before everything closes for lunch and the afternoon *riposo*. Things won't open again until after three."

Kitt followed her through the arched double door entrance of the *Municipio*, moving into an open hallway with a terrazzo floor. The brown door to the *Stato Civile*—the office of births, marriages, and deaths—was locked. Mae looked for the sign that displayed the opening times. On the wall to the left of the office entrance was a hand-painted, pictographic map of the Linguaglossa, the 'You Are Here' marked with a red M. The town's other municipal offices, information centre, churches, the train station, and notable villas were listed with icons on a painted yellow scroll. To the right was an old brass plaque with a sheet of paper taped over it, the printing faded. *Aperto: Mercoledi 8:30 dal 10:30.*

Mae sighed with resigned irritation. "The office is only open for two hours on Wednesdays. That's six days from now. Welcome to Italy."

Kitt shrugged and knocked hard on the brown door. "Nothing ventured."

"You think knocking's going to work?"

Two seconds later, a portly man opened the door. "*Che?*" He looked them both up and down. "*Ma, siamo chiusi.*"

She huffed. "He said they are closed."

Kitt slipped his arm about Mae's waist, turning her slightly. He said, in halting Italian, "*Buongiorno. Mi sposa...e io...cerco...*how do you say the office of information, darling?"

"Close," the man said, brushing his hair back into its wispy comb-over. "We are close. The tourismo office not here."

Mae waved a hand and said, in Italian, "We don't want tourist information. We want information about the municipal cemetery, specifically information about some of my family buried there. Can you help us?"

With one hand on the door, the man pointed to the paper taped over the brass plaque. "Come back Wesday," he said in English.

"And what, make an appointment to come back the following Wednesday to look at the birth and death records." She put a hand to her throat. "It's *my* family and we are trying to find a family member match for my brother's bone marrow. He has leukaemia, and we are running out of time."

"Hai ham sorry." The man shook his head. "That is very crying, but *non posso aiutarti*, hai can no help."

"Are you certain?" Kitt held out a folded wad of Euros.

Blue eyes grew large in a chubby face. "No! No, no!" He shook a finger. "*Che cos'è*...What you think? Hai can no help."

Kitt added a few more Euros. "Five minutes."

The man gestured, his hand moved from the door, something dark and metal swung down beside his knee. "Hai no *segretario*. Hai *idraulico*, the plum-ber. Hai make *il lavandrino*, the...the...sink hopen! You go Wesday." He pointed at the sign again. "*Capsice*?" He stepped back and closed the door with a bang.

Kitt gave Mae a pat and let her go. "The leukaemia bit was a nice touch."

"I thought so too," she said, rubbing her forehead in frustration. "So, do we bang on the door again and offer him more money?"

"No," Kitt moved to look at the map mural, reading street names.

"Should I bang on the door and you bully him into letting us inside?"

"Why would I bully him?"

"Isn't what you do?"

"I'd never bully a man with a pipe wrench."

"He had a pipe wrench?"

"Plumbers often do." Kitt looked at her over a shoulder and then returned to study the map. "He's a plumber, an honest plumber it turns out, and we're not going to get anywhere with him.

"What then?" She leaned against the wall. "I distract him and you go and look for the records on Torrisi and Russo? How do you suggest I distract him, unbutton my dress and show him my breasts?"

"You've watched too many spy films, Mae. Just relax."

"Relax? I may not have remembered, but have you forgotten the conditions of my bail? We need to do this as fast as we can."

"You needn't worry." Kitt located the *Carabinieri* on the map as well as the *Pro Loco*, the place she'd told him he could book a trek to see Etna up close. "I've made a call."

"What do you mean, you made a call? To whom?"

"The appropriate authorities. Perhaps you've noticed I know a few people in the police service back home."

"Yes, I've noticed. And when did you make this call?"

He turned his attention to her fully. "This morning, after I left you to finish your breakfast."

"But this means it's going to take more than a day or two. And even if we get in on Wednesday, we may have to schedule an appointment."

"A situation like this is why you wanted my help. There are other avenues to gather information in this town, but you needn't worry about the other end. There have been strings pulled, favours called in and such back home. All is in hand. Your appearance is not until the first of next month. Bryce is covering for me so you can take your time here. You are, after all, in my company and I am in your employ."

"Yes, for a whole five pounds plus," she snorted disdainfully, "expenses."

"And I have Riviera tastes. Seeing as I like to earn my keep, who do I need to attempt to bribe to find us lunch?"

"Sometimes, sir, I think your stomach is more a bottomless pit than your soul."

Mae took him to a little shop she knew for a *girarrosto* chicken. Ten minutes later, food bundles in tow, she drove down a very narrow dead end street and parked. She ushered Kitt to a pock-marked grey building where she unlocked a roll-down metal shutter and shoved it up to reveal pretty paned glass doors and a large picture window. "Your dining room and accommodation, sir." She opened the door for him.

Kitt went inside the tiny flat. It was, as Mae had mentioned, rather spartan. There was a sofa, a small table with two chairs in tiny kitchen space, a small bathroom, a wardrobe, a bookcase stacked with board games and a few books. A spare folding chair was tucked beside the bookcase. Mae put the food on the table and slid the window across a track to air out the place while he went to get the other bags from the car. As he returned, a short woman appeared at the open door ahead of him.

The woman wore a pale blue twinset with a charcoal skirt, and low-heeled blue-black shoes, her hair a sandy-brown bob streaked with silver at the front. "*Bedita! Bedita!*" she called out as she went inside the flat. Kitt watched the woman embrace Mae, squeezing her tightly, kissing her repeatedly. And then she let go and put her hands to her cheeks, suddenly horrified, shaking her head. "*Cos'é successo?* Who belted you?"

"*Io era scippata,*" Mae said, grinning at Kitt as he came inside and put the bags on the sofa.

"Mugged? No!" The little woman spun around to look at Kitt, hands on her hips. She was older than he expected, much older, and she eyed him up and down, frowning darkly. "Who this man?"

"This is Major Kitt, my employer. Sir, this is my dear friend, Fiorella."

A smile lit up Fiorella's softly creased face. "Ooo-hoo *Major*. American friend?"

"British." Kitt found himself being cuddled and kissed by a tiny woman whose powerful hands held his face as she smooched his cheek over and over. He glanced over at Mae and she laughed.

Fiorella let him go suddenly. "Have you eat *pranzo*, Major? I make pasta. You come."

"We have *girarrosto*, Fiorella," Mae said from the kitchenette. "*Girarrosto*, *patate*, and *caponata*."

The woman turned, mouth pursed. "Where you buy chicken?"

"The place on Via Roma."

"No!" she chopped a hand in the air. "That man is a dirty rat crook. His father cheat my father. He give that man milk to make cheese an' nothing. No cheese. Nothing." She chopped the air again. "No!" Fiorella shook her head. "You eat. I no eat. I come back with *frutta*, cherry, peach. I bring you *lenzuola* for bed an' good *ascuigamani* for bath. You like grappa, Major?" Before he answered, she whirled on her heels and departed, muttering, "Dirty rat crook!"

Mae burst out laughing.

Kitt chuckled. "I've experienced vendettas concerning livestock, land, and lost limbs, but that's my first vendetta over cheese." He ducked into the small bathroom to wash his face and neck, drying off with the tea towel Mae had left there earlier. When he'd finished, she'd already set out the lunch on dishes from the kitchen cupboard. He took a seat across from her and proceeded to devour half of a well-spiced and very tender chicken.

"You think this has merit, or are you humouring me?" Mae said.

"Maybe a bit of both. We could do this from home, but it would take longer, and I doubt it would be as delightful as this Vendetta chicken."

"Where do we go next?" She picked at a thigh and a roasted potato.

"Next we try church records, baptisms, marriages, that sort of thing."

"Do you know how many churches there are in this town?"

"I counted eight, and two convents, on the mural at the *Municipio*."

Mae pushed her potato aside. "So we'll get started after the afternoon *riposo*, when things reopen at three, four o'clock."

"You should take advantage of the siesta and have a rest. You look tired."

She looked over to the sofa and then at him. "And where would you sleep?"

"I don't need a rest."

"You rest just fine, don't you, anywhere anyplace?"

Kitt nodded once.

"Does it bother you at all that I killed a man in your home?"

"I don't like that it happened, but as moody and brooding as I appear to be, I can't say that I've spent much time dwelling on it. To fret over the incident serves no purpose. It's not..." he smiled softly, "...productive."

She sucked her bottom lip for a moment. "I'm not fretting or fixating on what happened. I don't think about it, then Sal's face pops into my mind. I hate the fact I know his name. I hate that I'm glad he's dead. I hate that it happened in your home. I hate that I don't know and...what I'm trying to do, Kitt?"

"You are looking for answers."

"Answers. Right." She got up and went to wash her hands in the kitchen sink. "Did I mention that O'Toole, the skinny woman from

Suisse Global Bank, rang me to let me know she's put someone on to follow up on Caspar's trust?"

"No, you didn't."

"Seems the bank takes the allegation of fraud rather seriously, even when they have no record of a client or an account."

"*Bedita!*" Fiorella called out as she came inside. She carried an open basket, a bowl of cherries and peaches, a book, bed linen and towels, a bottle of grappa poking out the top. She handed the basket to Mae and drew out the fruit, the book, and bottle. When Mae took the towels into the bathroom, Fiorella put the other things on the table. "*Malu vivanda,*" she said, and swept what was left of the chicken and potatoes into a plastic bag, even though Kitt hadn't quite finished. After she tied the top, she tossed the bag through the open door, and sat in the chair Mae had left vacant. Pointing, she said, "I bring peach an' *ciliegie*. This cherries nice, Major. Beautiful." Fiorella pushed the bowl towards Kitt, and grabbed a handful of ripe, bright-fleshed red fruit. She swivelled in her seat to face Mae as she returned. "*Allora.* Time for business. You do inspection now. I show you *contabilità*, an' then maybe you visit Caspar." She spat cherry pips into her hand and looked at Kitt. "She never visit her husband."

"I've visited Caspar this morning." Mae gathered the bed linen.

"You did?" Surprised, Fiorella smiled and glanced at Kitt again. "Ah-ha. I see. Now I know why you appearance so tired." She clucked her tongue and looked at Kitt. "She need to rest. Okay?"

"I won't argue with that," he said. Then Kitt frowned slightly and leaned a little closer to the elderly woman.

"Why you look at me that so? You wanna kiss me, soldier?"

"Well," he cut his gaze to Mae for a second, "I do like older women."

"Me too." Fiorella grinned.

Mae made a soft *tst* of amusement and placed folded bedclothes on the arm of the sofa.

"Sorry to dis'point. You can kiss Mae."

"I work for the Major, Fiorella."

"*Ma.*" Fiorella shrugged and gestured with both hands. "*Amore proibito*...forbidden love is so much more fun."

"I won't argue with that either." With a smirk, Kitt selected a peach and asked, "You've lived here all your life?"

"*Si.* Is a nice town. Everybody know everybody an' nobody care what you are—unless you goddamn Nazi. Everybody hate goddamn Nazi."

"You remember when the Nazis were here?" Kitt bit into the luscious, ripe fruit.

"Yes. I was thirteen when they come an' sixteen when you British an' Americans come an' say, 'Hey Hitler an' Mussolini, kiss my ass, *Ba-Boom!*'"

Laughing along with Kitt, Mae eased off her sandals and stretched out on the sofa. "What did I tell you?" she said. "She sounds like an American GI in an old war movie."

"*Ba-boom, ba-boom, ba-boom!* There were many bombs. Americans open the road from Randazzo to Linguaglossa, an' goddamn Nazis got push outta Sicilia. An' why you look at me that so again, Major?"

"You've lived here your whole life." He cocked his head, glancing over at Mae. She had an arm across her eyes. "I was wondering, Fiorella," he said, watching the older woman stuff a cherry into her mouth, "if you know much about the families who have lived and died here."

"Everybody," Fiorella spat the pit into her hand, "know everybody, an' everybody business. This a dinky small town."

Mae sat up. "Do you know anyone named Russo who died in the last twenty years?

"*Bo.*" Fiorella shrugged. "There are many Russo in Sicilia and many in Linguaglossa."

"Stefano Russo, did you know him?" Mae asked, sitting up. "He's buried next to Caspar."

Fiorella shook the cherry stones in her hand. "Stefano Russo... Stefano... Ah! He marry the little woman, Lina Cavallaro. I know her. They both *maestri*, schoolteachers. They die young, fifty-six. Car crash, like Caspar. Sad. The son, also name Stefano, has his daddy blue, blue eyes. When his mama an' papa die, he go to live with family in San Giovanni, near Macchia. They bread baker. Stefano make bread."

"What about Biagio Torrisi?" Kitt said.

Fiorella chortled. "Your Italian bad. No *Bye-ah gee-oh*. Is *Bee-ah-jo*, Major. I know him. I know his sister-in-law, Rosa. We go to haircut school together. They my age. Rosa have a son. Biagio have no children. He...*come si dice 'baccelliere'*, Mae?"

"Bachelor.

"Si, bachelor. Like me. Everybody know Biagio love his sister-in-law. Even Giuseppe, his brother, know. Know what I mean?"

"Are they related to the Torrisi coffee family?" Mae said.

"No. The coffee Torrisi family in Catania. Biagio was postman. He a nice man. His nephew, Little Giuseppe, 'Pippino' name after his papa. Every boy here name after his papa or gran'father. Pippino is a big shot *avvacato*—lawyer in Taormina." Fiorella opened her hand and, like shrivelled dice, the cherry stones rolled onto the table. "People think he turn his back on family, an' marry girl from the north, but he nice, a good man like his uncle. Rosa an' her husband die maybe *tre ani fa*. Three years. Big Giuseppe die first, then she go, then Biagio, *affranto*, with broken heart. Rosa an' Big Giuseppe bury in same cemetery with Caspar, but in fancy *mausoleo*, not in ground like Biagio." Fiorella inspected the peaches and chose one. "Why you wanna know 'bout Biagio Torrisi an' Stefano Russo?"

With a cough, Mae rose from the couch and went to the table. "They are entombed beside Caspar. And I've been thinking," she said. "I'd like to take Caspar back to England. If I do, it might disturb the graves beside his. Of course, I have to talk with the cemetery caretaker before I contact the Torrisi and Russo families, but I want to make sure that they would find my plan reasonable and know that I'd compensate them for any trouble it causes. I supposed I could talk to the families first." Mae put a hand on Kitt's shoulder. "So, the Russo family are bread makers in San Giovanni?"

"Yeah." Fiorella smirked at the location of Mae's hand. "The *panificio* old, time machine old. Not pretty, not fancy-schmancy like in Milano or Roma. *Rustico*, but bread nice. I buy there when I see my friend Carmela in San Giovanni." She looked at Kitt and pursed her lips for a moment before she smiled brightly. "I call Stefano and tell him you come visit the *panificio* today because the Major like old things. You don't ask on phone. You go see him. Good manner that way."

THE *PANIFICIO* in San Giovanni had opened its doors early in the twentieth century. The two wood-fired ovens in the bread shop had been in operation since then. Barring modern stainless-steel equipment that mixed the dough, the Russo family still kneaded the bread by hand, baked everything in the ovens, and the shop itself remained unchanged in its alleyway position.

Kitt paused in the shop's entrance. It was similar to a garage, the metal door rolled up overhead. Below, a line of black volcanic ash and flour showed that the door had been closed during the morning's eruption and then opened again to patrons who left behind shoeprints of gritty black mixed with off-white. Larger volcanic pebbles had tumbled inside, some crushed into powdery black splotches as they'd been trod upon.

Mae glanced at her watch. "The end of the afternoon *riposo* is usually around 3, although it's not unheard of for some shops to reopen at 4. This place stops baking for the day after lunch, but Fiorella said Stefano Russo would be here because the fires in these ovens are never extinguished. Somebody always has to tend to the ovens." She pushed up the sleeves of her dress, the still-lit open furnaces heated the *panifico* to a temperature just a few degrees below that of the molten lava that might spew from Mount Etna at any time.

On the right side of the *panificio*, where dough proved on wooden shelves, industrial bakery equipment *ka-chunked* and whined. Bags of durum wheat flour were piled high, protected from the heat by a stone wall that looked as if it had been hit by shrapnel in World War II. The rest of the bakery was clad with white tiles that reached halfway to the ceiling. Flour clung to the tiles, dulling them. The machines squealed and clanged as she fanned herself and looked around at the arched doorways of the bakery. They went farther inside, leaving footprints in the flour that scattered and swirled across the brick floor.

"What a stink," Kitt frowned. A burnt smell hung in the air, and it was an unusual aroma Mae didn't associate with overbaked bread, but then she'd never baked anything in an open wood-burning oven like the ones she stood looking at. Enormous, soot-edged hoods made of metal topped the two old, domed wood-fired ovens. The far one raged, drawing flame and wisps of smoke up and out. The closest oven had been cleaned out recently, but tremendous heat radiated from it still.

She called out, "*Buongiorno, Signor Russo!*" No one responded above the din of the dough-mixing machines or the roar of the fire.

Kitt ducked into the machinery room and Mae ventured into the open space to where the ovens crackled and glowed. Loaves of crusty bread stuck up out of dusty white laundry baskets that sat on the flour-coated stone floor. Round loaves of bread were stacked on a flour and semolina-dusted stainless-steel table that separated the room and the two ovens. A flour-sprinkled pink basket was filled with bread that had been burnt black, explaining the charred odour in the air.

Mae went toward the blackened bread, around the loaf-stacked bench closer to the oven on the other side. She inspected the fat charcoal shapes, pulling out a loaf that had once been bread, the staff of life, and then she looked into the flickering, roaring fire that had baked the life out of the staff. Sweating, she stood, mesmerised by the colourful dancing, curling fire in the old brick and stone oven. Then she realised the smell heavy in the air had less to do with the blackened bread lining the wall, and more to do with what lay at the mouth of the flaming oven.

Not quite believing, she took a few hesitant steps forward to the flour-dulled tiles, to the searing heat licking out of the arched furnace, to a smoking, black-spotted hand that was backlit by red-and-orange-glowing bricks and burning loaves of bread. The noise she'd heard in the Major's kitchen a few days ago returned, drowning out everything except for the thickened blood coursing in her head, engulfing the din of the fire and the machines in the other room, rushing, roiling, deafening her.

Something gripped her elbow and she swung the baked-to-charcoal thing in her hand as a muted shout registered in her sound-blunted ears.

A bread baton shattered against Kitt's chest, coal-coloured flakes and crumbs spilling down his pale blue shirt. "Did you touch anything?" he shouted a second time into Mae's white face. She turned to look at the oven and he followed her gaze to a sight that was grotesque but didn't match the sickening horror of what he'd found wrapped around the dough mixer in the other room.

"Did you touch anything?"

She covered her mouth with both hands, and when she shook her head, Kitt propelled her to the garage-like entrance then slowed. Outside, beneath a blazing sun, his arm through hers, they walked down the little alleyway, to the car out on the street. And then they were in the car and he was driving, following the twisting streets out of the village. He pulled off the narrow road, into a driveway overgrown by Queen Anne's lace and purple wildflowers. He opened his door, got out, and was violently ill.

"Christ," he muttered into the weeds. As he retched again, he felt her trembling touch on his arm.

"A hand. There was a hand in the oven," she murmured. "It was a hand, wasn't it?"

He nodded, wiping his mouth with the back of his fist. "The rest of him was in the other room. What the hell are you mixed up in, Mae?"

CHAPTER NINE

K itt said nothing as he drove a short distance and into a little town called Macchia, where Mae had once worked for the Gelsomino family. Volcanic sand had fallen more heavily here. The small piazza in front of the church was blackened with thick grime. A statue of Saint Vito and his dog rose on a pillar above the piazza. The patron saint's outstretched hand protected the locals from the more horrifying dangers of Mount Etna. Mae looked up at the statue as they drove by, the ash crunching beneath the tyres.

With his jaw set, Kitt slowed and pulled along the kerbside to park near a petrol station with a sign showing a red, stylised six-legged dog. He climbed out of the Volkswagen, pulled his mobile from his pocket, and tapped on the screen.

Three black sand-layered car lengths up from the VW stood a small kiosk café overlooking a wooded park. The shopkeeper had brushed away grime from the tables and collected it in plastic bags, forming a little pyramid against the side of the dark green kiosk wall.

Mae let her eyes wander back to Kitt. He put his phone away as he walked past a spread of shady palm trees. She followed. Colour had returned to his face rather quickly after he'd been sick, and so had his appetite. With his traveller's Italian, he ordered two *caffè Americanos*, pointed at two ricotta-filled cannoli, and headed for an aluminium table in the shade, shooing away pigeons. She joined him, wondering how he could be hungry.

Her chair made a hollow scraping noise as she slid it across recently washed bricks and took the seat beside him and a purple bougainvillea. He sat facing the volcano, watching, she supposed, the swelling black cloud of volcanic ash drifting north, or gazing back in the direction they'd come, down the twisting hill road from San Giovanni, a mere five minutes away. She watched him watching, and wasn't game to say anything, to be the first to talk because she decided she didn't want to know what she was mixed up in. She didn't want to find out where the rabbit hole went. She wanted to run away. She wanted to go to New Mexico, or Mexico, or someplace in the Caribbean where it was always warm. She wanted to be anyplace but in Sicily or back in London. And she wanted Kitt to come with her.

It was funny. The burnt hand in the oven had been frightening, but seeing him be ill had terrified her more. He held himself with an exterior of imperturbable confidence and had a soft underbelly after all. The man, the bully, hero, and saviour had become human, but was he really? The contradiction of his confidence and vulnerability had shifted so rapidly. Detached, he went on watching the volcano and she went on watching him until the barista called out. Then Mae watched Kitt try to brush off a few remaining cinders of burnt bread that clung to the soft blue of his shirt as he got up to collect the tray with the coffee and pastries. He set one of each in front of her and took his seat.

She watched him reach for a cannolo and bite into it. Creamy sweet cheese oozed from the cracks he made in the crispy shell, icing sugar dusted over his fingers, landed on his shirt beside smudges of charcoal, and drifted onto the table. She watched him savour the bite, take his time, let the sweetness roll across his tongue. She watched him consume the dessert. Boorishly, he ate the entire cannolo and made a mess doing so, drank his coffee in between bites, licked and sucked his fingers, brushed crumbs from his lap, and then reached for the pastry she hadn't touched. He ate and licked and sucked, sloppily, and continued to drink coffee as if nothing had happened.

As if nothing had happened.

Scared, confused, disgusted, and surprisingly furious, she snatched up the coffee in front of her to have a sip and then put it back on the table, hard. Coffee splashed up and over the edge of the cup to form a pool in the saucer and puddles on the table. Pastry crumbs became minuscule islands surrounded by sugar snow bright on aluminium. She glared at him. "How..." she began. "How can you..."

Kitt gazed back, his eyes direct, cold, his tone matter-of-fact. "How can I what, eat after finding a man with his neck twisted around an industrial dough hook?"

Hand to her throat, she said, "Is that what you meant by 'the rest of him'?"

"Yes," he said coolly.

"No wonder you were...squeamish."

"Yes. No wonder. Listen, Mae. I've seen sickening things in the work I do, and what I've learned, from being stuck in war-torn countries to dealing with families trying to kill each other over a piece of land no bigger than this café, is that everyone processes their trauma in different ways. Sometimes I eat. Sometimes I run. Sometimes I drink. Let me put it in these terms for you. It's more productive to do something else. Whatever happened, I don't hold on to it. My point is if you change your behaviour, you change your thinking, or you *start* thinking. I needed to think, Mae."

Mae looked at what remained of the cannolo, the crumbs scattered, the tiny blobs of ricotta, the sprinkling of powdery white sugar, the coffee she'd slopped on the table, and Jaysus, she wanted to clean up the mess, to put something in order when everything around her had turned chaotic. "I don't think I'm going to process this by eating." She lifted her dripping cup of coffee and took a careful sip. And she had another, trying to concentrate on what she tasted, the way he had when he ate his pastry. She was surprised that it helped. She breathed in the coffee's aroma and had another sip, catching a hint of caramel and syrup, with molasses and slight burnt overtone. Then the flavour vanished, replaced by the invasive memory of a burnt hand. Carefully, Mae set the coffee down. "Do you think the man was Stefano Russo?"

Kitt gave a single nod. "He did have very blue eyes."

"What am I mixed up in? What have I got you into? Oh, God." She exhaled. "We have to go to the police."

"No. We don't," he said, watching the road, or the volcano, or the palm trees.

"Of course we do."

"No. We don't want to do that. You're not supposed to be here, remember? We don't want to draw attention to the fact that you are here, regardless of what I managed to arrange at home." Kitt brushed powdered sugar from the front of his shirt and watched a white and blue *polizia* sedan pass by.

She huffed. "You're not supposed to be here either. You're supposed to be doing paperwork. You're supposed to be spending time with Miss Astor. You're supposed to be going to Wimbledon. But instead you're finding dead men in kitchens."

"Yes," he said and the table wobbled. When he looked at Mae, her mouth was tight, her lips pressing together as she wiped away the cannoli-coffee-crumb mess on the table. "Who knows you're here?" he said. "Did you tell anyone you were coming to Sicily?"

"Only Fiorella and Mr Stephens."

"You told Stephens?"

"I only told him I would be away and his new front door key was in his postbox. Why, do you think Mr Stephens is involved?"

"No, I don't thin—"

"This has to be about money and Daniel Pierce. This has to be connected to Pierce and Caspar's trust somehow. What other explanation is there? It can't be a coincidence that Daniel Pierce and now Stefano Russo are dead. It *has* to be tied to Caspar's money, but how?"

"I don't know, and I think you're right. This whole thing is about money. And I am not letting you out of my sight. Not now. Not after what we found." He lifted his chin. The *polizia* sedan had turned around and stopped at the front of the café.

Mae followed his line of sight. "Maybe they're here to have coffee?"

"Maybe, but they turned around and stopped after pointing at the Volkswagen." He swiped tiny crumbs from the corner of his mouth. "Oh goody, they're getting out of the car."

"I made a bollocks of all this. You should run, Kitt. Just run. Go home. Shag Miss Astor."

"And miss out on making five pounds?" Kitt took her hand and kissed it, which startled her. He met her eyes and watched her swallow. "Why would I run?" he said. She tried to pull from his grasp, but he kept hold and kissed her hand again, and she drew in a breath, lips parted, breasts rising. He leaned close to her, drawing near enough to catch the scent of coffee and the perfume she wore. He liked her perfume. "Can you work with me?"

"What?" she said, her mouth a few inches from his.

"Can you work with me?"

"Yes," she whispered, and the way she'd whispered the word—not frightened or uncertain, or contrary—surprised Kitt, gave him an odd little thrill. She held his gaze, and he would have sworn she smiled when she murmured, "Yes, change my behaviour to change my thinking, but Kitt, how clichéd."

"Clichéd?" he said.

"*Scusate*," one of the police officers said.

Head turning, Kitt felt Mae's lips brush his ear. With a spark of unexpected delight in his bloodstream, he looked up at the redhead who wore a handgun on his hip.

The policeman's expression shifted from slightly officious to concern as his eyes settled on Mae. Kitt had never wished that she'd worn make-up before, but it would have been helpful if she had caked on some to cover the bruising that remained on her face. "Uh, *buongiornio*?" He turned back to Mae, smiling. "Does one still stay *buongiorno* at this time of day, darling?"

"I think so. Or you could say *salve*."

"*È sua l'auto verde*?" The redhead pointed over his shoulder.

"Wait. Maybe it's *salvo*."

Kitt glanced up at the policeman and held up his index finger. "Check the phrase book."

"I thought you had the phrase book," she said, drowning out the officer's words.

"I thought you did."

"You put the map inside the back of the book."

"Oh, bollocks!" Kitt released Mae's hand and began to climb to his feet. "I think I left the phrase book back at the cemetery we visited."

"Okay. Stop." The policeman held up his hand. He paused for a moment, scrutinising Mae's bruises before his hard gaze shifted to focus on Kitt. "Is that your green Volkswagen there?"

"Oh, you speak English." Kitt settled back into his chair. "How nice."

The redhead smiled at his partner, translating what Kitt had said, and adding that they were dealing with an English wife-beating tourist, not a *Babbu Americano* wife-beating tourist. "Yes," Red said. "I speak English. Is that your green Beetle?"

"Well, yes, but not really." Mae shook her head.

"What does she mean 'not really'?" the policeman said, eyes on Kitt.

Mae gave an impatient snort. "*I* mean we hired the car. It belongs to the Hertz Hire Car company in Catania. Why? Have we done something wrong?"

Kitt refrained from grinning. Mae sounded like an irritated Princess Anne. "Was the car reported stolen?" he said. "Or did you catch me speeding? Going by the way people drive 'round here, and the accident we had in our last hire car, I was under the impression there *is* no speed limit in Sicily, even if it's posted at 110." Rubbing his forehead Kitt turned to Mae. "I wonder if Sicily is anything like Alabama or Mexico, Jane, and we have enough cash to make a contribution to the Mother and Fathers Italian Association."

"Oh, good, God, Ian!" Mae said, eyes rolling. The *Mothers and Fathers Italian Association*? Really?"

"*Che cazzo*," Officer Red swore, teeth clenched. "What are your names, please?"

"Leiter. Ian Leiter and this is Jane. Did you need to see our pass-ports or something?"

"Mr Leiter. You weren't speeding and the car isn't stolen."

"Well, then what is it?" Mae frowned. "We didn't try to order cappuccinos in the afternoon. We learned that was a crime when we were in Florence."

"You can't park there at this time of day."

Kitt frowned. "What do you mean?"

"I mean you can't park *there*." Red pointed at the VW. "That section is for deliveries only."

"I wonder why the barista didn't say anything about not parking there." Mae said.

"*Perché siete imbecilli*?" Red said under his breath.

"He could have said something," Mae grumbled.

"We'll move the car immediately, officer." Kitt reached for Mae's hand and pulled her to her feet.

"But Ian," she whined, "I haven't finished my coffee!"

"Do you want them to give us a ticket, or a fine, or whatever, Jane?"

"Lady, listen to you husband."

"Oh, all right!" Mae let Kitt lead her toward the car as the two policemen made comments about *stronzo di merda Inglese* tourists.

She slid into the passenger side, hands shaking, and drew on her seatbelt.

When Kitt climbed in he leaned across, bussed her cheek. "Well done, Jane," he said and sat back, starting the engine.

"I'm glad you think so, because I'm barely holding it together, Ian."

He pulled from the kerb and watched in the rear-view mirror as the lights of the police car winked on, red and blue flashing. The sedan sped off in the direction of San Giovanni. "Keep holding it together, Jane. Breathe in and out." Kitt made a U-turn and drove by the little café, following the same route as the police.

She took a breath. "We're going back to the *panificio*, aren't we?"

"No, we're going to Linguaglossa. Why would we go back to the *panificio*?"

"Fiorella spoke with Stefano and his wife. He was expecting us." She turned, listening as a siren approached. "Someone could have seen us or the car. There were a few people on the street when we got to San Giovanni."

The siren grew louder and louder and the *Carabinieri* were behind them. Kitt slowed and moved aside to give the *Carabinieri* space to charge by on the narrow street. "If we were seen it's easy to explain, Mae. We walked in. No one was there. We walked out and came here. We even spoke with the police."

Mae watched the black and red sedan scream around a sharp curve and head toward San Giovanni. "Then what are we doing?"

"We're driving back to the flat. I have to collect a few things, and then we're going to find Torrisi. Hopefully no one's killed him yet."

SHADOWS MOVED across fields of wildflowers, over lemon trees, and crumbling stone cottages. Light and dark patches traded places as clouds travelled overhead and shrouded the sun. The VW rounded a bend, shifting their direction east to frame Mount Etna and the ballooning plume of smoke and ash drifting north amid grey curtains of rain.

"Who is it?" Mae said. "Who does this start with? Me? Daniel Pierce? Caspar?"

Kitt glanced at her. "What do you know about Pierce?"

"He was fifty-two, divorced, and had an adult daughter who lives in Australia."

"How did you meet?"

Mae watched tiny raindrops dot the windscreen. "He sent me letters about Caspar's trust. I thought it was scam. Then I went to the bank, and Daniel showed me that there really was a trust. He wasn't what I expected."

"What did you expect?"

"I don't know. I didn't expect flirty. From the start he was...interested, flirty, but not in an obsequious way."

"You sound surprised he flirted."

She snorted. "Well, I'm not exactly an ingénue."

"Why would you want to be?" He gave her a sidelong glance. "You're not insecure about ageing, are you?"

"No, but I'm aware men have a preference for younger women."

"I do believe you are a little naïve about men, Mae. When a man is attracted to a woman he shows his interest."

"That may be true, but I was there to discuss Caspar's trust and Daniel's flirting didn't strike me as particularly professional."

"Ah, professional." Mae watched the edge of Kitt's mouth curve into a smirk. "The cornerstone of your existence. However did he convince you to have dinner with him?"

"Go ahead and mock me. It may be rigid, but there's a time and place for things, a time for work and a time for play. I liked Daniel. Perhaps he wasn't professional, but he was...sweet."

"I'm pleased to know you're not closed off to the idea of having a relationship with someone sweet." Kitt switched on the windscreen wipers.

Mae removed her sunglasses and turned to look at him. "I'm not closed off. I may not have what I did with Caspar, but I'm not closed off to dating or even sleeping with other men. I'm happy to date or sleep with other men."

"When was the last time you went out with a man, besides Pierce?"

"Three or four months ago."

"How long did it last?"

"About two weeks."

"So you're happy to date, but you avoid long-term relationships."

She burst out laughing. "What's that they say about pots and kettles and black?"

"If you can't trust a friend to tell you the truth, who can you trust?" Kitt shrugged.

"Why are you concerned with my dating habits?"

"I'd like you to be happy, Mae."

Mae wondered if she'd gasped out loud because she certainly had in her head. She didn't understand why it was so shocking to know Kitt wanted her to be happy, but it was shocking and something else she couldn't name, something akin to a witch's brew of anger, fear, desire, and delight. Confused by the inexplicable emotional concoction, she turned back to watch the light rain sprinkle against the windows and decided not to pursue any sort of meaning to his words, beyond the fact that it was an insult to women everywhere. She said, "I'm not unhappy. And I don't need a man to be happy."

"I only meant I'd prefer if you didn't live your life in mourning," he said softly.

"That's very sweet of you," she sniffed. "But I think I liked you better when you were sick in the weeds."

"Right." He laughed and fired off a round of questions. "How long were your meetings with Pierce? How many times did you meet with him? What did you talk about? What did he tell you?"

Mae watched out the window. "He explained how a trust is structured, that Caspar set up the trust with Suisse Global Bank acting as trustee. Monthly deposits were made into the trust from investments in what we assumed was the share market. The details of the trust stipulated the assets were to be distributed to his beneficiary sixteen years after his death. Daniel said it took some digging to track me down. Before I signed any papers transferring the trust, I had to show proof that Caspar and I were married, show his birth and death certificates. I did that the Friday afternoon before you returned home. I thought Daniel held off on my signing the transfer papers to Monday because he wasn't sure I'd meet him for dinner that Saturday."

"He wanted to see you again, even if you stood him up."

"I suppose so. I guess I found that enchanting."

"And because Pierce had held off on your signing the transfer documents is why it seemed reasonable to you that Largo was legitimate after Pierce died."

Mae let that all sink in before she answered. "Yes. That's why I let him help me carry things into your flat."

"Are you still dwelling on that?"

"I fell for the oldest ruse used by thieves and con men, and it's what got us here, isn't it? Somehow, it's why Russo had his neck broken and his hand cut off, isn't it?"

"I don't know."

She made an impatient noise in the back of her throat, a guttural, German-sounding *ach*! "We're back where we started. We know nothing. We've learned nothing."

Kitt turned to look at her. "I've learned that you like sweet men and you dwell on the past."

"How do you not dwell on a man dying in your home? How do you not dwell on finding another man with his neck broken and his hand cut off?"

"I'm forward thinking."

"Yes, you are, you're forward thinking, but right now you should be forward *looking*." During the earlier drive to Linguaglossa he'd done something similar and pointed at the road. This time she did.

The sky had grown much darker ahead of them, and it wasn't rain falling on the other side of Linguaglossa. A steady, soft shower had painted the Volkswagen with glistening drops, but the wind had changed direction, blowing northeast, rapidly shifting the direction of the ash cloud. They'd drive into it soon. "How bad do you think that's going to be?" Kitt said.

Mae leaned forward with the ridiculous notion that being six centimetres closer to the windscreen would somehow give her telescopic vision. "Hard to say. Could be like the hailstones we had before or could be more like sand. We won't know until we get closer. Hopefully it won't damage the car's paint or shatter the windscreen. Did you get insurance for volcanic ash damage to this car, Kitt?"

"Are you saying we should turn around?"

"Five more minutes and we're there. It's twenty back to Macchia, so keep going. We'll put the car in the garage next to Fiorella's."

It got darker the closer they moved to town. Kitt switched on the car's lights. "Why don't you tell me how you met Caspar?" He glanced at her.

She smiled faintly. "I was in the employ of the Countess Von Klein at her home in Weybridge. There was a sick chestnut tree that the she wanted to save. She couldn't bear having something else die so soon after her son had been killed in a skiing accident. The problem was every arborist in London said it needed to be removed. The countess and I consulted over a dozen different arborists from across Europe and they all told her the tree had to come down—except for one man who'd grown up harvesting chestnuts in Sicily."

"So Caspar was a master gardener and an arborist?"

She dug into the handbag she had on the floor beside her feet. Kitt thought she was looking for a tissue to dry tears, but she took out a small iPad and then a metal container of tiny mints. She put the tablet back and offered him a mint. When he declined, she continued, "He was an arborist, gardener, landscaper. The Countess flew him in for breakfast once a week. He came to the house at Weybridge for eight and a half months to look after that tree, trimming it, feeding it, overseeing that the roots grew stronger by having the tree anchored by cables. One morning, before I served breakfast, he asked about the coffee I made. He said it was the best coffee he ever had and wondered, in a town as wealthy as Weybridge, why the coffee was so terrible. I made sure he had coffee the next time he came to check the tree, and the time after that, and the time after that, too."

"What did you talk about in those times?" Kitt caught a soft whiff of peppermint.

"Coffee, food, family, travelling, everything, anything. He had striking eyes that were a...singular shade of brown with little dabs of gold, and he wasn't conventionally handsome."

"You mean like me?"

"Do you want to hear about Caspar or would you prefer a story about yourself?"

He chuckled. A tiny black pebble *tick-tacked* into the windscreen. "Go on."

Mae shifted in her seat. "Caspar went to university in Palermo and wound up in a position at the University Botanical Gardens. Eventually he became the master gardener there. He was the master gardener for a monastery in Malta and master gardener for a private estate in on the Croatian island, Vis. He liked being consulted, he liked travelling from one garden to another, but what Caspar enjoyed most was gardening. He loved to work the earth and study how things grew. He had no interest in finance or politics, or social causes. He liked getting dirty, and I suppose I liked that. My brother Sean thinks I held some kind of Lady Chatterley fantasy for Caspar, that he was the outside chaos to my inside order. And maybe he was. All I really know is that I loved him. I quit my position with the countess, married Caspar in Ireland, and took employment with the Gelsomino family." She gave a sad little sigh and said, "Tell me about the woman you loved."

Kitt gave a sad, soft little laugh. "No." A handful of pebbles tapped against the windows, plinking as they hit the Beetle's domed roof.

"Well, that's unfair. Why not?"

"I don't wish to be reminded of my...shortcomings." He turned

146

down the narrow laneway beside her spartan flat and stopped the car.

"You have shortcomings?"

"More than you could ever imagine. Where's the garage?"

"Under the geraniums. Follow me." Mae threw open the door, dashed through the pebble shower, and jerked open an old wooden door that would have looked more at home on a barn than it did beneath a balcony covered in white and red geraniums.

Thirty seconds later, Kitt grabbed a small black canvas case from the Volkswagen's boot and darted inside Mae's flat.

She drew heavy blue drapes halfway across the large window and went into the bathroom to shake the grit from her hair. When she came back into the kitchenette, she dug her glasses and little iPad from the side pocket of her handbag. Then took a seat at the table, beside the black case Kitt had placed there. Once the tablet had powered up, she slipped on her reading glasses and typed *Giuseppe Torrisi, Sicily* into a search engine. There were 182,000 results—all in Italian. She added the Italian word for lawyer, *avvocato,* to the search. The search came back with 27,000 results. When she included Taormina, the results showed 158,000.

She read through the first ten. "If this is the right Giuseppe Torrisi, then he's a lawyer and advocate for refugees and asylum seekers."

Kitt read over her shoulder as he emptied his pockets, leaving change and a stubby fountain pen on the table. "Does that say something about the UNHCR, the United Nations High Commissioner for Refugees?"

Mae moved her finger across the screen. "It does. Torrisi specialises in EU law and policy. And he plays guitar in a band."

Kitt laid a tea towel flat on the table's top and reached for the black zip-case. Mae watched him unzip the heavy canvas and draw out something black. He set it on top of the towel, beside a small expensive thing she'd seen before. She blinked, first at the black fountain pen then at the other black thing she'd also seen before. "Is that—"

"My Beretta."

She found it bizarre that he'd said 'my Beretta' like the thing was a well-loved pet. Mae picked up the weapon and examined it, careful to keep it pointed away from them both. It was heavier than she thought it would be, and wasn't warm, fluffy, or cuddly in any sort of way that a pet was. "This is the same piece you had that night in my flat."

"You're correct." Kitt took the weapon from her and set it back on the tea towel.

"How...how did you get it through customs when you flew here?"

With a laugh, he opened another section of the black case and pulled out a second handgun and placed it beside the first. "I work in risk assessment for a rather large organisation with close ties to the British government. The job comes with certain licence."

Disconcerted yet fascinated, she said, "What made you bring these things here? If you came here to have a holiday, what made you bring your Beretta and...what's this one?" She reached for it.

He picked up the weapon before she touched it, ensured the chamber was clear and that the weapon was unloaded, and returned it to the towel beside the Beretta. "A Walther PPS."

"What made you bring a Beretta and a Walter—"

"Walther."

"What made you bring two weapons with you on holiday?"

He examined the Walther the same way he had the Beretta. "Force of habit. I always travel with them. They're always packed and ready to go in a bag."

"I have packed and unpacked your bags. I have never come across guns, ammunition, or that case."

"You never touch this case or the other I keep at home. I may leave bags at the door, but I always secure this case."

The room grew a little dim as the ash cloud moved to shroud the sun. Mae rose, switched on a lamp, and sat again, staring at him with her mouth slightly agape—and he went about sorting through his things; things like clips or magazines or whatever one called the thing that held bullets. "I think I should be terrified of you, Kitt. Shouldn't I?"

"But you're not, are you?" Kitt pulled his charcoal-soiled shirt off, yanking it over his head. He shook out the long-sleeved cotton button-down shirt he'd taken from his largest bag and hung the pale green garment over the back of the other chair.

"No," she said. He stood less than a hand's span away, closer than she'd ever been to such an expanse of his naked skin. He had scars on his chest, old scars faded with time, a newer scar that was pink and puckered, a long white scar that slashed down his abdomen. There were a few nicks that reminded her of vents on a piecrust, and a round, lumpy-looking scar at his right shoulder. Was it odd that she wanted to touch that roundish lump? What did *odd* mean anyway when everything about today was odd, when every-thing that happened in the last week was odd? Kitt slipped on the new shirt and she stopped thinking about what was odd and what that lumpiness would feel like.

She looked back at the two semi-automatic firearms, and then met his eyes when she realised what those weapons meant. "You've killed people, haven't you?"

He'd begun to button the blue-green fabric and his fingers paused at a buttonhole mid-chest. The amused glint in his eyes faded. He exhaled harshly. "Mae, there are things I'm not ab—"

"Yes. Your time in the military." She raised a hand and shook her head. "I'm sorry," she said. "I'm quite self-absorbed at the moment, Kitt. I have no regard for what comes out of my mouth. I say before I

149

think. I do understand. I understand that 'war is hell,' and with what Sean went through as a chaplain with UN Peacekeepers in Bosnia, I ought to know better than to pry about what you experienced. Let me pry about this instead. I've never stumbled across where you store your weapons when I've been cleaning. Where do you keep them?"

He finished buttoning and rolled up his sleeves, giving her a very measured look, as if he were gauging how much he trusted her. "There is a kick plate beneath the window seat in the sitting room. It houses a lockbox." His mouth twitched. Apparently, he found it humorous that the pistol safe had been right under her nose for years, but his amusement didn't quite reach his eyes.

"There was a gun within reach when Sal tried to kill me?" She lifted the Beretta by the butt, keeping the nose down.

"You did well enough with a toilet brush." He took the weapon from her. "Stick with cleaning equipment." He tucked the Beretta into the right side of the black case, shoved the magazines back into the middle section, securing them with Velcro straps, and then slid the Walther into the left. Then he zipped the case shut and set it beside the couch.

Mae stared at the case. "Do you think we might need those?"

"I hope to God not, but it's better to be prepared." He went to the window and pulled the drapes back. "Well, that's no good," he muttered.

She hurried to his side and looked through the glass. The light rain had mixed with tiny black gravel. Day had turned to a foggy grey twilight. "I don't think we're going anywhere," she said.

CHAPTER TEN

It was a drink typically served in winter, but Kitt poured more grappa into a glass meant for a shot of espresso and drank it. He suspected Fiorella was cheating, but how did one accuse an elderly woman of stealing money from the bank in a game of Monopoly, especially after she'd braved falling volcanic sand to deliver the best *fritelle di melanzane* and *spaghetti alla puttanesca* he had ever eaten?

"Winner, winner, chicken dinner," she said, as she had every time he landed on Park Place, which was far more often than he cared to note. "So, Major, you and Mae stay here an' I bring you *colazione* breakfas'—if *il volcano* does not essplode an' burn us in our sleep."

"When was the last large lava flow that worried the town?" Kitt tipped more grappa into his glass.

"Two-thousan' tree. It destroy tourist station, an' then in two-thousan' twelve we have lotta hash...*ash*. Little more like today. Last time was very hot. You could not open windows. This time is cooler. Is funny summer. You worry 'bout Etna, Major?"

He raised an eyebrow and knocked back the grappa.

"I think he's more worried that you've won." Mae slid reading glasses down her nose.

"I have win. See?" Fiorella pointed to the board and all the hotels and houses she owned. Then she pointed at his lone twenty dollar note and Mae's measly two hundred and fifty. "I have kick your asses." She lifted her glass. "One more nip, Major. No, no, not the grappa. You drink grappa. Give me limoncello. Is nicer. Please."

Kitt obliged and watched the woman down the yellow liqueur and set her glass on the table.

"Winner, winner, chicken dinner!" Fiorella said again, and looked at her watch. "Is late! Past my bedtime." She rose abruptly, lifted the board and slid the hotels and houses into the game's flat box in a shower, the top hat, tiny shoe, and sports car tinkling against red and green plastic. She took the money Mae had gathered, dumped it inside, shoved the board on top, and, rather hastily, put the lid on top. She returned the box back to the bookcase where it usually sat. Patting her skirt, she moved to Kitt, kissed his cheeks, did the same to Mae, and hurried to the door.

Mae went with her. She pulled the door open and looked outside. "What do you think?" she said.

Fiorella, peered outdoors. "I see worse *sabbia*, sand, but this not good to drive. Very slippy, like bad ice. Glad you stay here. Finish that fruit. I bring more in the morning." She lifted her empty basket, raised an umbrella over her head, and stepped out into the falling sand. "*Buonanotte, ragazzi.*"

Mae watched her cross the street to her little house and go inside. Then she shut the door and turned to Kitt, squinting. "I think she cheated."

"Yes. And rather cleverly. I only just worked out how as she was packing up."

"What did she do? How did she get all that money? I was the

banker. I didn't give it to her. Okay, I did give it to her, when I landed on her property, so did you."

"Mm-hm." Kitt went to the bookcase and slid out the Monopoly game. He took it back to the table and removed the lid. The board inside was humped up in the centre and didn't quite fit inside the box. He lifted the hard cardboard, looking beneath it. "As I suspected." He turned to show Mae. "We were set up."

She shrugged. "What do you mean?"

"There's a tremendous amount of Monopoly money in this box."

"Define tremendous." Mae collected the glasses and used plates from the table.

"I'd say three or four times the usual."

"What's the usual?"

Kitt put the game on the table, beside his glass, which he refilled with grappa. "Fun fact. Old American versions of the game, like this one, have approximately fifteen thousand one hundred and forty dollars. Newer games have twenty thousand. There's got to be at least sixty thousand here."

"That doesn't mean Fiorella cheated." Mae stood at the sink, filling it with warm soapy water, tying a tea towel around her waist.

Kitt watched her smooth the towel down over her hips the way she did whenever she tied on an apron. He shot back the grappa and poured more. "Who insisted we play *this* game instead of cards? Who talked about playing Monopoly with American GIs? Who said she had two old American Monopoly sets at home? She came supplied with money from one of her games. She set us up."

"Your analysis is dizzying." She chuckled, tossed him another tea towel and plunged dirty supper dishes into the water. She washed the glasses first and held one out for him to dry. "Yes, Fiorella played us. She played us so well. If only all crimes were this easy to solve," she sighed.

Kitt swallowed another measure of liqueur, left the game on the table and began to dry the glass. "We'll sort it out, Mae."

"Maybe we will tomorrow." With a nod, she scrubbed cheese crusted on a fork. "The best way to get to Taormina is to catch a bus because there's no place to park. If the roads are clear, and the buses are operating, we'll go in the morning."

"Yes, that will work. Was Caspar your last lover?"

Her head came up from the fork. She looked up at him over the frame of her reading glasses then returned to washing. "That's an interesting shift in conversation. Is that what you say to win over women? I've seen you with them and wondered how you did it. I never imagined asking about a last lover was the answer, but what would I know when a man wins me over by being sweet?" She gave a very Italian shrug.

"You're curious. I never knew you were curious about me."

"Not about you." She shook soapsuds from her hands. "About them." She pushed a wet plate to his chest. "Don't they get angry? Don't they get jealous or bent out of shape? What is it you have that they find so attractive?"

Kitt dried the plate and put it on the worktop beside the other clean dishes. "Besides my unconventional handsomeness? I suppose they find me charming."

"I suppose they do."

"Don't you find me charming?"

"I don't have to find you charming." She held out another damp plate.

He laughed, a loud whoop of a sound. "You're always honest." He dried the dish. "You're honest with me. I have no need to look in the mirror. I only need look at you. I like how you see me. Plainly. You see me and see it all. And yet you never judge me. Never. You're not like other women, even if you're just my type."

She pulled the plug in the basin. Water snorted as it drained. "I am the antithesis of your type," she said, eyeing him as she wiped her hands on the tea towel she pulled off. "Exactly how much of that grappa have you had, sir?"

Sir. She'd tossed out the reminder that there was a professional barrier between them, but that barrier wasn't quite as high as the other wall she lived her life behind. "Enough to know you're still married, albeit to a dead man. You're so very married and in love with a dead man, and even that kind of married is married. I like married women. You are wholly my type." He left the towel beside the sink and went back to the table—and the grappa. "Why is it again you don't judge me, Mrs Valentine?"

"I work for you."

"Yes, yes. I pay, you care, we've discussed that before, but you're on a leave of absence now. There is no money changing hands. You are not in my employ at present."

"No, sir. You are in my employ." She folded up the spare chair Fiorella had used and slid it beside the bookcase.

"Mm, yes. The five pounds. So by all rights I should call you *ma'am* and you should call me by my first name instead of *sir* or *Major.*"

"I suspect you like that I call you *sir.*" She moved to the table, sat, and began to play with the little band of gold she wore on the third finger of her left hand.

He looked at her, shooting back the last of the grappa. "Do you? Do I?"

"Oh, yes. I believe it makes you feel...superior, dominant."

"Dominant? I can assure you, I am not the dominant one here in this room." He looked at the empty glass and the bottle before he took the seat across from her. How many shots had he had?

Brows arching, she crossed her arms. "You're suggesting I'm dominant?"

"Yes. I'm suggesting I'm submissive, not you. I'm bottom, you're top. I've submitted to you, without the hackneyed leather facemasks and games that call for whips. After all, here I am in your employ and all I can think about is Fiorella suggesting I kiss you, and *Mr Spielzeug*. Yes, I'd like to be your plaything, and I wait in vain for you to tell me that I may, Mae—I mean, *ma'am*. I suppose since I am now your employee, my kissing you is still not an option."

"Was it ever an option?"

"No. Never. Except I find I should like very much to kiss you. You liked that I kissed your hand today, didn't you?" He smirked.

"You are quite drunk and talking nonsense. Nonsense is new for you."

He nodded once. "Yes. I'm drunk and talking nonsense. I've had rather a lot of grappa. I'm very, very drunk and drunk me wants to kiss you, Mae, and when this is all over and I no longer work for you, you'll work for me, and I'll be in this same position."

"You could fire me."

"Now why would I fire you? If I let you go, who'd cook my breakfast? Who'd scramble my eggs? You could quit, but the questions would remain the same. If you quit, who'd scramble my eggs? Who'd cook my breakfast?"

She took off her glasses and placed them on the table beside the bowl of peaches and cherries. "You do know how to scramble eggs, don't you, sir?"

"Of course I know how to scramble eggs!"

Mae picked a cherry from the bowl. She played with the little red orb, spinning it by the stem. "I would really love some cherry gelato right now."

"Know what I'd love?"

"Yes. Béarnaise, coffee, wheat toast, jam..."

"No. No."

"What then, you'd add bacon?"

"Bacon? I don't want bacon. Do I ever have bacon? No, no. I want to kiss you."

She tilted her head. "Are we back to that again?"

"Bacon." Kitt sniffed with disgust and rose, moving around the table. "I want to kiss you and kiss you and kiss you 'til I don't know where we are, or where you are, or I am, or know anything about this stupid mess you're in. I want to kiss you long and soft and slow and deep. I want to kiss you until that cherry you're clutching is squashed in your hand. And then I want to kiss you more. I don't suppose you want to kiss me, do you?"

Mae put the cherry back into the bowl. "Shall I be honest with you?"

"Mrs Valentine, we have established that you are always honest. Honest and plain with me, so I shall be honest with you. They mean nothing, you know, those other women. I am being honest about that with you, as honest as I am with myself. They mean nothing. I like honesty. So, in your honest way, will you kiss me, Mae?"

She began to laugh. "I don't know if I have ever seen you drunk like this before, but you still don't move like you're drunk. You talk shite, but you don't stumble, you don't slur your words. I don't know how you do it."

"Simple. I drink a lot. A body habituates to the alcohol."

"Go to bed, Kitt."

He rolled his head on his neck and grinned because she'd finally dispensed with the *sir*. "Yes," he said, walking from the kitchen area to the sofa on the other side of the room, knowing his gait was steady, his posture perfectly upright. "Bed. What an excellent idea. Let's go to bed." He lifted the seat of the sofa until it clicked and then pulled it forward so that it flattened into a something slightly larger than a single bed. He took the folded bed linen from the sofa's arm, shook open a sheet, and let it drift down upon the bed.

Then Kitt realised one small detail. He grimaced and squeezed his eyes shut for a second before he turned around. "Mrs Valentine," he said, opening his eyes to look at the kitchen chair he had vacated several moments before, and at Mae.

Her arms were still crossed and she had the gall to smile. The woman looked at the bed, at the bloody straight-backed wooden chair, and then smiled at him.

He muttered a rather creative string of curses.

Still smiling, she rose and moved toward him; brushing against his arm, she sat on the edge of the bed and took off her sandals.

He swore again, this time a single word.

Mae laughed. "You think I'm that cruel?"

"I think I am just discovering the depths of your cruelty."

"If you can talk drunken nonsense then I can have fun at your expense, Mr Spielzeug."

"I don't think you're at all funny."

"Maybe I'm not amusing, but I am practical."

He rubbed his chin. "I'm *not* going to sleep in that chair."

Laughing again, she twisted and stretched out on the bed, looking up at him. "I realise that if you don't quite comprehend what I am suggesting, despite how you move about like you're sober, then you must be very pissed indeed." She waved her hands over the couch. "Look. I've made space. For you."

"Mrs Valentine, I am not simply pissed. I am positively, irrefutably, unrelentingly *hammered*. I am intoxicated to the point where I would be incapable of rising again if I sat down." He watched her shut her eyes before he lay beside her, saying, "I am inebriated to the point that, should you be at all concerned for your virtue, I can assure you the grappa has rendered me impotent."

"I'd prefer it render you unconscious," she said.

Kitt listened to the soft, even cadence of her breathing as she ignored him, as she lay still on her back, her hands clasped below her breasts. He listened to her, smelled that soft perfume she wore, felt her warmth, and closed his eyes. Despite the fact neither one of them had switched off the lamps before they'd climbed into bed, he let the blackness of sleep take him. Then, sometime before dawn he felt her warm body press into him. Her arm slipped across his abdomen. She slid a leg over his hips. A moment or two passed before she opened her eyes. Mystified, even a little hopeful, Kitt rose on an elbow and looked at her, his brow furrowing.

With a frown of her own, Mae lifted her hand and tucked it under her chin. "Forgive me." She removed her leg, turning over. "I thought you were Caspar."

"No harm done." He moved, chest against her back. "Do you mind? It's a little less cramped this way."

It may have been inappropriate, unprofessional, and unorthodox to take comfort from him in such a manner. His hand on her hip was unbefitting too, considering the inklings playing at the back of her mind; Mae didn't care. Although an awareness of him had poked her subconscious in the years since they'd met, the shifting, emotional edge it had now irritated her, but she wanted to go back to sleep, with his arm about her, without dreaming of anything. She had slept for a few hours because he was beside her, and despite the annoyance, however unprofessional, unsuitable, or silly, Mae wanted, needed the sense of consolation Kitt gave her. With a huff of resigned weariness, she took his hand and dragged it beneath her chin. "If you start talking rubbish again, it's the chair for you."

He gave a little sniff of a laugh, the air puffing over her ear as he tucked his knees behind hers.

IT HAD BEEN years since she'd slept in the clothes she'd worn the day before. Clad in a rumpled dress and yesterday's knickers, Mae stood at the open door, waiting for Fiorella, staring out at the few centimetres of piled-up volcanic sand the older woman had swept very early this morning. She'd dusted off the geraniums too and their bright white faces shone in the sun.

The flowers shifted Mae's thoughts to Kitt vomiting into white wildflowers. Then her mind passed to an image of a burnt hand amid burnt bread, a fleeting glimpse of Caspar's grave, the sight of a scrap of yellow paper with names written on it, before shifting back to Kitt—and his thoroughly bizarre drunken declarations last night.

She had come close to playing along, to challenging his suggestions, and maybe even making a few of her own. She wondered what the surprise would have looked like on his face if she had. She also wondered what he would say if she told him that she had the key to the furnished two-bedroom house next door, the house Caspar grew up in, the house she still owned.

She heard him come out of the bathroom. "Good morning, Mae," he said.

Mae liked the sound of his voice all gruff and hungover. It made him seem vulnerable. She didn't know why seeing him as vulnerable was appealing but suspected it had something to do with how vulnerable she felt. It was nice to have vulnerable company. She turned and watched him rub a towel through his damp hair, ruffling up the collar of a black tennis shirt. "Good morning, Kitt," she said, wanting to fix the collar—and smell his neck.

The absurdity of smelling his neck made her laugh.

Wincing, towel draped over one shoulder, Kitt moved to his bag, rummaging through it until he found the packet of paracetamol. "What's so funny?"

"I ought to feel sorry for your hangover." She grinned. "But I don't."

"I'm in agony. Agony, Mae." He downed the tablets with a glass of water and then grimaced again as Fiorella arrived and shouted out a greeting.

Mae cackled and he pressed fingers to his temple.

Armed with her basket, Fiorella took out pastries, a metal container, biscuits, and a bottle of blood-orange juice.

"Do you have any rainbow-coloured money in there, Fiorella?" Kitt watched the woman hand Mae a change of clothes and toiletries. He couldn't recall ever seeing anyone more grateful for receiving a change of clothes and a toothbrush. "The bus leaves in forty-five minutes, Mae," he said as she darted into the bathroom.

"You need money, Major?" Fiorella filled an electric kettle with water. She switched it on. Then she opened the metal container and spooned ground coffee into a Chemex filter carafe she'd taken from a cupboard.

"No, I need your coffee." He sat at the table where she'd put all the food, and tied his shoes, his eyes on the slow drip of the coffee into the carafe. "But you did clean me out last night."

"You want to rematch?"

Kitt said, "I imagine you'd bleed me dry."

Smirking, the woman ran a strand of polished black beads through her fingers, adjusting them against the lavender twinset she wore. She gave him a humourless stare. "The airport in Catania close today. The ash blow that way. Now we alone, soldier, you tell me. I am not stupid. Mae come early. She finally go to see Caspar. She stay here with you instead of the house she own next door, an' she sleep late. She never sleep late. You ask questions. Lotta questions. You want to know Russo an' Torrisi stuff. I see her an' I hear news. Lotta stuff about refugees, refugees drowning, protests about refugees, but also news about the baker Russo. Russo is dead, an' someone beat up my Mae before you come here. This is not a vacation, is it?"

His mobile buzzed in his bag. "It's certainly not the holiday I hoped Mae would have," he said, rising to retrieve the phone.

Fifty-five minutes later he was sitting in the middle of a bus, twisting and turning downhill, the way his stomach wanted to. Instead of watching the terrain outside pass by or taking more than a brief notice of the stripes of black ash pushed to the side of the road, Kitt kept his eyes fixed on one or two points inside the bus. He watched the back of the seat in front of theirs and the way Mae's left hand gripped it. Her wedding ring glinted as sunlight hit it, the tiny flash burning a streak in his retinas, reminding him that he'd made one foolish confession last night and did not need to make another this morning. Mae did not need to know everything. There was no point to her knowing everything.

The window beside him was open. The last two days had been more like spring than the middle of summer, but a band of heat had wrapped around the morning. The breeze coming through the window had only the slightest cool touch. By noon it would be stifling.

Kitt put his hand into the pocket of his cargo trousers, pushed aside the pen, and felt for the coins he had. He gathered them. "Would you mind if I tossed this change in your handbag, Mae? The jingling is driving me mad."

She drew the tote-style handbag from where she'd tucked it between her feet and held it open. He dropped in a few gold euro coins and a shiny copper American penny, and returned the bag to her side.

The phone in his other pocket vibrated.

"About what you said last night, Kitt," Mae said.

"Ah. You remember. How nice," he grumbled, and he responded to Bryce's second text of the morning. *To hell with him.*

"Is your head still sore?"

"Not as sore as my pride and, I believe, my arse is about to be.

Do be gentle with me, Mrs Valentine." He typed *He can wait until I am finished.*

"Have I ever caned you?"

"No. Perhaps it's time you did."

"Oh, yes. I forgot. I'm the dominant one."

Maybe today or tomorrow, he typed and his mouth quirked, then pursed, then he grinned. "So, last night? You were saying?"

"You got me thinking."

"About what?"

"The last time I had a decent kiss."

His finger paused over the mobile's screen. "Are you asking me to kiss you?"

"No, I'm segueing into confessing I agreed to meet Daniel Pierce for dinner because I thought he looked like a good kisser."

He'll know when I know. Kitt sent the message, shoved the phone back into his pocket and slipped on his sunglasses. The dark lenses softened the pain in his eyes. "I see. You turned down my offer because I don't look like a good kisser. I am wounded, Mae," he said, his grin fading. "Mortally."

She wrinkled her nose. "One's imagination can hurt more than words. The choices we make are sometimes based on facts, previous experiences, gut feelings, but first impressions matter, and what we imagine about someone based on what we see that first time matters. We make a judgment on our perception of what we see or think we see the first time we meet someone. Her skirt's quite short —she must be a whore. He's well dressed and very tidy—he must be gay. He has a lovely full bottom lip—he must be a good kisser."

Kitt thought her gaze lingered a moment on his mouth before she stared beyond him and out the window.

The bus juddered as it hit a pothole and she bumped against him. "I am here because I judged Daniel to be a good kisser based on how his bottom lip looked. I am sitting here on this bus, going to see a man I've never met, after another man I've never met was killed because I judged someone's worth by the shape of his mouth and the colour of his eyes. He had pretty brown eyes."

"Eyes can say a lot about a person."

"I suppose they do. Except your eyes. You're hard to read. Surprisingly hard to read. I seldom know what your eyes are saying or what's behind them."

"Seldom isn't always." He took off his sunglasses and squinted against the harsh glare. "What do my eyes tell you now?"

She turned back to him, studied eyes he knew were bloodshot and aching, and surprised him with a previously concealed knack for mimicry. "Christ, I need coffee and scrambled eggs."

"It's not polite to mock the hungover, especially when you've never mocked the hungover before. However, you have quite a gifted tongue. And ear, I should add. No wonder you speak several languages."

"Flattery will not make you easier to read."

He gave a small laugh. "Fiorella's clothes look very nice on you."

Mae pulled at the stretchy, form-fitting, scoop-necked yellow dress she wore. "Have I mentioned what a horrible liar you are?"

"You have."

"The cardigan is Fiorella's, the dress belonged to her goddaughter. So do the knickers I'm wearing. The yellow in the dress matches the shade of my bruises." She touched her jaw and sighed. "As soon as we get to Taormina I am buying new knickers and a dress."

"I think you mean I am buying you knickers and a dress."

"I can buy my own pants, Kitt, thank you." She reached into her bag and pulled out her iPad, glancing back at him.

He smirked and rubbed his temple. "Twenty minutes ago we agreed that you would not use your credit cards and keep your cash. No credit card means no trail for anyone to track, remember? We want to keep a low profile."

She tapped the small screen, brought up a map, and made a face. "We know nothing. Daniel Pierce was a banker. Caspar was a master gardener. Russo's parents were teachers, and he was a baker. Torrisi is a lawyer, and his uncle was a barber. The only thing these three men have in common is that they're from Linguaglossa and buried in the same cemetery."

"And we have Mr or Miss Bianco, the third name you saw."

"What are we doing?" she said. "I should chuck this all and hire a private investigator. I should go home and hire a private investigator."

"That would cost more than five pounds." He squeezed the bridge of his nose and squinted.

"I'm serious, Kitt."

"So am I." He put his sunglasses back on. "All we're doing is asking if Torrisi would be opposed to you making changes to your beloved husband's grave. Questions of that sort need no private detective. You are being respectful to dear departed Uncle Biagio and to his nephew. I'd suggest you play your widow card here, Mae. It could be...useful, but if you prefer a different tactic, we're doing genealogical research. A lot of people do that on their own, without a private investigator—or with one that costs them five pounds, a new dress, and pair of knickers. By the way, have you contacted anyone you know in Taormina, anyone in the Gelsomino household?"

"They would be in Lugarno this time of year."

"No chance of running into them then?"

"I doubt it." She placed the iPad in her latte-coloured handbag and took off her reading glasses, tucking them into the neckline of her dress.

"Did you say anything to Fiorella?"

"No, did you?"

"I didn't have to. She knows something's going on."

Mae frowned and licked the corner of her mouth. "Shit."

He pulled his sunglasses down his nose a little. "The stitches look ready to come out." He touched the thread with the edge of his thumb, fingers brushing her jaw.

She drew back slightly, regarding him, her frown turning into something quizzical. "I hope you don't think you're pulling anything."

"Not anymore." Kitt slid his sunglasses up. "What is the problem with the knickers anyway?"

Mae laughed. "Do you really want to know?"

"Why not."

"Besides the fact they are someone else's knickers, I don't think one can really classify them as actual knickers, as much as a disturbingly binding and amazingly hot torture device made of fishnet. Who makes—or wears—underpants made of fishnet?"

A rare broad smile blossomed on Kitt's face and Mae knew his amusement was genuine.

He said, "I am so glad I am not the only one sitting here in relentless misery."

"I think I hate that volcano," Mae said and went back to looking out the window, clinging to the metal rail at the top of the seat in front of her.

Kitt switched his focus from watching her grip the seatback to watching her. The screaming citrus orange and yellow dress rode up high on her thighs, which gave him a better view of her Southern Cross constellation of freckles. When she shifted and pulled at the dress again, he laughed. And then he winced a little and shut his eyes. "Yes," he said, "a new dress."

CHAPTER ELEVEN

The narrow switchback route uphill to Taormina had almost been his undoing, and the new dress Mae had chosen to replace the ill-fitting yellow thing she'd worn drove him even closer to ruination.

Kitt was accustomed to her usual appearance, to her navy shirt-dress and crisp white apron, her sturdy Mary Janes, the reading glasses she wore on a chain, her neat French braid. Despite the sensible nature of her specific attire, her work clothes suited her and fit her without any hint of dowdiness. There was nothing remotely Pygmalion-esque about seeing her in different clothing. There was no startling transformation that had taken place. Mae was an attractive woman and would be an attractive woman regardless of what she wore—even a too-bright clinging dress left over from two decades earlier. He'd taken greater notice of his potential downfall the evening they'd met at the Baldessare, when she wore the little black dress with a bit of lace, her hair loose and soft. That had set him off kilter because, like yesterday's pink dress and today's 50s-influenced new dress, seeing her in something other than the garments of her profession showed him the barrier that stood between them was made of nothing more than fabric and occupations sewn together by a single word: truth.

Unaccustomed to persistent reminders of an obstinate quixotic nature he never knew he possessed—until recently—Kitt glanced at Mae again. The capped-sleeve dress fit to her waist, flared out over her hips, with the hem of the floral printed cotton a few centimetres above her knees. The neckline showed the curving swell of her bosom. She'd swept her hair into a little knot, leaving wisps free to frame her face. She had been right that the garish yellow dress had accentuated the yellow of the slowly fading bruises on her jaw. The heat of the day made the pink of her cheeks brighter, toning down the mottling more, yet the variegation remained, and reminded him of how that colour got there. The moment of having an impractical disposition shifted back to having a very efficient, shrewd, and practical nature that was now tinged with irritation.

"You know you're a nuisance, Mae," he said.

She added another dress, this one a wrap-around in leafy green, a pair of espadrilles, three pairs of plain knickers, a slip, and a floppy sun hat to the things on the boutique's counter. "I'll reimburse you."

"I don't want your sodding money."

"Not even your five pounds?"

"Do you *want* to visit the lawyer or shop?" He handed over his credit card and, in tentative Italian, asked the boutique shopkeeper where he might find a chemist. "*Dov'è...una...farmacia?*"

"You'll find the British Pharmacy Di Verso Giovanni five buildings up, on the left, just before the piazza," the clerk replied in English, giving him a kittenish smile.

Mae rolled her eyes.

"*Grazie*," Kitt said, taking his card and the shopper bag full of new things.

Mae followed him out the door, onto the Corso Umberto, Taormina's high street, and headed for the building that bore a large green cross. "Do you still feel unwell?" she said. "Are you after more pain relief or something to tame your stomach?"

"I'm fine," he snapped. Then he paused near the pharmacy's entrance, his tetchiness softening. "I'm fine, but might I make a suggestion?"

Mae angled her head. "Is this something I want to hear?"

His eyes traversed her face. "I think you need a little make-up to go with your new dress."

"That was not what I was expecting." She touched her jawline. "I'd prefer if people didn't assume I bashed you."

"I understand, but I'm hopeless at applying the stuff."

"I'm not."

"Why does that not surprise me?" She brushed past him and went inside the pharmacy.

Ten minutes later, they stood with tourists in the centre of the black and white paved Piazza IX Aprile, looking out over the spectacular vista of Mount Etna and houses dotting the rocky hill, falling away to the Ionian Sea. Behind them was the old stone San Giuseppe church. The Porta di Mezzo, a stone clock tower with an archway beneath it was to the left. Mae made a sweeping gesture. "Welcome to the Sicilian Rivera." She scratched a spot near her nose.

"Stop touching your face, you'll rub off the Max Factor camouflage."

"I feel like I'm wearing Hollandaise."

"Is that more or less comfortable than fishnet knickers?"

To hide her amusement, she faced the inside of the small square. "The GPS on my tablet has the lawyer's offices in a building up the steps, near the white one with all the windows," she pointed, "just above the Café Wunderbar sign. I hope climbing the stairs won't make your head hurt more."

"What makes you think my head still hurts?"

With a sniff, she left Kitt, giving the skirt of her dress a flounce as she walked toward the café.

"Eggs," he said, following. "I need scrambled eggs."

At the top of the staircase, beside San Giuseppe, they made a left turn and entered a small area shaded by palm trees. A black and white paved path led out of the shade and to the front of a pale-yellow house with a stone arch over a black door. Vivid red geraniums spilled out from boxes on the two black balconies above the arch. A small round, blue sign beside the door read *Corso Umberto 23*. A tile plaque below bore a hand-painted image of a lawyer and his client standing before a judge, with the word *L'avvocato* at the bottom.

Her palms had gone clammy. Then her pulse began to rush. Mae gazed at the black and brass buzzer in the middle of the door. She gave Kitt an uneasy look, her lips pressing together. "What," she said, "do we do if we go inside and find a lawyer who's been fed through a paper shredder?"

"What do we do if we find a lawyer stapled to death?" Kitt said.

He had a point, but Mae's heart hammered wildly anyway.

"There's only one way to find out. Will you ring, or shall I?"

Mae rang the buzzer. Two seconds passed and a loud hum released the lock. Kitt pushed the door, took her hand, and led her inside.

The office was well appointed in a minimalist Sicilian Baroque style using shades of cream, black, and soft sea blue. A thin, dark-haired man sat behind a carved oak wooden desk adorned by modest gilt edges. He looked up from his computer screen and waited with an expectant lift of one eyebrow.

"See?" Kitt squeezed her damp hand. "Not a staple in sight. Go on."

Mae gave him a dry, sidelong glance. "*Buongiorno,*" she said.

The man gave a nod. "*Buongiorno. Posso aiutarla?*"

"*Posso parlare con il* Signor *Torrisi?*"

"*Chi è Lei?*"

"*Mi chiamo Mae Valentine.*"

"*Hai un appuntemento?*"

"What did he say?" Kitt set the shopping bag at his feet and removed his sunglasses.

"He asked who I was and if I had an appointment."

"Tell him we'll only be ten minutes." Kitt said.

The man set his gaze on Kitt, his dark brown eyes skating from head to shoes and up again. He smiled faintly, his focus entirely on Kitt. "I am sorry, sir," he said in English, his accent tinged with a slight American pronunciation. "Mr Torrisi is not here. May I inquire as to the purpose of your wish to speak with him?"

Mae released a very soft snort.

Kitt squeezed her hand and let go. "It is something of a personal nature regarding a cemetery in Linguaglossa and disturbing the graves of Mr Torrisi's late uncle, and Mrs Valentine's late husband."

"Disturbing graves?"

"Moving them, actually. Mrs Valentine wishes to disinter her husband and take his body to England. That might affect the grave of Mr Torrisi's uncle. We won't require much of Mr Torrisi's time. No more than ten minutes."

"You are?"

"Mrs Valentine's brother. And your name is?"

"Luca. One moment." Luca lifted the handset of a telephone and pressed a button. "I will check with Mr Torrisi's personal assistant." After a brief pause, he said, in Italian, "Vivienne, an Englishman and his sister are here to speak with Pippino... Something about exhuming the grave beside his uncle in a cemetery in Linguaglossa... Yes...exhuming her husband...to take to England... Yes...I don't know... They did not say... No...I'll tell them... Yes, *fine*, Vivienne, I will.... I *said I will*." With a huff, muttering something about Vivienne breaking his balls, he fixed his frown on Kitt and switched back to English. "At present, Mr Torrisi is in Messina with the Libyan refugees who survived last week's boat capsize. He may be back later this morning or this afternoon. You might catch him then."

Kitt drew a cream-coloured Regents Park Consortium business card from his back pocket and offered it to Luca. "If you would, please have Mr Torrisi ring me so that we can arrange a time to meet. The number is on the card. As I said, it shouldn't take more than ten minutes."

Luca scanned the card, set it on his desk, and handed Torrisi's business card to Kitt. "Good day to you both." He shifted his attention to his computer's monitor, glancing back up at Kitt once.

Kitt tucked Torrisi's card in a pocket, grabbed the shopping, and shepherded Mae outside. She let go of his hand immediately and he followed her to the paved black and white pathway, through the shade to the staircase they'd climbed. He paused at the top of the stairs as she began to descend them. "I bet you hated that," he said. "Not so much his dismissal of you, rather how he deferred to me."

She was one step down when she turned and looked up at him. "I think I was more amused by how taken he was with you."

He tipped his head. "It wouldn't be the first time that's happened."

"Of course it wouldn't." She frowned and resumed her descent.

Kitt slipped on his sunglasses and watched her go down the stairs, captivated by the sway of her hips in her new dress. He pondered the immeasurable trouble she was and mulled over the last message he'd sent to Bryce. Then she was at the bottom of the staircase and he trotted down to meet her. A group dressed in white, carrying various signs of protest against illegal migrants, separated them for a moment longer. She was in front of the Café Wunderbar when he caught up to her.

"What do we do now?" she said. "Go back to Linguaglossa and wait to see if Torrisi rings you? Stay around here for a bit to see if he rings you, or forget it all, go home, and pretend none of this ever happened? Jaysus, Kitt. What the hell am I doing here? What am I hoping to accomplish? It's only money, money I never had, money I don't need." Mae huffed, pulling at the stitch in her lip. Maybe she ought to let him tug it out. Yes, let him tug it out, call it a day, go home and let the chips fall where they might. It was only goddamn stupid bloody money.

She huffed again and looked at Kitt.

He cast his eyes about at their surroundings. One hand held her shopping, the other was in his pocket, and he gazed about the patrons dining at the café, reading a poster on the wall, at peace with the world.

Mae knew, no matter how he appeared to be, no matter how he regulated his behaviour, Kitt was still hungover, his head still hurt. His sunglasses may have been dark enough to hide the fact his eyes were bloodshot while they stood outdoors, but she'd seen how bloodshot they were inside Torrisi's office. Despite those little glimpses of vulnerable, his level of nonchalance could be, as it was now, maddening. His detached coolness was maddening. He was maddening.

And she was short-tempered and confused, frightened, amused, *moody*, and barely keeping her grip on things.

"There's a party here tonight," he said, eyes on the poster. "And you have a new dress."

"You want to go to a party tonight?"

"You have a new dress."

"So we're going to stay here all day, hope that Torrisi rings, and then go to a party at the Wunderbar tonight."

"You have a new dress." He held up the shopping bag.

"What," she said, crossing her arms, "do we do in the meantime, find some scrambled eggs to detach the tenacious bite of your hangover?"

"No. We get a room someplace and do a little more research on Russo and Pippino Torrisi. But since you mentioned scrambled eggs..."

THERE WERE TWO TWIN BEDS.

Kitt found himself standing amid Baroque-influenced opulence in a splendid suite in the Belmond Grand Hotel Timeo. There was a spacious private balcony, views to the sea, a marble bathroom, a living area, fresh cut flowers, and...two twin beds. "Are you happy, Mrs Valentine?" he said.

"You said you had enough of spartan living and wanted a suite. This was the only suite available."

His mouth pursed and he dropped the shopping bag onto a green silk sofa. "Twin beds. How quaint."

"Quaint, perhaps, but I would not call this spartan."

"That is because you have an inexplicable fear of large beds."

Mae crossed the room and went to the desk. She set her handbag down and removed the iPad from the side pocket. "This would be rectified if you'd let me have my own room."

"I told you yesterday. I am not letting you out of my sight. Why is it you fear adult-sized beds, Mae?"

"I don't like sleeping alone. The larger the bed, the more alone I feel."

He regarded her for a moment and gave her a little smile.

"There's an odd sense of logic to that." Kitt's phone buzzed. He dragged it out of his pocket.

"Is it Torrisi?"

"No," he said, looking at the screen. "It's Llewelyn."

She went to the sofa to retrieve the dress from the bag and moved to the wardrobe for a hanger. "Who's Llewelyn?"

"My employer. Will you excuse me?" Kitt opened the glass-paned door to the balcony and stepped outside.

Double-glazed, the windows let in no sound from outdoors, but as Mae hung up the dress she watched Kitt for a moment. His flat expression grew even duller while he spoke to his employer. His slide into stone-faced was—she knew now—a good indication that he was angry, and she understood why. In all the years she'd been in service, she'd never had an employer intrude on her holiday time. There was something irritating about an employer or company that felt as if they owned an employee, going so far as to keep tabs on them. It was understandable in Kitt's work as a risk assessor that his company would monitor his whereabouts for reasons of safety when he was on an assignment, but monitoring him while he was on holiday was...was...exactly what Kitt was doing with her now. His 'not letting you out of my sight' comment, something she'd construed as a turn of phrase, was Kitt stating, directly, that he was keeping tabs on her.

She watched him grip the balcony railing, the sun on his back, his hair shining more ginger than dark blond. She thought of how he looked the night in front of the Nepali embassy, when he'd broken a man's nose, when his face was cast with the same lack of expression as now. Then she thought of him when he'd stood behind her, looking at her in the reflection of the medicine-chest mirror in his bathroom. Finally, she thought about the frown he'd worn when he'd told her she was a nuisance, and she was glad he was keeping tabs on her.

Leaving him to finish his conversation, Mae found her iPad and reading glasses. She sat on the green silk sofa and began a search on Stefano Russo. By the time Kitt came back inside, she'd read the first search result four times. It was a news story about the Sicilian bread maker who had been murdered in his bakery.

Local police said this dashed the hopes of the *Addiopizzo* movement—citizens standing up against the Mafia and refusing to pay protection money. The report also noted that a few days before Russo's murder, a journalist from local paper had been attacked with a tyre iron, and the mayor of Nunziata had fish heads left at his door. The most startling line of the story mentioned that witnesses in San Giovanni saw a man and a blonde woman leaving the hundred-year-old bakery shortly before Russo's body was found.

A man and a blonde woman.

Real. This was all real. Being in the news made it real.

Mae shivered, suddenly cold. It was a sweltering outside. Fifteen minutes ago she'd been sweating, and now she was freezing, and it had nothing to do with the climate control. Ice had tiptoed over her, nestled into her bones, soaked into her bloodstream.

"Mae?"

Mae handed the iPad to Kitt. "Read this."

He scanned the screen. "Fiorella mentioned something about seeing the news," he said. "The good old Mothers And Fathers Italian Association."

Mae pulled off her glasses. She rubbed her forehead and the silly nervous laugh she'd developed in the last handful of days ploughed through her snowy chill, and she tittered. "Police think Russo was made an example of by the Mafia."

"Lucky for us."

"Yes, their thinking the man and blonde woman seen leaving the bakery were Mafia assassins rather than tourists is lucky."

"Take a deep breath, Mae."

"I know," she said and breathed in, deeply. "I know. I feel it. I'm teetering. I'm teetering. I keep thinking about Russo's black hand, Sal's blood, squashed sausages, you breaking that man's nose, and the names on that feckin' yellow sticky note! And then I read about Russo and fish heads, the *Addiopizzo*, and the Mafia. I know I said the Mafia is alive and well in Sicily, but...do you think the Mafia killed Russo? Did we stumble into something else?"

"Maybe we found the link to Caspar's money."

Mae blinked, incredulous. "Don't be ridiculous."

"It's not that far-fetched."

She shook her head. "You didn't know Caspar."

"Perhaps neither did you."

A streak of heat spiked through the cold enveloping her. Glaring, Mae rose, snatching up her handbag, and stalked to the desk. "Caspar never would have...he had nothing to do with... Yes. Take a deep breath. Change my behaviour to change my thinking."

"What can you tell me about Caspar's trust, besides the amount? Where did the money come from?"

She tossed down her spectacles and rummaged through her handbag, looking for nothing in particular except something to occupy her hands. "A pension fund tied to the share market. Equity income, shares in medium and small cap companies. From what I can remember, dividends varied in size, but regular deposits were made. Automatically. For years."

"Where did the pension come from?"

"I have no idea. It wasn't a government pension or one affiliated with his position at the university. Caspar had several jobs when he was a teenager. He worked on a ferry, he packed sardines, and he harvested chestnuts. My guess is the pension came from one of those companies. It could have been something set up for all employees."

He switched off the device and brought it to her, looking at her with his maddening detached, cool blue-grey gaze that she simultaneously hated and admired. Then a tinge of warmth crept into his indifference. "I apologise," he said. "I didn't intend to be insulting. It was a clumsy way to say that one very rarely knows anyone that well. As you said before, everyone has secrets. Even you."

Kitt expected that she'd snatch the iPad from his hand, but she took it gently and pushed it into her handbag, taking a deep breath, and then another.

She said, "It seems I don't know myself. I know I don't know you, and I think I may be losing my mind. Jaysus, I should wear a sign around my neck: *twenty-five minutes since the last mood swing and meltdown.*"

He regarded her and made a confession of sorts. "The truth of it is, Mae, I do know you. You're the one constant in my life. In my travels, the people I deal with in my employment, constancy is rare. In spite of what's happened to you, you remain constant. To Caspar, to your work, to me, you remain constant. You know me better than you think. Better than anyone else actually. And I like that," Kitt said.

She met his gaze and shivered. "Yes. I'm your true north."

"You could say that."

"I just did."

"Do you still want to smack me for suggesting Caspar had Mafia ties?"

"I never wanted to smack you." She wrapped her arms around herself and shivered again. "I wanted to punch you in the eye."

"Smack, punch, what's the difference? I do know you. You are not losing your mind. Given your circumstances, and whether you believe it or not, you are doing very well."

"Thank you for the rousing speech." She snorted. "I think I'd rather have the same sense of detachment that you have."

Kitt ran a hand though his hair. "Because I don't ruminate over the dead man in my kitchen or finding Russo with a broken neck does not mean I am insensitive or unconcerned."

"How do you not ruminate, Kitt?" She frowned. "How do you get beyond the invasive images and fear and anger?"

"Breathe."

She dropped her arms. "Breathe?"

"Yes. Breathe."

"Is that all? Breathe? Not down a quarter of a bottle of grappa, eat two cannoli, and a go for a good run?"

"No. Deep from the belly breathing." He lifted her latte-toned handbag, a simple, medium-sized tote with two pockets and a centre pouch with a zip. The bag was as efficient and unpretentious as Mae. He held it out to her. "Come on. You can practise breathing while you play Taormina tour guide."

THE *TEATRO GRECO*, Taromina's ancient Greek theatre, was built in the early part of the seventh century BC. Constructed of bricks, the theatre stood fifty metres wide, one hundred and twenty metres long, and twenty metres high. A section was missing from the centre of the wall behind the main stage and it framed a panoramic view of the Bay of Naxos and ash-billowing Mount Etna. The dusty cloud spread out in the direction of Catania, where the airport was. Mae put on the sun hat she'd purchased earlier and watched the cloud of ash drift.

"I gather this is still used for music and stage performances and film festivals?" Kitt said.

"It is. The Taormina Film Festival and the *Nastro d'Argento*, one of the oldest film awards, are presented here."

"Well, it's a magnificent backdrop for any ceremony."

The *Teatro* was Taormina's most popular attraction. Tourists moved up and down the stairs, taking photos, pointing out Corinthian columns, admiring the magnificent setting. At the top of the theatre, on the cavea, were raised, old brick seats that would have been as uncomfortable centuries past as they were now. Kitt shifted on the hard seat, took in the view, and watched other tourists arrive.

Mae sat beside him, pulling up dark green weeds that grew in the midst of where they were. "Is it common for your employer to check up on you when you're on holiday?"

He glanced at her. "No. I left a bit abruptly, and there were some issues Bryce wasn't able to resolve for me, as I had hoped. What *is* that you're picking?"

"Wild arugula." She smelled the weeds. "Would you like to taste it?"

He lowered his sunglasses and squinted one eye. "Considering the number of tourists who've most likely trodden on it, I'll pass. You should too. It might give you further nightmares about doing things with papers."

She tossed the arugula aside and chuckled, removing her hat. "What do you dream of?"

"Getting a new, less girly car, retiring to a tiny, private island somewhere in the Caribbean."

"I mean when you sleep. What do you dream about?"

"Scrambled eggs."

She laughed again. "Are you still hungover?"

"No. Hot and hungry. It's getting too crowded here. Let's find a charming trattoria someplace in the shade." He rose, extending his hand, and when she took it he helped her up and didn't let go until they reached the bottom of the stairs.

They paused at the entrance to let a small group of Chinese tourists by, and again when a woman in a straw sun hat stepped on Kitt's foot and her hat fell off. She lost the tourist brochures and map under her arm as she grabbed for the hat's broad brim and missed. The hat bounced left, in front of Mae. Mae retrieved the hat, the blonde woman bent to pick up the map, and cosmetics from her open handbag spilled onto the bricks.

Kitt crouched to pick up lipstick, eye pencil, and mascara while the woman's companion, an American man in a New York Yankees baseball cap, said, "Apologise to the man, Simone," and continued to read whatever he was reading on his smartphone and head for the stairs.

"Thank you for your help, Ronnie, ya dickhead!" Simone said, shoving the map into the brochures. She straightened and looked at Mae, then at Kitt. "Sorry...um...*mi...mi dis-dispiace... Grazie*," she stammered in Italian, trying to nod politely.

"I'm fine," Kitt said.

Simone looked as if she were melting. Her heavy eyeliner smudged into heavier make-up that had gone shiny in the heat. She managed a smile as she took her hat. "Oh, thank you. I hope I didn't hurt your foot too much."

"Just my little toe, but no one really needs that." Kitt gave her the lipstick and other make-up. "That should be everything," he said.

"Come on, Simone, quit fart-assin' around!" Ronnie from Brooklyn New York hollered from the middle of the cavea stairs.

Kitt gave Simone a small smile. "Perhaps I could accidentally kill him for you?"

"I'd say 'please, yes,' " She glanced back at the man glaring down at her, "but I can't do without the dickhead." Simone winked, stuffed her hat, brochures, and make-up into her handbag, and hurried after scowling Ronnie.

Mae put on her own hat and Kitt reached for her hand. They took a short walk past their hotel, through the street packed with tourists, shops, cafés and art galleries. His hunger and the lure of a wood-fired pizza drew them to a restaurant with shady awnings and a view of busy Corso Umberto.

He'd eaten three-quarters of a Margherita pizza when his phone buzzed in his pocket. He checked the screen, found a number he didn't recognise, and lifted the mobile to his ear. "Hello?"

"Mr Kitt, this is Luca, Mr Torrisi's office manager," he said, his voice soft and smoky. "Miss Vivienne has spoken with Mr Torrisi."

Kitt touched Mae's arm. "Thank you for contacting me. My sister is keen to speak with Mr Torrisi regarding what may be a delicate matter."

"Yes. I understand. Mr Torrisi is happy to meet you and your sister, to speak about her wishes, but there was an ugly incident at our office in Taormina late this morning. Some anti-immigration protestors made a bit of a mess."

"I'm sorry for your troubles."

"Yes, thank you. That being the case, if you are still interested in meeting with Mr Torrisi, are you able to meet him tomorrow, at *Il Marino* in Aci Trezza? That is his restaurant. He is an excellent cook and welcomes you to join him for lunch. If you are in Taormina, I can arrange a car to take you. Otherwise I can give you directions."

"Please, give me a moment to speak with my sister."

"Of course."

Kitt hit mute and looked at Mae. She had been listening intently, frozen with a slice of pizza in her hand. He said, "Torrisi wants to meet us tomorrow, to make us lunch, in a place called Aci Trezza."

Mae set the pizza on a plate. "That's about forty-five minutes south."

"Luca said he'd send a car."

"Do we go?"

"Do you want to go?"

She hugged herself, as if she were chilly. "I have never been more ambivalent about anything in my life," she said.

"Would you like me to go?"

"By yourself?"

"Yes. It would make me feel as though I am doing something to earn my five pounds."

Her laugh was genuine but thin. "Part of me wants to say yes, while the other part of me wants to say something about your awful Italian."

"It's not that awful." Kitt unmuted the phone and lifted it to his ear. "Luca, please thank Mr Torrisi for being amenable. We can arrange our own transportation. Please send me directions and we will meet you." He ended the call and looked at Mae. "Aci Treza, *Il Marino* restaurant, noon tomorrow for lunch." Two seconds later his phone vibrated with Luca's directions to the restaurant.

Mae rubbed a hand up and down her arms. "So we're going back to Linguaglossa for the car?"

"That's not necessary." Kitt dialled a number.

Bryce answered after one ring. "Are you coming home, Kitty? Llewelyn will be so pleased."

"I need a car," Kitt said.

"Llewelyn will not be so pleased. Is she still with you?"

"The car, Bryce."

"Did you find your butler's money?"

"The car, Bryce."

Bryce exhaled. "Yes. Yes. Time?"

"Eleven tomorrow morning."

There was a pause and the sound of typing. "Take the cable car from Taormina to Mazzaró Bay by the sea below. This time it's a blue convertible."

"Thank you."

"Honestly, Kitty."

Kitt ended the call and pocketed the mobile.

"What do we do in the meantime?" Mae said, twisting her wedding ring around on her finger.

"Finish lunch, have some gelato, a long afternoon sleep out of the heat, and get ready for the party tonight."

"The party tonight," she echoed, looking at the pizza and the bubbles of condensation that had dribbled from his bottle of Peroni beer onto the table. She swept crumbs away and soaked up the water with a paper napkin.

"It's all right to do something fun, to do something normal, Mae. Not everything has to be productive."

"I like productive," She said. "Productive is fun. Productive is straightforward." She lifted her eyes to his and smirked. "Don't look at me like you think I have Obsessive-Compulsive Personality Disorder."

"I don't believe I thought anything along those lines about you."

"I like neat, and all of this is anything but neat."

"You said you liked Caspar because he got dirty, and now this is dirty, and this is about Caspar." He held her gaze.

She chuckled, crumpling the napkin and tossing it on top of her plate, "I admire your knack for reframing things."

He sat back, his eyes still fixed on hers. "I'm so pleased that you admire my knack."

"That sounded incredibly filthy."

"Did it? Lucky for me that you like dirty men."

She set her elbow on the table, resting her chin on the back of her hand. "Are you flirting with me, Kitt?"

He leaned forward. "Would you like me to?"

Her hand shifted from her chin, her fingers touching the gold hoop earring in her right ear. "I don't know."

Kitt felt himself smile and signalled the waiter for another beer.

WHILE KITT EMBRACED the Italian afternoon *riposo* with gusto and slept in the other room, Mae sat at the desk and admitted to herself that she had reached a dead end.

Internet research could only take her so far. She made a list of what they knew: Stefano Russo, a baker, was the son of a teacher who died two years before Caspar. Giuseppe "Pippino" Torrisi was the nephew of Biagio Torrisi, a postman who had died two years after Caspar. Pippino Torrisi was a lawyer and advocate for immigrants, refugees, and asylum seekers. For more information she needed death records, cemetery records, obituaries, probate wills, information from the *Ufficio di Stato Civile*, and had access to none of that until Wednesday.

It was wrong, she knew, to pin all her hopes on meeting Torrisi tomorrow, silly to believe she and Kitt could figure out what, or whom this was all about, silly to think *why* mattered at all.

Earlier today what drove her to distraction had been an inability to focus or maintain an even mood. Now it was her ambivalence, the desire to wake up Kitt and tell him she wanted to go home, and the contrary, determined, angry part of her that still wanted to know *why* and 'solve the mystery' of the missing money—money she had no interest in keeping.

What was she interested in, then? Was it to clear her name? Find a reason to justify killing a man, beyond self-defence? Or was it to ascertain why Caspar had never told her about the trust? Why hadn't he ever told her about the trust?

Barefoot, she padded into the bedroom to rest, to breathe, to try to relax, when the only thing she knew would slacken the contradiction of her thoughts was ironing, except there was nothing to iron, besides a new dress and the shirt and trousers Kitt had purchased on the way back to the hotel.

Mae reached the edge of her bed and drew the sheets down, looking at Kitt asleep in the other small bed across the small gap.

On his side, hand beneath a pillow, Kitt slept in boxer briefs, which were dark-green with a grey band, and they moulded to his buttocks. She let her eyes travel the length of him. The light in the room was diffused, but she saw a thick scar high on his back and dappled spots that looked like skin that had blistered from sunburn. His lashes were long and thick, his mouth, so usually hard, was soft with sleep. He was handsome. He was ugly. He was beautiful. He was looking right at her.

She saw the little twitch of his mouth, the tiny sign that meant he was amused, and she knew if she wanted him to he'd sleep with her. If she wanted him to he would kiss her, use his hands, make love to her, or fuck her. All she had to do was act first, move first, touch him first. All she had to do was ask.

And he wanted her to ask.

He wanted her. That should have made her uncomfortable. The way women were disposable to him should have made her uneasy, yet knowing he wanted her was empowering. Mae looked back at him and laughed. Then she turned, slipped off her dress, and got into bed in her bra and underpants that didn't fit her nearly as well as his fit him.

Despite a clear demarcation of their roles, she looked at Kitt differently now. She was accustomed to their positions, to the delineation of employer-employee and landlady, accustomed to what she held for Caspar. She was unaccustomed to possibility, unacquainted with curiosity and fascination. Kitt fascinated her, made her curious, and he was right. She did know him. She saw through him, maybe even saw into him, to the place where he was...well, not exactly empty, but filled by shadows and a weird sense of conciliated acceptance of a life lived in eternal dusk.

He knew all these things about her as well, and he wanted,

genuinely, for her to be happy. It wasn't that she didn't want to be happy or that she didn't want to be happy with someone else; it was that, having lived so long without that particular sort of happiness, she recognised futility when blue-grey eyes looked at her from a bed little more than a metre away.

It struck her then that she'd stopped thinking about dead men in kitchens and bakeries. She'd stopped thinking about mysterious trust funds and immigration lawyers and Austrian men with expensive pens. She'd stopped thinking about Caspar.

CHAPTER TWELVE

A crowd filled the black-and-white tiled piazza. People were bathed in the glow of street lamps and party lanterns. San Giuseppe, the church, was lit from below and stood out bright. Tiny lights twinkled and winked from Mazzaró Bay and Gardini-Naxsos, the town below Taormina. Mount Etna glowed red in the distance, lighting up the cloud of ash above it. There was laughter, the scent of fine food, and old music played. People danced and drank and ate.

A shot of Disaronno in orange juice over ice was a new drink for Mae. The liqueur tasted of apricots, spices and, almonds, despite containing no nuts of any sort. It was refreshing, perfect for a hot summer night. Kitt was on his second. She was on her third. Mae had a large swallow of her cocktail and set it on the table. "That man," she pointed, "is Swedish."

"And you say that because...?"

"He's wearing yellow trousers. Only Swedes wear yellow trousers."

"Why's that?" Kitt craned his neck around the leggy brunette in a tight pink dress to get a better look at Mae's 'Swede.'

"Because their winters are so long and dark, and yellow reminds the Swedes of the sun."

A whoop went up from the crowd when the little band near the staircase began to play *Tu Vuò Fá L'Americano*. People clapped and sang along. Kitt leaned closer to Mae. He caught the hint of the hotel's bath gel, Penhaligon's Lily of the Valley. He wanted to touch her, to tuck a swathe of hair behind her ear, and run a finger across her lips, and she knew it, which amused and irritated him. This was a delicious game of cat and mouse, where the mouse had the upper hand, saw him for the tomcat he was, and didn't tease him for it.

This mouse played other kinds of games, games that were distracting, innocuous fun, like 'Guess the tourist's homeland and occupation.' He said, "You do realise one could apply your Winter Yellow Trousers Theory to all Scandinavian countries, Siberia, Iceland, Greenland, and Canada?"

She gave an Italian-style shrug. "Yes, but he's a Swedish writer."

"Why is here in Taormina?"

"He's come to commune with the spirits of Cervantes, Goethe, D.H. Lawrence, Truman Capote, and Tennessee Williams."

"What's his name?" Kitt finished his cocktail. It would be his last.

"Axel Klinckowström." Mae reached for her drink and gave him a satisfied little smile.

"Axel Klinckowström was a Swedish explorer and playwright."

"And there he is in yellow trousers, dancing with Svetlana, the Ukrainian spy in the pink dress."

The music turned soft and traditional and Kitt leaned even closer. "If you want to know who the real spies are," he said, "they're arguing at the bar."

Mae drank and glanced to the left, finding the American couple they'd run into earlier. She laughed, nearly choking on a chip of ice. "Yes," she said, after a cough. "Loudmouthed Ronnie and Simone from New York are spies."

"Trust me. The Hawaiian shirt he's wearing is standard CIA dress. Would you like to dance?"

"With Ronnie? I'm afraid he'd step on my feet."

"I meant would you like to dance with me."

"I know." She played with the straw in her glass. "You don't think Ronnie and Simone are here on their honeymoon and realise they've made a terrible mistake marrying each other, do you?"

"No. They're here to make sure I don't drink too much and make an arse of myself."

"I admit it." She pushed the straw up and down. "There is something strangely endearing about what you said last night. There is something strangely endearing about how you are when you're— what was it you said—*unrelentingly hammered*."

"Are you still thinking about that?"

"I'm thinking about all sorts things so I don't think about other less pleasant things. I'm thinking about what you said about me being happy. I'm thinking about why you know how to apply make-up so well. I'm thinking I'd like another one of these, please." She rattled her empty glass.

He took the glass from her and set it beside his. "I think you may have had enough."

"I've never been *unrelentingly hammered*, but I think I'd like to be. You made it look rather fun. Freeing, I guess. Would you like to dance?" she said.

"Yes."

She smiled and leaned in close, meeting his eyes. "Go and ask Simone because Ronnie left her and she's looking at you. Longingly."

His gaze unwavering, he said, "Simone is not my type."

Mae arched a brow. "She's married, isn't she?"

"She's on her honeymoon."

Mae tipped her chin to the left. "Why married women, Kitt?"

"It's less complicated."

"I should think it's more complicated."

"It's never a long-term complication."

"Have you ever wanted a long-term complication?"

His head tipped, mirroring the angle of hers, and his mouth twitched. "Would you like another drink?"

"I thought you'd never ask."

With a laugh, he got up and went to the bar. Mae watched Kitt move across the space with easy confidence, and she laughed when Simone intersected his path. The woman gave him an open-mouthed smile. They had a few words. Simone played with her pale hair, tucking it behind her ear. He leaned in close to her for a moment. Mae saw Simone's flirty smile widen just before an older gentleman stopped beside the table and eclipsed the view.

The band shifted tempo into a bossa nova, playing *Quando, Quando, Quando*. Kitt ordered tonic and lime for himself and an orange juice for Mae. When he turned, she was a few feet away, dancing with a well-dressed, short gentleman old enough to be her father. The little man had a moustache and wore a red carnation pinned to his vest. He chattered away to Mae and had the easy confidence of a man who loved dancing with beautiful women.

The elderly gentleman wasn't alone in that pleasure.

Kitt watched a moment longer. He left the drinks on the bar and picked his way through the couples dancing. Then he tapped the older man on the shoulder. Crestfallen, the man gave a nod, kissed Mae's hand, and placed it in Kitt's.

Head shaking, chuckling, Kitt led her to a spot at the edge of the dance area, where the lights were low. He slipped an arm about her waist, holding her loosely as he began a series of steps, slow, quick,

quick, forming a box. Mae moved forward when she should have gone back and bumped into his chest.

"I'm not very good at this," she said, glancing down at her feet.

"But I am," Kitt said.

She raised her gaze to his. "Yes. It's part of your deadly-to-women charm."

"There's no way I can charm you, is there?"

"No. So stop trying."

"You think I'm trying?"

"You are very frustrating."

"I frustrate you, Mrs Valentine?" He moved, slow, quick, quick, his hand on the small of her back.

"You distract me. I am tipsy, and you are distracting."

"And you are flirting."

"Is that what I'm doing?"

"Well, you're not dancing," he said, and changed direction, turning her to face the crowd instead of the church. "You're a shocking dancer. Didn't you ever dance with Caspar?"

"You didn't want to talk about complications, I don't want to talk about Caspar," she said. "I haven't thought of Caspar all day. That's a first."

"How does that feel?"

Mae considered the question for a moment. "Lightweight."

"Unlike you on my feet."

"And tipsy."

"Exactly like you on your feet."

"You *are* charming.

"And I didn't even try." He gave her a small twirl and pulled her close.

She laughed up into his face. "Do you know this song, *Quando, Quando, Quando*?" she said. "*Quando* means *when*. The song asks when will you come? When will I see you? When will you kiss me because my life without you means nothing? Somewhere, at the back of my mind, I think, once the tipsy passes and I stop treading on your toes, I'll be wondering *when* about Caspar again." Mae put her cheek against Kitt's chest. He was a bully, he was a hero, and right now he was man. "But for now, I don't mind that you're a little distraction."

"I am curiously happy to distract you." He nuzzled his nose into her hair. "Especially when you smell so nice."

Mae lifted her cheek and looked up at him. "I know you're curious. You've made that clear."

"Aren't you? Even the slightest bit?"

"Of course." Her eyes traced a path around his face, moving from his eyes to his forehead, his cheek and his jaw, to his mouth and back to his gaze. "Of course I'm curious. But when this tipsiness passes, and this is all over, and you stop working for me, I want to go on working for you as much as you want me to continue to work for you."

"Spoilsport."

"Think of all the scrambled eggs you'd miss out on. Imagine what a hellish life that would be."

Kitt stopped dancing. He drew back, holding her at arm's length. "You'd do that?" he said and took one look at her sly grin. "Yes. Yes, you would."

"You know what they say about curiosity and the cat."

Kitt laughed. "You're no cat, Mae. You're a cunning mouse." He resumed the bossa nova steps, moving slow, quick, quick, his hand in the small of her back.

"Thank you. Every woman wants to be thought of as *mousy*," she said and stepped on his toes.

"I'm sorry. Moose may be more accurate."

Mae laughed and he took her by the hand to lead her to the bar and their waiting drinks, but she remained rooted to the spot where they'd stopped dancing. Lips parted, she watched something at the front of the brightly lit church. Kitt followed her line of sight through the crowd, to see a woman.

Fashionably dressed, the diamond point hemline of her tangerine dress swished above her knees. She had a striking profile, a head of blonde ringlets, and a very ugly pair of vividly coloured shoes.

Mae pulled Kitt's hand, and they followed the woman, keeping a discreet distance. Her pace was even. She travelled further down Corso Umberto and began weaving through the tourists and locals out on the warm summer night. She paused twice to have a look through shop windows, and they paused too. As she continued, the street narrowed slightly, and she halted in front of a strip of restaurants with outdoor dining and shook her head. Turning about, muttering to herself, the glittery shoes caught the light, and she began swishing back in their direction.

Mae glanced left to Vicolo Stretto, a long anorexic staircase with uneven steps crushed between two buildings. Barely wide enough for one person, the stairs led to a wine bar and restaurant on the street above. One might pass by the opening thinking it was a tight alleyway where rubbish bins were hidden away, but in another two weeks, during the high season, tourists would crowd about at the bottom of the stairs and wait their turn to have their photo snapped while standing on the narrow old stone steps. Lovers might pause there too, for a moment's privacy.

She yanked Kitt into the skinny stairwell, moving up four steps. When she stopped, he stood on the tread below, putting them at an equal height. She pushed him against the wall, hooked an arm around his neck, and pressed her cheek to his, eyes fixed on the curly Goldilocks at the front of the eatery on other side of the street.

Kitt shifted their positions, putting her back to the wall so they could both see, closing the tiny space between them, mashing into her, crushing her breasts and handbag, his thigh wedged between hers. He was warm, heat radiated from his chest. The agitation of seeing the woman with the ugly shoes joined curiosity and the primitive excitement of his body pressed to hers. Mae lifted her head and looked at him.

His blue-grey eyes regarded her. "I think," he said, "I prefer you without the make-up." He ran his nose across the tip of hers, his breath a whisper of a kiss over her mouth, saying, "Move your head a little."

When she did, his nose tickled along her neck. His lips nuzzled into a tiny spot, and it made her shudder. "Can you see her?" she said.

"Now I can." In the half-shadow of the narrow staircase Mae trembled in his arms. Fear, revulsion, excitement, whatever she felt that made her quake, it wasn't lost on Kitt that she was giving back as good as she got and she pressed closer. "Yes, and those are ugly shoes," he said, a thrill tickling up his spine.

"Where did she go?" Mae said, her mouth a hair's breadth above the shell of his ear.

"Just to wait..." Kitt's breath hitched, "...at the place across the street facing us. She's looking over here. Did I mention that you smell nice?"

"Enjoying this, are you?"

"It's always a pleasure to have an attractive woman poke her tongue in my ear."

"I didn't poke my tongue in your ear."

"I'm hoping you will."

"Cheeky monkey." She nipped his neck.

"Cheeky vampire."

"Careful, or I'll draw blood."

"Promise?"

"Kitt, I don't want to give the wrong impression, but you do that rather well."

"What, this?"

"Yes," she said, digging her nails into his side, her breath catching the way his had, "and I wish you'd—"

"I'm so glad you're liking this as much as I am, but before you scold me, make a speech regarding employer-employee relations, and ruin this very pleasing distraction for us both, take a look at the men who just arrived. Anyone you recognise?"

Mae rubbed her cheek against his and peered through half-closed eyes. It took a split-second to forget how farcically erotic their spontaneous surveillance had turned. Goldilocks spoke to a lean, tall man with light brown hair. "That's Ernst Largo!"

"That's Largo. Right. What about the big man shaking his hand, have you seen him before?"

The dark-haired Asian man was built like a rugby player, one who was all muscle and no neck. "I don't know who that is, but I recognise the other bastard. You broke his nose."

"Yes, I did."

Introductions were made. Polite smiles all 'round, the foursome went into the restaurant and found a table outside.

The unobstructed view of the players in his game made Mae shake with indecision. She wanted to rush down the stairs, cross the street, grab a chair and smash it over the heads of the two men and a woman who had started it all. She wanted to run away with Kitt, forget two men had died, and ignore that she was somehow responsible. She clenched the back of Kitt's shirt in her fist. "What do we do?"

Furious, his ability to respond in any sort of way that would satisfy his needs hindered, his hands bound by his career and international laws that frowned upon personal vendettas that involved killing, Kitt stared through a thin curtain of Mae's hair, watching the group talk, watching money change hands surreptitiously. "I don't like this," he murmured at her ear. "If the volcanic ash hadn't closed the airport I'd put you on a plane and send you somewhere far away, somewhere safe, but we both know that you wouldn't go." He pulled back, eyes narrowed as he looked at her. "Would you? Would you leave this to me? Would you go if I asked you to?"

She met his gaze. "No. And you're the one who should leave. You should take your five pounds and go. This doesn't involve you."

"The hell it doesn't. I'm involved, Mae. More than you know."

"You have a very misplaced sense of loyalty."

"You're right." He looked back at the table where Goldilocks sat with her three bears. A waiter in a short white apron, the kind Mae favoured wearing, set a plate of food on the table.

"What do we do?" Mae said again.

Kitt turned to her. "We watch them. It doesn't look like they're going anywhere for a while, but we can't stay here." He pulled his arms from her waist. "Let me have a look at that little *trattoria* on the other side of where they are. I'll be right back."

"Wait." She huffed. "What do I do if they leave?"

"Pay attention to the direction they take and stay here and wait for me." He left her on the steps and darted across the street.

Mae watched him pull out his phone and take a photo of the restaurant while pretending to take a photo of a menu on a wrought-iron stand. Then he moved up the street and she lost sight of him in the mass of evening tourists and diners.

As she watched, Largo, the man with the broken nose, Goldilocks, and the big man ate and argued. It only took a moment to work out who was in charge. Mae was surprised, and somewhat annoyed with herself for automatically thinking it would be Largo or one of the other two men. Goldilocks ruled the roost. One by one, she levelled each man with a word or a single glare, and Largo looked away sheepishly, the big one shoved bread into his mouth, and the man with the broken nose guzzled wine.

A couple appeared at the bottom of Vicolo Stretto, obscuring her view. Mae came down the steps and let them pass. She stood at the mouth of the alley staircase, in a shadow beside a lighted menu fixed to the wall beside the stairs. She looked for Kitt in the moving crowd, watched the four dining in the place diagonally opposite where she waited in the half-light, and heard the sound of fist cracking bone. She heard Largo telling her it would be like falling asleep, and Sal's high-pitched slow scream, and she smelled that bizarre odour of burnt bread and burnt flesh, as she stood beside Caspar's grave looking at three names. But before fear set in too deeply, before she began to hyperventilate, before her judgement was clouded, she took a slow breath, from her belly. Then Kitt was there. He pocketed his mobile and took her hand.

The bar Kitt had chosen was crowded, noisy, and perfect for surveillance. Barely speaking, he sat beside Mae. Hidden in the crowd for over an hour, nursing drinks, they both watched. The man with the broken nose got up first. He dropped a wad of money on the table. Goldilocks grabbed his wrist and said something that made him nod before he hurried off. He walked by the bar, glancing in their direction without noticing them.

Mae leaned close. "Do we follow him?"

"No," Kitt said, eyes on the man. "As much as I'd like to kill him, I think we're better served by following the woman or Largo."

"Would you really kill him, Kitt?"

He turned to her. "Yes. If allowed the opportunity, yes. I'd kill him. Does that surprise you?"

"What surprises me," she said, "is that I'd like to watch you do it."

"What if I merely knocked out his teeth?"

"I'd watch you do that too." Mae looked at her wedding ring for a moment. "Does that make me bloodthirsty?"

"It makes you human."

Mae sat back, hand to her mouth.

Kitt thought she looked as if she were about to cry, and it made him jealous. Tears, he knew, were not a sign of weakness. Tears were a rather healthy way to dispel and process stress and emotion that a good portion of the male population tended to bottle up and ignore—until a heart attack or something equally dramatic forced them into the socially acceptable masculine explosion of rage. Kitt was full of rage, so full of suppressed rage he would have appreciated the release of a good cry. Or a heart attack. Instead he had to sit on his frustration and roiling emotions and do nothing. He loathed doing nothing even more than he hated paperwork.

Largo got up next. His eyes lingered on Goldilocks, his adoration for her plain. He made no polite or rude gestures and bid no one a goodnight before he departed. He simply walked away from the table.

"Damn it," Kitt said. "I was hoping they'd leave together."

"You follow him. I'll wait and follow the other two when they leave." Mae rose.

Kitt jerked her back into her seat. "That's not going to bloody happen."

She glared at him, but then the irritation softened. "Are you afraid something will happen to me, Kitt?"

He put a hand on her neck, his thumb on her cheek. "You're so angry, exasperated, and bewildered by what's happened to you, I don't think you have any sense of your own safety. You rushed to Sicily without a thought and you're again rushing now. I don't think you realise how dangerous this is. We don't know what we're dealing with, Mae. You want to put puzzle pieces together to form a picture that makes sense, but there may not be sense to any of this.

Yes, I'm afraid something will happen to you. Something already happened to you, and I don't want something to happen again." He slid his hand away and fixed her with a hard stare. "We follow Goldie and the Asian man. Together. Do you understand?"

She clamped her teeth together, grabbed her handbag, and rose again. "I can't decide if you're being bossy or if you're being a bully."

"Decide in a minute because they're on the move and coming this way." He stood, arms going around her, pressing her face to his chest. She squirmed, her protest vibrated against him, but he held her fast. With his nose to the crown of her head he watched the muscle-bound man and his curly-topped blonde companion pass by. Then he released Mae and she scowled. He took her hand, pulled her along, and wove a path out of the bar, keeping an eye on the couple moving just ahead. Zigzagging along Corso Umberto, they travelled back toward the black-and-white tiled Piazza IX Aprile, San Giuseppe, and the party at the Wunderbar, where the crowd had thickened.

Earlier, the dancing had been limited to the area near the staircase beside the church. The dancing had now spilled across into the piazza. The party had become a festival. The music played on and people danced everywhere. Pulling Mae along behind, Kitt became a plough snaking a trail through a mass swinging and twirling to *Mambo Italiano*. The blonde and her muscular companion picked their way through the throng, and he kept them in his sight. The pair headed across the front of the clock tower and Kitt pushed through the sea of dancers. Mae hollered at him in the crush, her hand jerking from his. Irritated, he fixed on the couple's heading.

When he turned around, Mae had vanished.

CHAPTER THIRTEEN

The two young men apologised for knocking her down and helped her up. Mae craned her neck around them to see Kitt and began to pick her way through the gambolling horde. She was jostled hard, spun about, and tumbled into a tall man in an ugly Hawaiian-print shirt.

Smiling Ronnie-the-American-from-New York reached for her. He stank of beer and perspiration and pressed her to his sweaty chest as he began some kind of mash-up of tango and waltz. He squeezed her tightly and laughed, shouting in her ear, "So your husband has a lot of money?"

Mae tried to pull away, but hands roamed up her back, and Ronnie yelled above the music, "Did you know all marriage is not about two people spending their lives together? It's about the wife spending all her husband's money." He squeezed her closer, mouth at her ear. "Why don't you show me what kind of good time we can have with your husband's mon—"

Mae grabbed his bollocks.

Ronnie squealed, let go, and Mae shoved him hard. He bounced against others dancing. Amid protesting and angry shouts, she twisted around and tried again to find Kitt, jumping up to see over the tops of heads. She waded into the mass, winding a way toward the Wunderbar, peering around arms and backs and gyrating bodies. A flash of vivid tangerine caught her eye as it moved beyond the band playing near the stairs beside San Giuseppe.

The woman was alone.

Mae pushed her way to the outside, skirted the edge of the revelry, and followed the bright colour up the stairs and into the dark. She and Kitt had crossed this palm-lined pathway this morning. Dappled moonlight shone on black and white pavers now, palm fronds casting shadows. Mae stuck to the dark spots. She'd lost sight of Goldilocks at the top of the stairs, but there was only one way the woman could go. The path led out of the shadows to the front of a pale house with a dark stone arch over a darker door. Geraniums that had been bright red in the morning light were black now as they spilled out from boxes on the two balconies above the arch. A broken window had been boarded over, the result of the anti-immigrant protest earlier in the day. The moon lit up the small, round sign beside *Corso Umberto 23*. Someone had spray painted *BASTA CLANDESTINI*—stop illegal immigrants—across the front.

Mae's palms went clammy. Her pulse began to rush. She gazed at the moonlight glinting on the brass buzzer in the middle of the door that was ajar. A dim, bluish light shone inside.

She a poked a toe against the door to open it wider and went into the office.

Soft music came from speakers that lay on the pale carpet. Beside the speakers sat a pair of hideous platform heels that were a cross between rubber Crocs and Birkenstock sandals with a ribbon ankle strap and a fur pom-pom on the toe. Papers were strewn across the floor. The wooden filing cabinet and drawers of a carved wooden credenza gaped open, files scattered about. A bright orange *Stop Invasione* defaced the wall behind the desk. The computer monitor lay on its back on the desktop, the light from it shining on the ugly anti-refugee words, shining on the ceiling, shining on Luca, the young man she'd met that morning.

Mae moved closer, forgetting about Goldilocks and her Asian companion. Luca sat behind his desk in the high leather office chair, head tipped to the left. His pants bunched at his knees, genitals exposed. Shirt unbuttoned, he clutched the phone receiver, eyes bulging, tongue protruded from his mouth, his necktie gouged deep into his throat.

She waited for the shock, for the thunderous rush of blood in her head to dampen her hearing, but she was mesmerised by the way his tie had twisted into his skin, rolling flesh and fabric together.

Had it just happened or had he been strangled hours ago?

She touched the back of his hand. He was tepid, not ice-cold. She was tepid too, not frozen or overheated or much of anything beyond lukewarm.

Handbag pressed close to her side, she backed up, two, three steps. A hand closed over her mouth and nose. Chin forced up, she was yanked snug against a shoulder and a hard chest, her left arm jammed to her waist. Boosted off her feet, she thrashed wildly with her free hand, raked her nails down flesh, and kicked a heel into a shin.

"It's me," Kitt hissed into her ear, lifting his palm.

Mae stopped squirming. Angry, relieved, eyes narrowed, she looked up and back at him. He released her, pointing to the torchlight bouncing about down the hallway to the right of Luca's desk.

Shin smarting, Kitt led her across the carpet, around the papers and the upended wine glass she'd been about to step on, and through the door she'd left wide open. Outside, he headed for the entrance of the house next door and the dark, recessed doorway. He pushed Mae into the corner, pressing her to the wall with his back as he stood in front of her. Hand in his pocket, he closed his fingers around the outrageously expensive little fountain pen, and watched the big Asian man pause in the threshold of Torrisi's law office. The man looked in each direction down dim cobblestones, at the balcony above his head, at the doorway where they sheltered. Kitt unscrewed the top of the pen. The man looked a moment longer, then stepped back inside the law office and shut the door.

Kitt replaced the cap, let the Montblanc fall back into his pocket, and hurried Mae down a laneway, between a large building and a small, empty café. They rounded a corner and found a staircase to take them back to Corso Umberto.

Mae halted abruptly at the top of the stairs. "Aren't you going to be sick?" she said.

"No."

"I think I could be sick, but maybe I'll jog instead." She started down the steps, taking two at time.

He caught up to her at the bottom of the first flight, latched onto her shoulder, and spun her about. "Goddamn it, Mae, what the hell are you doing?"

"Running away from here." She pushed back from him and glared. "Running from the death I seem to attract. Running from whatever it is I started."

Glaring back, Kitt pulled a handkerchief from his pocket and wiped a small trickle of blood from the scratches on the back of his hand. He wanted to shout at her, but he moored in his frustration and shoved aside the fear twisting in his gut. He looped her arm through his and hurried with her down the remaining flights. They pushed through the still-crowded streets. Within six minutes they were in the lobby of the hotel. Within eight minutes they were in their room with the two twin beds.

Immediately, she went about the room straightening things, pulling the drapes shut, smoothing pillows on the sofa, remaking the beds, *dusting*, and it cut loose his tethered exasperation. "Oh, stop it!" He tore a face washer-dust cloth from her.

Livid eyes stared at him. Kitt waited for her to fly at him, to slap and pummel fists against him, yet she simply stared. Her unwavering, odious gaze tipped out drops of the larger ocean of rage he'd held dammed. He swore and she blinked at the crude vociferousness of his words. He broke off to stare back at her and grit his front teeth. "Damn him. Damn that man. Damn Caspar. Damn him for putting you in this position."

Mae covered her face with her hands and shook her head. "Don't," she said.

"Why? Why would he do that? Why would he hide thirty-seven million pounds? What sort of man keeps secrets from the woman who loves him? What sort of husband does that to the wife who loves him?"

Her hands came away. She gave an incredulous laugh and squinted at him. "Hide? What do you know of being a husband? Nothing. You know nothing. Caspar died. Through no fault of his own, he died, along with seventy-five other faultless people in a foggy wreck outside Padua sixteen years ago. He died. And you blame him for all this?"

"Yes. I blame him for all this. I blame him for setting up a trust that you knew nothing about. I blame him for keeping that from you. I blame him for your broken heart. I blame him..." Kitt ground his molars together. He had gone too far and not far enough, not nearly far enough. Prudently, he staunched the flow of his ire, inhaling slowly. "I apologise," he said. "I am sorry."

"Yes, you are very sorry."

"I'm not a very nice man."

"I just said as much." Mae took the balled-up dust cloth from him and shook it out.

Kitt noticed a smear of blood on the inside of his wrist. He rubbed at the brownish stain. "Do you know why I wasn't sick back there on the steps?" he said softly. "I was sick when I lost you, when I couldn't find you."

"How nice that I make you sick." She snorted.

"I don't know that I've ever vomited because of a woman before. You realise you make me care, don't you? Caring makes me sloppy. Caring means I've been watching you instead of watching what's going on about us. I don't like caring, I can't afford to care, but here I am, caring. What does that mean?"

"It means you are human."

"Yes. Right. My words. Thank you for feeding them back to me," he said with a nod. "Did you touch anything in that office?"

"I want to go home, Kitt." Mae resumed her productivity. She gathered up the few items she had left out, taking her dress from the wardrobe.

"Did you touch anything? Back there."

Mae froze. His words about Caspar had finally struck home, repeating what she'd thought earlier in the day, but the tirade was not what had immobilised her. Had she touched anything in the office? She'd read the slogan written on the wall, glanced at the boarded-up window, and she'd toed the door open, but had she touched anything? Had she touched anything inside? She squeezed her skull with both hands and exhaled. "Only Luca."

"Why."

She dropped her hands and rested her head against the wardrobe door. "I wanted to know how long he'd been dead, if it had just happened or if he'd been that way for a while. Does it matter if I touched him?"

Kitt knew his tone was matter-of-fact and he watched her

dispassionately, hating himself for the detachment she'd said she wanted. He'd never hated himself before and was not detached from the sense of self-loathing. For some reason, recognising how contemptible he was made him smile. "This is two dead men in Italy now," he said, brushing fingers over his grin to wipe it off. "If you touched anything else in that office, the fingerprints will lead the police to you in England, where you were arrested for killing a man."

"I wasn't charged." Mae shifted from the wardrobe and wandered in a small circle, the spring green dress in her hand.

"That won't matter. You come to Sicily every year. A blonde was seen leaving Russo's bakery. Someone may have seen a blonde entering or leaving the law office. That blonde could be you or Goldilocks. Either way it will be easiest to pin on you." Kitt had a seat on the sofa. "Why did you go after her yourself?"

She stopped pacing.

"Was it to prove what a bully I was to you? You see why, don't you? You understand?"

With a swallow, she moved into the sitting room where he was, and ran a finger over the stitch in her lip. "I was knocked down. The American, from the Teatro Greco, Simone's husband, he grabbed me. He wanted to dance and wouldn't let go. I shouted for you to stop, but you kept going, and I lost you. I couldn't see you anywhere, but I saw her. And I went after her, single-minded, without thinking. Did I frighten you?"

He looked up at her, one brow arching. "Shall I take you to the spot where I was violently ill?"

"I am sorry." Mae sank to the sofa beside him, the dress in her lap. "The Mafia being involved seems reasonable now. Sort of. I still don't know why. I don't know what ties it all together or ties it to me beyond Caspar. It does hinge on Caspar, doesn't it?"

"I agree that he appears to be the lynchpin."

Hands shaking, she combed fingers through her hair. "Do you think that woman is a Mafia assassin?"

"It's possible, but it takes some skill and strength to strangle a man the size of Luca that way. Just like it took some strength to put Russo into the dough mixer. I doubt Goldie and the other two have the upper body strength to have killed either man. I'd say our friend Luca died at the hands of the big Asian man, and it was set up. It was set up to look like a sexual encounter that turned into a robbery because Luca wasn't the target. Torrisi is. Luca was simply in the wrong place at the wrong time." Kitt turned to her. "This is some kind of extermination, Mae. The names on that list you saw are slated for execution. And you were at the top of the list."

"Over money or something else?"

"Money is the most likely reason." He ran his thumb over the scratches she'd left down the back of his hand. "The papers that Largo took, what were they?"

Mae pulled floral printed fabric through her fingers. "The letters that Daniel Pierce sent me. Account documents. A lasting power of attorney, a revocation of power of attorney, release documents, standard banking papers with an account number and a balance. And no, I don't remember the account number. That's not something I committed to memory." She gave him a frosty, smile. "Caspar may have forgotten about the account, or not even known about it, because what teenager is concerned with his retirement?"

"Mae..."

Rising, she tossed the dress where she'd been sitting and looked at him. "If the airport wasn't closed I'd get on a plane and go home."

"If the airport was open, I'd get on the plane with you." Kitt took her hand and got to his feet.

"What should we do?"

"We go to Torrisi tomorrow and warn him."

KITT HAD BEEN asleep when Mae had started her bath. He woke up fully when she finished and the bath water gurgled and choked as it drained away. Quickly, she closed the bathroom door, deadening the sound.

It was after midnight. He heard her move, heard the soft tap of a tumbler being placed on a silver tray beside the bottle of Disarrono she'd had sent to the room after they'd returned. He wondered how much of the bottle she'd drunk while she'd soaked in lily of the valley perfumed bubbles and watched her through half-shuttered eyes.

Noiselessly, she crept into the bedroom wearing the slip they'd bought earlier in the day. The illuminated face of the clock on the bedside table cast a bright glow between the two beds. Freshly scrubbed, her damp hair combed back, Mae stood at the foot of her bed and stared at it sourly, her skin pale and oddly shadowed by the greenish hue of the clock. After a minute, she lifted the bed linens and slid beneath them. She turned on her side and stuffed her hands under the pillow. It took a moment before she realised he was looking at her.

"I'm sorry I woke you," she said.

"You feel better?"

"I tried to pull out my stitches."

"Did that make you feel better?"

"No. It hurt. Maybe I should let you do it."

Kitt rolled onto his side. "What makes you think it wouldn't hurt if I did it?"

"You would have redirected my attention. You would have distracted me with some odd fact about yourself, confessed that you have a weakness for older women."

He sighed. "Yes. I find Dame Judi Dench astonishingly attractive. Helen Mirren, too. They're smart women. Smart is sexy."

"Margaret Thatcher is your idea of a Page Three girl?" she said.

"I make it a rule to steer clear of politicians. Is this enough of a distraction for you?"

"I don't know yet. What can you do to get rid of my thoughts of dead men?"

"Come here," he said softly.

"No."

"Do you want to be distracted, Mae?"

She looked at him for a long while. "Yes. And no. Not like that. Not that way."

"I'm sorry I'm not Caspar."

"I don't want you to be Caspar, sir."

"What do you want then?"

She said nothing, which said everything.

"All you have to do is ask."

"I don't want to ask you anything, Major."

"Because that wouldn't be appropriate, would it?" Kitt grabbed his pillow, climbed out of his bed, and got into hers. Despite the scent of toothpaste, he caught the fragrance of spiced, sweet spirits on her breath when he gathered her close. Half atop him, his arms around her neck and waist, she stiffened, drew in a breath to chastise him, but before she could he said, "Shut your eyes, Mae."

"This isn't the same as last night, Kitt."

"Yes, it is."

"You are not drunk."

"But you are."

"And why is that the same?

"Because I know the difference between drunk and sober, between sense and nonsense, between curiosity and certainty. I know the difference between taking advantage and being accommodating, between comfort and distraction. And I know what you want from me but won't ask. This is the same as last night, when you could have gone next door to sleep in the house you own or stayed with Fiorella."

"That woman talks too much."

"Go to sleep, Mrs Valentine," he said, closing his eyes.

It took a few minutes, but she softened, relaxed and fell asleep in his arms. Then Kitt was awake for more than an hour. And when he woke far too early the next morning, he did not go back to sleep at all. He got out of bed, careful to not to disturb her, and went out on the balcony to speak to Bryce.

MAE ROLLED over and found what she'd never realised she'd been looking for. Just like Caspar, Kitt wasn't there beside her, but a phantom of him remained. The space he'd occupied was still warm and smelled ever so faintly of him. She pulled a fistful of the sheet to her nose, breathing in the slightest scent of Kitt, and found him somewhere he had no cause to be.

It wasn't because they'd shared a bed or that they had endured traumatic incidents together. It wasn't even simple curiosity. No, Kitt was there before any of those things happened. He had been there much longer than a few days, longer than a few weeks.

He had been there for years.

Hidden, waiting, germinating beneath layers of landlady and tenant, the mantle of employer and employee, Kitt had been sown, stuffed into a place, crammed inside where she thought there'd been no room, gestating until he filled it so completely he burst through. It was a startling, breathtaking live birth.

When the shock wore off, the grim reality burned her eyes and Mae began to cry. Then she began to sob. The noise of water running in the bathroom as he showered was loud enough to drown out her small gasps, but she grabbed the pillow that had been under his head, dragged it over her face to muffle her moaning, and curled into a ball.

Stupid. She was stupid and irrational and overwrought and furious and utterly without hope. There was no avoiding the thoroughly inexplicable truth.

Mae was still in bed when Kitt came out of the bathroom. She'd cocooned the sheet about her and had a pillow wrapped around her face. Despite the insulation of the cushion and how quiet he tried to be, she heard him dressing. She heard him move to the bed, and when he sat on the edge she said, "I don't want to."

Kitt tugged the pillow from her and rolled her onto her back. He seemed surprised. Perhaps, she guessed, because he'd expected to see a face creased by sleep and bedclothes, not a red nose and tears. Mae knew it wasn't uncommon for a situation like hers to take a toll on one's state of mind. Her behaviour had been erratic; it was something she was aware of and tried to control, to rein in and think through, but physical and emotional trauma contributed to her emotional dysregulation—the mood swings she kept having—despite her best efforts to hold it all together. The chinks in her resolve were just as plain to him. She blubbed, and, after a slight hesitation, he smoothed hair from her forehead.

"Was it a nightmare about dead men or another bad dream about papers? Did the papers bury you this time?" He stroked her hair.

She pushed his hand away and blinked out fat tears. "I don't want to," she said, her tone petulant as she hugged the pillow to her chest from the childlike safety of bed. If he hadn't been sitting on it, she would have pulled the sheet over her head. "I don't want to."

He rose and crossed his arms. "You think I wanted to? You were soft and warm and very delightful, despite how you crushed me in this pea-sized bed."

Tears trundled sideways into her ears. "I don't want to."

"Neither do I, but we can't stay here all day, Mrs Valentine. However much I like that idea, we've an appointment with Torrisi. Come on. Get up."

Face awash, her nose streaming, she gasped and hiccupped, gazing at him, she imagined, the way people gaped at disaster zones.

He thought she didn't want to get out of bed.

She hiccupped another sob, and then began to laugh the way she had the evening they sat in Skinny O'Toole's office at the Suisse Global Bank. "I woke up and there it was, staring me in the face. I don't want to look. I don't want to look at you. I don't want to look at myself."

"Yes. The harsh light of morning can be so vicious. I'll get you some aspirin."

She covered her face as she laugh-cried and sat up.

"There's a good girl," he said.

"There's a good girl," she mimicked. Hands fell away. Sniffling, half-laughing, angry, she swabbed hard at her tears and swung her legs over the side of the bed.

"It was quite a nightmare, wasn't it?"

"I don't want to talk about it." She looked at him again, frowning, shaking her head. "Jaysus. What the hell do I do now?"

"Your hair is a good place to start. Your hair is a mess. You went to bed with it wet."

"Yes, doing my hair is going to fix everything."

"You'll feel better after some lunch. Your hangover will pass after a good lunch. Come on. It's nearly ten-thirty and we have to meet Torrisi for lunch in ninety minutes."

Mae flopped over and yanked the sheet over her head.

CHAPTER FOURTEEN

The overblown curves of the blue Volkswagen Beetle were painted with bubbles and goldfish. "Bloody Bryce," Kitt said stuffing the key fob into a pocket of his khaki cargo trousers.

"The blue matches your shirt," Mae said and pressed a finger over her mouth to disguise her amusement. "But you cannot drive this."

"Not if I want to hold on to any shred of manhood." Kitt moved to the passenger door.

"Then I'm not even sure you should *ride* in this fishbowl."

"I have little choice, Mae." He climbed into the Beetle.

Mae pulled the driver's door open and slid into the seat. "I take back what I said about your Bentley." She started the engine.

Kitt lowered the roof with the single touch of a button. "Yes, that's completely better. Now it's less like an aquarium."

"And more like a clown car."

He gave her a dry look and slipped on his dark sunglasses.

A minute later she drove along the seaside, took a hooked

entrance onto the *autostrada*, and headed south, moving closer to the ash cloud raining down volcanic particles that had closed the airport at Catania. "You know," Mae said. "I could turn back and drive us to Palermo, to the airport there. We could get a plane or take a ferry from Messina to Reggio Calabria and go home, or someplace else."

"Are you asking me to run away with you or just to run away?"

It depends. How much trouble will I be in when I get back to London?"

Kitt didn't say anything.

"That much trouble?" She glanced at him. "I knew you were keeping something to yourself. "I haven't merely put you in a difficult position with the law, I've put your job in jeopardy, haven't I?" When he still said nothing, she took her eyes from the road and saw he had opened the glovebox.

Kitt pulled out the black leather travel case he knew would be inside the compartment near his knees. However ridiculous the car looked, Bryce was thorough. Kitt unzipped what some referred to as a 'manbag' and removed a map, leaving the other standard things Bryce arranged to be in the case. He unfolded the map and began to read it.

"I should have guessed you'd be old school," Mae said.

"Old school what?"

"You could just follow along on the GPS."

"A GPS, while precise, isn't always accurate. How many times have you put a street into the GPS, followed the instructions, and wound up at the destination only to find that number 7 Bunt Street is a duck pond? A map gives a wider, and, in my opinion, better mental picture of a place than a GPS, which may only cover a few blocks at a time. You turn on the GPS and glance at it to follow a route. That's fine. I'll do that as well, once I have looked at the big picture. A GPS screen doesn't give a location and a destination at the same time. For the big picture, I trust the paper more than the gizmo."

She shifted in her seat and changed her grip on the steering wheel. "How long would it take us to get to Palermo?"

Kitt pinpointed their location on the map and calculated the distance. "A little less than three hours." As he searched the map for another route they weren't going to take to Palermo, he felt Mae accelerate. She began overtaking cars. The paper in his hands fluttered at the edges. He looked up from the colourful flat image as she sped by a large refrigerated lorry. Tiny bits of gravel and volcanic sand skittered the VW's undercarriage. Windswept streaks of black volcanic ash lined the motorway. The dim, greyish cloud billowing from Mount Etna to the east cast a softer grey net beneath it to the southeast, showering Catania with fine dust. Kitt watched road signs and distance markers whizz by, *shush-shush-shush*. Rather than his usual agitation and distaste for being a passenger, he admired her driving skill and understood the reason for her pace. "Yes," he said. "Let's get this over with."

"How do we get this over with?" she said, after passing a tourist bus that chugged out puffs of black exhaust. "How does one, without proof of any sort, tell a man they've never met that somebody is trying to kill him?"

"Very politely." Kitt folded the map. "And you are exceptionally polite, Mae."

"Yes, I am well-trained in etiquette for all occasions, but I missed the lesson in acquainting a lady or gentleman of their inclusion on a hit list. This means I am open to any suggestion you may have."

"Let me do it on my own."

Mae gave him a sidelong glance. "Has your Italian magically improved overnight?"

"Then we improvise."

"Isn't that what we've been doing?" She flipped down the sun visor and soared past a little Fiat like the one she had at home.

SMALL FISHING BOATS and smaller rowboats lay along the entrance to the small bay, their backs to the sun. The beach of Aci Trezza was made of black volcanic pebbles rather than sand. The dark shoreline set off the sparkling clear water of the Ionian Sea. Mythology said that the rock formations just off the coastline had been flung at Ulysses escaping the Cyclops Polyphemus. The road that led to the seaside restaurant narrowed. The emblem on the outside of the building showed a stylised version of a Cyclops. Mae parked the VW beneath the sign.

Hidden away by boat repair shops and fishing equipment, the one-time fish-processing factory had a run-down, seafaring appearance. A notice on the front door stated that the restaurant was closed for refurbishment and would reopen in a week's time. A young, giant of a man glanced at them as he washed bird droppings from the bonnet of a white Maserati parked beside them.

Mae tipped her chin to the sleek car. "See?"

"Yes. I noticed," Kitt said. He opened the glovebox and placed the map on top of the leather travel clutch.

"You don't suppose he'd like to trade, do you?" She squinted one eye and climbed out of the VW, handbag under her arm.

He shut the glovebox and got out of the car. "At least we know the little fishbowl handles well."

"You're welcome," Mae said.

The young man stopped cleaning and buffing. He was a big one and built like a professional wrestler. He turned and sighed, bulging muscles stretching his t-shirt taut across his arms and massive chest.

"Che bella," Mae smiled and pointed at the Maserati.

Nodding, he said, *"L'uccelli sono sporchi,* the birds, they are so dirty." He jerked his thumb to the open top of the Beetle. "The roof, you must *copiare,* cover, or the birds make shit all over the chairs."

Kitt muttered, "That might improve the Beetle's looks."

"Yes, your car is ugly." The man snorted as he watched Kitt turn back to raise the VW's roof. He plunged a fat sponge into a bucket of soapy water. "You are here to see Mr Torrisi, yes? Go inside, upstairs. Martini will welcome you, and I will clean bird shit from his car." He gestured, dribbled water, and set to scrubbing with his eyes fixed on Kitt, his manner raw, primitive as he washed the car haphazardly. His over-muscled physique cartoonish, like the Volkswagen's exaggerated goldfish. Amused, Mae laughed to herself. Kitt slid his hand to the small of her back. She took his arm and went with him into the old factory.

The door clanged shut behind them. "What's so funny?" he said in the little foyer.

She shrugged casually. "I was just curious."

"And what are you curious about this morning?" Kitt said, the corner of his mouth lifting.

"Enough," Mae muttered and faced him. She ran fingers through the sash of her green wrap dress, eyes narrowed as she exhaled another, "Enough." She rose up on her toes and kissed him, sweet and slow.

Kitt acknowledged the millstone he carried and let it slide from his grip. Mae was childhood Christmas, springtime sun, summer rain, earth, wind, and so much fire, an astounding amount of fire, and therein lay the weight, therein lay the danger. Therein lay the nuisance because Mae tasted nothing like he'd ever imagined how she would taste—and Kitt had imagined. Despite his practised discipline, her eternal devotion to a dead man, and interminable professional composure, for years he'd imagined how his butler would taste. He had been so sure she'd be pastry-sweet with a hint of coffee, but he was wrong. Her taste was unimaginable, wholly exhilarating, and utterly perilous.

She slid one palm down his chest and he keenly faced his peril. The stitches in her lip tickled. He drew her nearer, angling his head to take the kiss deeper, to gain more of her taste, to move closer to the precipice and flirt with the sharp edge of risk, but she pushed back.

"There," she said and settled on her feet. "Curiosity, loyalty, gratitude, distraction, however you want to think of it, it's out of the way. I know you've been trying to redirect my attention so I don't wind up rocking myself in a corner somewhere, but enough with the feckin' suggestions. Enough with the flirting and the questions about my romantic life. Shut your gob about that shite and let's focus on what we came here to do."

His laugh was wry. "Yes, ma'am," Kitt's equilibrium wavering pleasantly.

The smell of paint greeted them before they reached the top of the staircase. They turned a corner, walked by a pedestal holding a reservations book, and found that upstairs opened to a lavish restaurant that the building's rustic factory exterior did not suggest. Large windows showed off the view of the shimmering sea and the black rock formations created by the Cyclops' ire. Canvas drop cloths covered the floor. Tables, chairs and other furnishings were stacked up and draped with paint-spattered sheets. Paint trays, brushes, rollers, and scaffolding were pushed up against the wall.

A stout man, late forties, salt and pepper hair, approached them. He wore beige linen trousers and a crisp white shirt open at the neck. He moved past a large aquarium that was home to a lone fish, a silvery-looking bass, and offered his hand to them both. "Mr Kitt," he said. "I am Aurelio Martini, Mr Torrisi's associate. His secretary requested I meet you. He has been delayed and makes his apology to you and your sister. There was some unfortunate trouble at his Taormina office."

Mae smiled politely. "We were told there were protestors."

Martini gave a small nod and a pleasant smile. "Yes," he said. "Protestors. They did severe damage." He gestured to the dining room. "Please. This way. Tomelli will make us coffee while we wait." He led them further into the dining room, where another man set a tray of biscuits at a table beside another pyramid of paint tins.

The redhead laying out plates and spoons on a white tablecloth for a far-too-early afternoon tea had freckles and a heavy Sicilian accent. "*Su 'nglisi. Fossi volunu n'ti*," he said, sounding as if he had marbles in his mouth.

Martini hesitated. "Forgive me. You are English. Perhaps you want tea?"

"Coffee," Kitt said, "will be fine."

"It is no trouble. Tomelli will make what you like."

"Mr Kitt prefers coffee, Mr Martini," Mae said.

"Espresso then. And for you, Mrs Valentine?"

"Coffee, thank you."

"*Allora*." He held up four fingers and waved the redhead away. "Please, Mrs Valentine." He pulled out a chair for Mae and sat opposite her. "Forgive this great confusion...mess, I think mess is a better word. Forgive the mess in here." He lifted a white cloth napkin from beside his small plate and laid it in his lap. "The painters will not be back until Monday, but the kitchen is open, and Mr Torrisi is a fine cook. He hinted that he would make you *pasta con cavolfiore, uvetta e pinoli. Uvetta* are raisins, and *pinoli* are pine nuts. Do you know *cavolfiore*? Sicilians say *calisciuri*. I cannot remember the English word. It is a white vegetable, with little bushes, like broccoli, but shorter."

"Cauliflower?" Kitt took the chair beside Mae, watching her tuck her handbag beneath her seat.

"Yes, that is it." Martini looked over the selection of biscotti on the table and put two on his plate. "Have you tried *paste di mandorla*, these almond cookies? They are very popular in Sicily." He nibbled the sugar-dusted biscuit and glanced past them. "*Solo, li, per favore*," he said to the man who had been washing shit from his car.

Solo placed a brown paper gift bag on the empty seat beside his boss and sauntered out of the dining room.

Martini had a look inside the bag and nodded to himself before he put it back on the seat. "I hope you do not think me rude, but I am curious," he said, lifting the napkin to wipe sugar dust from his fingers.

"I am so glad I'm not the only one," Kitt rubbed a finger across his bottom lip.

"What makes you curious, Mr Martini?" Mae glanced at Kitt.

"Why you are here. It is not my business, and yet I am curious. Pippino—Mr Torrisi—tells me so little and sometimes asks for a lot."

"It's an awkward matter," Kitt said.

"Yes. It was mentioned you were awkward. *Oh.* I think I said that wrong. Didn't I? I believe I meant delicate, but I am not sure that is correct either. Ah, the coffee."

Tomelli had returned with espresso on a tray. With the ease of an experienced waiter, he set down a cup and saucer in front of Mae, the same for Kitt, and a larger *caffè Americano* for Martini, who immediately dipped his almond biscuit into the dark brew.

Mae reached for her little cup, and Kitt almost missed it. A foolish, impractical intention was the reason he was here, and that pointless notion had clouded his judgment. Like a volcanic ash cloud, Mae's kiss had dimmed his level-headedness even more. Instead of staying focused he had been distracted by her, and that distraction had brought them here. Then again, perhaps his real undoing was refusing to accept what Bryce suggested as a cold truth; he had passed his use-by date. Whatever the cause, he had almost missed it.

Almost, but not quite.

The shift of Martini's expression was subtle, nothing more than a simple, fleeting flick of the eyes to Mae's espresso. Sugar-laden coffee spoon in his hand, fear flared in Kitt's gut. He knocked the small cup from Mae's hand. A spray of black liquid arced and splattered Martini's white shirt, the china bounced on the floor, and Kitt grabbed her wrist, propelling her up and away. "*Run,*" he said, despite it being far too late to run. He heard the crack of the fist hitting his head above his ear before he felt the jolt of pain and staggered from the force of the blow, careening backwards into Mae.

With a yelp, she slammed into a table with him and tumbled over a chair, smacking her forehead on the edge of another table with a sickening *thud* before she hit the floor.

"Solo!" Martini yelled. "Solo!"

Kitt whirled and ducked Tomelli's left jab. Coffee spoon in his fist, he stabbed upwards and caught the southpaw in the soft flesh beneath his left arm. It didn't penetrate, but the man howled in pain as the spoon's handle dug into his body. The soft metal bent in Kitt's hand. He rammed an elbow into the man's gut, then slammed a knee into Tomelli's nose when he doubled over. Tomelli went down, the centre of his face streaming red.

"Get up, Mae! Run, *run!*" Kitt shouted. He heard Mae scramble to her feet, hollering a string of curses, and he threw himself across the table at Martini.

The legs of Martini's chair had tangled with the drop cloth as he'd stood. "Solo!" he bellowed, biscuits tumbling and scattering as Kitt's momentum pushed him back into his seat. The chair humped and skidded over the drop cloth and toppled them both arse-over into paint tins.

Rolling to his feet, Kitt snatched a tin by its wire handle. He saw

Mae bolt for the stairs, and he swung the paint tin at a rising Martini's head. The man bobbed, feigned right, and hooked left, landing a clout in Kitt's ribs. Grunting, Kitt swung the tin again. It glanced off Martini's shoulder, but set him off balance. Stumbling, his foot tangled in drop cloth, he fell.

Kitt turned, dashed for the stairs. Solo appeared in the dining room entrance with Mae by the hair. Kitt snatched the reservations book from the pedestal and threw it at the colossus. The book hit her before it hit Solo, but it startled him enough to give her an opportunity. Despite his handful of hair, she twisted around, shouting obscenities in Italian, and stepped toward the Sicilian giant, lashing out, her clawed hand raked across his face. He hauled her head backwards, and grabbed her around the throat, dragging her back into the dining room where he pressed a small knife just below her ear, and Kitt knew it was all over.

Solo smiled, his big face a Christmas ham scored by bright red lines.

"You're a goddamn bloody nuisance, Mae," Kitt stared at her, and she stared back at him, angry, frightened, and ready to bite. He felt the same way, but shook his head and flicked his eye to Martini.

She followed his gaze. "Oh, this has gone arseways."

"Yes," Martini nodded. "Good. You see. You understand." He held the empty brown paper packet in one hand and a small black pistol in the other.

Tomelli got to his feet and shook himself. Martini bent and picked up the napkin he had used a few moments before. He pressed it into Tomelli's hand. The man held it to his nose, crossed the room, and backhanded Kitt.

"This would have been easier if you had simply drunk the coffee," Martini sighed.

The inside of his cheek had been pinched between his molars. Kitt ran his tongue over the cut in his mouth. He rubbed his jaw as

Tomelli began to pat him down. The man took Kitt's wallet and mobile, the little Montblanc pen, and the single Euro coin in his pocket. When he came up with nothing else, he looked at Martini and shook his head.

Martini jerked his chin at Solo. Solo pulled the knife away from Mae's throat. He shoved her towards Kitt.

She lurched over bunched-up drop cloth. Kitt steadied her before she fell on her arse. "What did you put in the coffee?" he said, taking Mae's hand.

Martini tossed aside the paper bag and brushed off his creased trousers. He smoothed his hands down the wrinkles. "Lorazepam." He looked up. "You were worried it was sodium hydroxide?"

"Something like that," Kitt said.

"Oh Jaysus, feckin' drain cleaner." Mae swallowed. "So much for being polite."

Sniffling and dabbing his bloodied nose, Tomelli went and righted the table Kitt had upended. He put Kitt's things on the tabletop, pulled everything out of the wallet, then lifted Mae's handbag, turned it upside down, and shook out the contents. He looked through her wallet, poked through her coins, studied her driving licence, and rummaged through the cosmetics bag holding the make-up they'd bought yesterday. Helping himself to one of her mints, he tossed aside the napkin he'd used to staunch his bleeding nose, and lifted a tiny white object. He pulled off the cellophane and stuffed it in one nostril, leaving the tampon's pale blue string dangling above his lip.

Solo laughed.

Martini told him to go wash his face, put on a clean shirt, and come back.

Tomelli moved away from the table and left the dining room. The blue string fluttered as he passed by.

Mae knew she ought to be more frightened than she was. She

was plenty scared; the sweat on the back of her neck and between her breasts was cold, but foremost in her mind was how she and Kitt had been such trusting idiots. It was startling to realise precisely what a gullible fool she was. Kitt was here because she was here. Outrage that she'd been taken in by a seemingly helpful man *again*, and the indignation over her own idiocy, tipped the scale on fear. For now. She wondered when that would shift.

Kitt pulled her to his side and kept an arm about her waist. "Here's where I'd better earn my five pounds," he muttered.

"You are not her brother," Martini said.

"No, I am not." Kitt spat out a glob of blood.

"And this little gun?" Martini raised the pistol, nose pointing to the ceiling. "It was in inside your car."

"I hired the car. The Beretta is a standard feature."

"You are very humorous," Martini said, looking down at the crushed almond biscuits on the blood-dappled drop cloth beneath his feet. He crouched, picked up two unbroken *paste di mandorla* and rose. "I think you are a professional, Mr Kitt. You did not make the bruises on her face. You are here to safeguard such a thing does not happen again. You are her bodyguard."

"I'm her employer."

With a smirk, Martini said, "You show unusual regard for your employee. What does she do for you?"

Kitt glanced at Mae. "She scrambles my eggs."

"Forgive me. My English is sometimes lacking. Cos' è...what is *scrable*?"

"Scramble." Kitt gestured, gripping an imaginary whisk, his right wrist moving in a rapid circular motion.

"Ah." Martini and the other man laughed. "*Lei fa una sega.* Okay," Martini said. "How much *salario*, how much you pay her for that?

"*Cretino!*" Mae snapped. "Scrambled eggs. *Uovoa strapazzate.*"

Martini quit smirking and making crude remarks about hand jobs and blow jobs. He pursed his lips. "You speak Italian?"

"*Certo*. Of course."

"*Sai cucinare pasta al sugo*?"

"Yes, you bloody *bestia*," she said. "I can make pasta with sauce." Mae had forgotten where she was and what some of the men in this country could be like. She'd forgotten why she'd asked Kitt to assist her. Martini reminded her of the where, what, and why.

He grinned. "How nice. I like a woman who can cook. I like a woman who can keep her mouth shut even more." He looked at the two young men, at the large aquarium with its single fish, then at Kitt again, and his grin grew wider. "I would be so pleased if you would do both. I confess that Mr Torrisi is not able to join us to make lunch. I would prefer a simple sauce to his with cauliflower. I do not like cauliflower."

"Why will he not be joining us, is he dead?" Kitt tightened his arm around Mae.

Martini adjusted the collar of his shirt. "Is that why you are here, Mr Kitt? To kill Mr Torrisi?"

"This is diabolical," Mae said pulling away. "This is a nothing more than a terri—"

Kitt yanked her back, his arms around her waist, crown of her head at his chin. "Let him talk."

Martini nodded. "Yes, woman. Let the men talk or I will have Solo take your tongue." He blew fuzz off one of the biscuits, took a bite, and licked his lips. "Yes. I know it is *sessista* and *offensivo*." He brushed powdered sugar from his fingertips. "I do not like threatening a woman. It makes me uneasy, but believe me, it is not a concern for Solo. Nothing is a concern for Solo. That is why he is here. As I said before, it would have been easier had you drunk the coffee. We would have had lunch, you would have been relaxed, and remembered none of this. Now, Mr Kitt, you told Luca, Mr

Torrisi's office assistant, a story. You said Mrs Valentine wanted to move her husband's grave. You said you wanted to see Mr Torrisi because the grave is beside his uncle's. Am I wrong?"

"You are correct. That is what we told Luca, and that is why we are here. That is what we came here to discuss with Mr Torrisi. His uncle is in the grave beside Mrs Valentine's husband."

"Mm." Martini pulled down the corner of his mouth and bobbed his head, shrugging his shoulders. "Yes, we checked that. We checked the names in the cemetery in Linguaglossa. There is only one thing. This is a small place. News goes everywhere fast. A baker was killed in San Giovanni. A man and *una bionda*, a blonde woman, were seen leaving the baker." He looked at Mae. "Mrs Valentine is blonde and you are a man. A man and a blonde woman were seen at Mr Torrisi's office in Taormina before the protestors came. A man and a blonde woman were seen at Mr Torrisi's office after the protestors came. And now Luca is dead." He crossed his arms and gazed at them both. "You do not seem surprised to hear this news," he said.

"That could be because you've shocked us with your hospitality."

"Yes. Maybe, Mr Kitt. You see my dilemma. But what of the baker? I cannot remember his name." He looked over at the muscle-man. "*Come si chiama*, Solo?"

"Russo." Solo offered.

"There is a Russo buried in the cemetery beside Mrs Valentine's husband, but what of the Russo in San Giovanni? Did you tell him the same story before you cut off his hand and killed him? Which did you do first, kill him or cut off his hand?"

The sense of fury that had been leading the race inside Mae went lame, and fear crossed the finish line. She smelled her own stinking, lathering, ice-cold sweat. "We haven't killed anyone," she said, her mouth dry.

"I like this word, *scramble*. I must remember it. Mr Kitt. Remind your employee to stay quiet because another word and I will have Solo, my employee, take her tongue and *scramble* her brain."

"That won't be necessary." Kitt pressed Mae's spine close to his chest. "But she's right. We haven't killed anyone, and this is all an extraordinary mistake. You'll most likely see that explanation as something we are improvising to save ourselves."

Mae understood. He was improvising, doing his damnedest to keep her safe—to keep them safe. Now her sense of fear was a thing inside her brain and body screaming at her to fight, fight, fight, then run, run, run, and he was improvising. Just what the hell he was improvising, she had no idea, but she was smart enough to know that trying to run away could get them both shot. She looked back at him, at his maddening nonchalance and coolness and wished to Jesus that it would wash over her too. Maybe he knew that, maybe he was trying to do that, because he bent around and kissed her cheek.

Martini placed a hand over his heart. "I see. That is how it is for you," he said. "I should have guessed. My vulgar remarks were uncalled for because this is true love."

Mae made an incoherent sound.

"So then, Mr Kitt, you are saying this, you being here is *un coincidence*?"

Mae watched Kitt smile broadly. It was a casual expression she knew was fuelled by rage, menace, and hatred. "It's one hell of a coincidence," he said.

"It might be, but there is something you are not telling us." Martini smiled back. "This little pistol says you are not telling us everything we need to know. Why do you have this?"

"Someone tried to kill Mrs Valentine," Kitt said. "We think that same person killed Mr Russo, and we came here to warn Mr Torrisi we think he could be next."

Martini stroked his chin, his mouth twisting contemplatively. "That is quite creative. And why did you not go to the police if you feared for Mrs Valentine's life?"

"We did. The police refused to believe her."

"Convenient and *fantastico*, but no matter how *fantastico*, I am willing to listen to you explain further. *Allora*. I am hungry. I am certain we are all hungry. These biscotti—not something typically served before lunch. So we will have a simple pasta, a little discussion, and some fun for lunch." He waved Solo over. "Solo, let us take these two down to the kitchen," he said in Italian. "But first, show them the photo on your little smartphone."

"Get ready to run," Kitt said softly against Mae's temple. "Don't turn around, don't wait for me, just run. I'll be right behind you." He loosened his hold on her and ignored the contrary squint staring back at him.

Solo approached, a mobile phone in his hand. "Look, do you know this person?" he said, holding out the phone.

Mae's head swivelled around. She leaned forward slightly, for a better view of the screen and the image of an Asian man in profile. Tomelli re-entered the dining room. Kitt caught the man's movement, the upward swing of his left arm. So did Mae. She shoved Kitt hard, but not hard enough. The C2 Taser's metal probes struck his stomach and chest, just below his left clavicle. Fifty thousand volts jolted his sensory and motor nerves, shocking the neurological impulses directing muscle movement, disabling him. Kitt went down, screaming.

CHAPTER FIFTEEN

"Please stop doing that," Mae said through her teeth.

She sat at the table, her hands folded in her lap, Kitt opposite her, flanked by Tomelli and Solo, his hands cuffed behind his back, his forehead on the table. Despite this, despite the probes and the wires that led back to the Taser Tomelli had fired a third time, the two men played it safe and kept their distance from him.

"Yes, yes, stop now. Put it away," Martini said.

Kitt waited for the dizziness to fade, for muscle contractions to subside. Tomelli ripped the probes from his back and Kitt lifted his head. He watched Martini pull out the chair to Mae's left.

The man stroked his chin after he was seated. "Now, back to business. That was a fascinating tale from you both," Martini said. "One we will have to verify. In the meantime, I understand your Gandhi-style protest of peace, Mrs Valentine, b—"

"*I got the devil in me,*" Solo's phone announced. "*I got the devil in me!*"

Martini threw up his hands. "*Ma,* Solo, how can I be menacing when you've got Zucchero announcing you're possessed?" he said in Italian.

"*Scusi, scusi.*" Solo dragged his mobile from his jeans. "*Pronto?*" he said, the toothpick between his teeth waggling.

Fingers drumming, Martini waited.

Solo shoved his phone back into place. "Vivi is coming."

"That woman! I told her I would see to this!" Martini rolled his eyes and turned his attention back to Mae. "Where was I? Ah, your peaceful protest, Mrs Valentine. You are a fine-looking woman."

Tomelli snorted. "*Cia cinquanda anni,*" he muttered with marbles-in-his mouth Sicilian.

Martini's eyes walked all over her, appreciatively, lingering on peekaboo glimpse of her breasts in the criss-crossing neckline of her green dress. "You look good for your age." He held up a hand. "No. I said that badly. I do not know why this expression is used. That is very American thinking. One should simply say 'you are a fine-looking woman.' A woman's age is not a matter in Italy. You are a very fine-looking woman, like Monica Bellucci, but smaller and blonde."

Mae glanced at the two thugs near Kitt and swallowed.

Martini drew his chin back and shook his head. "Now you worry. I see that you worry." He waved his hand. "We are not professionals like Mr Kitt, and we are not *animali*. I am happily married, and I love my wife. Tomelli has just returned from the *luna di miele*, the honeymoon. And Solo, he likes boys."

"*Stu cazzo!* What the fuck, not boys, men!"

"Forgive me, Solo," Martini clasped his hands together and returned his attention to Mae. "I admire your passive demonstration, *Signora*," he said, "but I will tell you why you will be happy to cook for us."

He leaned close to her, blocking Kitt's view of her for a moment, until the man bent and put his mouth beside her ear. He said something, and Mae's head snapped up, her eyes shifted from Martini, and she stared at Kitt, her lips parting. Her colour had been high. Kitt watched the blood drain from her face.

Martini sat back and waited.

Blinking, Mae inhaled, clenched her jaw, and stood. "I'd like an apron," she said.

"*Splendido*," Martini smiled and clapped his hand together. Then he turned back to Mae. "I will take you to the kitchen, and the boys will introduce Mr Kitt to Shirley Bassey."

MARTINI SWITCHED on an old radio cassette-player tuned to a pop music station playing a song about Grace Kelly. The restaurant's downstairs kitchen was professional stainless steel and white tiles. Sound bounced off the gleaming walls. Unlike the old factory machinery they'd passed on their way to the kitchen, the kitchen equipment was glowing metal state of the art, save the long wooden table that was used as a work surface and a dining table for staff.

The food resources were limited, but Mae put together *pasta puttanesca*. The radio blared as she cooked and set the table for five under Martini's silent, watchful eye. Twenty minutes after she began preparing food, Tomelli and Solo returned, without Kitt. In his stead, Tomelli had a roll of silver gaffer tape, and Solo had a very heavy, very stupefying slap that made the universe explode inside her head.

At the edge of a glittering darkness Mae felt herself being manhandled. The bursting, spiralling universe shrank back down to a galaxy, then to a planet, and finally to a converted warehouse on an island in Italy as Tomelli dragged her down a hallway, across a factory floor, and tossed her inside a black room. She landed hard on her coccyx, and the door slammed. The bolt and padlock on the outside clattered and banged.

Head aching, tailbone smarting, gaffer tape pulling at her skin, she sat up and waited for the nausea to pass, waited for the throbbing in her jaw to subside, waited for her eyes to adjust to the dark. The room stank. A tiny red light shone in the dark and a crack of light came through the bottom of the door.

She had a few choices. There was crying and wallowing in fear and pity, which would solve nothing and change nothing. There was screaming with the hope that someone—besides the three men having their lunch—heard her. Then there was the practical activity of getting free of the gaffer tape.

It was a small step that might lead to something useful.

A little unsteady, she got up. Her bottom was wet. Mae stood, feet apart, knees slightly bent, and brought her bound hands up over her head, elbows to her ears. Sean had once described having to do what she was about to try. It sounded simple, and she hoped to Jesus Christ Almighty her brother hadn't been lying.

She took a deep breath, jerked her arms down to her sides and pulled back at the same time. She punched herself in the stomach, but the tape ripped. Her hands were free. She peeled off the sticky strips and let them fall to the floor.

Her fingers reeked of the garlic she had chopped twenty minutes earlier. Stinking hands thrust out, she moved toward the door, touched the wall beside it, and felt about until she found a light switch. Then a dim light painted the room with a ghastly, catacomb-like glow that reflected off puddles on the floor. The humid, smelly space was stocked with large bottles of cleaning products. Buckets and brooms were gargoyles and grotesques watching all, the red light on a rechargeable hand vacuum fixed to the wall a staring evil eye, the mop leaning in the corner a freakishly bony Medusa with wilted hair.

While eerie and unpleasant smelling, the room was not as disturbing as the sight of Kitt, as limp as the mop, slumped in a chair he'd been secured to.

"Kitt?" she said, prickling with fresh terror. She waited for him to make a dry comment, to moan, to something, to *anything*. Head down, Kitt remained hunched forward, lifeless.

Rankling fear infused with a jolt of desperation, and Mae hurried to him, tripping over an upended bucket, falling hard on warm, wet concrete, splitting the skin on her kneecap. "Please," she murmured on her hands and knees, ignoring the sharp pain, "please. I don't want do this again. I've already loved one dead man. Don't you be dead. Please don't be feckin' dead."

His head lifted and fell back between his shoulders. "I'm not bloody dead, Mae."

Heart drumming in her chest and temples, Mae rubbed the stinging knee she'd split open. "You look dead."

"I'm," he groaned, "resting."

"Resting, like that?"

"I was a little tired. Why the hell are you still here?"

"I wasn't exactly able to leave."

"Where are they?"

"In the kitchen. It's lunchtime. This is Italy. Pasta trumps work. They'll eat, have a rest, and then kill us."

"I love Italy." He tilted his head to the left and then right, stretching his neck, sucking air between his teeth. "Lunch means we have time."

Mae got up and wiped her hands on her dress. "Time for what, to sit here and ponder dying? She was responsible for him, for what happened to him, for his being trussed up and beaten, for the blood that oozed from the cut on his head and crusted around his nose. Every part of this was on her—and he made jokes. "We are going to die, aren't we?"

"Yes. We're going to die." Turning, he looked at her over a shoulder. "But not today." He started to laugh. "That was terribly hackneyed, wasn't it?"

Mae would have been sick if there'd been anything in her stomach.

"They may hurt us, but they've no intention of killing us. They simply mean to put the fear of God into us," he said.

"This may be a shock, but I don't find you amusing at the moment."

"I find your profession of love for me amusing. Let's talk about that."

She stared at him and came closer. "My profession... Did you have a dream while you were slumped there lifeless? Were we walking along a beach, sipping piña coladas as the sun set when I declared feelings of deep and enduring tenderness for you?"

"I don't like piña coladas," he said, twisting his hands, feeling his fingers. "And I dreamt nothing. You said you love me."

"I said nothing of the sort."

"You did. I heard you. Maybe you didn't use those exact words, but your meaning was clear, and it is rather...sweet." He kept on laughing, his hands twisting. "Mrs Fairfax? No, you're Jane Eyre."

"You may not be dead, but it's obvious you are punch-drunk."

"Are you hurt badly, Mae?" His hands stopped twisting for a moment.

"No. Martini was very polite when he forced me to make lunch. I would have spit in the spaghetti, but I didn't have any spit."

"Forced you how? Held a gun to your head, sexually assaulted you?"

She was quiet for a moment.

"Mae?"

She rubbed her face with her garlicky hands. "Before you get angry and tell me I should have run whenever I had the chance, let

235

me tell you what Martini said before they took you out of the room. He told me if I tried to fight or run, Solo would peel off your face with a fish scaler and feed it to the bass in the aquarium in the dining room. He said Solo would cut off your hands and use them as bait. He said Solo would hang you upside down and slit your throat while I watched the blood drain from you. So I cooked them lunch."

His hands began moving again. "I'm sorry."

"You're sorry? You're only here because of me. What did they do to you?"

"They gave me a thrashing and tried to drown me in the fish tank with Shirley Bassey. That's the name of the fish in the tank upstairs. Then they brought me here, secured me to this chair, wrapped a towel around my head, and poured buckets of water over my face."

"Oh, God."

Kitt looked to his left, to where she stood beside him, weirdly backlit by a nightlight tinged with red. She breathed deeply, inhaling and exhaling slowly. "That's good," he said. "Do that. Keep breathing."

"Is that what you did when they tried to drown you, practiced deep breathing?"

"No. I held my breath."

Her question had been stupid, and his comment was smart-arsed. Mae moved closer and laid a hand on his cheek. "Jaysus. Oh, Jaysus. What did I get you into?"

"It's not the first time I've been beaten, Mae. I've had worse. You've seen me."

"And always you're so cool about it. Have other eejits tried to waterboard ya? Has that happened to ya before?"

"Yes." He kissed the inside of her wrist and smelled garlic. "I like you angry. You're so Irish. I'm waiting for you to say '*what the feck are ya doin?'* The answer is, getting us out of here by picking the lock on these handcuffs."

She pulled her palm away and bent to have a look at his hands. The hardwood chair he was secured to had a criss-crossed back, his hands fed through and cuffed on both sides of the X. "What are you using to pick these things?"

"The toothpick Solo gouged into the back of my hand."

"The toothpick he had in his mouth?"

"Yes."

"Well, that's disgusting."

"And so far, it's too soft, but one just needs a pin or a sliver of something to shove...into...the...lock."

She sighed. "There it is, that supreme confidence of yours. To think I used to like it, but at the moment I find it irritating."

"You doubt that I can pick the lock? Think positively, Mae. Picking the mechanism on handcuffs is easy, but I need you to find something sturdier than this damn toothpick. It's far too soft and if it breaks... Do you happen to have a hairpin?"

"No." Trickles of perspiration dribbled down her back and between her breasts. The room was airless, smelled faintly of fish and wet mop in need of disinfecting. Mae found it odd the strongest odour wasn't her garlicky hands, or fish, or manky mop, but her own sweat. Fear had a definite smell, a sharp, vinegary smell that held a tinge of something metallic. She went to the shelving and began to feel the edges for loose screws or wire. "All right. I am positive that you've picked handcuffs before, but even if I find something, I don't know what good that's going to do us since we're locked in a storage room. Can you pick padlocks on the outside of a door as well?"

"The door may not be a problem."

"Because your skill to pass through doors is equal to your ability to read minds. I'm so glad to hear that." She snorted, wiping sweat from her mouth with her shoulder, shoving bottles aside and feeling around on the shelves.

"I might surprise you this time."

"You constantly surprise me, Kitt."

"I like to think that's a good thing because I've surprised myself. I suppose because I've never had to be concerned with anyone's welfare besides my own. I don't seem to be very good at looking after anyone but myself. Or maybe I'm merely getting old and slow." Kitt ran his tongue over the cut inside his cheek. The inside of his mouth felt like an old man's mouth. All over, he ached; he ached like an old man who couldn't remember if he'd ached this much when he was younger—although it had been a while since he'd been thrashed, and even longer since he'd been and half-drowned, and recalling how it felt to be thrashed and half-drowned wasn't something he ever committed to memory when he was younger. Kitt exhaled. "The door is hollow. We can kick our way through it. Are you scared, Mae?"

"I'm terrified. Aren't you?"

"Of course. I'm very afraid, and I was very afraid for you, but fear has energy. Use it, act on it. Don't let it get the better of you."

She groaned. "You sound like Sean."

"How long has your brother been a priest?"

"Thirty-six years. Don't change the subject. Have you picked the cuffs yet?"

"No," Kitt laughed. Have you found anything I can use to pick them?"

"No.

He exhaled. "Try the metal bucket, Miss Eyre."

"Sir, please."

"Sir? We're back to *sir*, Jane?"

"This is not funny." Mae moved to the bucket and pulled out the stinky mop and dropped it on the slippery floor. She lifted the metal pail and searched for anything she could break off, trying to bend the handle.

Kitt gave a little chuckle. "It's a fitting way for me to meet my end, you declaring your love for me."

"You said we weren't going to die today."

"These people don't want to kill us. If they wanted to kill us we'd be dead already. They wanted to find out what we knew. They wanted to scare the hell out of us because someone already tried to kill Torrisi. Try the mop."

Mae grabbed the smelly Medusa-like mop. "We know fuck all."

Kitt ignored her comment because the overhead fluorescent light flickered on and continued flickering as the padlock rattled on the other side. Kitt swore. "Lunch appears to be over. I wonder what's for dessert."

Solo entered the room, a baseball bat in his chubby hand. Breathing heavily, he wiped his nose on his shoulder. His dark eyes darted from Mae to Kitt.

Mop tight in her hands, she stood in front of Kitt. "You said these people wanted to scare us, and hurt us a little, but he looks like he wants to kill us."

"I stand corrected. Move, Mae. Get out of the way."

"Like hell I will," she said, standing her ground as if she were an Amazonian.

Solo, the Sicilian Goliath, took a deep breath, blew it out though his pursed lips. He took two steps and swung, striking the mop handle Mae used to deflect the bat's blow. The mop snapped in two. Holding the bat vertically, with both hands, he rammed forward into her chest and drove her back into the shelves. She hit the metal unit hard, bottles of cleaning liquid tumbling down onto her, and bouncing and rolling. The man kicked them out of the way before he kicked her in the stomach.

Bat raised, Solo turned for Kitt.

Gasping, nauseous, Mae threw a bottle at Solo, an arc of pink liquid sprayed out of the open top and splattered across the floor. The scent of roses filled the air.

Kitt had jerked sideways, tipped over the chair, and crashed to the damp concrete. Hunched over on his feet, the bat struck the chair instead of his head. The chair's back broke and Kitt tore his arms free of the wood.

Solo lifted the bat again and slipped on the wet and soapy floor. Kitt scrabbled backwards, lurching and skidding on the slick underfoot. He used the wall for leverage to get to his feet. Another bottle of cleaner exploded when it hit the ground. A thick streak of pink splattered Kitt's neck and chest as he dropped, swept out with his left foot, and took Solo down. The man hit the hard floor beside him. The bat spun through the viscous goop and stopped beneath a shelf. Kitt tried like hell to gain some kind of traction on the slippery concrete. The instant he was on his feet again, Solo was on him, huge hands driving him against the wall and down to the floor, pressing him to the slick, rose-perfumed concrete. Fat fingers squeezed, thumbs gouging into his windpipe. Arms pinned beneath his back, hands cuffed, Kitt shoved a knee into the man's abdomen and planted a foot in his hip, pushing and twisting. The heavy man went with him and threaded his legs through Kitt's knees, locking his ankles around his shins, pelvis on his stomach. The choking pressure increased, cutting off Kitt's breath, cutting off the blood to his brain.

There was a fleck of parsley in Solo's teeth. Kitt watched the blot of green shift to dots of grey. The dots turned to fog. Amid the darkening haziness he saw Mae with the broken mop, the head of it limp. She swung the sharp end, aiming for the man's skull.

And missed.

The handle struck Solo's back and Mae skated one way, then the other, and fell. Broken wood pierced Kitt's shoulder. The wet, dank end of the mop skimmed over his face. Through the rushing noise in his head, Kitt heard Mae scream. In his dealing with the matter of his butler, he'd failed her. Miserably. He'd tried to keep her from harm and put her directly in harm's way. Now she would likely die the same way he was—only he wasn't dying. Christ, he was angry. He was angry and disappointed and frightened for Mae, so frightened. He bucked and twisted and pushed and wondered why it was taking so damned long to die.

CHAPTER SIXTEEN

Kitt tasted perfume. Something whined beside his ear and something very heavy sat upon his chest, making it quite difficult to breathe. He was lying on his arms, his hands fizzing as if they were asleep.

He opened his eyes.

Disoriented, a weight pressed on his throat, the cloying scent of roses assailed his nostrils. Mae knelt beside him. The howling rechargeable hand-held vacuum she gripped looked like a science fiction space weapon—a broken space weapon. The barrel of it was sheared off so that all was left was the handle and the motor. A tuft of bloody scalp from the man collapsed on his chest was stuck to the carbon fibre motor-head. Blood streaked Mae's chin, splattered stripes of red stained the front of her green dress. Kitt remembered the last few minutes and why he had a muscle-bound lad on his chest. He offered Mae a smile of sorts.

She switched off the vacuum, half-laughing, half-crying. "Oh, thank Jaysus,"

"Get this thing off me," he said, hoarsely.

Mae tossed the machine aside and began to shove Solo's inert body. Kitt bent a knee and twisted. Solo flopped onto the concrete, rolled onto his back, and stared vacantly, one eye askew. His head was a mess of blood and brain and matted hair.

Kitt wondered how many times Mae had hit the man before he fell.

Grunting as he sat up, he felt the splinter of wood embedded in his shoulder. Before he made the suggestion, Mae was already going through the dead man's pockets, pulling out loose change, a spent tissue, a folding knife with a bone handle, and a little key. When she'd freed his hands from the handcuffs, Kitt groaned, arms stiff and aching. With a snarl, he yanked out the wooden shard. Blood flowed and joined the stain of pink hand soap. Unsteady, he rose. She put an arm about his waist to give him support, and he turned, pulling her close, holding her for a long moment.

Shaking, she held on tightly, face pressed to his bloodied chest.

"Right," he said. "Right." He let her go, bent, and retrieved Solo's knife. There was blood on the bone handle. "Let's get the hell out of here." He grabbed her hand and took care crossing the soapy concrete. In a moment, they were walking across the floor of a factory that had once processed seafood.

"There." She pointed. "The garage door over there." The roller door in the far corner looked promising, but a chain and lock secured it. A short distance further, the emergency exit had been wedged open, but bickering voices on the other side meant the only option was to leave the way they had entered. They turned back toward the corridor that would lead them past the kitchen where pop music blared.

Tomelli sat with his back to the door. He ate the tomato and anchovy pasta Mae had cooked straight out of the pot, and thumbed through a pornographic magazine, nodding along to Cher asking if he believed in life after love. A small, black 9mm pistol—the same one Solo had appropriated from the VW and given to Martini—lay on the table beside a half-eaten plate of spaghetti.

Kitt pulled Mae from the doorway, backtracking a few steps. He pressed his mouth to her ear. "Wait here. And I mean *wait here.*"

She dug fingers into his arm and yanked him down, saying in his ear, "No."

He rubbed drying speckles of blood from her chin. "There's a gun in there, Mae. Wait here."

Mae watched him creep back to the kitchen. He looked back at her once and darted into the kitchen. Tomelli swore, "*Cazzo!*" There was a frightening *ka-blam-ka-blam* of gunshots. The man shouted "*Cazzo, Madre di Dio, ti mazzo!*" The gun fired again. Then came a series of metallic clicks. The small pistol hit the door's frame. Chairs scraped across tiles and feet shuffled while two men grunted. There was hollow-sounding *clang* that cut through Cher's autotune-manipulated, reverberating voice and then Kitt swore.

The pot that had contained pasta rolled across the kitchen tiles, past the weapon, and out into the hallway. There was a shout of pain, then a sharp cry. Mae snatched up the little gun and skidded into the kitchen, the weapon thrust out in both hands.

Nose bleeding, Kitt stood behind the shorter man, immobilising him with an arm around his chest. He twisted Solo's knife in Tomelli's throat and Mae choked on her own spit.

Strands of spaghetti hung from Kitt's ear, tomatoes and anchovies atop his head. He turned, his face awash with blood. "Oh, Christ!" he said over Cher's echoing *Afterloveafterloveafterlove* and lowered the twitching man to the floor. "Don't you ever bloody do as you're told?"

All Mae saw was blood. Beneath Kitt's feet, on his face, down his chest, his right side was a sheet of blood, and Mae couldn't tell whose blood it was. She lowered the pistol, took a long, deep breath, filling her lungs like the ship she stood upon was about to sink into a raging ocean, and went to him. Quickly.

"Where?" she demanded, inspecting him, pulling pasta from his skin, looking for a hole, a gash, a slice, for ripped flesh, for protruding organs...finding only blood. She ran her hand up his chest and down his ribs, across his abdomen and around to his back. "Where are you hurt?"

"I'm fine."

"You're *not* fine."

"Stop fussing. He only bloodied my nose," he said. "Now give me that thing." Kitt tried to prise the Beretta from her hand. "Come now. Let go."

"It's stuck."

"It's also empty. It's had its six shots. It's useless, unless you want a hammer. Let it go, Mae. My nose isn't broken. I promise I'm as fine as I can be." He held her troubled gaze, wrapped a hand around her wrist and squeezed tightly. After a moment, her fingers relaxed. He pulled the Beretta free and tucked it in the waistband of his trousers. "Let's go."

She nodded and hurried behind him, holding his hand, going up stairs to the dining room. Mae faltered as she passed the fish tank and puddles of water all on the floor beneath it. Then she stumbled to a halt when she saw Aurelio Martini sitting at the same table they all had before.

His once crisp white shirt had been stained by coffee, but a wet scarlet bloom covered the blemishes and gleamed in the overhead light. Tiny bubbles of blood sat at the corner of Martini's mouth.

Mae waited for some sense of horror to kick in, waited to have some kind of reaction to finding another dead man, but nothing remotely horrifying registered. In fact what she felt was the opposite of horror, and smug satisfaction was far more disturbing. She pulled away from Kitt. His mobile, wallet, the Montblanc pen, her handbag and all its contents lay in front of the man. She went to retrieve the things.

Kitt missed snatching her elbow. "What the hell are you doing?" he said, and Martini opened his eyes.

The man spoke in Italian, rasping. "*Devi lasciarmi.*" He took a breath and the hole in his chest made a sucking sound. "Leave me," he said. "Vivi is here. You must go. Solo will kill you as he has killed me, and then he will kill my friend Pippino." He breathed again and his chest slurped.

Kitt examined the man's injuries. He'd been shot twice. "You have a serious wound to your liver and a punctured lung."

"Yes. I am drowning," Martini said in English. "It is *ironico*, is it not?" He smiled. Blood stained his teeth. "I am sorry. It was a mistake. I know it was. I believe you. I believe what you told me."

"Why do you believe us now?" It was futile, but Kitt found a napkin on the floor and pressed it to the man's abdomen.

"Because he wants us to help him," Mae said, sweeping their things into her handbag.

"You cannot help me, can you, Mr Kitt?" Martini's face contorted.

"No." Kitt applied firm pressure anyway.

The man grimaced. "But I can help you. Maybe." Martini ran his tongue over his bottom lip. "There have been threats to Pippino before, but this time was different. I knew that it was. Before, it was neo-nazi *fascisti*, the anti-migrant factions who want to let refugees drown. The police thought the same, but I know the police are part of this. I know a man in the Anti-Mafia Investigation Department. There is corruption, a dirty cop, as Americans say." He hiccupped and coughed. "But Vivi, it is Vivi. His secretary is the architect."

"Vivi, Mr Torrisi's assistant?" Kitt said. "Luca said she made the arrangements for us to come here."

"*Si.* Her."

"She is with the police?"

"No. She is a pain in the ass. Pippino refused to see her as I have. He believes she is a tender-hearted young widow, but I know her. She is very smart. She has made me a good deal of money, but she is *doppiogiochista*, two-faced. She arranged this. She arranged it all. Solo is *nipote*, the nephew to her dead husband. So is Tomelli. The woman has many nephews." He drew in a harsh hissing breath. "Pippino gives them all jobs when Vivi asks. She has been a sweet little baby sister to him, and he could not say no, but she and Solo killed the baker and Luca. I do not know the reason why she would do this, but, Mrs Valentine, they spoke your name." He gasped. "She told Solo to kill you both."

Voices, a man and woman squabbling, travelled up from the rear of the restaurant, where the back steps led to the kitchen and factory below.

"Go," Martini rasped feebly pushing at Kitt's pressing hands. "*Amonini carusi.* They are coming, Solo, Tomelli, Vivi, and *il cinese...* the Chinese man she quarrels with now."

"Solo and Tomelli are not coming back," Kitt said. He placed Martini's hand over his abdominal wound and stepped back. "But the Chinese man, is he the man in the picture Solo showed us?"

"Yes."

"Who is he?"

The argument became more heated, but the pair had halted and squabbled in one place. "I don't know. I had hoped that you would." Martini's inhale was half-strangled; frothy blood spilled over his bottom lip and ran down his chin. "You must go."

"He's right, Mae. We need to leave."

She moved towards the breathless man. "Were you going to kill us?"

Martini licked at the blood on his mouth. "No. I was going to

247

pay you off. Vivi had other ideas. She let me know them when she got here, as you can see."

Mae swallowed and moved even closer. "We saw the Chinese man last night with a woman and two other men. One of them hit me, and the other tried to have me killed back in England. Do you know a German or Austrian man, a tall, thin man with light brown hair and brown eyes, his name i—"

"Ernst Largo," Martini coughed. "He is from Solda, in the Tyrol in the far north of Italy." He hacked and sprayed blood, stippling Mae's dress and handbag. "He is Pippino's accountant and Vivi's cousin. He is in love with her. They all love her." Gasping, Martini lifted a bloodstained hand and pushed a key fob over the table. "Go. Take my car. Solo disabled yours. Go. Go."

"We're not leaving you here like this," Mae said.

He smiled weakly. "But I am already dead."

Mae looked at Kitt, back at Martini, and shook her head. "We're not leaving you here."

"Tell her I am already dead, Mr Kitt," he said, and the wound in his chest drew and slurped.

Mae stared at Martini and the bickering grew louder, the pair advancing from the level below. "We can't. We can't leave you here."

Kitt swore under his breath. He grabbed Mae around the waist and half-dragged her towards the front stairs, taking her down the steps. He paused at the door, pushed it open and checked the area outside before he pulled her out into the hot summer sun.

A black Mercedes sedan dappled by seabird droppings had blocked in the Beetle. A dark-haired man stood hunched over, peering through the softly tinted glass, into the interior of the car. His head came up. He had a moustache, two black eyes, and a recently broken nose. He froze mid-inhale, a cigarette between his fingers. "*Cazzo Madre di Dio.*" A grey tail of cigarette ash dropping as he stared at them and the Beretta in Kitt's hand.

"That's exactly what I was thinking," Kitt said. "Tell him to lie on the ground."

"*Scendere sul terreno*," Mae hissed.

The man tossed aside his cigarette, brushed tobacco from his moustache, and stretched out on top of gravel, spent matches, and cigarette butts.

"Get in the car, Mae," Kitt said, giving her a little nudge.

"After you shoot him."

"You know I can't."

"Then knock out his goddamn teeth."

"Get in the bloody car, Mae."

She swore and went around to the other side. Kitt climbed into Martini's Maserati as she slammed the door. The black case, the one that had been in the Volkswagen's glovebox, lay on the driver's seat, the extra clip still inside. Kitt tossed it at Mae's feet, reversed, and drove off in a cloud of greyish dust.

Kitt didn't know where they were going. He simply drove away from the old marina restaurant, out of the town, and turned down the first road he came to. He followed the route for a bit then turned down another street that twisted through high grass, dilapidated stone walls, and trees. When he reached a dirt road, he took it and stopped when it ended at the front of a white painted hut half-hidden by a fruit orchard.

CHAPTER SEVENTEEN

Neither of them had said a word since they'd broken into the shack. They'd taken turns in the tiny bathroom at the rear of the furnished hut, showering off blood and God knew what else, leaving their stained clothes on the cracked edge of the old wash-basin before climbing onto the double bed inside, wearing damp old towels.

Kitt fell asleep quickly, his arm around her waist, as if to ensure she wouldn't go anywhere. Mae was too confused, too worried, her brain too occupied to be exhausted or give any consideration to leaving.

She rolled away from his comfort and slid from the bed. Kitt didn't stir. He remained curled on his side, towel still fastened around him. She watched him and wondered how in hell he could sleep so *deeply*. Her mind would not stop trying to put together this puzzle. Her mind would not stop identifying the players. Her mind would not stop replaying the day, the last few days, or the night everything began. Her mind would not stop rolling over the fact that she'd killed two men, had seen Kitt dispatch another, and they'd both left a man to die. Her mind would not stop coming back to the point that all these things had happened—and Kitt slept.

Soundly.

With a huff, Mae squeezed her temples between the heels of her hands. The one-room shack was better appointed than her spartan flat in Linguaglossa, and better decorated too. The large wardrobe at the foot of the bed divided the single room in two and provided privacy from the little kitchen. She went around to the front of the wardrobe and opened the ornately carved doors. One side held drawers of socks, boxer shorts, and tees. The other half was hung with shirts, trousers, and a few other things that belonged to a rather sizeable man.

To the left of the wardrobe sat a wicker basket of clean, rumpled shirts. Mae pulled off her towel. She chose a red-and-white-striped shirt from the pile and put it on. It was huge. She buttoned it, folding the sleeves to her elbows, and took the basket to the other part of the room.

In the kitchen area there was a small table, two chairs, and an upright pantry that had come from an old kitchen. Outside, beneath the covered patio, was a table identical to the one inside. She placed the wrinkled shirts on the outdoor table then went inside to the bathroom, collected the bloodied clothes from the basin and went outside, to the small concrete basin and washing machine on the other side of the French door. A tall cupboard to the right of the washer housed detergent, an iron, and ironing board.

She put Kitt's shirt into the sink to soak and shoved their soiled clothes and towels they'd used into the washer. As laundry churned through the cycle, Mae got to work. There was no thought involved, no concentration necessary; it was all straightforward, mechanical activity she could do with her eyes closed. She found a bottle of spray bleach and cream cleanser at the back of the kitchen sink and tended to the bloody mess they'd left in the bathroom.

When she had finished scrubbing and bleaching away blood and muck, she returned the bleach and cleanser to where she had found them. Then she went to hang the washing on a clothesline stretched between two lemon trees. She found a glass in the kitchen, filled it with water, squeezed in a lemon she'd picked from the orchard, and added mint she taken from a plant near the clothesline. She gathered the creased shirts she'd left on the table, set up the board, and began ironing, a mindless, mechanical, blood-less activity that hurt no one, that had a beginning, and an observ-able end result. Her racing brain began to slow as she sipped water, as she pressed collars and cuffs, as steam flattened wrinkles, as she sharply creased box pleats and placed shirts on hangers she'd found inside the wardrobe.

"Whatever are you doing?"

With a start, Mae turned. Kitt stood in the doorway, squinting in the late afternoon sunlight, the bruising on his neck vivid. He still wore the towel he'd fallen asleep in, wrapped low around his hips. She stared at him, at the contusions, grazes, and scrapes on his chest, at the lumpy scar on his shoulder and the gash she'd made beside it, at the cut above his eyebrow. "Ironing," she said. She turned back to the shirt and ironed around the buttons.

He moved out onto the patio. "What will the owners think when they come here and find the house has been cleaned and work shirts have all been pressed?"

"They'll think the feckin' cleaning and ironing fairy visited." She set the iron down with a bang and slid the shirt on a wire hanger.

He laughed. "Can't you sleep?"

"No, but I know you can, and I don't know how you manage."

"I'm tired. Being almost drowned repeatedly makes one very tired. I noticed you felt the need to scrub the bath tiles with bleach."

"It couldn't stay in the state we'd left it, now could it?"

"Why not?"

"I have some scruples remaining. We've broken into a place belonging to someone who visits it regularly."

He nodded. "On weekdays, mostly, judging by the newspapers I saw on the bedside table. But today's Saturday. Are you angry with me because I slept, Mae?"

"Go back to bed." She moved to a row of shirts she'd hung from the edge of the table. She shoved the shirt she'd finished into the line, jerked his blue shirt from a hanger, and stomped toward him. "Here." She thrust the garment forward. "I did my best with the stains, but I couldn't get them out completely, and there are holes where the Taser hit you."

"You washed my things?"

"There was so much blood." She looked down at the fabric in her shaking hand. She hadn't expected to be shaking. She looked back up to him, her eyes travelling over his chest, up to his mottled throat and into his cool gaze, which wasn't as icy as it had been four hours earlier. Perhaps that was because his eyes were red-rimmed and somewhat swollen. They'd bulged from his face before she'd grabbed the hand vacuum and bashed out Solo's brains. "There was so much blood."

"Yes," he said, tossing the shirt aside, his regard even, his tone matter-of-fact.

"There was so much blood, more than with that man in your kitchen." She walked backwards to the ironing board, staring at him, not understanding why she was so perturbed, because his injuries were nothing really. He'd said it himself. She'd seen him so many times before looking the worse for wear, all battered and bruised, but she stared at the thumbprint-shaped discolourations

253

on his neck, knowing that they were the reason his voice was hoarse, knowing she was responsible for that hoarseness and the gash on his shoulder. And the blood was different this time too because some of it was his, not hers. Some was from the man he'd killed. Some was from the man she'd killed, and that changed everything, that set accountability for death and injury in her hands. "You were covered with blood."

"Yes. But I'm not now."

"It was all over you."

"It was all over both of us, but it isn't now." Kitt knew then he'd made a mistake in thinking that she'd have the same post-adrenaline rush need to sleep that he had. She hadn't yet processed the anxiety or its after-effects. He wasn't quite sure if he had either. "You need some rest. We both do."

"I have to finish this." She pulled a shirt from a wicker basket. "I *need* to finish this."

"Go to bed, Mae. Switch off the iron and come to bed."

"Don't tell me what to do!" She snapped at him over her shoulder and reached back for the iron, grabbing it by the hot base instead of the handle, searing the heel of her palm. She yelped and stumbled into the ironing board, which wobbled and gave up the iron. The power cord stretched and popped out from the point in the wall, the nose of the iron hit the floor and cracked the terracotta patio tile. And then Kitt moved, dragging her to the basin, shoving her hand into flowing cold water.

Mae's Irish was up, and so was her Irish accent, every trace of carefully cultivated, proper Queen's English professional gone as she swore at him, "Ya pigheaded gobshite, why'd ya follow me here?"

"*I'm* pigheaded?" Kitt winced as she tried to wrench from his grip, but he held her hand under the tap.

"What in underfuck did ya think ya were doin'?"

"What did I think *I* was doing?"

"Oh, ya think it's funny repeatin' everythin' I say, do ya?" She squirmed, pulling hard, struggling to twist away from him. "For a risk assessment specialist yer shite assessing risk. Look at yerself! Look! Those yahoos nearly killed ya! I nearly killed ya!"

"Nearly isn't dead."

She went still.

Mae stopped trying to shake off his hold and stared at him, into eyes that were clear, bright blue, and held far, far more than a flicker of warmth. "Almost," she said. "Nearly. Look what I did."

Her breasts rose and fell in the open neck of the old, worn, cotton businessman's shirt she wore. Kitt wondered if she'd ironed the shirt before she'd put it on.

She looked at the top of his head where an egg throbbed and twinged every so often, at the smarting scratches on his cheek, at the blotches he knew mottled his throat. "I did this to you," she said.

"No. You did this to me." He pointed to at the gouge she'd put in his shoulder, just beside the scar from a shrapnel wound he'd sustained three years previously. He let her go and reached around her to shut off the running water. Her wet fingers touched his chest and cool liquid tricked down his skin. Feather-soft, her fingertips traced over abrasions and cuts. He flinched when she reached his shoulder. He shuddered when her thumb brushed over the little split in his chin. He took her damp hand, turned it palm-side up and looked at the burn, which was red, but unblistered. "Does it hurt?" he said, lifting her hand to his lips, blowing on the pad below her thumb.

"Ow," she muttered and met his gaze again.

Kitt liked the sound she made when their mouths met and he didn't pull away, the way he should have. He shifted back and wedged her against the concrete basin before he took her sideways and up a step, setting her against the frame of the open door, almost levelling their height difference. She tasted of lemon and mint, of fear and anger, of fire, so much fire, an astounding amount of fire. He knew which one of them would end up burnt and didn't care.

Mae ran a hand down his spine and tugged at the towel that kept tickling his knees. The cloth came away; she clasped his arse. He yanked at the buttons on her shirt, tearing it open, and she pressed herself close, closer, as if all that mattered was finding a way beneath his skin. Her calf slid up along his, up to his thigh, to his hip. She wore no knickers and that amused Kitt because he had expected to find knickers. He kissed her harder and deeper. Whiskers rasped against her chin, his tongue in her mouth. He pulled back slightly and looked at her breasts, watched his fingers trail over the full, silken skin, listened to her draw a breath, and then he lifted her.

Indoors, she locked her legs around him and bit into his neck, just above his collarbone, and when he reached the edge of the bed and pushed into her, she made the same sound that she had a few minutes before. She'd called him by name. Not *sir* or *Major* or *Kitt*, but his first name, and Christ, closer, he wanted her closer, wanted to be beneath her skin, to turn her inside out and back again, so she would know he was there.

It was an inelegant act, rough, wild, and urgent. Her breaths were short and sharp, like his thrusts, until all at once she was breathless. Then they were both breathless and grunting, and the word 'rutting' sprang to his mind before she called him by name again and a rushing release made him senseless.

He twisted, slipped his weight from her, and settled her alongside him. They lay together, catching their breath, her right leg across his hips, her head on his chest, hand gripping his shoulder. His fingers were buried in her hair, his other hand on her thigh. In a few moments she was asleep, breathing softly and evenly, her body limp.

Kitt closed his eyes. Romantic, idealistic, vain, and her favourite word, *inappropriate*; however he reasoned his actions, all he saw was windmills.

Ten minutes, thirty minutes, or maybe two hours later, he woke with a start as fingers moved across his mouth, down his chin and throat. "Mae," he said.

She sat beside him, the sheet tucked beneath her arms. Her fingers skimmed through the hair on his chest and she tugged strands. "Is this real?"

"It's not glued on."

"I don't mean your hair. I mean this day. It doesn't seem real, it doesn't seem like it's happening. It seems... it seems..."

"It seems what?"

"Like I'm outside myself watching an amateur 3-D thriller. The camera work is terrible." She pressed nails into his chest. Hard.

"Ouch." He pushed her hand away and glanced down at himself. She'd left little crescents in his skin.

"I didn't feel that," she said, frowning.

He sat up. "That's because it's customary to pinch one's self, not gouge others."

"I meant I don't feel you. I don't feel myself. It's as if I'm not here."

"Shall I pinch you?"

"I'd rather you kiss me."

Kitt leaned forward and kissed her softly, scarcely, and as before, even with the barest touch, it was childhood Christmas, springtime sun, summer rain, earth, wind, and all that fire. "Do you feel that?" His mouth drifted across her cheek, leaving a trail of the lightest kisses. When he reached her ear, he paused, took a breath, and then followed the outside shape of her ear. "Do you feel that?"

He kissed her mouth again, moved to the curve of her neck, and began a gentle, exploring descent, easing her back to the mattress.

Mae watched him kiss her breasts, watched him kiss down her bruised torso, watched him raise her knees, push them apart, and smile as he moved to kiss the inside of her thighs. He trailed kisses on her soft flesh until his mouth was buried and nuzzling and suckling. And Kitt watched her. He chuckled when she trembled and shuddered and her knees knocked against his head, and then she shuddered even more.

He lifted his head. "Ah, you felt that."

"Yes," she said.

He smiled with warmth and joy and passion she'd never seen light up his face before, his eyes a vivid blue, and Mae's breath caught in her chest for a different reason.

He crawled beside her, his arms going about her. "You're lovely to watch come undone."

"Would you like to see it again?" she said.

"I would."

She pushed him onto his back, slid on top of him. When she slipped him inside, he began to laugh until she began to move. Then Kitt caught fire and she took her time, letting the smoulder build. Slow, steady, she rocked against him, her hair spilling into her face. His hands went to her hips and she moved them to her breasts. He sat up and she leaned into him, kissing him hard, tangling her tongue with his. He matched her rhythm as she rose and dropped, rose and dropped. He watched her, and she watched him, until he cried out and she gasped, and they both burned alive in a way that made him forget he was a colossal fool full of pointless, tender ideas.

For a little while, the foolish world existed in a bubble neither one of them was ready to burst. He held her close and considered outlandish things, considered his life and the things he valued most.

What he valued most touched the scar above his left eyebrow, "How did you get this?" she said.

"A pub brawl in Haiti. Someone threw a chair. I was in the way."

Her fingers tickled over the bumpy flesh beneath his jawbone. "And this?"

"I walked into a champagne glass in a pub brawl in Macau."

"You walked into it?"

"In a matter of speaking."

She ticked over the scar that bisected the tip of his left ear. "What about here?"

"Ah, that's from a broken bottle of Kalik beer in a pub brawl in Nassau."

"And this one across the bridge of your nose? Did someone hurl a bottle of vodka at you during a pub brawl in Siberia?"

"Oh, no," he waggled a finger. "A *bar* fight in Miami. Man had alligator boots and a big knife. He started it. Actually, they all started it."

"Of course they did. You were just minding your own business, enjoying your drink when someone picked a fight."

"Exactly."

"M-hm. What about these spots here?" She touched tiny dark welts on his chest.

"Buckshot."

"Buckshot in a pub or bar fight?"

"Skiing in Switzerland. Well, skiing and maybe a little trespassing."

Her fingers traced the lumpy circle on his right shoulder, near the flesh she'd broken with a sliver of wood. "And what's this?"

"That. That was a hunting accident outside Istanbul."

"Were you hunting or being hunted? Was there a woman with a husband involved in all these...altercations?"

"I don't kiss and tell."

"No. You just break hearts, and I'm sure you broke their hearts."

"Those women weren't in love with me any more than you are."

She sniffed a tiny laugh and shook her head. "You're a heartache, you know. Nothing but a heartache."

"And you know a heartache when you see one, do you?"

"When it is written as large as you, yes."

"Have you had many lovers, Mae?"

"The things you ask."

"With you knowing my history, it seems a fair question."

Mae regarded him for a moment. I've had a few, but not as many as you." She sat up suddenly, holding the sheet between her arms to cover her breasts. Then she flattened a palm to her forehead. "Oh, what have I just done with you?"

The bubble burst. Or perhaps it merely deflated because she hadn't run screaming from the bed. Whichever it was, he'd ruined it with his talk of history, and it made Kitt oddly sad. "You did what you needed to," he said.

"What I needed to?" Her hand came away from her head, her brows arched. "I had unprotected sex with my employer. I don't think shagging you was something I *needed* to do."

"What you did, what *we* did, was respond to and process the aftermath of a horrifying situation."

"By sleeping together? Unprotected sex. Yes, always an excellent response."

"I assure you there's no chance of my impregnating you."

Her laugh was a single, nasal high note. "*Impregnating* me? Falling pregnant this late in my life, however improbable and potentially disturbing an idea, is the least of my worries. I slept with a man who has a rather long list of bed partners. That perturbs me."

"I am tested regularly and always use protection. Always."

"Except for this time."

"Except for this time. The situation didn't exactly allow time for me to dash to the chemist for a box of condoms."

Mae drew up her knees, clasping her hands around them. "You realise this means I can no longer work for you ever again."

"You're not working for me at the moment. You've taken a leave of absence."

"And a leave of my senses. I liked working for you. I liked it very much. It gave me a sense of purpose."

"These are extenuating circumstances, which I hazard to say are not likely to occur again."

"Twice was already *again*."

He chuckled. "Three, if you count what we did in the middle, but you have a point, and so do I."

"What you must think of me." She shook her head.

"You care what I think of you?" he said, his tone one of surprise.

"I'm concerned that I have somehow breached your trust, taken advantage of that trust, taken advantage of your friendship."

"I have been your employer, we have been friends, and we have been lovers. Now there is another degree of trust involved, an added sense of loyalty, of honesty."

Mae blew hair from her face. "I understand how this works, Kitt. I'm not a twenty-two-year-old girl with romantic fantasies about you. I have no expectations of moonlight, roses, or passionate declarations. I have no expectations of you at all. For anything."

"You should. You should expect that I would not hurt you any more than you would hurt me. The last thing I want to do is hurt you. Have I hurt you?"

"No."

"Did I hurt you?" He trailed a finger down her spine.

"You know you didn't."

"I had to ask."

She cocked her head. "Did I hurt you?"

261

"You have rather sharp teeth." He touched the sensitive spot on his neck, just where the curve of his shoulder began. He wondered if she'd left a bite mark. He liked the idea that she had. "They mean nothing, Mae. Those women. They mean nothing. They're comparable to a delightful meal and nothing more."

"A delightful meal." She scowled. "Why do you say that, why do you tell me they *mean nothing*?"

"Because you are not nothing."

"No. I'm your soon-to-be-ex-butler who sees all and says nothing."

"No, you are my friend." Kitt sat up, the sheet spilling into his lap. "Are you judging me, Mae, finally judging me?"

She licked the corner of her mouth, as if expecting to find a stitch still there, but he'd pulled it out when she'd asked him to after she'd showered. "I think this is more about self-judgment than it is about you. What does it say about me, that I killed a man, left behind another to die, and then toddled off to sleep with my employer? Mother Mary, I killed another man."

"Yes, you did. You killed a man, and then you ironed."

"I killed a man and I liked it." She looked at him, solemn-faced, missing his joke. "I killed him and I feckin' liked killing him."

"No, you didn't."

"Oh, yes." She nodded vigorously. "I did. I liked it. I liked bashing out his brains. It was very satisfying."

"You didn't like it. It was a necessary action. He was trying to kill me, and had he succeeded, he would have killed you. You defended yourself. You're no killer."

Sucking on her bottom lip, she stared at him for a long moment. "But you are."

He nodded, once. "Yes."

"Pub brawls. Bar fights. Guns, knives, and your bare hands... I don't know why I never guessed, how I never saw. You're not simply a retired military officer or a Risk Assessment Specialist, are you?"

"No."

"Then what are you, SAS? SIS, DI, NCA...CIA?"

"Yes."

"Which?"

"Does it matter?"

"How long?"

"Long enough to be thinking I should consider retirement. Especially after yesterday's cock-up."

She unclasped her knees and massaged her temples for a moment. "I meant how long have you been covering your own tracks? That's what you people do to stay covert, isn't it? It seems so bloody obvious now. I bet you started suppressing everything before Sal the Italian died on your kitchen floor. It all began the night outside the Nepali embassy because you couldn't be seen to be part of any confrontation. You took measures to ensure near-silence, made things go away, quashed incident reports, had me released on bail, leaving enough residue behind to explain your involvement in events in a way that's plausible to the police and the public."

"Yes."

"Yes?" Her eyes widened.

"Yes. It's standard practice when a civilian is involved in any incident with an intelligence officer, even a traffic accident," Kitt said. "It's to maintain cover. What happened to you tripped an alarm of sorts. But there's something else to this. You stumbled into an action in progress. *We* stumbled into an action in progress. I didn't know until after the fact, when I was told to follow procedure and stand aside. There were consequences if I did not comply. I was told if I didn't stand aside, I would be forced to move and live elsewhere. I don't like being told where to live. So I followed procedure until I decided that procedure was unacceptable. Then I followed you."

"Procedure. It's standard practice to drug civilians so agents—"

"Intelligence officers, not agents. Anonymity is crucial for intelligence officers. And, as much as I hate to admit it, so is procedure."

She worked her jaw back and forth and glared. "And the rest of us are fair game for anything the government sees fit to keep that anonymity and procedure. That day in the kitchen with Sal and Largo, you knew I hadn't had any bourbon. I was drugged, wasn't I, injected with something so that the police would think I was drunk and you could keep your feckin' anonymity?"

"No. You weren't drugged. Hindmarsh simply tainted your blood sample so the police would think they were dealing with a drunkard and I could keep my cover. I thought it was uncalled for. I thought all of it was uncalled for. Bryce and I nearly came to blows over that."

"Bryce. He works for you?"

"Yes. With me, for me, in my section. He's my secretary, my aide, my sergeant. I am active duty military reserve. As is Bryce. We served together. He was my squadron sergeant."

Her laugh was thin and high-pitched. "Bryce is your Moneypenny?"

"Bryce wouldn't find that at all amusing." With a grin, Kitt rubbed his chin, feeling the whiskers that had sprouted there. "But I find it tremendously amusing. There's a theory, you know."

"A theory about Bryce?"

"No. About James Bond. Bond is a code name used by the intelligence officer who steps into the 'licensed to kill' position when the previous man dies—or retires."

She made a face, shaking her head. "Right. Yes. You're James Bond."

"I didn't say that."

"No, but that's what you're implying, and what a pack of nonsense. I've read the books. I've seen the films. There's continuity to Ian Fleming's character throughout them all. And you live in Maresfield Gardens, not in a flat off the Kings Road in Chelsea."

"I once lived in Chelsea, and you do realise book Bond has a housekeeper named May, don't you?"

"I'm a butler and she's a surly, grey-haired elderly Scotswoman who—"

"You perform housekeeping as part of your duties and you have grey hair." Kitt's eyes wandered over her untidy hair and picked the strands of silver amid the blonde. "We both do."

"Yes, and that is where any similarity ends." Mae looked at him flatly, "Why then," she said, "are you here? You cleared the way for yourself. You kept your," she snorted, "identity secret. Everything was nice and buried. Why did you really follow me here? And don't tell me it's because you needed a holiday or that it has anything to do with bail."

"You don't know?"

She snorted again. Then she went quiet and chewed her thumbnail. Finally, she said, "My coming to Sicily made me a loose end for you, not quite as tied up and tidy as I should be."

"That's one way of putting it."

"And now that I know, my employer, my friend, my lover, that degree of trust, the added sense of loyalty and honesty, you have an expectation that I will keep my mouth shut about what you are?"

"Yes."

"Or what, you'll kill me?'

"Yes."

"Nice."

He laughed. "I'm joking."

Her expression was flat. "I don't know what to do. I don't know how to respond or react or what to think about this, about you."

Kitt dipped his head. "What you and I do. It's not that different. We both clean up after someone's made a mess."

"I hardly think killing a man is the same as cleaning a house or looking after a wine cellar."

Kitt reached out and cupped her cheek, half-expecting her to recoil. "You have to trust me, Mae. I followed you here because you were a loose end. You're a very loose end. But there are things I am not able to tell you, actions I am not able to talk about. Ever. You have to trust me and let me do what it is I do." His thumb ran over her bottom lip.

"Are you trying to seduce me?"

"Would you like me to?"

She placed her hand over his. "I think we're beyond seduction. Was seduction something you intended, was sleeping with me how you thought you'd gain my trust? Is that why you confessed you wanted to kiss me, is that why you offered to be a distraction?"

Kitt frowned. "I never intended to sleep with you."

"But you wanted to?"

He pulled away and lay back, hands tucked behind his head. "You're a very attractive woman. Yes, I wanted to sleep with you, in spite of our arrangement, however inappropriate and unethical. I told you I was curious because I was curious. It was pleasant to learn you were too, but however drunk I got, however inappropriate my admission and suggestions, I knew you'd never cross the line. I knew you'd shut me up and shut me down before anything happened."

"Until today."

"This is different, and you know that."

"And it changes everything for us."

Kitt bent his knees. "Because of our newfound intimacy, or the work I do?"

"Both."

"Please explain why."

"I don't know, but it does. It has to." Mae tucked hair behind her ears.

"Meaning when we get home you will cease to work for me?"

"I don't know."

"Then nothing has to change. You remain in my employ, I remain your tenant, and we remain friends who were once lovers."

She squinted one eye at him.

He drew in a slow even breath, and his mouth quirked. "I suppose I'm asking that you don't decide what you're going to do until we are actually home. Our routine works. It suits us both. Why should we alter it simply because we've slept together? It was for here, for now. We both know that."

She squinted both eyes. "This is all about access to scrambled eggs for you, isn't it?"

"Am I that transparent?"

"Right now, I don't know what you are." Mae looked down at the ring on her left hand. "And I'm not very sure what I am either." She twisted the slim gold band on her finger. "Do you think I'm in love with you?" She looked up at him.

A laugh rumbled low in his throat. "You shoot your arrows very straight," he said. "There's that insecure part inside of every man that hopes the woman he beds loves him just a little. I know you're fond of me, but I'm not foolish enough to think that you'd love me, or any man besides Caspar. You're done there, Mae. That's game, set, and match for you. What was it you said a few minutes ago— I'm nothing but a heartache? No. In spite of what we've done, I've never held any notion that you'd love me. You're too smart, too practical for that."

"Oh yes, I'm so smart and practical I shagged you because I couldn't cope with killing a man and process what I'd done simply by ironing." Mae looked away for a moment. When she met his eyes again, she touched the dark spots where buckshot marred his skin. "Are you in love with me? I hadn't thought of that until now, but are you in love with me?"

Kitt knew where his future lay. There was no sad surprise there and no sense in pondering otherwise, but he could be honest with himself, and even if there was no sense to it, he could be frank with her. "Would it help if I was? Would it change anything?"

"No. But it would at least offer me a measure of having some power in a powerless situation."

"Well, then," Kitt trailed fingers down her arm, "from the bottomless nothingness of my black soul and charcoal lump of a heart. I love you, Mae."

Her laugh was soft as she nestled alongside him, her head on his chest. "What was her name?"

Kitt slid a hand into her hair. "Whose name?

"The woman you never got over."

"Mrs Valentine," he said. "Go to sleep."

CHAPTER EIGHTEEN

C hildren's stories were an odd thing to ponder. Kitt mulled over *Pinocchio* and *The Velveteen Rabbit* and then got to the fairy tale *Beauty and the Beast*. The fact he'd settled on that particular narrative was amusing, telling, and quite vexing. People often overlooked the fact that many fairy tales were alarmingly violent, that liars had their eyes plucked out, that traitors were shut up in spiked barrels and rolled downhill, that cruelty's reward was being boiled in oil.

Kitt wanted to stay in bed, wrapped around Mae's rounded curves, the fullness of her breast in his hand, her hair tickling his nose. She was soft as a woman was meant to be, shapely in all the best places. She was affectionate, thoughtful, passionate, sensual, and far more intelligent than he could ever hope to be. She was a thorn in his side he would never be rid of. He deserved that thorn. He'd looked at Mae and seen a different tomorrow, hazarded thoughts, fleeting and inane thoughts, of a different tomorrow, and had no right in doing so. A quixotic fool, a quixotic fraud like him deserved to have his eyes plucked out. A quixotic fool, a quixotic fraud like him deserved to be shut up in a spiked barrel, rolled downhill, and boiled in oil.

More than anything he wanted to stay in the nest of sheets and pillows they'd constructed, but he was careful not to wake her because if he did he would make love to her again—and more than anything he wanted this, *he* wanted to be...real.

The sun had barely begun to rise and it lit the room with pale, dull light. Kitt slipped from the bed. He turned and looked at Mae. His hand shook when he brushed a lock of hair from her face. The tremor was a manifestation of the self-deception that he could keep her from harm, when he couldn't keep her safe from himself.

He found a green shirt Mae had ironed and a massive pair of boxer shorts and put them on, tying a knot in the waistband to keep them up. He laid out a tee for Mae at the foot of the bed. His hands shook when he did that too.

His mobile and other belongings were on the table with Mae's handbag. She'd taken her things from the bag and tried to sponge off bloodstains. Martini's blood had dried dark on the latte-toned leather and was a sharp contrast to the brightness of the copper American coin beside it. Kitt exhaled, lifted the shiny one-cent piece, and dropped it back into Mae's handbag. Then he grabbed his mobile. The phone's battery was low. He went outside, walked across dewy grass and into the orchard to where he'd left Martini's car.

Brownish fingerprints dappled the car's exterior. Inside, the seats and leather steering wheel were sticky with half-dried blood. Kitt used the power cord left in the Maserati's console to recharge the mobile and rang Bryce. When he finished reporting events and making arrangements, he found a bucket near the washing machine, filled it with water from the concrete basin. Unable to find rags, he took off the shirt and began to clean the car with it.

The sound of trickling water pushed into Mae's dream. In the twilight of morning somnolence, Mae knew the pattern of the last sixteen years had altered. She did not, as she had every morning, reach for Caspar, because Caspar was dead. Her semi-conscious mind understood he was gone and had been gone for nearly two decades. When she rolled over, Mae reached for another man, and he was gone too.

She was alone, at sea in a bed too large for one small woman and she was sinking, going down, drowning. The last three days washed over her breathless, submerged languor. She came awake and confusion ebbed into a different sort of pain, a different sort of reality, a new, very strange bleakness to her future. A thick sound pushed out of her throat as she opened her eyes and looked at the empty space that surrounded her, at the depression in the feather pillow beside hers, at the rumpled sheets, at a blue t-shirt laid out near her feet.

It was the morning after. It had been quite some time since she'd had a morning after, and never had she had a morning after quite like this one, a morning after that juxtaposed the violence of the day before with the fierce desire and tender passion of the night before. Thinking about the day before was wholly unpleasant. Thinking about the night before was a mixed bag of delight, disbelief, and wretchedness. Mae didn't want to ruminate about either.

She sat up, reached for the blue shirt and pulled it over her head. Holy Mother, she was sore all over and wondered how bruised she was this time as she crawled from the bed. The tee flopped around her knees and she shuffled around the front of the wardrobe to the kitchen.

Kitt sat outside, at the table on the patio, bare-chested. She went to join him. He'd drawn something on a sheet of paper. His mobile lay beside a small pile of hollowed-out oranges, an old ceramic juicer, and a glass of orange juice. He said, "Good morning, Mae."

Mae wished him a good morning too, as she always had, but

called him by his first name—and wished that she hadn't. It was a stabbing reminder of ridiculousness, a poke in the eye of reality. It was easier to deny than accept the futility of what had become a very strange truth.

She swallowed. "I don't suppose you found anything to eat besides oranges?" she said, and her voice cracked because as she came around to the table she saw his neck was a mass of bruises, *he* was a mass of bruises, cuts, welts, and scrapes. Mae swallowed again as he went inside.

How often had he come home like this? How often had his injuries been covered by a dressing gown or pyjama top? Odds were, he'd come home like this in the future. That is, once they left here and life returned to normal—if life ever could return to normal. He seemed to believe it could and it would.

But his normal involved killing people.

Yes. It was easier to deny it all than accept the futility of what had become a very strange truth.

He returned with a bowl of nectarines and peaches, and clothes he had taken from the line earlier. "Have you decided if you will work for me once we get home?"

"The only thing I've decided is to wait to decide what I'll do until we are home. Who knows what will happen before now and then?"

Kitt dropped her dress and knickers over the back of a chair before he split a nectarine in two. "About now and then," he said. "I'm sending you someplace safe."

"You're not sending me anywhere, Kitt." She took half of the nectarine.

"We're not arguing about this. The Italian police, however corrupt Martini suggested they were, are looking for you. The DIA —the Anti-Mafia Investigation Department—are looking for you. The British government is looking for you."

"You're the British government. You know where I am, and I'm curious.

He gave her a sly little smirk and removed the nectarine's stone. "You're still curious?"

"Yes." She gave him a sly little smirk of her own. "I'm curious why you want to send me somewhere else now, after we've almost got this figured out, and you said you didn't want to let me out of your sight."

"We've got nothing figured out, and I'm trying to ensure your safety." He bit into his half of the nectarine.

"And who's going to ensure your safety?"

"I can take care of myself." Kitt licked juice from his bottom lip and had another bite.

Mae looked at the bruising on his throat, at the nicks, cuts, scrapes, lumps, bumps, and scars that marred his bare skin. "Ha!"

He swallowed fruit flesh. "Ha?"

"I think that you're a terrible spy or intelligence officer or whatever it is you call yourself."

"This morning I call myself lucky," Kitt moved to take a seat. "I admit I've had better days. I've done far more competent work than recent events suggest. Clearly it is not in my skill set to take care of anyone else other than myself. I was a fool to think I could keep you from harm."

She said nothing. She simply began to eat her portion of the fruit.

"You're not going to contradict me?"

"Do you need me to?"

He gave her a quizzical look. "I think I might." He reached for another piece of fruit, a peach this time, and began to cut it.

Mae watched Kitt slice out the peach stone and dispose of it. She thought of yesterday, when he'd shown a similar proficiency with a knife. She blinked the image away and looked at the sheet of paper on the table. "What's this?" She turned the paper about to have a better look at the drawing. Then she went inside to get her reading glasses.

When she returned and sat, he tapped the point of the knife on the paper. "It's who we know, so we can connect the dots to what we know."

"Which is?"

He scooted his chair closer to her. "Let's start with Pierce, here, then move to the others." He slid the knife like a pointer. "You. Russo, Torrisi. The principals are Largo, Vivi, and the Chinese man, but Vivi appears to be the head of the monster."

"Nice rendition of a Hydra."

"I was going more for diagram than a mythological creature, but Hydra fits. Solo, Torrisi, and Sal, the man in the kitchen in my flat are secondary players. Martini said Vivi had a lot of nephews. Let's assume Solo, Sal, and the man in the restaurant kitchen are related." Kitt began to eat the peach.

"Now let's marry it up." Mae said. "What do these people have in common?" She drew her finger across the page. "Three dead people with no connection to each other except the proximity of their grave sites. Pierce was a banker. Largo is an accountant. Torrisi is a lawyer and advocate for refugees. I don't know if that means anything. I'd say Russo and I are random victims in this, Luca and Martini too, but bankers like Pierce and accountants like Largo mean money. Bankers and accountants and trust funds that go missing...what do you bet Russo had a trust, Torrisi too, or his uncle Biagio, and those trusts vanished like Caspar's?"

Kitt sucked peach juice from his bottom lip. "Assuming there were other trusts." he sat back. "If we go with that theory, then this could be a cover up of theft. Whatever it is, I'm still sending you somewhere safe."

"Where is it you want me to go?"

"Albuquerque."

"Albuquerque?"

"Well, just near there."

Mae forced herself to finish off the nectarine that she'd left sitting on the table since Kitt had given it to her. "Will I be going alone?"

"Bryce will take you. I'll get you to Palermo and Bryce will meet us."

She made a face. "I don't think so. I'm not leaving Sicily without you."

"Do you think I'm giving you a choice?" Kitt held out a peach quarter. She didn't take it.

"The bully is back. How wonderful!"

"Albuquerque. With Bryce, Mae. Will you go?"

"Are you asking me to?"

"I don't think you want me to force you to go."

"Force me?"

His head cocked. "I am a bully."

She crossed her arms. "How do you know the Italian police and the DIA are looking for me? Wouldn't they be looking for both us? Shouldn't you be coming along with me to lie low or something because the heat is on?"

"No one in my profession talks that way."

"Well, what *do* you say?"

"No more stalling." Exhaling, Kitt put down the peach and reached for his mobile. "Bryce sent this about twenty minutes ago." He showed her the news story: *British Butler Sought for Three Murders*. It was in English, on the first page of the online version of *The Times*. The headline the *Mirror* carried was worse: *The Butler Did It*.

Mae swore. "Martini was a banker."

"He was on the board of directors for the United Nations Credit

275

Union, and based in Geneva. He was very well-connected." He watched Mae reread *The Times* on the small screen. "Neither article," he said, "makes any mention of a male accomplice."

She handed him the mobile and took off her glasses. For a while she was quiet. Birds chirped, a breeze rustled through the trees. The morning sunlight dimmed and brightened as clouds rolled along. "Why don't I go to the police and explain everything, explain it all from the start?"

"Because Martini said the police were involved. I am inclined to believe that since people are trying to kill you."

"They're trying to kill you as well."

"I don't matter."

She blinked. "You matter to me."

"I'm touched," he said, smiling.

Kitt's broad smile was sincere, and it surprised Mae. These last few days her moods had swung in all directions, yet somehow she had managed to stay upright, on her feet until this smile. The colour of his eyes took on the shade of a welder's blowtorch blue and the look he gave her set her more off balance, despite the fact she was seated. The smile and the look shook the ground, rattled her brain, and loosened her tongue. "Maybe ya enjoy your work. Maybe ya think you're selfless and heroic. Maybe spy training taught ya to think you're expendable. Maybe ya think you're not worth a shite. Maybe you're fishin' for reassurance because some woman never loved you. Maybe ya never stopped to think someone cared about ya. I don't know what it is, but you're dear to me," she said. "You must know that, ya bloody bastard. You're dear to me. As much as ya don't wish to see me hurt, I don't want any harm to come to you. Any further harm. You matter and ya are touched." She tapped her temple. "You're absolutely bonkers."

"As if that is news to me." Kitt bit into the peach. "This is what we're going to do," he said, the fruit flesh as sour and unripe on his tongue as the plan was in his mind. "I'm going to dress and move the car. I found a big Ducati on the other side of the shack. We'll use that."

"Please don't say you expect me to ride a motorcycle to Palermo to meet Bryce."

"Don't be daft," Kitt said, rising. "We're going to ride it to Linguaglossa, get the Volkswagen from Fiorella's garage, and drive to Palermo to meet Bryce. Then you're going to get on a plane with him, and this time tomorrow morning you'll be in a safe house outside Albuquerque, New Mexico enjoying green chile stew."

Mae pursed her lips. "And what," she said, "will you be doing?"

"Taking out the rubbish."

Head shaking, she swallowed. "That's stale. You can do better. What will you be doing?"

"Settling the account."

"Shite."

"Making a deposit at the blood bank."

"That's shite too, but I like how you lowered your voice. Very menacing."

Chuckling, Kitt went inside to dress, leaving her grumbling about shite to herself. "Can you be ready to go in twenty minutes?" he said, pulling on his trousers. "I'm going to move the car as far into the orchard as I can, then I'll get the bike ready. In the wardrobe is a big leather jacket I'm going to force you to wear."

"What are you going to wear?"

"We'll probably both fit into the jacket. It's nearly the size of a whole cow."

"Ya think you're a comedian, but you're not," she said, all Irish-intoned as she came into the shack.

She moved past him and made up the bed as he buttoned the shirt she'd laundered and pressed yesterday. He watched her go into the bathroom and then he retrieved his shoes from under the bed.

He'd been about to tell her to find a pair of trousers or something to cover her legs, but as he sat on the mattress to tie his shoes he noticed the bathroom door hadn't quite shut. He found himself staring at her, at her bare body, with naked longing and an ache more painful than he expected. "You're very beautiful, Mae," he said.

When she realised he was looking at her she made no move to cover herself. She offered him a little smile; the kind schoolteachers give to very small children. "There now, Kitt. We're done with that, aren't we?"

Kitt dropped his eyes and finished tying his shoes. Without a word, he left the shack and went to move the Maserati deep into the large orchard.

Mae put the water on in the shower and climbed into the tiny space barely big enough for one person, pulling the little curtain across. She didn't want to think about Kitt or how she felt about him. She didn't want to mull over how he felt to touch, how he smelled, how his hands had been on her, or how he was leaving her in the care of Bryce. It was a strange trade, but the hopelessness of Kitt wasn't that different from the futility of how she had been for Caspar. Both men were heartaches.

She wanted to focus on something real, something normal, something routine. For a long while she let the hot water rain down on her, and stood beneath the soothing jet before she finally washed her hair and body. She reached for the plastic razor she'd found on the edge of the washbasin and shaved her legs because shaving was mundane. Amid the mugging and missing money, amid the two murdered bankers, the strangled office assistant, the people who wanted her dead for whatever reason, and sleeping with a man she had no intelligent reason for sleeping with, shaving her legs felt like an ordinary, harmless activity.

Over the sound of the water's spray, she heard the shuffle of

Kitt's shoes on the other side of the curtain, and normal became something else. God help her, but she liked the idea that he had come back. She liked knowing that he still wanted her as much as she wanted him.

He'd talked about things between them being 'for here and for now'. They were still here and it was still now. Maybe there could be one last 'here and for now' before she left because she had already made up her mind to leave in every sense. She would stop working for Kitt. Not right away. She'd wait until she could find a replacement for the position. Then she would hand over property maintenance of his flat to a company she sometimes used, and go back to Ireland to live, to be closer to Sean. Her brother was her only family, and family was important, but for now, for here...

"I was wrong. We're not done quite yet, Kitt, are we?" Razor in one hand, Mae turned off the water, wondering if she'd find him wearing his little smirk, or rare, heart-stopping smile. She pulled the opaque curtain back halfway, and her heart jumped.

There was no smile beneath the two black eyes and swollen nose that made a moustache seem darker than it was. "I am very sorry," the man said in Italian. "I was sorry before, and I am sorry now." He pulled down the towel she'd tossed over the curtain railing. "It was most unfortunate for you." He pressed the towel to her.

Mae slashed sideways, slicing the twin blades of the razor across the back of his hand. He drew back by reflex, and she grabbed the shower curtain, threw herself at him, hurtling him back into the washbasin. The curtain tore from its rings, covering him. He was a ghost wearing a white plastic sheet and towel when the back of his head struck the mirrored cupboard.

Dripping wet, hair dribbling, Mae ran from the bathroom. Another man, hazel-eyed and quite handsome, grabbed her around the waist and forced into the kitchen, against the sink. She bit into the hand he clamped over her mouth. Spitting out blood and skin, her flailing fingers closed around the bottle of dish soap beside the basin. She squeezed the bottle in the man's face and a spurt of bright yellow spattered into his eyes. He reared back, swearing, began flushing his eyes with water from the tap, and she shot to the open door. A big man with no neck approached from the side. He met her elbow with his eye. Slim and short, nothing more than a kid, rushed into the scuffle. He shrieked when she grabbed his ear, yanked out the hoop he wore, and darted for the orchard.

No-neck snatched her wrist and jerked hard, twisting her. His big arms forced hers back. He clasped his hands behind her head, shoving her chin down, and pushed her to the ground beneath a lemon tree. On her knees, arms forced up and apart, shoulders screaming, flailing, she spat and called the men every insulting, filthy Italian name she could think of, disparaging their mothers, sisters, and wives, belittling their manhood.

"*Che bocca vergonosa!*" a new man said. Bent forward as she was, Mae could only see the man wore woven leather sandals. Burrs from weeds stuck to the leg of his trousers.

"*Fatti una pugnetta, mange merda e morte!*" she shouted for him to have a wank, eat shit and die.

"*Zitto!*" he hissed and jabbed something sharp and cold into the back of her neck.

Mae heard the first high note of her own scream, then everything dulled, her muscles slackened. The strong man let her go, and her head was so heavy she could barely lift it. Pulled to her feet and carried to the patio, "Kitt," she mumbled rather than shouted. "Kitt." Limp, her limbs uncooperative, Mae wondered if she might have been dead or dying. Maybe that's why she wasn't screaming and kicking as the kid and the red-eyed handsome man lifted her legs and slid her knickers on and up her thighs. They pulled them up so snugly and she mumbled, "Backwards. You've put my knickers on backwards."

They ignored her and handed her to the man with the broken nose and bleeding hand. He was hot and sweaty and apologetic as he held her. "I am sorry," he cooed in Italian. "Truly. You got in the way. I had no choice."

Mae knew she ought to bite him, to grab his bollocks and twist them off, but as much as she thought what a great idea it was, she simply couldn't be bothered. Broken nose went on cooing as the handsome man lifted her arm and slid green fabric up one shoulder and then the other. Broken nose kept her upright, turning her in his arms so that Handsome could cross and tie the front of her dress. "What did you do to Kitt?" she murmured.

She was in the back seat of a large German car. Boneless, she flopped against the door. The handsome man dragged her upright. When they went around a sharp bend, she listed the other way, plopping against him. They'd dressed her but forgot her shoes. Her right foot was stuck through the handles of her handbag and her knickers were wedged in her bum crack. "You put them on backwards," she muttered.

"She's awake," Handsome said.

Awake? Mae didn't remember falling asleep. It was a little dark in the car. Was it nearly night, or was it raining? Her view was skewed; everything listed to the right. Her head contained lead weights she couldn't quite hoist fully or hold steady. Head bobbing, she shifted her gaze her and looked ahead, through the windscreen. The wipers left pasty black streaks as they *swish-swished* over the glass. "It's hot as hell in here," she said.

"My name is Francesco, Mrs Valentine," the man in the front passenger seat said in Italian, as he turned around.

Mae looked at the man who'd stabbed her with a needle full of whatever it was that made her floaty, queasy, drunk, weak, and not give much of a feck about where she was. She knew she ought to be trying to throw herself from the car, thinking about how to get away, but it was so hot, and curly-haired Francesco was middle-aged and had a salt and pepper goatee that made her think of Mephistopheles. "You don't have horns," she said, half in English, half in Italian.

"But you have a very foul mouth."

"And very sharp teeth," Handsome muttered from her left side.

"I've been told that before," she said. "Where are we going?"

"Your Italian is beautiful, Mrs Valentine. You speak like you were born here. We are going someplace you've been before," Francesco said as the car fishtailed. "Vitali, slow down, there is too much ash."

Her knickers dug in and sweat trickled down her neck. Or was it water? They had taken her when she had just showered. Her hair had been wet. "It's hot in here. Will you please open a window?"

Vitali, the driver and man with the broken nose, said, "I am afraid there is too much volcanic ash falling for that."

Mae looked at Vitali's profile. "You. Kitt is going to kill you," she mumbled. "Where is Kitt?"

Francesco shrugged.

"Is he dead? Did you kill him?"

Francesco shrugged one shoulder and smiled very softly. "I think it's fair to say we ruined his day."

"Oh," Mae said. "Oh," she said again, feeling...nothing. It should have been disturbing to not feel anything about Kitt being dead. It should have been disturbing to not feel anything, but nothing felt like much of anything at all.

"Tell us about your husband, Mrs Valentine." Francesco reached for the handrail above the passenger door and held on.

"Caspar?"

Francesco nodded. "Yes."

"He's dead." Mae blinked. It seemed to take forever for her eyelids to travel up and down.

"Yes, we know."

"He died years ago, in a car accident."

"We know that too."

Mae sighed. "Then why did you ask?"

Swearing, broken-nosed Vitali braked hard, and Handsome's arm crushed her back against the seat before she flopped forward. Mae looked down at the bronzed, hairy forearm across her breasts and thought about biting it. Then she noticed something that should have been surprising, except it was barely even perceptible. Handsome eased her back against the seat so that her head rested on the leather. "I don't know how I feel about Caspar," she said, peering at Francesco through eyelids that wanted to close.

Francesco, grasping the handrail, dabbed his sweaty face with a handkerchief. "Where is the money, Mrs Valentine?" He told Vitali to take the next left.

Mae sagged against Handsome when the car turned. The man beside her was hot and sweaty, as she was, and he wore an oriental vanilla-patchouli-based cologne that made him smell like a big scented candle someone had lit to cover the stink of sweating male. She wanted to wrinkle her nose and sit upright so that she wasn't pressed so firm to him, but then the heat and perspiration were gone, and the inside of the car smelled more like hot wax and candle wick than vanilla and patchouli and sweaty man. The elastic of her knickers burrowed into her unpleasantly and was made worse by the hard, wooden church pew she'd been seated upon.

When had they arrived at a church?

Oh, yes. There had been a time between the car and here, a moment when they were outside, the sun so bright it had washed out the top of the obelisk in the row of graves after Caspar's, so bright it made the tiny bits of volcanic soil sparkle when Handsome had brushed off Caspar's grave and Francesco had asked her something, so bright she shut her eyes because they burned. It had been so bright and oven-hot in the Linguaglossa cemetery.

Only now it was cool. The sanctuary had whitish walls. There were long alcoves open on one end. The spaces, she realised, were empty burial vaults. One vault was being prepared for a funeral. Was it to be her funeral? Was she to be shut up inside a tomb?

Francesco sat beside her on the pew. He put a hand under her chin and lifted her head. "Yes. You are in the cemetery. We know you were here before, but you still haven't told us why." He patted her cheek. "I asked you a question, Mrs Valentine."

Yes. He had. He had asked her another question about Caspar, said something about *death do us part* and *graves* and *other wives...* "Caspar was never married before he met me."

"Of course he was not." Francesco patted her hand. "You were his first wife. The woman in Malta was his second wife, and the Croatian woman on the island, Vis, was his third." He shook his head. "All three of you at the same time. For some men that is a fantasy. For me it would be a nightmare. Perhaps you were his favourite and that is why he never gave the money he took to the woman in Malta. So is this where you put the money, favourite wife? Is it in Malta or on the Croatian island, where your husband toiled beneath the sun? Where is the money from Aurelio Martini? Where is all the money, Mrs Valentine? Is it here in the cemetery?"

"*Cazzo che ti fotte,*" Mae mumbled.

With a frown, Francesco shook his finger and pursed his lips, going *tsk tsk tsk*. Then Vitali wadded up a handkerchief and stuffed it in her mouth.

CHAPTER NINETEEN

The dead were interred six high, from floor to nearly the ceiling. Slim windows and tiny skylights let in a modest amount of light. Dull yellow shone from wall sconces beside every other burial vault. It was cool inside the crypt. In some ways it was like a dank church. There were pews and kneelers at the end of each hall, crucifixes and statues, and the scent of candles mixed with the odour of flowers rotting in vases. In places, browned petals, leaves, and stems sprinkled the white tiled floor.

The crypt was also something of a maze with several levels. As frantic as he was, Kitt was methodical. He moved through the chambers quickly, hall by hall, going up and down each metal stair-case he came to, moving down every part of the crypt until he reached a room that contained a chapel, two burial vaults and an exit to the cemetery at the top of the stairs. Below, a single pew and kneeler stood in front of a small altar.

"Oh, God damn it," Kitt said.

Mae lay on the cool, tiled floor in front of the altar, on her side, hands cuffed behind her back, gag in her mouth, handbag near her shoulder. She was very, very still.

Kitt went to her, tucked his weapon into the waistband of his trousers, and pulled off the leather jacket that was three sizes too large. Charcoal grey dust wafted up and around him, and he threw the jacket aside. Bits of windscreen glass that he'd smashed slid from the bunched-up sleeve and *tick-tacked* on the tiles.

He didn't want to jump to conclusions. He'd done that when he'd returned to the shack and found that Mae was gone. He'd kicked over the kitchen table, broken crockery, and shattered a pane of glass in the French door, slicing open his knuckle. In a rage, cursing her for leaving, he'd gone into the bathroom and then forgot about tending to his self-inflicted wound because there was blood on the washbasin, blood on the floor, blood on the white plastic shower curtain pulled from the railing. Mae hadn't taken off. She had been taken. He'd promptly vomited.

Then he went to look for her handbag. The latte-toned bag was gone too. He fished his half-charged mobile from his pocket, remembered the conversation they'd had about his preference for using maps over GPS, and changed his mind about which one he preferred.

Hot and sour nausea rose again as he moved toward her and his eyes burned. There was no blood on her. Her neck was not twisted at an unnatural angle. There were no ligature marks on her throat. Her legs were not bent in odd directions. Bones did not poke out anywhere. Nothing on the outside indicated that she had been injured when she'd been taken from the shack. Nothing on the outside indicated that she was dead now, but...

"Mae?" he said, and before his fingers touched her to feel for a pulse, she opened her eyes. Relief pushed out his breath in a rush and he gasped, tears trickled down his face, his nose ran. Sniffling, he swore under his breath and tugged out the gag.

"Are ya cryin'?" she said hoarsely.

"Yes."

"Did ya think I was dead?"

"Yes."

"I didn't cry when I thought you were dead."

He helped her sit up. "No, you didn't."

"You're not dead now, are ya? We're not both dead, are we? I feel dead all over."

"No. We're not dead. I'm so sorry, Mae. I didn't see this coming."

"You're a terrible spy."

"I am." His arms went around her and her lifted her to her feet.

She sagged against him and her head dipped and bobbed up as she looked at him, licking her dry lips. "I don't seem to be workin' properly."

"I noticed." He held her close and tightly, her face pressed to his chest.

"Please tell me that's a gun in your trousers."

"That's my Beretta. But I am delighted to see you," he said softly.

"Why are ya so dirty?"

"I rode a motorcycle through volcanic ash to get here. There was no ash cloud when I left to look for you. The wind changed direction."

"Mmm. Ya taste a little crunchy. Are ya gonna uncuff me and then start shootin' up the place?"

"No."

"No, you're not gonna uncuff me or no, you're not gonna start shooting?" She lifted her chin and her head wobbled around on her neck.

"Yes."

"Yes what?"

"Both."

"Both what?" she said. "They put my knickers on backwards."

Her speech was thick and slow and all Irish-intoned, her eyes glazed. She was unsteady on her feet, as though she were drunk, drugged, or had a head injury. Hoping it was not the latter, he slipped a hand into her hair, his fingers feeling the back of her head for a lump or a soft spot. They both heard the *squee-squee* of heels with rubber soles approaching.

She said, "You're mighty, Kitt. I don't care if ya kill people. You're mighty. Kiss me and then shoot the fuckers who're comin' down here."

"I'm sorry. I can't," he said. Then he swore and said in Italian, "What did you give her, Francesco?"

Mae brought her dry slack lips together and looked at him, blinking twice, slowly.

The man behind them on the stairs replied in Italian. "A little benzodiazepine and propranolol. She has a mouth. Gutter talk. I don't like her mouth. Women shouldn't talk like that. I warned her, but she did not listen."

As much as Kitt wanted to pull out his Beretta and squeeze off one of the six shots he had, he let Mae go and stalked toward Francesco when the man reached the last step. "She swears, so you decide to drug her?" Kitt glanced back at Mae. Unable to stand for long on her wobbly legs, she wilted to the floor. "The handcuffs and gag weren't enough?"

Francesco crossed his arms. "We drugged her because she was not compliant—and she bites. We administered a very small injection. She's a little sedated and calm. Coherent, not comatose."

"And the handcuffs?"

"Well..." Francesco shrugged. "I did not like what she called me."

"I told you I'd bring her to you."

"We got tired of waiting." Francesco exhaled. "I wanted to know why she came to this place and you were not forthcoming with that information."

"I *said* I'd bring her to you when I knew more," Kitt said through his teeth.

"I don't care for your tone at all."

"I don't give a damn."

"You forget yourself, Kitt."

"We agreed. We agreed on this, and I don't approve of your methods."

"You have your methods, we have ours."

"And waiting one more day to use your methods would have killed you?"

"No, Kitt. It appears that it might have killed you. In fact, from what I've been told about yesterday's events in Aci Treza, it very nearly killed you both."

"No thanks to you."

"Did you find the money?"

"I might have if you'd let me finish what I was doing." Kitt turned back to Mae. Sitting on the floor, she stared at him, mouth slack, a shadow in her glassy eyes. "How much benzo did you give her?" he said.

"Enough to calm her anxiety and take the fight out of her, not to impair her or make her forget. We wanted her to talk. The boys were surprised a middle-aged woman would be so aggressive. She's come around in the last hour; the effects are wearing off."

Francesco was right. The drug was dissipating. Like a drunkard, Mae was ungainly, but she gazed up at him. "Ya said ya only spoke tourist Italian," she said.

Kitt cocked his head. "Yes, I'd say it's wearing off."

"You speak Italian," she said again.

"Yes."

"You speak Italian very well. And ya know him. That's not right."

Mae tried to climb to her feet but only managed to get as far as her hands and knees.

Kitt watched her sway. When she began to crawl, he bent, pulled her upright, and walked her backwards to the pew. With a *plop*, she sat. "Why'd ya lie?" she said. "That man there lied to me too." She looked over at Francesco. "He said the most outlandish things, like the police did back home. He said I planned this. He said I stole Caspar's money. Caspar had such warm brown eyes. I thought I liked blue eyes now, but then ya lied. Like that man says Caspar lied. Ya lied. Why do ya lie? Why are all of ya lyin'?" She may have been drowsy and drugged, her thoughts may not have been completely focused, but there was nothing wrong with her hearing.

Kitt gritted his teeth. "What did you two talk about, Francesco?"

"Trust funds, bankers, and dead men in kitchens."

"I told you to wait. I told you we were piecing this together." Kitt turned and glared at the other man. "What else did you tell her?"

"What I thought necessary. We had to find out for ourselves what she knew about the origin and route of the money."

"Yes, and to hell with cooperation. To hell with our agreement. Did you send the two Americans into this?"

"Ronnie and Simone are just as interested as we are. Unlike you, they want to cooperate."

"Take the bloody cuffs off and we'll discuss how they tried cooperating."

Francesco tossed him the key. "May I remind you? You are responsible for her."

"Why do you think I'm here?" Kitt bent around her and unlocked the handcuffs.

"Please. You had no intention to bring her to us. No intention at all. We know you chartered a plane in Palermo. Did you think we'd let you keep the money? And really, did you have to smash my windscreen? Breaking into a car to set off the alarm is not much of a diversion."

"It got you out of here, didn't it? And I had no way of knowing you were the one who had taken her, now did I? You didn't exactly leave a note."

Three very quiet men appeared near the top of the stairs. They came down the metal staircase, single file. "As you see," Francesco said to them, "we've been discovered. Did the groundskeeper protest about the noise?" he asked a good-looking lad with a large plaster wrapped around the web of his hand. The beige flesh tone stood out brightly against his olive complexion.

"No, he asked if we would be gone before lunch," a younger man answered, touching a bandage on his earlobe.

The last man on the staircase had two black eyes, the result of a recently broken nose, and he swore when he saw Kitt.

"*Bongiorno*, Vitali." Kitt said as Mae pawed at his abdomen, trying to grab the Beretta.

Kill him," she muttered. "Kill him."

Kitt pushed away her weak hands and took a step back. "Your hired help is incompetent, Francesco."

"Kitt, kill him." Feebly, Mae pointed at Vitali. "Shoot him. *Segailo. Ce l'hai piccolo.*"

Francesco waved the other men back upstairs. "Oh, that mouth!"

Kitt found Vitali's red-faced reaction to being called a wanker with a little penis most amusing—until the man said, "Shut up, lady, or Francesco will make me gag you again."

"Touch her and your teeth come out, Vitali." Kitt smiled, chin down, eyes up.

"I'm trying to help her," Vitali gestured with two hands, thumbs to fingertips, "and you threaten me."

"No, no, I'm not threatening you. I'm assuring you. You will lose teeth."

"If you two," Francesco said in English, "proceed with this any further I'll shoot you both and dump your bodies in the sea. I don't care who it pisses off." He drew a packet of cigarettes from his jacket pocket. "*Madonna*, the mouth on this woman. Did you hear her?"

With a hand on her shoulder to keep her from trying to get up again, Kitt said, "Yes. I heard her. Now, you hear me. You don't like it when she uses naughty words, and," he set his eyes on Vitali, "I don't like Vitali. If he comes near her he loses teeth. Are we clear?"

"Don't bully him," Mae mumbled. "Kill him." She squeezed her eyes shut. Bizarrely, the last few minutes and foggy hours formed a hazy picture of something that should have been disconcerting. Yet what registered as a feeling was a trickle of nausea, which in itself was strange since it was a physical sensation without any sort of distress or discomfort.

Kitt's palm slipped from her shoulder. Mae opened her eyes. This was frightening without any actual fear, this was another moment where she ought to flee or fight, like when she'd thought Francesco had planned to seal her alive in a burial vault. And yet, exactly as she had then, she sat again on the pew with sloppy, unco-ordinated muscles and an unresponsive disposition. Being kidnapped, thinking Kitt was dead, believing she was going to be entombed alive, and being told Caspar was a thief who had other wives should have been like a shovel in the guts, but these things only registered as curiosities.

Kitt moved away from her. She watched him. He said, "If or when it's necessary, *I* will deal with her. Not you, Francesco, and not," he jerked his chin at Vitali, "some incompetent twat who doesn't comprehend the value of subtlety."

Mae watched Francesco shake a cigarette from the pack. "We

didn't ask for you to participate. In fact, we made it very plain we did not want you to participate."

"You didn't give me much choice now, did you, seeing how that imbecile let it escalate from the start." Kitt tossed the handcuff key aside. "You should have left all of this to me."

As they argued about Vitali's shortcomings Mae looked at Kitt's back. Beneath that ash-smudged sky-blue shirt, high on his back was a short, thick scar, one she hadn't asked about.

Wait. What had she been thinking about before that scar? What was it Kitt said a moment ago? He would deal with her? He would *deal with her when it was necessary*? No, before that...what was it he said before that? What was it? He would *bring her to Francesco*. He'd said it in Italian. He'd said everything in Italian. Kitt knew Italian. He was speaking Italian. And there was something else.

Kitt knew Francesco.

Kitt knew Vitali.

Kitt had known Vitali when they'd left the restaurant yesterday, had known him when he'd appeared with the blonde woman in Taormina.

Kitt had known Vitali back in England.

Sucking her bottom lip, she blinked and pushed to her feet, holding on to the top of the pew, kicking over her handbag. Cigarette smoke drifted in her direction. The trickling urge to be sick grew insistent as tobacco haze began to rise in the air, and the heaviest fog lifted from her mind. Her eyes wandered from Kitt, to Francesco drawing on his cigarette, to the man who'd bashed her in front of the Nepali embassy, and back to Kitt. "No. Oh, no," she said, tripping over her own feet as she headed for the stairs where Vitali stood watching his boss argue with Kitt.

"Your butler is trying to run away." Francesco laughed and waved his smoking hand in her direction.

"I'm going to be sick," Mae muttered. "I'm going to be sick."

Kitt's arm went around her waist. He hauled her up the staircase, past Vitali, past the other two men, to a door, shoving it open, taking her out into the glaring sun and stifling afternoon heat. He half-carried her past headstones and monuments, to the shade of a tree where she sank down and heaved. The bits of pinecones and dusty black volcanic sand and pebbles were hard and scratchy under her palms and knees.

"I'm sorry, Mae. This shouldn't have happened." Kitt crouched and wiped her mouth with the bottom of his shirt.

She looked at him. Her eyelids were heavy. Not sleepy heavy, simply heavy. All of her felt heavy, except for her brain. Every cog and spring in her mind whirred and ticked, as if being ill wiped away dust and cobwebs. "Tell me why," she said, tongue thick, and turned her leaden body to sit with both hands on the abrasive ground to support cumbersome limbs.

Once Kitt made certain she wasn't about to collapse, he sat beside her. "Impatience, perhaps. Idiocy is more likely," he said.

The four other men had come out into the heat to watch. They stood nearby, behind Mae, in the shade of a statue and monument, listening.

"Yes, idiocy. Mine. Trust me, ya said," she muttered, her affect almost flat, her Irish roots discernible. "There were—what was the phrase ya used?" she said. "Activities? There were activities you couldn't talk about, but ya asked me to trust ya, so I did. I trusted ya, and you took advantage of my trust. So did Caspar. At least that's what Francesco told me." Her hand rose in slow motion, and she wiped her mouth. "He said Caspar was a thief."

Her gaze, however sleepy, fixed on him, and everything Kitt had tried so hard to preserve had been pulverised. "Yes," he said, glancing at Francesco over her head. "I wondered if he'd tell you that."

"All the lies. All the lies should be infuriating. I should feel some way about the lies, but I don't feel anything. Well, I do, but it's not quite the rage that it should be. Why is that?"

"It's an effect of the injection Francesco gave you."

"Oh." She regarded him as she nodded. "I see," she said. "It's really quite strange. I know I should be ranting."

"You have every right."

"I do." Her gaze shifted to her hands. "At least ya fixed my knickers. They're not up in my bum crack anymore, so that's a small victory."

"This is my fault," he said.

She gave a wobbling, drunk's nod. "Yes, it is, but there's somethin' that's my fault. I told ya I hadn't had a decent kiss and that left ya free to think of me as a lonely, middle-aged widow who needed a good fuck. You probably always thought of me as a lonely, middle-aged widow who needed a good fuck. I bet ya thought ya were doin' me a favour. Only I wasn't lonely, and ya weren't that good."

Francesco and his men laughed. Vitale sniggered. "*Addesso lei rompe sui palle.*"

Kitt ignored the comments about Mae breaking his balls and wiped back hair from her damp forehead. "You're wrong about that."

"No, I wasn't lonely and ya weren't that good."

"I meant how I thought about you. You are wrong about that. I thought about you. I think about you, al—"

Mae shoved his hand away. "I liked ya, rather a lot. I don't so much now." She looked at him again.

With an exhale Kitt sat back, hard black little stones poking the backs of his thighs. "You don't like me?"

"No more scrambled eggs for ya, ever," she said, her expression not entirely flat.

"That's not exactly fair," Kitt's mouth compressed. "This isn't wholly my fault. We had a bargain and they reneged. They wanted you before today. They wanted you back at home, but I refused. It would have been easier if you hadn't left England. Once you did, the game changed."

"A game." Mae's headshake was rubbery. "I don't know why I didn't see it," she said. "Maybe because I didn't open my eyes wide enough, but it was right there in front of me. I told ya about Caspar's trust, and then this game of yours began. I left my bank documents in your home. You could have looked at them any time, but I guess ya thought they were at my place. If you wanted money, Kitt, I would have given you money. All ya had to do was ask. You didn't have to try to have me killed."

"*What*?" Kitt stared at Mae. "I didn't have to *what*?"

CHAPTER TWENTY

Roaring laughter reverberated off headstones and monuments. Vitali's laugh was loudest, and when he caught his breath he shook his head, grinning. "*Hai un problema.*"

Yes. Kitt was aware he had a problem. He directed his attention to the four amused, sweating males fascinated by this train wreck. "Give us a minute," he said.

Francesco lit a cigarette. "Give me your word you won't try to leave with her."

"You have it."

The man jerked his head at his sniggering merry men. Kitt watched them head back into the cool mausoleum.

Mae played with her wedding ring, turning it 'round and 'round. She had an inkling of searing hurt in her chest, of internal bleeding, the twinges anaesthetised by new shock and what remained of the drug. She ran her tongue around her lips and took care when she spoke. "Why didn't you just kill me yourself? That would have been easier. Is it because you needed me to sign the papers that Daniel Pierce kept aside? Or was that another part of the ruse?"

His frown deep, Kitt moved closer. "I didn't try to have you murdered, Mae."

She twisted and turned the small circle of gold she wore as she looked up and out over the rows and rows of gravestones, monuments, and mausoleums. "I may be doped to the gills, but I heard you and Francesco. You know Vitali. You pretended that you didn't speak Italian. I don't know why you would do that. The lies. All the lies. Them. You. For money. Bloody money. I killed two people so you could get money to play your game to get more money, but you all need me to find the money. That's why I'm not dead, isn't it? You need me."

"I do," he said. "I need you."

Betrayed. She'd been betrayed and deceived, was blindly trusting, and was a blindly trusting and loving fool for men who kept secrets. Anger was there, but it wouldn't rise as it should and it was distressing without palpable distress. Mae tried to get to her feet, but she faltered and sagged to her knees after two steps. Undeterred, she began to crawl away from him on her hands and knees across pine needles, volcanic dust, and hot concrete.

Kitt grabbed her around the hips, pulled her back into his lap, and squeezed his arms around her. "Stop."

"Let go," she gasped. "I can't breathe."

"You can breathe, and you're wrong. Very wrong about me, about this bloody farce, and you're not thinking clearly." He loosened his grip, spat her hair from his mouth, and slid her from his lap. "You've got Francesco's little drug cocktail floating in your bloodstream. It's clouding your judgment, altering your perception. All right, you heard us, and what you heard makes you think I set you up and tried to have you killed. I work for the British government. We established that. We discussed that at great length, Mae. Do you remember that?"

"Yes."

298

"Right then. Let me explain this to you."

"I don't care for your tone. I'm stoned, not a child."

Kitt exhaled. "This *is* a game, but it isn't the kind of game you seem to think. It's a crapshoot. Governments gamble, banks gamble, and when international banking is involved governments play on the same team to bring down the cheater. Listen to me. Francesco Casino and his team—that includes the bastard in there who hit you—are with the GdF, the Italian *Guardia di Finanzia*. The British government is cooperating with the Italian government in investigating tax evasion that involves prominent European families, and maybe something more."

"Tax evasion?" She worked her mouth open and closed. "This is about tax evasion?"

"Yes."

"How do I know you're not lying?"

"You know my bank balance. You tend to my household accounts. Does it seem like I need money?"

She gave a meekly defensive shrug.

Kitt spooled in his incredulity with a single shake of his head. "You thought I wanted your money and tried to have you killed?"

Mae looked away, ignoring the man watching them from the mausoleum front, choosing to follow the south-easterly drift of the volcanic ash cloud in the not-so-far-off distance. After a long moment she said, "Given the circumstances of how I got here, what I heard you say to those men, and seeing the man who bashed me with them, are you really that surprised I'd believe otherwise, Kitt?"

He looked at her, eyes narrowed. "I can't believe you'd think I set you up."

"I can't believe you're insulted."

"I'm not insulted, I'm angry."

Mae turned her head quickly and blinked as if she were dizzy. "*You're* angry?"

A stone crucifix rose above the grave across from them. Jesus, with his arms outstretched on the cross, looked down upon Kitt as he ground his molars together. Yes, he was incensed, with Mae, with Francesco, but mostly he was furious with himself. "You had to come here, didn't you? You had to be contrary. The morning you left I was told to let it be, to let it play out, to let Francesco and the GdF do their job and keep you under surveillance. I damn well should have done as I was told."

She wore a ghost of a frown. "I was being watched?"

"You've been under surveillance since Vivi stole your handbag, Mae. That set this all in motion with the GdF."

"You knew I was being watched?"

"No. I found out ten minutes after I came home and found a dead man in my kitchen."

She looked at him and then past him, mumbling to herself, about lies and truths. "Caspar," she said. "Francesco told me Caspar was a polygamist. Is that true?"

Christ, there it was. He'd tried like hell to preserve what she valued most: the unsullied memory of her beloved dead husband. Now the grenade was about to detonate. He wanted to set the blame for the impending devastation with Francesco. He wanted to use all six rounds in his Beretta on the four men who had pulled the pin, but Kitt knew that if he had done a better job, if he had acted professionally, as Mae always did, they would not be here. The fault was his. Unequivocally. "Yes," he said. "It's true."

"How do you know it's true?"

The crucified Jesus on the cross behind them was suddenly disquieting. Kitt drew in a breath and exhaled hard, perhaps not as Godless as he'd always thought he was as he confessed his sin. "I've always known. Before you began to work for me, before I moved into the flat you own, you were vetted. Every aspect of your life was scrutinised. That included Caspar. I've always known, Mae, but when *this* happened the office went back in for another look, and found he'd embezzled money from the Santa Liberata Monastery in Malta. He gave back the money, and the Santa Liberata Brothers saw no point in proceeding further. It was forgiven, forgotten, until Caspar's trust appeared..."

She stared at him blankly.

Her empty reaction was far worse than tears or ranting. The hollow look was a shard of glass piercing his chest. "Mae, I—"

"Yes. You were angry yesterday. Was that yesterday? You said you wondered why he put me in this position. You said, 'what sort of man does that to a woman he loves?' You did know. Why didn't you ever tell me?" she said.

"I very nearly did tell you, but to what end? You love the man, Mae. Why would I destroy that? Why would I take that from you? His death is painful enough for you, why would I add to your heartache? Why would I hurt you that way?"

Again, the empty reaction, the cool, detached stare. Kitt kept his mouth shut. It would have been so out of place to point out she was behaving very much like him, like she once said she'd wanted to.

"I see," she said.

"I don't think you do."

"No, I do. Not telling me anything was all part of procedure."

"Yes."

"I don't like your procedure, and I don't like you." She went on looking at him, dispassionately.

His frustration got the better of him. Kitt rose and glared down at her. "I was informed how this would work. I was instructed that I would not participate, but I presented a reasonable argument to have you released in my charge. My participation then was limited to that. I could keep an eye on you, report back, and everyone was satisfied. But then you left for Italy, which convinced everyone, except me, that you were involved. Even the Americans were interested. I didn't relish the idea of turning you over to the GdF. So I made a deal. I made a bloody deal and I came here *for you*."

"Are you expecting me to be grateful? Wait. Wait. Turning me over to the GdF for what?"

"I came here for you, Mae. Do you understand that?"

She shook her head slowly. "You don't get to be angry about this, Kitt. You don't get to argue either. Turning me over for what? Tell me."

"Uncovering a sizeable money laundering network that appears, on the surface, to involve you, your husband, a baker, and an immigration lawyer."

A half-second spark of shock lit her eyes. "Before you said it was tax evasion, now it's money laundering? You know I'm not involved in anything of the sort."

"I know you're not, but the British government thinks Caspar *might* have been, given his previous embezzlement. They shared this information with the GdF. Now, I'm somewhat prejudiced in the view I have of my prized butler. I protested most vehemently about your involvement, I asserted your innocence, but I was considered to have a conflict of interest. As I said, your leaving England didn't bode well. It reinforced the supposition that you were involved. I came after you because if it hadn't been me, it would have been someone else. I couldn't let it be someone else. Someone else would have been unsympathetic. Someone else would have taken you straight to Francesco. Do you understand?"

"No."

Kitt was quiet for a moment. This was not the time, and he knew there never would be a time to explain the intricacies of his lying, of his omitting particular details. He said, "I had hoped we could get this sorted out before Francesco intervened." He glanced at the good-looking man keeping watch from the doorway of the mausoleum. "We almost got there, Mae. I think we're close. Nobody could figure this out. The only thing obvious is that it hinged on you, somehow, you and your paperwork."

"There was never any bail, was there?"

"No. I let you assume there was."

The ghost of a frown that had been there once before returned, looking a little less like an apparition. "So after you told me what you were, what you are, after we had that little talk about you maintaining cover and national security and bloody James Bond shite, why didn't you tell me about Francesco and the money laundering? Why didn't you tell me when you showed up at the Castello di San Marco and said you were a tourist on holiday? Why didn't you tell me that night at the Four Seasons? Why didn't you tell me when you came home and found I had killed someone? Why didn't you tell me anything then?" She held up a finger. "That's right. I know. Procedure. Killing and lying, it's what you do for a living."

He said, very quietly, "I've been trying to protect you, to prove you're not involved. Whether you realise it or not, that's what I've been doing, protecting you."

"Do you ever tell the truth?" she said, wearing a phantom sarcastic smile.

"Yes. Often. The truth is vital. Whether you believe it or not, I have a high sense of justice. I lied to protect you from Caspar's unfaithfulness and larceny. I lied to protect you from being unjustly prosecuted for murder, even if the British, and now the Italian government, are well within their rights to charge you for the deaths of two men. I had to find out what you knew, if it was anything at all, however small, however seemingly insignificant, to help you uncover whatever we could find, to keep you safe, to keep you... I've done a terrible job." He shoved his hands into his pockets. "The bloody Americans snatched you right out of my hand. I let you out of my sight long enough to move a car and charge my phone, and Francesco's men took you. I've done an appalling, miserable job.

You're a nuisance, you bloody distract me, and there's no room in this work for distraction. I've been inattentive to what was most important, which shouldn't have been how good you smell. I've lied to you. Omitting details is lying. Letting you make an assumption is lying. I've lied to you, but I won't ever lie to you again. Do you understand?"

Mae poked her tongue into the crease of her mouth and then swallowed. "No one has ever been direct. Instead, it's assumed I'm guilty. I was told what I did. No one ever asked me what I knew, and no one asked me to help. No one asked me to cooperate, not even you. I'm threatened with prosecution so I'll comply. I'm drugged so I'll comply. You lie so I'll comply. You sleep with me and say I can trust you so I'll comply. Is that about right?"

"All except the last part. And I'm asking you now. Please help me help you."

She sighed. "The stuff must be wearing off because I'm starting to feel like I really want to bite you."

"You have bitten me. I quite liked it."

She made a face of sorts; her insipid lip-curl not quite in synch with an anaemic frown. "So did I, and that's what irritates me."

Kitt's hand came out of his pocket, his chuckle faint.

The dim frown remained. "I thought I was dead," she said. "I thought you were dead. How did you find me? How did you know where I was?"

"I had no idea where you were. I got back to the shack and you were gone. I thought you'd thumbed your nose at me and left. Then I realised you'd been taken."

"So how did you find me?"

"The same way I did when you vanished in Taormina. Basic equipment carried by all intelligence officers."

"What, like a tracking device?"

"Exactly."

"I was joking."

"I wasn't. I dropped a tagged coin in your handbag, one you couldn't spend in Italy. The American penny has a little GPS tag embedded in it. That's how I found you." Kitt brushed dust from his legs. He offered his hand, Mae took it, and he brought her to her feet. She was unsteady, still clumsy and weak. He kept a hand on her elbow and refrained from pulling her into an embrace to support his own unsteady, clumsy weakness.

FRANCESCO'S MEN stood at the top of the stairs. Kitt sat beside Mae on a church pew at the bottom of the cool mausoleum. Her arms were crossed and irritation had begun to find its way through her mantle of dullness. Francesco had agreed not to arrest her if he was satisfied with the explanation she gave.

Kitt glanced at her folded arms. "I would appreciate you giving me a few details before I tell you what Mrs Valentine and I have found," he said.

Francesco mulled over the request. "What is it you wish to know?"

"How does Aurelio Martini fit into this?"

"Didn't you ask him that before you killed him?"

"I didn't kill him."

"Did Mrs Valentine?"

"No," Mae said. "I killed Solo."

"Mae." Kitt put his hand on her thigh. She shoved it off.

"Which man was Solo?" Francesco looked over at Vitali.

"The big one in the supply room," Vitali said from his place on the bottom step. "The smaller man in the kitchen was his brother. They are Gallia's nephews."

Francesco tilted his head, his expression doubtful. "You knocked out that big man's brains, Mrs Valentine?"

She drew in a breath to reply, and Kitt put his hand back on her thigh. "Don't say another word, Mae."

"Very wise, Kitt. *Allora.* We have been investigating Martini for collusion with UNFed Credit Union clients to conceal undeclared 'black' accounts for heirs to some of Europe's biggest fortunes. Vitali had been assigned to Martini, undercover. He has been acting as bodyguard and driver. Several times during his investigation, Vitali travelled to London with Martini and a woman named Vivienne Gallia. She works for Pippino Torrisi. She is his personal secretary but has at times assisted Martini with his financial activities. Often he would ask Vitali to look after Gallia while she tended to some financial dealing for him, as a matter of her protection. Vitali went along, as he had in the past, but it appears this woman had another project ensuing, one Kitt insists is separate to Martini's. I believe his first night in London was when Vitali knew something else was operating. Is that not so, Vitali?"

"Yes. That was the night."

"And that was when Vitali met you and Kitt, Mrs Valentine." Francesco looked over at Vitali. "You can see the man is horrified he injured you, Mrs Valentine."

His dark eyes earnest, Vitali clasped his hands together in supplication. "I am deeply sorry I hurt you. I only meant to slow you down so that I could continue with Vivi's action. She said your husband had stolen from her," he said contritely, as if a shameful expression and penitent tone made up for a split lip and battered face. "I did not expect you to fight back, Mrs Valentine."

"Oh, gosh, I did not expect I'd want to kill you."

"Mae." Kitt said.

"I did not expect I'd want Kitt to kill you either."

"Mae."

"He's an arse, Kitt." She gestured at Vitali, her index finger and pinkie extended. "*Gavone. Maleucato. Cazzo che ti fotte.*"

"Please." Francesco sighed. "If you are going to talk again like a sailor, I will click the handcuffs, gag you, and continue this at the *Carabinieri caserma,* the station in town."

"Mae," Kitt said softly.

Mae crossed her arms again.

"Thank you," Francesco said. "The man you killed in London, Mrs Valentine, Salvatore Tornatore, he was a policeman with the *Direzione Investigativa Antimafia*—but a corrupt policeman we know was assisting Martini. Vitali uncovered evidence of this. We now believe Sal Tornatore was also aiding Vivi Gallia. We think there are two cases in play, and since they share a few suspects they fall under our jurisdiction. Martini executed the transfer of vast sums of money that moved through Italy. No taxes were paid on any of the funds. It's large-scale tax evasion and Italy has one of the highest rates of tax evasion in the European Union. The country is being bled dry. People have died, money has vanished, and you are still at the centre of something, Mrs Valentine."

"How can I be at the centre?"

"Because of your husband's trust account."

Mae did her best to glare at Francesco. Faking anger was easier than mining for submerged fury. "Which I knew nothing about until ten days ago. And what about Caspar's...other...wives? Have you painted them as criminals the same way you have me? Did you kidnap them as well?"

"Those women are dead, Mrs Valentine."

Hand to her throat, Mae said, "Were they murdered? Did Salvatore Tornatore kill them? Or do you suspect me for that as well?"

"No." Francesco shook his head. "One woman had cancer. The other had a congenital heart defect. Both died several years ago."

Mae's bogus glower collapsed. "How convenient for me."

Kitt said, "What about Torrisi, is he involved with Martini's venture?"

"No. We are not interested in Torrisi. He and Martini are, *were*, close friends, but Torrisi is clean. We have found no evidence to incriminate him. Martini sheltered his friend from anything illegal. Torrisi's personal assistant, however—we are very interested in her now, particularly since Martini is dead. We know you did not kill him, Mrs Valentine. Vitali verifies that. Before he died, Martini stated he had been shot by the big man you say you killed. We are not sure who killed the man at the *panificio*, but we speculate his business was a front for money laundering. We have yet to find the body of Torrisi's office worker, the man Kitt said you found dead. He has disappeared. Gallia has also disappeared. Everyone, except you, has dispersed. We are very interested to know what you do know about Vivienne Gallia, Mrs Valentine."

"She wears ugly shoes," Mae said.

"Is that a British idiom or a joke?"

"It's what I know about Gallia," she said, leaning forward. "Her shoes are ugly."

"Have you been friends for very long?"

Mae's features formed a decent frown. "Why would you ask if we are friends? She tried to have me killed for money I never knew existed."

Vitali rubbed his forehead and rose from the steps. "I am very sorry for hurting you, Mrs Valentine."

"You can stay where you are," Mae said.

"Gallia said her accountant had papers that showed you had stolen money." Vitali smoothed his hair. "She wanted your keys so she could get the papers from your house and prove you were a thief."

Francesco brushed tobacco from his chest. "Is that what led you to seek out Torrisi, Mrs Valentine, the money you thought he stole from you?"

"No. My husband led me to seek Torrisi."

"*Si*, your husband. We are here, in this cemetery because of him. Where is his money, Mrs Valentine? Is it here, buried somewhere? Or did you give it to the baker to launder?"

"Why do you persist...where do you get the idea I launder money?"

"The British government suspects you." Francesco laughed. "Did you not tell her that either, Kitt?"

Mae glanced at Kitt and pushed hair from her face. Her anger was muted into the sort of frustrated irritation one had with a persistent buzzing mosquito. These men were all mosquitoes. "Jaysus, the money was stolen before I even signed for it to be transferred, and ya all want it. Well, if ya want it, you'll have to ask Vivi Gallia or Largo for it because my guess is they have it tucked away somewhere in an offshore account. So stop lookin' at me and look for them."

"Refresh my memory, Vitali. There are so many. Is Largo one of the nephews?"

Kitt pulled his mobile from his pocket. "This," he showed the screen to Francesco, "is Largo. We thought he was a friend of Vitali's. He said he was an employee of Suisse Global Bank. Martini told us Largo is Torrisi's accountant and Vivi's cousin. He is the man who instructed Salvatore Tornatore to kill Mrs Valentine. In my flat."

"Which is why you take this so personally, Kitt?"

"How would you feel if someone tried to murder a close friend in your home, Francesco?"

"A close friend?" Francesco arched his brows. "I thought Mrs Valentine was your butler."

"Po-ta-toe, pa-tah-toe."

"I'm not familiar with that expression." Francesco jerked his head to Vitali. "Is this the cousin?" He tossed the phone to Vitali, who caught it and came forward, keeping a safe distance from Mae.

Vitali nodded. "Yes. That is Ernst Largo. He left after dinner the other evening. He's Vivi Gallia's cousin. He is in love with her. They are all in love with her."

"Do you know the other man?" Kitt said.

"Yes. I was there the evening you took this photo. His name is Man. Li Man. He is a cleaner."

Mae huffed and massaged the back of her neck. "*Man.* That's one of the other names on Largo's list. Man and Bianco."

"List?" Francesco narrowed his eyes. "What is this list?"

Mae began to rub her temples. "Don't you people share information?" she said. "When Largo and I were talking in the Major's kitchen, I noticed he had a list of names stuck beside the papers he wanted me to sign. The papers were so Suisse Global would release and transfer the money to an account in my name. I signed the bloody papers and I saw the list stuck to the papers." She stopped massaging her temple. "Three of the names are in this cemetery, Russo—that's the same name as the man at the *panificio* in San Giovanni—Valentine, my dead husband, and Torrisi, but not the Torrisi you know—are on the list. I think, *we* think the names might be linked to bank accounts that vanished like Caspar's has, and that is what we were tryin' to find out. I wanted to know if Russo and Torrisi had been approached by Largo like I was. Two others names on the list, Mr Man and Mr Bianco are not, as far as I know, in this cemetery."

"How do you know Russo and Torrisi are in this cemetery?"

"I shared this information with you already, Francesco," Kitt said.

"I want her to tell me. How do you know this, Mrs Valentine?"

"Because the graves for Russo and Torrisi are beside Caspar's.

Martini knew that too, and that is why he is dead." Mae sat back and crossed her arms again and eyed Francesco. "Don't tell me ya haven't bothered to look for yerself?"

Vitali and Francesco exchanged glances.

"My hole, ya call yerselves feckin' professionals."

Francesco shouted for someone at the top of the stairs to go and look.

Mae hollered as a man moved to head outside "Five rows down from the front gate, four graves in! You're probably gonna have to dust off the volcanic ash!" She exhaled. "I didn't make the connection when I first saw the names," she said. "I've been to this cemetery three times. The first was the day my husband was buried, then last Thursday, and today. I didn't recognise the names on Largo's list as anything important until I was standin' in front of Caspar's grave last Thursday. Caspar, Russo, and Torrisi are all buried in the same row. My...husband is buried between Russo and Torrisi. I never took the time to see if a Man or Bianco were nearby."

Vitali stroked his chin. "*Ascolta*, listen. Mr Man I know, but was the name you saw Mr Bianco or *Misterbianco*."

"What's the difference?" Kitt said.

"Two words, Mr Bianco, or *Misterbianco*, one word."

"Sorry?" Kitt said, glancing at Mae.

She stared at Vitali. "Misterbianco is a town outside Catania. Sicilians call it *Mustarjancu*."

"*Si*. That is the place. And this is what I know of Misterbianco. It is where Li Man has a property, a beautiful villa. I have been there many times to fetch him and drive him to Taormina to meet Vivi." Vitali stroked his chin again. "Listen. Please. Listen. That night you saw me with them, Vivi was furious because Salvatore, the man you killed in London, had failed to kill you. They are not aware Sal is dead. They believe he is touring the UK. That made Viv's anger grow. She said she should have taken on the task

311

herself since she had to finish it now. There was *no* discussion of what she planned to do. Largo said he did not want to know the details, and Man only wanted to eat and be paid. The conversation turned to Martini. Vivi said it was time to bring Martini into the flock, as she called it. Early yesterday morning, she instructed me to drive to Misterbianco to pick up Man and bring him to the *ristorante* at Aci Treza. I thought we were there to deal with Martini. We arrived a little late. Vivi was very unhappy because her nephews said Martini had not waited. I did not know you would be there. I did not know you were there until I saw you come out the front."

"Am I supposed to be impressed you have a conscience?" Mae shook her head.

Vitali sighed. "Man has cleaned up. It is what he does, the dirty things for Vivi and others who pay him well. She could have sent him to you in London, Mrs Valentine, but he has such little finesse. Finesse is Largo's specialty. Sal was already in London, on holiday, so it was simple. Vivi likes simple. The police will find nothing to incriminate her at the restaurant in Aci Treza, just as they will find nothing incriminating at Torrisi's office. They will never find poor Luca, and they would not ever find Martini, but I was there and know where he is."

"Kitty!" Bryce's voice bounced off the crypts and tiled floors. Vitali drew a weapon Mae had never noticed he had.

Bryce appeared with his black hair tousled, hands raised. He smiled. "Francesco Casino, *Che piacere vederti!*" Francesco made an Italian gesture, Vitali holstered his gun, and Bryce started down the stairs. "Llewelyn wants your head on a pike, Kitty."

"That's today. Tomorrow he'll buy me a bottle of bourbon. Thank you for coming."

"We all need a little help sometimes." Bryce shrugged. "You're looking better than the last time we met, Mrs Valentine." He gave her a smile that lit up his amazingly green eyes. Then he turned to the Italian man, his hand out. "It's been a long time, Francesco."

"We all have a few more greys, Timothy." Francesco Casino clasped Bryce's hand.

Seeing the two men chat like old school chums was a strange little confirmation that this game was indeed a joint investigation. Mae didn't like any of the players. Angry, frightened, sickened and sad, ripples of emotion seeped through her in a muddied mix. She dug fingers into Kitt's wrist. Not quite strong enough to squeeze very hard, but her fingernails poked into his flesh. "What do we do now?" she said.

"We?" Kitt rose from the pew. "This stops here for you. These men are going to suggest we use you as bait to draw in Vivi Gallia, but you'll say no."

"That's not your decision to make."

He smiled, coldly and deadly serious. "You are going with Bryce to Albuquerque, as you agreed you would, and I will give these men a happy ending. Was that suggestive and clichéd enough for you, Mae?"

She glared at Kitt. No matter how sickened, frightened, sad and angry she was, no matter how she detested his bullying insistence, no matter how this turned out, there was no happy ending in this— for anyone. She'd had enough; enough of blood, and killing, and being responsible for it all because she'd wanted to make sense of what had happened to her when there was no sense to any of it. There was no answer to *why*. All she'd done was uncover murderous greed, duplicity, and the futility of loving a man with a black soul. That was the one very clear, very painful truth she felt.

She dug her fingers deeper into Kitt's arm. "This is never going to be over."

He slid his hand over hers and detached her burrowing fingers ever so gently. "It's over for you, Mae."

313

"No, it isn't." She worried the corner of her lip where the stitch had been and met cool blue eyes that were ablaze with contradiction. Then Francesco's man reappeared upstairs, out of breath, shouting, "*Loro sono li*, they are there!" and Kitt's gaze shifted to Bryce.

Bryce glanced past Francesco and raised and flicked his eyes to the stairs.

"Why is Bryce helping you?" Mae said. "Why has he been helping you all this time?"

"I suppose he feels he owes me. Are you suspicious of Bryce now?"

"I'm suspicious of everyone. Owes you for what?"

Kitt slid his hand into a pocket. "I got his wife out of North Korea."

Mae snorted. "Did you sleep with her too?"

"They weren't married then, and—" He clenched his teeth for a moment. He looked at her. "That is, no, I did not sleep with Nari. It was a straight extraction, over twenty years ago. I led a team. And I do believe you have something of a mean streak, Mae."

"Can you blame me?"

"No. And if I could erase it all I would."

She fixed her suddenly wet eyes on him. "I wish we could erase it all and go back to how it was, how we were. All these things I don't want to know, about you, about Caspar, about myself. How do I move on? You do this all the time. How do you move on? How do you go back to your normal life?"

He smiled, genuinely. "I come home to you."

"And there I am, a faithful dog waiting for you."

"You are justifiably angry, but that is my normal life, Mae. I come home *to you*. That is my routine. That is my life. I come home to you and you are there. I realise I have never thanked you for being there, but I am grateful for your dogged loyalty. Please do go on being loyal." Kitt pulled her to her feet. And let her go.

Mae swallowed. "Is that what it is, loyalty? I thought it was all about the scrambled eggs, but loyalty, yes that makes sense." Her frown took better hold. "No, it doesn't make sense. None of this makes sense. Whatever it is, I don't want to know. It doesn't seem right that I should be so angry with you and so...so...afraid at the same time. Do you know why I'm so afraid?"

"Well, I am dear to you," Kitt said, and noticed she was shaking. He was too.

Her eyes, clear at last, spilled tears that meandered around the curve of her nose, over her mouth to drip off her chin. "I've been mugged, stitched, and almost killed, my hair's been pulled, my face slapped, I've been drugged and kidnapped, I saw you nearly die, and learned Caspar was a thief and a polygamist. Do you know what the hardest thing was?" she said, crying without screwing up her face. "Finding out about you, about what you are, about myself, and I don't want to. I don't want that. I can't want that. When you come home, you will have my resignation."

His lip curled, baring his teeth. "Two weeks. You owe me two weeks' notice."

"Yes. I do." She nodded. "Anything less would be unprofessional."

"Damn it. Damn it all." Kitt tore his gaze from her. "She's done here, Francesco."

The man tipped his chin and shook a cigarette from an empty packet. "*Allora*. I see no reason not to agree. We do not prosecute victims. Our apologies to you, Mrs Valentine."

Kitt put his hands on her shoulders and turned her to Bryce. Immediately, she spun around. "I need you to check on Fiorella." Mae swiped at her nose with an arm.

"Yes." He took her hand. "Of course I will," he said. "I'll tell her you are safe." Kitt slid an arm around her waist and drew her to Bryce. "Take her, Bryce. Get her out of here. And don't let her out of your sight."

"That's it?" Bryce arched his brow. "Take her, Bryce? Without even a goodbye kiss?"

Francesco raised a hand. "*Aspeta*, wait. There is to be no goodbye for anyone. I said she is done here, yes. That is true. But she is not finished. This is not over."

"It is for her," Kitt said.

"You are mistaken. I agree she did not commit murder and is a victim of fraud, but we need Mrs Valentine to identify those involved."

Kitt's eyes narrowed. "Vitali can identify those involved."

"Vitali is still our man inside. We cannot reveal him. Surely you understand the importance of her participation, Kitt?" Francesco turned to Mae. "Mrs Valentine, I apologise for the way we treated you. It is regrettable, but the nature of this work can be a dark shadow that sometimes envelops the innocent. We need your help in this shadow. Please. Will you help us complete this investigation?"

"Christ, no. You are not going to use her as bait."

"But is that not what you did, Kitt?" Francesco rubbed his chin and smiled.

"What is it you want me to do, Mr Casino?" Mae said.

Kitt whirled her about. Teeth clenched, she glowered, eyes bright with unmistakable fury. He stared back. "Let me guess. I'm a bully and he asked nicely?"

CHAPTER TWENTY-ONE

"Do you like killing people?"

"Stop fidgeting with the tape."

"It's pulling my skin."

Kitt frowned and leaned over to adjust the microphone she'd unstuck. "Why did you agree to participate in Francesco's plan? Because Vivi Gallia disappeared?"

"You didn't answer my question."

"No. I don't relish ending a life, but I admit I would enjoy killing this man. Now hold still and...well, now I've got it stuck to your bra and your décolletage is askew. You're going to have to take off your dress s—"

"I think I can manage without Francesco's men poking my breasts again." Mae huffed and rose, and the bottom of her red dress parted, offering Kitt a glimpse of her upper thigh. She refastened the button and moved to the corner of the room to fix her neckline.

Kitt watched her and tried not to think about her little constellation of freckles. That sort of astronomy was amateurish. She had resolved to be angry. He had resolved to be professional, yet she was the one acting like a professional, which made him feel even more an amateur for thinking about the Southern Cross on her skin.

"Excuse me, Mr Spielzeug?"

Kitt turned around. The receptionist gave him a tense smile. "You may go in now. Should I get you coffee?"

"Yes. Two Americanos, thank you."

"Of course. This way, please." The young man gestured toward the broad door and ushered Kitt into a brightly lit office decorated in retro-style furnishings.

The trim gentleman behind the desk wore a fashionable three-piece suit with a modern fit. Glass-topped, his desk was accented by a red blotter, a red clock and a black leather compendium embossed with *SGB* in gold lettering. There was no hint of recognition in the man's eyes as he rose and came around the front of his desk, offering Kitt his hand. "Good morning, Mr Spielzeug," he said in Italian. "I am Ernst Largo."

"A pleasure, Mr Largo." Kitt replied in English and shook Largo's slender hand, careful not to twist and snap it. "I apologise. My employer will be a moment. You know how women are."

"Not a worry." Largo switched to English and nodded at his assistant. "The usual, please, Nino."

The young man departed and Kitt cast an eye about the office and its floor-to-ceiling windows. It would be quite satisfying to toss Largo out of one of the windows. "You have a quite a view of Milan from up here."

"*Ach, ja*, it is splendid." Largo joined him beside the wall of glass.

Kitt looked out over the panorama of the city. He had been well-briefed on a few of Largo's better-known clients. "Dame Maud-Louise sends her regards," he said, tucking a hand into his pocket as the requisite small talk ensued.

"Such a fine actress. I enjoyed her work on *The Prince Regent* series."

"I haven't seen it yet."

"Then I won't give anything away. It is excellent intrigue."

"I love a little intrigue."

"Then you must not miss the series."

"If only I had time, Mr Largo." Kitt ran his fingers through the few things in his pocket, turning coins, and other slim, rounded objects. "My work keeps me quite busy."

"Such is the curse of a twenty-first century man. How is it I can be of assistance, Mr Spielzeug?"

Kitt looked across the skyline to the Duomo di Milano, the city's cathedral. "My employer is looking to ensure her security."

"Understandable and wise."

The door opened behind them. Largo moved away from the window, gesturing to a straight-backed charcoal sofa, a chair, and coffee table. "Shall we sit?" he said as he turned around. And froze.

"Mr Largo." Mae walked across the carpet, her heels leaving indentations in the nap. She seated herself on the sofa and crossed her ankles, hands in her lap, composed, as if she weren't wearing a wire beneath her right breast.

Largo swallowed, his face going pale. "How much do you want?"

Kitt chose the matching chair across from Mae and watched her watching Largo. "My employer isn't interested in extortion."

"Then what does she want?" The man swallowed again.

"Ask her."

"What is it you want, Mrs Valentine?"

She patted the sofa cushion. "Please, Mr Largo, come sit down beside me. We are not here to kill you or divest you of your money. I've forgotten about that. Mostly. There is no reason why we can't be comfortable and have a discussion."

Largo ran two fingers around his top lip, as if he were smoothing a moustache. He walked across the oval rug, sat, and repeated the lip smoothing. "What do you want, Mrs Valentine?"

"Besides having my employee beat you senseless? You're lucky I see your value, Mr Largo. I'd like three things."

"*Ja?*"

"I would like coffee."

"It is on the way," Largo said. "Go on."

"I want to know how this works."

"How what works?"

She leaned toward him.

He recoiled.

Kitt laughed as she picked a ball of grey carpet fuzz from Largo's dark suit and flicked it away. "I have a number of acquaintances like myself, widows," she said, "all of us interested in our future security. I'd like you to show me how my dead husband amassed thirty-seven million pounds. I'd like to learn how it is done." She sat back. "Naturally I'd compensate you for your guidance."

"You wish to...*ja*, I can see that you do wish to." Largo looked at them both, studying them, considering his options. He straightened. "You are very shrewd, Mrs Valentine. Very shrewd."

"Thank you."

"Why should I trust you?"

"That's a good question. Would you be more comfortable if Mr Spielzeug stepped out of the room?" She smiled over at Kitt.

It was same smile as when he thought he'd been about to spend the night sleeping on a hard, wooden chair, only this time she was angry. Three days ago, he'd left one volcano and now found himself with another. Christ, Mae was angry. He'd been distracted by the constellation of freckles on the inside of her thigh, and she was blinded by her rage, her contrary, stubborn, rage that insisted she see this through. Kitt had never been quite so afraid in his life. He gave her a flat, hard stare.

She went on smiling.

She turned back to Largo. "He does have a better head for this business than I, but if you must know, Mr Largo, I do confess that after our last...encounter, I prefer to have someone else present."

"As I said, you are shrewd, Mrs Valentine."

The assistant entered with coffee on a tray, which he placed on the low table between the sofa and chair where Kitt sat. The man gave a nod and departed, closing the door softly. Kitt had taken notice of the beads of sweat on the young man's brow.

"Now then," Mae said. "How did you manage it?"

Largo sat back and smiled. "I have banking experience and...associates."

"It's never what you know, but who you know?" Kitt said.

"*Ja*, something like that."

Mae had a swallow of bitter coffee and set the cup back on the tray. "You mean knowing people like Daniel Pierce or like Sal, the man you had kill him? You realise Sal and I came to something of an understanding, don't you?"

"And that is why you are here. Very shrewd indeed." With another cool smile, Largo tipped his head. "I was once an auditor for Credito Popolare. I understand the banking system quite well. I have banking connections with Suisse Global Bank. I have a connection in London. Not the banker Daniel Pierce, the unfortunate man who contacted you. Had he been as amenable as you, we would not be having this conversation. My associate is the Relationship Manager for Suisse Global's London branch. I believe you met her. Before she rose through the ranks in Suisse Global, she worked for me at Credito Popolare."

"Do you mean Tiffany O'Toole, the skinny woman at the Cabot Square branch?"

"Ah, *ja*, O'Toole. That is correct." Largo reached for his cappuccino and sipped it. "I can make arrangements for her to assist you, so that you have someone closer to home. She is very good. It more or less comes down to opening accounts and moving your money, Mrs Valentine, transferring small portions that are within the regulated limits, from one account to another. It is done all the time. I can show you how to do it, walk you through every step." He returned his cappuccino to its saucer. "I can support you as I supported Dame Maud-Louise, and then place your parcel in capable hands closer to home."

"Thank you, Mr Largo. I think I can live with this."

"So there are, as Americans say, no hard feelings?"

Mae leaned closer to him and brushed off a bit more carpet fibre. "Mr Largo, if this works, I'll harbour no feelings about you whatsoever."

He gave a very continental nod of his head. "You said there were three things. What is the last thing you want?"

She leaned closer still and said, "Vivienne Gallia."

Largo lunged, his thumbs pressed into Mae's throat as he shoved her down to the seat of the button-backed couch. His feet kicked coffee cups across the table as he squeezed. All at once, he was gone.

Kitt pressed the man's nose to the sofa, his left arm twisted up high between his shoulder blades, one palm flattened on the charcoal upholstery.

Coughing and sputtering, Mae saw something black gleam in Kitt's grip. Largo shrieked. Kitt released him and the man shot to his feet, stumbled back across the room, the hand that had been behind his back now clutched to chest. Blood poured between his fingers, scarlet drizzled the pale grey rug. He knocked into the edge of his glass-topped desk and hit the floor, wailing and moaning.

Kitt pulled Mae to her feet. She was trembling just as much as he was. "What did you do?" she said.

"Gave him back his pen."

"Oh," she swallowed, "that's a very good line."

"Yes. And now you're done," he said, as Francesco Casino's men crashed into the room, weapons drawn.

MAE STARED across the juniper and piñon woodlands of the Sandia-Manzano mountains somewhere outside Albuquerque, New Mexico.

The green-eyed Welshman took a place beside her on the rough-hewn wooden porch bench. "We'll be going home soon." Bryce tucked away a satellite mobile. He held one of the cocoa biscuits she'd made that morning and he leaned against the wall looking out over the wooded canyon vista as he ate the biscuit.

She watched hummingbirds buzz about purple sage. "Did they find Vivi Gallia?"

"In Hong Kong. But they didn't find Man. Kitt's debriefing. He's a little banged up, but that happens sometimes; people poke you with chopsticks or other pointy things when they don't want to be captured."

Mae looked at Bryce. He had a chocolate biscuit crumb sitting just at the top of his chin cleft. "Can you tell me anything else?"

Bryce grinned. "Just a little. Some of it you won't like, something in particular I really shouldn't mention, but I think you ought to know. Let's walk." Bryce waited for her to rise and come down the front steps and start walking alongside him on the dirt path. "Largo and Vivienne Gallia opened local accounts in Sicily using the stolen identities of dead people. The accounts were used for transferring money."

Aromatic pine needles crunched under Mae's feet. "Where did all the money come from?"

"The usual. Extortion, gambling, drugs, prostitution...and people smuggling."

"People smuggling?" Mae stopped walking. "Then Pippino Torrisi was involved? His work as an advocate for refugees was merely a front?"

Bryce backtracked a few steps. "No. Not at all. He's a well-respected, decent man. Vivi Gallia, on the other hand, operated the ghastly, inhumane business right under his nose. She took advantage of his work. She had access to boatloads of desperate people she found ways to exploit. And she had help from her large family who all seemed to think Vivi was an angel for looking after them all so well."

With a heartsick laugh, she began walking again. "Keep going. Tell me every horrid thing."

Bryce cleared his throat and fell into step beside her. "The accounts were used to receive transfers and payments. Shell companies were set up. The money was laundered through several small businesses, like the bakery Russo operated. He received a monthly sum for his participation. The bulk of the proceeds were funnelled into other countries, and then back into Italy and England. It was all recycled. Gallia, Largo and O'Toole worked as a trio under Gallia's direction. There were hundreds of thousands of transfers, all of them under the €1,000 limit, which is why it was so hard to detect, but there were two missteps here. One was that Gallia opened an account using the personal details of Torrisi's deceased uncle."

"What was the other misstep?"

"Your husband's account was rather substantial, much larger than the other two. Things probably would have continued to operate as they had. You never would have known of your husband's account. O'Toole dealt with these accounts personally, but she fell gravely ill—*E coli* or something—and Pierce took over her position while she was sick. He picked up irregularities with your account, reported his findings to O'Toole, and mentioned they might need to contact the Serious Fraud Office and HM Revenue and Customs. O'Toole, who was in hospital at the time, panicked. She contacted Gallia and Largo. Those two, they set to work trying to cover their tracks, meaning they meant to eliminate you, Russo—who wanted more money for his silence—and liquidate the accounts."

Chipmunks skittered across the path and scurried over rocks. "Why was Caspar's account so large?" Mae said.

Bryce swatted away a horsefly. "The private holdings for Gallia's rather large family. They've accumulated millions in euros and even more in property."

Mae gave him a sidelong squint. What she saw made her smile, despite the repugnant tale he recounted. "You have biscuit stuck in your chin."

Bryce brushed at his chin.

She watched him and wondered. Did Kitt count Bryce as a friend, or simply a colleague? Did men like Kitt have friends? Perhaps it was unprofessional, unorthodox, and unwise for a man like to Kitt have friends of any sort. She looked at Bryce again. The chocolate biscuit crumb was still on his chin. "May I ask you a question, Sergeant Bryce?"

"I am not at liberty to discuss anything about Kitty, Mrs Valentine."

"No. It's about you."

"Then ask away."

"Do you often get things trapped in your chin cleft?"

Bryce's loud laugh bounced off the bottom of the canyon wall in front of them. "You know," he said. "There's something good that's come from exposing murderous, unbridled, rampant greed."

May snorted. "Yes. Murderous, unbridled rampant greedy

thieves go to prison. Now, what is it that I'm not really supposed to know?"

Still chuckling, he said, "The newspaper stories that Kitt showed you?"

"Yes?"

Bryce's mouth compressed for a moment. "They were fake. I mocked them up for Kitty so that you would agree to come here with me. Murder was never on the books. It was quite clearly self-defence." Bryce laughed as she came to a dead stop to stare, mouth agape.

The bird calls, buzzing and chirping of insects, the wind in the trees faded out as she tried to pinpoint how she felt. Anger rated high on the spectrum of emotions, as did disbelief. She had to make peace with the things she'd done, had to accept that she might be bloodthirsty, merely human or both. The lies in her life were astounding. She wanted, desperately, to put this event behind her. She wanted to move on from the strange tale of Caspar's infidelity and embezzlement, to move on from Caspar. She wanted to move back to a normal life but had no idea what a normal life was without lies—including her own.

THE TEXT MESSAGE he'd sent was brief: *Home. Breakfast at 7. Please.*

Fresh food and other supplies in tow, Mae arrived at the rear entrance of her employer's Maresfield Gardens flat at 5:30 and let herself inside. She found his luggage beside the front door, which meant he'd only be home a short time and was likely to depart for another destination quite soon. Or he'd been preoccupied by something soft and perfumed and hadn't bother to unpack. She tended to the things that indicated the former, hanging up the jacket that had been left on the chair beside the front door, returning throw pillows to the window seat in the sitting room.

In the butler's pantry adjoining the kitchen, she slipped off the messenger bag containing her laptop and stored the items in a cupboard that also housed cleaning supplies, aprons, and two extra sets of work clothes. Once she'd tied on a fresh apron, she organised the groceries, and set the breakfast table near the big bay window in the sitting room. She arranged gilt-edged blue and white Minton beside the Jersey butter and her homemade orange and ginger marmalade.

By 6:40 the coffee was ready and the Béarnaise was done. By 6:55, Mae took out eggs to scramble and the Major ambled into the kitchen in his dressing gown, in need of feeding, a purplish welt beneath his right eye, a white plaster visible just below his collarbone.

It was a morning like any other. A morning so usual it was as if nothing had happened. *Had* anything happened?

"Good morning, Mae," he said, gravelly voiced.

Mae didn't ask how he was. It was all so usual, so typical of so many mornings. It was common to see him with a black eye or split lip. As an intelligence officer the Major's job sometimes sent him to remote and often dangerous parts of the world. He met with all sorts of hospitality in his travels. At times, the hospitality turned hostile and resulted in his harm. There was also the fact the man had two vices: the drink and women. Mae suspected that a few of his injuries were sustained by his use of alcohol and his attraction to married, attached, or widowed women with ties to murderous, money-laundering international bankers, and people smugglers.

"Good morning, sir," she said, smoothing her apron over her hips.

"Did you miss me?"

"How could I miss you with so much of you here to haunt me?"

"Did Bryce give you the details?"

"Sergeant Bryce told me many electrifying facts, sir."

Kitt stopped beside the cooker. There it was again. *Sir.* The navy-blue dress, the apron, her hair in a French braid, her shoes, and the *sir*; the barriers had been put back into place. The routine re-established. Except... Her wedding band hung now from the same gold chain that held her reading glasses. "You're making scrambled eggs with Béarnaise." Kitt poked a finger into the Béarnaise, sucked the sauce from his fingertip, and a low, appreciative sound vibrated in his throat. "You're very thoughtful. Well, this puts me in a rather awkward position, Mrs Valentine."

"Of course. The five pounds I owe you, sir." She reached beneath her apron, into the side pocket of her dress, pulled out a pale green and yellow banknote. She held it out to him.

He looked at the money for a moment before he took it and dropped it on the worktop beside a glass bowl. "Yes," he said. "Yes. And with that exchange we've re-established the routine and taken our places. Nearly. There's one more bit of awkwardness to tend to, Mae."

"Your rent is not due for another fortnight."

A fortnight. She'd be gone in a fortnight. "No, it's something else," Kitt said. "Would you come with me?"

Mae followed him into the little sitting room, to the bay window. Well now, he was going to show her the weapons safe beneath the window seat, where she'd replaced the pillows earlier. She didn't want to see the safe. It was enough to know the bloody thing existed. "I don't want you to tell me where it is, sir. I don't care to know. I've had enough of guns and such."

Her employer gave a small laugh. "I'm not telling you anything." He handed her a box she hadn't seen him pick up because she'd been too busy studying the moulding around the bottom of the window seat. "I'm giving you something."

The box in her hands was just big enough and heavy enough for Mae to be worried. "I appreciate the thought, I appreciate that you continue to look out for me, and I don't wish to be ungrateful, but I cannot accept, I will not accept a gun."

Laughter lit up his face. "Why would I give you a weapon?"

"Thanks be to Jesus. What is it then?"

"Open it and find out," he said. "I did my best to track down what you'd lost. I'm sorry it's not in better condition."

Mae placed the box on the dining table beside the butter and pulled off the lid. She parted the tissue paper, and her throat constricted.

Inside was a copy of *Jane Eyre*. Not simply a replacement for the *Jane Eyre* Caspar had given her, but *the* copy Caspar had given her. It was stained, pages rippled from being someplace damp, but it was whole. Eyes burning, she looked up at the Major, croaking, "You found this?"

"Yes. I'd intended to give it to you before you went on your holiday." His smile was slight, a little sad. "I didn't stop to think you might not want it now. Is it all right?"

"I...I...you..." Her hand went to her throat as she swallowed. "You are...you are a surprisingly thoughtful man, and I don't know what to say."

"You could say you'd stay on with me, but '*Thank you*' is customary."

"Thank you," she said, then stood on her toes, laid a palm on his cheek, and kissed him softly.

Kitt ran a hand about her waist, tightened his arm around her, and pulled her up higher on her toes, drawing her closer as he deepened the kiss for one long, last lingering time. She made a small noise. Or maybe he did. Her touch skated down his arm to intertwine her fingers with his. He lifted his head and her cheek came to rest on his chest. "You're welcome," he said.

"You are dear to me. So very dear, sir," she murmured.

"And for that I am glad."

"Yes, I'm sure it lights up the darkness of your soul."

"More than you could imagine."

"Now, that's the end of that." She began to pull away. "I'll get your breakfast."

"Eggs. Scrambled, not shirred."

"Oh, aren't you in fine, fictional spy form this morning." Mae moved, their fingers slid apart slowly until their touch was nothing more than haunting warmth. She left him in the sitting room and went to the kitchen. Usual, typical, routine, everyday... She moved to the cooker, set a pan on the hob, switched on the gas, and took a wire whisk from a magnetised strip above the cooker.

"Are you going to leave?" Kitt had followed her into the room and moved behind her as a shadow. "Really going to leave?"

"I see, the book was bribery so I'd stay, sir?"

"No. Of course not." Kitt watched her crack eggs into a bowl. Clarity was obnoxious, inopportune, and unexpectedly liberating when it came to the matter of his butler. He'd accepted her as ever-present, a perpetual arctic winter dawn in his life, only she had moved out of the half-light to stand beside him for a little while and he was damned. However quixotic, however foolish, however painful, he bathed in the bright warmth of her. He was a condemned man in two ways. The personal condemnation was far worse than the professional. "Did I mention I've been censured, Mae?"

"You mean you've been demoted due to your actions regarding me?" she said, whisking whites and orange yolks together.

"No, I mean reprimanded, temporarily suspended from field service, and reassigned. I can't say I mind so much. I'm tired, and I need a rest. I suppose that means I'm getting old."

With a small laugh, she looked at him over a shoulder and then continued whisking.

"You're not going to contradict me?"

"I recall you saying something about considering retirement. To where have you been reassigned?"

"The Home Station."

"I wonder how you'll survive the boredom and paperwork, sir."

"I'll be a field instructor and consultant for a while. It'll be tick a box, scribble an evaluation, pass along to a secretary. What do you think of that, Mae?"

"It will be nice to have you home more often."

"Yes. It will be nice," he said, and then exhaled sharply. "It seems it's a habit of mine when it comes to you, but I've lied again, Mae."

"Yes, the fake news story you had Bryce concoct. 'The Butler Did It.' Was that headline his idea or yours?"

"No, it's—Bryce told you about that? That bloody ba—"

"You didn't track the book down yourself, did you, sir?" She stopped beating the eggs and put the bowl aside, wiping her hands on her apron, chuckling softly.

"No, b—"

"You had Bryce find it. The poor man dug in rubbish bins, crawled through sewe—"

"Will you let me finish? Bryce didn't dig or crawl anyplace. I found the book in the bushes near the Japanese embassy. I'm not talking about the news story and I don't mean I lied about the book. But in a way, I did because you're not Mrs Fairfax, you're Jane Eyre. As moody and brooding as you say I am, I am in love with you. I love you, Mae. My soul is black and whatever lump I have that passes for a heart is yours because I love you. Other than tell you, other than be honest with you, and honest with myself, I don't know what else to do. I love you, and you're a nuisance, a nuisance I find necessary to my...existence."

"Necessary to your existence?" she said, looking over her shoulder, arching a brow.

"I am aware how trite that sounds."

Mae turned around and gazed up into the grim blue-grey eyes of a man who killed for a living. Hand in one pocket, he stood very still in his white terry-towelling dressing gown, his scraped, bruised face asserting his lethal occupation. It still surprised her that she wasn't afraid of him, but what surprised her more was that he looked hungover, annoyed, and something she never imagined possible about him. "Are you afraid of me?"

"Christ, yes." He wore a very faint, wry smile. "Afraid of you, of what you do to me, of what I do for you, of how you make me feel, of making declarations of love. I'm unaccustomed to making such declarations."

"But you thought I should know?"

"Yes."

"Why?"

"I said I wouldn't lie anymore."

She lifted her chin. "Is that the only reason?"

"Because you have no agenda. Because you make no demands. Because I am not Caspar. Because I don't know what else to do."

"No." She shook her head. "You are not Caspar."

He narrowed his eyes. "You do know that's why I came after you, don't you, because I love you? It had nothing to do with keeping my cover or government secrets. I obviously cannot keep secrets from you."

She took the frying pan off the flame and switched off the gas. "Perhaps then you should quit your job."

"As you are? I don't quit anything. I never quit, although I am getting tired."

"And you're getting old."

"Thank you for the reminder. Do the five years between us concern you, Mae?"

Head cocked to one side, she smirked. "So you're afraid of me. Are you afraid of getting older too, or are you afraid of being alone in your old age, Mr Spielzeug?"

"You've made me realise how large my bed is." The puncture wound below Kitt's collarbone ached in the dull way his pebble-sized heart did, but she wanted honesty. She deserved honesty, so he went on being honest. "I can't let you quit. I cannot accept your resignation, particularly when I know you happen to like working for me. Even if I'm making an arse of myself now, it is fair that you know where I stand. I know you; I know you are fond of me. I know I am dear to you, and I know, no matter the outcome of my foolhardiness, I can count on you being professional and making me scrambled eggs."

Mae looked at the bruise beneath his eye. The lies. All the lies. She was done with the lies, with deception of any sort. "Yes," she said. "You know me." She put the frying pan back and relit the flame. Then she took an unbroken egg from the carton, set it on the worktop, and chose another implement from the magnetised strip beneath the exhaust hood. She waved the spatula as she spoke. "You're not Caspar. I never really knew Caspar, at all. I loved a phantom of a man who never really was. I should be devastated by his deceit. I should be, but he's dead, so why does it matter? I loved him. I'll always love him. That's true enough. It's also true that I know you. I know you like you know me. You kill people and deal in lies for a living. By rights that ought to sicken me, that ought to send me packing. Yet here I am, in your employ. Maybe what you and I do isn't very different." She placed the spatula in his hand. "We sweep things away. Maybe we should do that now, clean the house, or at least get the house in order before we move on."

"Move on?" Kitt glanced at the flat-edged utensil in his grip and then at her. "You're going to quit?" His mouth compressed. "You're going to quit."

"You say all this like I should know what to do, when it's something I shouldn't do. I shouldn't *want* to do. I really shouldn't. But I do. I have for so long. And there it is. Right there. That's all there is to it." Mae took off her apron. "I know you're hungry. I'm hungry too and the frying pan's already warm. Go on."

Kitt looked at the cooker, at the frying pan, at the flame beneath it, at Mae. "Are you saying you want me...to cook breakfast? This is what you're saying after I lay myself bare to you, Mae? That's very harsh."

She sighed. "What I'm saying, is that I've spent these past years with a futile attachment to a dead man, and you and I have both been feckin' liars."

Kitt squinted. "How do you mean we've both been liars?"

Mae shrugged. It was unprofessional. It was unorthodox. It was unwise. It was undeniable. "You think I'm so honest. You see me as a paragon of honesty when weeks ago you asked me point-blank, and I lied." She laid a palm in the small of his back and gave him a little push towards the waiting pan. "What I'm saying is, I love you, Hamish," she said. "And I like my eggs fried."

ACKNOWLEDGMENTS

None of my writing would be possible without my bearded Sicilian's love, support, and encouragement. *At Your Service* is the first book of mine he has ever read, and I am so pleased that he enjoyed it! Thank you to my tall, little love and editor Belinda Holmes. I owe a debt to Sicily, Anna Cleary, Ainslie Paton, Lily Malone, Cindy Siverly-Hollabaugh, Annette Christianson, Megan Whalen Turner, my darling Lisa Barry, Wendy Knerr and Jon Stacey for their hospitality, damson jam, and keen British eye. Thank you to Gavin 'The Professor' and Trisha 'Wolverhampton' Kendall for keeping my English *English* instead of a mash up of Australian/American/UK English-isms.

I am obliged to Rebekah Turner for my covers and grateful to Amy Andrews' understanding of the need for Chelsea bun, to Salvo Costarelli's schooling me in the Sicilian dialect and furthering my education of Italian swearing, and Ian Fleming, Alistair MacLean, Robert Ludlum because *spies*.

But mostly I am indebted to Elle Gardner for wanting to read more, and to Daniel Craig and Toby Stephens for being ugly-handsome.

ABOUT THE AUTHOR

Thank you for buying this book! I hope you enjoyed reading *At Your Service* as much I enjoyed writing it!

I come from the land Down Under, drive a little Italian car, live in a little house, and I love little dogs (why you see a blonde, bespectacled dog avatar on social media). All my books present women over the age of 40 as lead characters. I am so interested in dispelling the myths and "Hollywood" stereotypes of older women you so often see in fiction and film, I did a doctorate on the subject. You can call me Dr Sandra.

My novels *A Basic Renovation*, *For Your Eyes Only*, *Driving in Neutral*, and *Next to You* are romantic comedies and romantic comedy-mysteries, available online at all e book platforms via www.sandraantonelli.com

www.ingramcontent.com/pod-product-compliance
Lightning Source LLC
Chambersburg PA
CBHW071155100726
47908CB00002B/391